Janet Ross, Enrico Morozzo della Rocca

Autobiography Of A Veteran

1807-1893

Janet Ross, Enrico Morozzo della Rocca

Autobiography Of A Veteran
1807-1893

ISBN/EAN: 9783337029845

Printed in Europe, USA, Canada, Australia, Japan

Cover: Foto ©Raphael Reischuk / pixelio.de

More available books at **www.hansebooks.com**

THE AUTOBIOGRAPHY

OF A

VETERAN

1807-1893

BY

GENERAL COUNT ENRICO DELLA ROCCA

Translated from the Italian and Edited by
JANET ROSS

LONDON
T. FISHER UNWIN
PATERNOSTER SQUARE
1899

INTRODUCTION

At the request of my wife and family I begin to-day, Sunday, the 15th January 1893, to dictate my memoirs. I shall incorporate with them historical events in which I had a part, or which passed under my eyes. Until my eightieth year I read without glasses, but gradually my sight has failed and I am almost blind, so my wife will be my secretary. I shall dictate and recount—she will write. We shall make use of the letters I regularly wrote to her during the campaigns of 1859, 1860 and 1866; and also of some hastily-written notes, jotted down, chiefly at her request, between 1870-1885, of impressions and thoughts, of facts witnessed by me, and details about the celebrated men who were my contemporaries.

The work will not, I think, be easy; as having never thought of transmitting to posterity any account of my own times, and still less of my own life, I never collected or arranged my numerous records or the documents bearing upon them. I have narrated much and written a few things, but always in a desultory fashion; and my secretary will have enough to do to keep me in order and make me attend strictly to chronology. However, I will do my best in order to please my dear ones.

I shall try to recall the memories of a past which I love for several reasons—my good fortune at witnessing the awakening of the noble idea of an independent and united Italy—seeing it realised, chiefly by the exertions of men belonging to the small and gallant country where I, my forebears and my grandchildren were born—and for the active part I took in nearly all the important events which have happened between 1848 and 1870.

But I particularly wish to remind those who one day may read these memoirs that they were written solely in deference to the wishes of my own family, and that I never had any idea of making a historical or a literary work, or of imposing my judgments or appreciations, still less, of weaving panegyrics or destroying idols. I consider that some of my contemporaries were superior to the reputation they enjoyed, while others were praised beyond their deserts. I have always, without adulation for the first, or bad feeling towards the latter, expressed my opinion frankly and in all sincerity.

October 1896.

CONTENTS

CHAPTER I

1807-1820

PAGE

CHAPTER II

1821-1825

CHAPTER III

1825-1840

CHAPTER IV

1840-1841

CHAPTER V
1842-1847

CHAPTER VI
1848

CHAPTER VII
1848—*continued*

CHAPTER VIII
END OF 1848. BEGINNING OF 1849

CHAPTER IX
1849—*continued*

CHAPTER X

END OF 1849-55

CHAPTER XI

1855-1857

CHAPTER XII

1858. BEGINNING OF 1859

CHAPTER XIII

1859 (SECOND PART)

CHAPTER XIV

1859 (THIRD PART)

CHAPTER XV

END OF 1859. BEGINNING OF 1860

CHAPTER XVI

1860

CHAPTER XVII

CHAPTER XVIII

1861

CHAPTER XIX

1861-1864

CHAPTER XX

1864

CHAPTER XXI

1865

CHAPTER XXII

1866 (FIRST PART)

CHAPTER XXIII

THE DAY OF CUSTOZA

CHAPTER XXIV

1866 (THIRD PART)

CHAPTER XXV

1866-1867

CHAPTER XXVI

1867-1870

Autobiography of a Veteran

CHAPTER I

1807-1820

I WAS born in Turin on the 20th June 1807, a few days after the battle of Friedland which Thiers pronounces to be *la plus belle de tous les siècles*, and on the eve of the day when those arch-enemies Napoleon and Alexander embraced on the Niemen. On the 20th June was, and still is, celebrated at Turin the feast of a miraculous image of the Virgin, the Madonna of Consolation, and my mother, a pious and excellent woman, consecrated me to her, fully persuaded that her fourth son's happiness was thus secured. I can hardly affirm that her hopes were entirely realised, but I must admit that my life has relatively been a happy one; perhaps because I am endowed with a certain amount of philosophy which prevents my attributing more importance to men or to events than they deserve.

After the enforced abdication of Charles Emanuel IV. in 1798, Piedmont passed under the dominion of the French Republic with a fictitious semblance of liberty and independence; then, thanks to the Austro-Russian intervention, or more correctly speaking, to that of General Suvaroff, she returned for a short time to legitimate monarchy under a regency lacking decorum or power. After the battle of Marengo she again fell under the French yoke. Divided in 1802 into four departments, she formed part of the Republic, and afterwards of the Empire, until the Restoration. In 1807 Piedmont was ruled by a general who was at the same time head of the 28th military division and civil governor. In the following year he was succeeded by Camillo Borghese, husband of Pauline Bonaparte, sister of the Emperor, who lived in Turin until 1814, when the Empire was overthrown. I was therefore born a French subject in the capital of the department of the Po.

My father, Charles Philip, was the second son of the Marquis Gaspar Morozzo of Bianzè, and of Irene Scarampi of Canino, whose eight sisters, with the exception of one who became the Marchioness of Bevilacqua, were all married in Turin, so we had innumerable cousins among the Piedmontese nobility. Marquis Gaspar and his wife had five sons: Charles Emanuel, Marquis of Bianzè; Charles Philip, Marquis Della Rocca, my father; Louis, abbé Morozzo; Joseph, chevalier Morozzo, finance minister, who kept that title till he died, and was director of the hospitals and charitable institutions of Turin; and one daughter, Christine, who married the Marquis Taparelli d'Azeglio and was the mother of Massimo d'Azeglio.

The Marquis Gaspar would now be accounted very eccentric, but in those days he represented the common type of the eldest born of noble and rich families. Brought up to regard himself as superior to his brothers and quite above ordinary mortals, he was persuaded that by divine and human laws he was sole representative of his ancestors and sole master of their large fortune, which by right would go to his eldest son. No other member of his family was to marry. They were to enter the army or the government services, take holy orders, or become Knights of Malta. To a man imbued with such notions, the new ideas introduced by the French Revolution were odious. Intensely hostile to the Republican government, which he, with many others, considered to be simply revolutionary and not likely to last, he was subjected to all kinds of vexations by our French rulers in the shape of taxes and fines. Once they seized the fifteen horses in his stable, saying that it was good for the health of *Citizen* Morozzo to walk. My grandfather, who never replied unless addressed as Marquis of Bianzè, immediately gave orders to his numerous factors to collect the finest mules they could find on his estates, and drove them, splendidly harnessed, four-in hand through the streets of Turin, especially under the windows of the governor's palace. It can easily be imagined how angry he was at the announcement, in spite of his opposition, of the marriage of his second son, Charles Philip, in 1799.[1] His bride was Sophia Asinari of the Marquises of Gresy, charming and of noble birth, but poor. Marquis Gaspar immediately altered his will, and divided what he had set apart for Charles between the abbé and the chevalier Joseph. All he gave him was a cottage with a dairy farm at Valfenera near Asti, which brought in about £160 a year, and a small apartment in the palace at Turin. He never relented towards his second son or gave him another penny, and died in 1813 without having known his grandchildren. If by chance we met our grandfather in

---

[1] Charles Philip, my father, was *aide-de-camp* to General Costa di Beauregard in 1796, and went with him to Cherasco on the 28th April, when the conditions of the peace of Cherasco were settled. They were dictated by General Bonaparte, and afterwards copied in the office of the Sardinian head of the staff. The young *aide-de-camp*, who probably had to make several copies, kept one, which is now in the small archive where I have collected the documents which will be used in these memoirs. I shall henceforward call this the *small Della Rocca archive* to distinguish it from the large and dusty archives of the Counts Morozzo and the Marquis Della Rocca, which contain documents dating from 1300.

the street we were made to bow most respectfully, but our salute was never returned; the Marquis Gaspar invariably turned away his head and walked straight on. Very different from the good King Victor Emanuel I., who, on his return to the capital in 1814, resumed his favourite walks under the porticos of Via di Po, accompanied by his first equerry. When he met us, and recognised the children of his faithful servant the Marquis Della Rocca, he always returned our bows and often called us to him and caressed the smaller ones; bidding us tell our father that he had stopped us in order to send him an affectionate *boundi* (good day).

As I have already said, my grandfather Gaspar died in 1813 without leaving anything to my father, and in the same year my seventh and last brother was born.[1] My parents brought up their large family with the strictest economy, giving us the example of a regular life, without luxuries or elegance, but contented and good-humoured. My kind and gentle father, who was delicate, left everything to his wife, in whose judgment he had implicit confidence. Healthy, robust and resolute, she ruled our small army with perfect success. There were no schools, or at all events we never went to any. Our father taught us reading, writing and arithmetic, and an excellent priest, towards whom we were sometimes wanting in respect, gave us Latin lessons and made us recite our catechism. Both of my parents were passionately fond of music, and in spite of manifold household occupations my mother found time to play the harp, then the fashionable instrument among ladies and young girls. My father sometimes accompanied her on the spinet, but oftener played his own compositions, when our elder sister Louisa, born in 1800, was charged to stop the diabolical noise we made in the small apartment. Woe betide him who broke the

---

[1] In 1819 my sister Caroline, who is still alive, was born.

silence ordered by my mother, or who left the place where he was seated with his back to the wall. Poor Louisa was our victim, and her shins might have told more eloquently than she did the number of kicks received when trying to impose silence or immobility on us. If my mother noticed any movement, or heard whimpering or naughty words addressed to Louisa, she came to her aid, and, administering one or two good boxes on the ears, put the offender into the corner with his face to the wall. Such discipline was an excellent preparation for the college, and for the army into which we were all to enter. None of us ever dreamed of complaining about our parents, or thinking they were harsh, nor did we ever expect the fondling which I see is the foundation of modern education, and which renders young men intolerant of every privation.

In 1814 the possessions of the House of Savoy were returned to them by virtue of the Treaty of Vienna, with the addition of the city of Genova and other Ligurian towns. Charles Emanuel IV., who in 1799 protested from Sardinia against the abdication forced upon him by the French, had voluntarily resigned his crown in 1804 after the death of his wife, Maria Clotilde, sister of the unfortunate Louis XVI. of France. He retired to private life in Rome, and ceded all his rights to his brother, the Duke of Aosta, afterwards King Victor Emanuel I. I perfectly remember every circumstance connected with the entry of the king into Turin, as far as a child of seven could see it. He was to pass along the Via di Po, so we went to the balcony of the Countess Ferrari's[1] house at one corner of the street. Thence we saw the king, mounted on a Sardinian galloway, dressed in his old uniform of

---

[1] Sister of the Countess of Castelborgo, my godmother; both descended from the Marchioness of San Sebastiano and of Spigno, morganatic wife of Victor Amadeus II.

1798,[1] blue with broad red facings a long waistcoat, white breeches and big jack boots, a Prussian hat, and a wig with a bobtail which hung down his back. The king was received' with loud and enthusiastic cheers; the people crowded round him, and all wanted to grip his hands, but only succeeded in kissing his boots. This was the first popular demonstration I witnessed ; afterwards I saw many in the suite of Charles Albert and Victor Emanuel II.

Immediately after the king's return he restored things to the condition they were in before the departure of Charles Emanuel IV. Sixteen years of exile spent among the bare rocks of his island—often badly informed about the course of events, and therefore incapable of understanding their importance—had seemed to him a dream, a cruel and oppressive nightmare. Awaking amidst the joyous demonstrations of his subjects, he felt impelled to destroy every trace of those sad years and to restore the old condition of mutual love between people and king. He did not perceive that all was changed, that individuals and ideas had progressed and could not turn back. A kind and excellent man, he was wanting in discernment. He immediately recalled, not only the faithful adherents of the monarchy, but, consulting old almanacs of the years preceding the abdication, he reinstated all the old functionaries. It was absurd, and at the same time sad, to hear of dead men being gazetted to their old posts. All this caused considerable dissatisfaction, particularly in the army, where officers retrograded in rank, and lost the steps they had gained under the French government. But others have written about this, and I shall return to my

---

[1] It was the uniform of Victor Amadeus III., *i.e.*, of a general of the Guards. Charles Emanuel IV., who was no soldier, had changed nothing in the uniform worn under his predecessor.

reminiscences. My father was one of the first to be reinstalled in his rank and pay as captain of the King's Dragoons, but owing to the heart disease which at last killed him after great suffering, he was forced to exchange into the bodyguard. He was named quarter-master, corresponding to the rank of major, so our poverty was a little alleviated.

The return of the queen from Sardinia, and of the young Prince of Carignano from France, was the subject of conversation in every household of Turin. Victor Emanuel I., obedient to the call of the allied powers in 1814, had come post-haste from Cagliari to Turin, but would not allow his wife to join him until peace was assured in Europe. After the battle of Waterloo and Bonaparte's exile to St Helena in 1815, the queen, impatient to see Piedmont and Turin, where she had reigned supreme as the beautiful Duchess of Aosta[1] in 1789 and the following years, left Sardinia to join her husband. Disembarking at Genoa, where she was received with acclamation, she entered Turin, accompanied by her four daughters: Beatrice, already married to her uncle Francis IV. of Modena; Maria Theresa and Marianne, twins of fifteen; and little Christine, born in 1812. Fifteen young girls of the first families of Piedmont awaited her arrival, with nosegays and baskets of flowers, on the new bridge of the Po, which she inaugurated.

Maria Theresa was still beautiful, and the sight of her, surrounded by those four youthful faces, touched the hearts of the enthusiastic crowd. Her popularity did not, however, last long. Murmurs and complaints soon began, accusing her of pride and hardness, of incapacity to understand the changes which had taken place during the exile of the royal family, and of using her great influence

---

[1] Maria Theresa d'Este, who married Victor Emanuel, Duke of Aosta, afterwards King of Sardinia, was sister to Francis IV., Duke of Modena.

with the king for party purposes and in favour of repression.

Victor Emanuel I. had also summoned to Turin the
young Prince Charles Albert[1] of Carignano, heir-presumptive to the throne if the queen or the Duchess of Genevese[2]
had no male children. He was seventeen, a sub-lieutenant
in the French army, but, on arriving at Turin, the king
made him quit foreign service and its uniform. Tall,
lithe, and handsome, gay, and full of fun, he became the
cynosure of all eyes, the subject of much talk, and the
centre of many ambitions, when the favourable impression
he had made upon the king was known. At the head of
his household, as governor, was placed old Count Grimaldi,
who fulfilled his duties too conscientiously to please the

[1] Charles Albert, Prince of Carignano, was a direct descendant, but of the
second branch, of Charles Emanuel I., the Great.

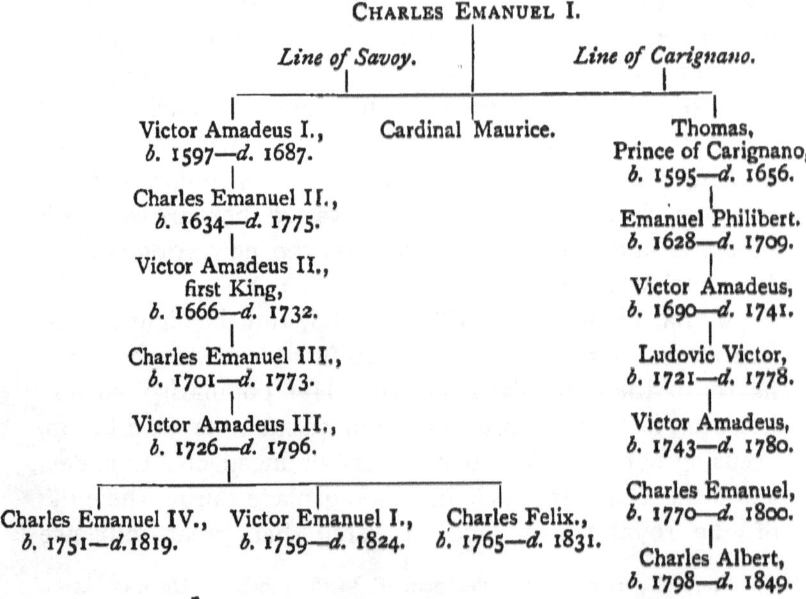

[2] Maria Christine, daughter of the King of Naples, and wife of Charles
Felix, brother of Victor Emanuel I.

young prince. He liked the first equerries no better; if not antediluvian, they at all events dated from those famous Court almanachs of 1798. The king, whose affection for Charles Albert increased daily, soon named younger and more acceptable men to the post. All Turin was astonished at the favour shown to the young prince, and it was rumoured that Victor Emanuel wished him to marry one of the twins, but that the Prince of Carignano was alarmed at the idea of Maria Theresa as a mother-in-law. Yet she was not a bad or a heartless woman. No one knew this better than my father, who was generously and kindly tended by her when seized with sudden illness in the royal palace at Genoa. But irritated by the worries of a long exile, and saddened by the loss of her only son, which destroyed all hope of seeing her descendants on the throne, she had become soured, and by her frank, sometimes even rude, speech she daily offended those around her, and showed too plainly her bitter disappointment at finding the popularity she had enjoyed as Duchess of Aosta no longer existed. Although intelligent and superior to the princes of the House of Savoy of that generation, she could not seize or make allowance for the great changes which had taken place in Piedmont during the French occupation. The royal family, completely isolated in Sardinia, were like that princess in the fairy tale who, on awaking from a hundred years' sleep, was astonished to find things were no longer the same—those sixteen years of sleep in Sardinia counted for more than a hundred in olden days.

In 1816 two young equerries—Count Gerbaix de Sonnaz and the chevalier Silvano Costa di Beauregard— were added to the Prince of Carignano's household. And as the king had twelve pages, and his brother, the Duke of Genevese, six, five were chosen for the service of his nephew, of whom I was one. My four companions, all between nine and twelve years of age, were Victor di Seyssel d'Aix, Faussone di Germagnano, the son of Count Filippi, and Coccognito di Montiglio. Our uniform, not to say livery, as Camillo di Cavour, who became page a few years after myself, called it, was of scarlet cloth with silver embroidery. We wore white silk stockings and shoes with buckles, and our hat was boat shaped. Our duties consisted in accompanying the princes and princesses to all Court functions, to church, to the theatre, to balls, following them upstairs, walking by their carriage, holding up their trains, and waiting on them in public. The Prince of Carignano was always pleasant and kind to us; in those days he was full of life and gaiety, fond of talking, and could be sarcastic; I suspect he often wished to join us in a game of romps. He undertook to have us taught riding in his riding school, and often lifted the smaller boys into their saddles or made the bigger ones trot and gallop by his side.

The military college was reopened by the king in 1816, and I was one of the first scholars. The idea was to educate a corps of good officers, who were to be not only instructed in the art of war, but inured from childhood to fatigue and privations. Our first swallow-tailed uniform was of blue cloth with crimson pipings. We wore short breeches and cloth gaiters up to our knees. In summer our breeches were white, and cold or hot, rain or sun, summer began for us on the feast of *Corpus Domini.*

In 1817 Victor Emanuel determined that the Prince of Carignano, heir-presumptive to the throne, ought to marry. His choice fell on the Archduchess Maria Theresa, daughter of Ferdinand III., Grand Duke of Tuscany, whose fair hair, youth, magnificent complexion, and courteous, dignified manners had pleased Charles Albert. The marriage took place at Florence in September 1817, and early in October the young couple came to Turin. I remember going with the other pages and equerries to meet them at the Valentino Palace, once the residence of Christina of France called Madame Royal. This pretty palace, then surrounded by shady walks and groups of old trees, was the first halting-place of royal visitors outside Turin. Now it is in the town. The prince and his bride entered a state carriage with large glass windows, drawn by four horses; three footmen stood behind and the two youngest pages, Filippi and I, stood on either side of the front windows on small steps added for the occasion. Whose idea this was I do not know, but we boys traversed the town with our hearts in our mouths. The State entry, probably arranged more in honour of the bride than of our young prince, was the cause of great future annoyance to him. Charles Felix, Duke of Genevese, who had just returned from Sardinia where he had been acting as regent, was jealous of the position given to Charles Albert. He regarded it as a personal affront, and so pestered the king and queen, and the master of the ceremonies Marquis Pamparato, that he obtained a rectification in the archives of court ceremonials kept by the grand master. He was ordered to register that the honours rendered to the Princes of Carignano were addressed, not to Charles Albert, who was only a Serene Highness, but to his bride, who as an Imperial and Royal Highness and Archduchess of Austria had a right to them. The obvious thing would have been to create Charles Albert a Royal Highness, but Charles Felix, and, they say also, the queen, who both still hoped for an heir in the direct line, were so hostile that King Victor abandoned the idea. From that day began the underhand, but unceasing and active malevolence of the Duke of Genevese towards the Prince of Carignano. Some years later, when Charles Felix was king, and he was advised to grant the title of Royal Highness to Charles

Albert, he replied, 'I cannot; one is born a Royal Highness, one cannot be made one.'

In 1820 the breath of revolution from Spain and Naples reached Piedmont, and the new ideas of constitutional government were first broached. *Carbonari* arrived in small bands, and members of the first Piedmontese families, the Dal Pozzo della Cisterna, the Perrone di San Martino, Collegno, Moffa di Lisio, Santa Rosa, Verasis di Castiglione, etc., were affiliated. They were joined by the officers who had fought under Napoleon, and under the restoration had been deprived of a step in rank. People talked openly about the *Carbonari* and the malcontents. The young men, always greedy for any novelty, were divided into two camps—the French Constitutionalists and the Spanish. The more fashionable and frivolous, led by the Marquis di Priero, were for the former. Gay and noisy, they dressed with the greatest care, according to French fashions. Sombre, nay even dramatic, wrapped in large cloaks, and wearing broad-brimmed white hats, the Spanish Constitutionalists stalked through the streets of Turin without attracting the attention of the king. Perhaps as it was Carnival time, he thought, or pretended to think, it was a Carnival joke.

On the 14th March the Princess of Carignano gave birth to a son, who was to be the future King Victor Emanuel II. Born during the first revolutionary movements for the unity and independence of Italy, *clairvoyants* might well have hailed him the Hope of Italy.

We pages were among the first to see the new-born baby, as we held torches round the font while he was being baptized. Some time afterwards, finding the door of the nursery half open, I entered, and absorbed at the sight of the baby in his cradle, was standing by him, when the Princess of Carignano came in. She scolded me well and forbade me ever to come near those rooms again without special permission. Twenty years later, when I was first equerry to Duke Victor Emanuel, I told him how I had been turned out of his room. He laughed heartily, but deplored his mother's love for strict Court etiquette, which bored him, and which he abolished on coming to the throne.

In the same year, 1820, I began my studies in the Academy for entering the general staff. The course of instruction lasted five years, and I must confess that the lessons of French and Italian literature left much to be desired. They were not calculated to teach even those who were extraordinarily gifted, like Camillo di Cavour, to write really well. Cavour often lamented how difficult he found it to express his thoughts in elegant Italian.[1] Mathematics and military tactics were, however, admirably taught, and those who failed in after years to distinguish themselves had only their own laziness or incapacity to thank.

[1] 'Dans ma jeunesse on ne m' a jamais appris à ècrire ; je n'ai pas eu de professeurs de rhétorique ni même d'humanité ; aussi ce n'est qu'avec la plus grande appréhension que je me decidérais à livrer un manuscrit à l'imprimerie. . . .' (Cavour. *Lettere*, Vol. I., p. 330, Collezione Luigi Chiala.)

CHAPTER II

1821-1825

THE political horizon in the beginning of 1821 was
gloomy; even we boys were conscious of the growing
agitation in Turin without understanding what it meant.
During a Court ball at the end of Carnival a fire broke
out in the Palace Ciablese, now belonging to the Duke of
Genova,[1] which forms one wing of the royal palace. We
afterwards heard that there had been riots, not only in
the capital but also in the provinces, for some days, and
that the fire was supposed to be the work of the *Carbonari*
and the Revolutionists, who hoped in the confusion to be
able to approach the royal family and to demand reforms
and the Constitution. What I saw (as all the pages were
on duty) was that the Prince of Carignano left the ball, and
returned in about an hour with his Court suit all blackened
with smoke, and high boots over his silk stockings, to

---

[1] The Duke of Ciablese, uncle of Victor Emanue I., left his palace to
Charles Felix, Duke of Genevese, brother of Victor Emanuel I., who succeeded him as King of Sardinia.

report to the king. A second time he left, and then came back to announce that all was safe and the fire extinguished. I and all my companions noticed that Victor Emanuel listened attentively and talked graciously to the young prince, while the queen frowned and glanced sneeringly at his boots and dirty coat. The Duke of Genevese, who was in the royal circle, did worse, for as Charles Albert approached he deliberately turned his back on him and walked away. He was suspected, unknown to himself, of being on good terms with the *Carbonari*, and Charles Felix was on the point of accusing him of incendiarism.

I forgot to say that the year before, on the birth of Prince Victor, the king had named the Prince of Carignano Commander-in-Chief of the artillery. This important post threw considerable power into his hands, and the constitutional Monarchists, then considered revolutionists, among whom were many *Carbonari*, centered their hopes in him. They expected that the young and liberal prince would put himself at the head of a party whose ambition was, with an enlarged and strengthened Piedmont, to form a kingdom of Italy, ruled by a constitutional king of the House of Savoy.

From 1818 to 1821 were perilous times for Charles Albert. The various parties who looked upon the restoration, or rather the resurrection of a dead past, as a farce, were searching for a personality—a name—in whose honour to unfurl the constitutional flag, and thought they had found him in the Prince of Carignano. So convinced were they that to him the idea of a constitutional Italy, united under his sway, would prove irresistible, that they made sure that he shared their notions. It appears, however, that the prince had never been approached on the subject. In the first days of March 1821 all eyes were turned on him, but whatever may have been said or written during those fateful days and even afterwards, it is certain that Charles Albert was affiliated to no secret society, and that in the beginning of 1821 he was ignorant of the plot hatched by the *Carbonari*, the nobility, and the Piedmontese officers. He declared it by word of mouth and in writing at various times, and the few around him who were not sectarians always said so, and have left it on record in letters which still exist.

I was then too young to understand what was going on, but some years later, when I got my epaulettes and left the Academy, it was still the subject of conversation. Charles Felix was then king and omnipotent, so most of the nobility naturally adopted the ideas of the Court, who looked upon the Prince of Carignano as a traitor to the Royal House. At the same time, he was decried as a traitor by some of the Liberal party. It was believed, or at least generally said, that he belonged to the *Carbonari* and had plotted with them in favour of a constitutional revolution; but becoming alarmed lest instead of helping him to a larger kingdom his companions might prevent his ever ascending the throne of his uncles, he had forsaken and betrayed them. In short, the poor prince was accused and abused by everyone, and even after he became king many still believed in his guilt. Only when the archives and documents of that time, as well as his own letters and those of his contemporaries were published, was light thrown on the events which I shall try to explain.

It was in the beginning of March that the prince first had cognisance of the revolutionary movement, and was surprised to discover that nearly all his artillery officers were in the conspiracy. To his astonishment, one morning Count di Collegno one of his equerries, introduced Counts Santa Rosa and Lisio and the Marquis di Caraglio into his study. They were, together with Collegno, the leaders of the movement, and came in the name of the Constitutional party to beg the prince to place himself at their head, and plead their cause with the King Victor Emanuel. Horror-stricken, Charles Albert remained dumb. It had never crossed his mind that the liberal sentiments he so frankly avowed to those about him could have led to his being chosen as the leader of a revolutionary political party. On recovering from his surprise he rejected their propositions, but probably not with the energy he ought to have shown, and dismissed the conspirators. They only wanted a figurehead, not a leader, and knew that the young prince lacked the decided character, the intuition, and the vast ambition of a Bonaparte. They hoped to compromise him—to seduce him with the idea of an enlarged and independent kingdom of which he was to be the founder. Taken unawares, and naturally irresolute and undecided, Charles Albert found himself in cruel perplexity—he must either be a traitor to the king who had been kind to him and laden him with benefits, or betray men who were his friends and had confided their secret to him. He chose the worst thing—a middle course. He tried to persuade the officers that their duty lay in fidelity towards their sovereign, and that their demonstrations were inopportune and dangerous, while he warned the king to be on his guard, and to take precautions against possible disorders. Whether, fearing to compromise some of his friends, he spoke too vaguely, I know not; anyhow, the king failed to grasp the situation and did nothing, while the revolution gained ground.

The Prince of Carignano spoke more openly to Saluzzo, the Minister of War, who was dismayed, but took no measures to forestall the revolution which broke out in Turin on the 8th of March. A cannon shot from the citadel was the signal which roused the whole population. The king, who had gone to Moncalieri the day before, immediately returned, and on the 10th he was presented with a *pronunciamento*, Spanish fashion, by the garrison of Alessandria, followed by those of Vercelli, Pinerolo, etc.

At first Victor Emanuel declared that he would not cede to violence, but when he understood that the revolution was spreading and civil war would be the result, he hesitated. A council was summoned, consisting of the ministers, their predecessors, several leading men such as Balbo, Vallesa, the Marquis Brignole, and the generals in command. Several of the latter declared that they would not answer for their men. A few of the councillors were in favour of granting concessions and reform, but the majority advised resistance. All those of the Liberal party who could obtain access to the Prince of Carignano were urging him to use his influence with the king and persuade him to grant a constitution. Among them were Vallesa, Saluzzo and Balbo. The prince declined to interfere unless called before the council and assured of the active support of the two last-named gentlemen. Summoned by the king, who asked his opinion, Charles Albert, strongly backed by Balbo and Vallesa, advised granting concessions, to which Saluzzo and Brignole assented, but all the others voted against them.

Meanwhile the revolution was spreading. Many of the troops quartered in and near the capital deserted and joined the garrison of Alessandria. The king, gradually becoming convinced of the aspirations of the majority of his subjects, was on the point of granting a constitution, when the Marquis of San Marzano[1] arrived from the Congress of Laibach,[2] to which he had been sent as minister plenipotentiary the year before. He declared that, in obedience to his instructions, he had assured the repre-

---

[1] Father of the Marquis of Caraglio, one of the heads of the Revolutionary party.

[2] Called at the instigation of Austria to arrange with the other great powers the right of intervention in countries which had risen in rebellion.

sentatives of the other powers that the King of Sardinia would never grant a constitution or make any change in the treaties and conventions of 1815. On hearing this, Victor Emanuel I. resolved to abdicate, and as his brother, Charles Felix, was at Modena to receive the King of Naples on his return from Laibach, he named the Prince of Carignano regent. Charles Albert at first refused, but on the representations of the ministers and servants of the crown present at the ceremony of abdication, he reluctantly accepted. The prince was deeply moved by the farewell words addressed by the king to him and to his faithful servants, and hardly less at Maria Theresa's cutting, but hardly undeserved, remarks to the ministers of war and public security,[1] who had allowed things to come to such a pass. Among those present at the leave-taking was my father, and he often told us that, on leaving, the king exclaimed, ' J'emporte avec moi le regret d'avoir inutilement travaillé au bonheur de mon peuple.'

Victor Emanuel I. left for Nice during the night of the 12th March, escorted by the whole light cavalry regiment Savoia, mounted on excellent little Sardinian horses. In spite of the entreaties of the king they accompanied him to Racconigi, where they took leave, and went to join the royal army under General La Tour at Novara.

Many people thought that in naming Charles Albert regent, the king meant to give a tacit assent to the promulgation of the Constitution. It was like saying, You are free, I am not ; do what you think best for the people and the monarchy. Unfortunately the young prince was inexpert, hampered by countless ties and duties, and had no man of strong character and intellect near him. He was overwhelmed by the revolution and became its martyr.

On the departure of the king all the ministers resigned,

---

[1] The queen's last words to Count Lodi were, ' Nous vous avons payé bien cher, monsieur, pour une police que vous faisiez bien mal.'—*Translator's Note.*

and their places were difficult to fill. The regent met either with a decided refusal or an acceptance negatived by impossible conditions. Meanwhile the revolutionary wave surged higher and higher. For want of sentinels who had abandoned their posts, or through the treachery of servants, the Carignano Palace was invaded by a mob, which declined to leave, and the prince was interrogated and advised by men unknown to him. When summoned to his assistance the Monarchists either turned a deaf ear or advised the proper course—the only one which Charles Albert could not bring himself to adopt—an immediate order to the troops who were still faithful to clear the streets. The soldiers in the citadel had exchanged their blue [1] cockades for tricolour ones, and some of the commanding officers threatened to fire on the town unless the Constitution was proclaimed. Under these circumstances, a prince of only twenty-three, with Liberal tendencies, and surrounded by Revolutionists, can hardly be blamed for conditionally signing the Constitution, pending ratification by the new sovereign. Couriers were immediately sent off to Modena with detailed accounts of the situation, and a request for explicit orders.

The answer was an order to go immediately to Novara and join Field-Marshal Baron La Tour, commanding that part of the army which was still faithful to the king. Charles Albert left Turin at nightfall, running the danger of being murdered by Revolutionary assassins, who called him cowardly, vile and treacherous. When he reached Novara, the field-marshal handed him a letter from the king, ordering him to go to Florence with his family. The prince went to Modena to see King Charles Felix, who refused to receive him, and, heart-broken, Charles Albert went into exile.

During the riots in Piazza Castello on the 12th March,

---

[1] The colour of the House of Savoy.—*Translator's Note.*

we boys were assembled in the chapel of the Academy at a funeral service in memory of our late governor, General Robilant. We understood that something was going on, but against whom, or for whom, there was fighting, we only learnt by degrees. A portion of the garrison of Turin and the suburbs had joined the Constitutionalists at Alessandria, so our governor, Chevalier Cesare di Saluzzo, mindful of what had happened in a Spanish town on the rebellion of the garrison,[1] marched us all off to the large buildings adjoining the church on the Superga Hill.

Shouldering their guns, the older pupils were placed as sentinels at every door, while the youngest amused themselves in the big room. The others, I among them, conspired—we wanted to join the army! One of our servants had just left to join his regiment at Alessandria, saying he was going to fight the Austrians. Fight the Austrians! Those three words fired our heads and legs, and we determined to run away into the woods, taking with us our silver spoons, forks and mugs to sell, and thus pay for our journey. No sooner said than done. Silently we slid down a steep slope through the wood towards the river. But our flight had been discovered and our older companions were sent in pursuit. They ran faster than we did and soon caught us, and with kicks and cuffs brought us back humiliated. On the 8th April the Constitutionalists were beaten at Novara by Marshal La Tour, aided by the Austrians, and their leaders fled to Switzerland and other countries, while the soldiers dispersed to their homes. The Austrians occupied Alessandria and Vercelli, and the governor of Turin, Count Thaon di Revel, named regent by the new king, Charles Felix, soon reduced the town to order.

Charles Felix prudently remained at Modena until October. Charles Albert, in disgrace, was exiled to Flor-

---

[1] The rebels seized all the pupils in a college for youths of good family, and held them as hostages.

ence, and Victor Emanuel I. was staying at Nice. On receiving news of the battle of Novara, Count Hannibal Saluzzo, commander of the garrison of Nice, went to inform his old king, who immediately exclaimed, 'Alas! My brave Piedmontese, they gave it to those cursed Austrians, did not they?' His grief was terrible on hearing that they had, on the contrary, been beaten. The good king hated Austria bitterly, to whom he attributed, far more than to France, the misfortunes of his country. Saluzzo seized the opportunity to urge Victor Emanuel to return to Turin, escorted by his regiment, assuring him that the whole army would at once rally round him. But the king refused.

Towards the end of 1821 Charles Felix returned to Turin, where everything was quiet owing to the vicinity of the Austrians. Called into Piedmont by Marshal La Tour in obedience to the king's orders, the latter found it no easy matter to get rid of them. 'Diplomacy moves so slowly. The Austrians are like pitch, which sticks if you touch it,' said the king. At least so it was reported. Two-thirds of the Austrian troops were withdrawn a year later, after the Congress of Vienna, but the last four or five thousand men only left Piedmont at the end of 1823.

Charles Felix was one of the few of his race who had no military tastes; but after ascending the throne he always wore a general's uniform. Intensely autocratic, he firmly believed in the divine right of kings, and exacted the greatest deference, not only to the crown, but to all belonging to it. He once placed a staff officer who reprimanded a servant of the palace under arrest for disrespect to the royal livery. Otherwise he was simple, almost infantine, in his tastes and habits. The theatre was his favourite' amusement, and he went there nearly every night.

Very different was Victor Emanuel I., who loved his soldiers. The presence of the Austrians at Alessandria and Vercelli was a bitter grief to him, and he regretted his beloved Turin. He had taken up his residence at Moncalieri,[1] and often drove or rode to the gates of the capital. There he would stop, gaze at the old walls, the green bastions, the Po and the Valentino Palace, and then slowly and sadly return to Moncalieri. He never approached the royal palace, not even to visit his brother.

From the spring of 1821 until that of 1823 the Prince of Carignano was an exile in Tuscany. No prayers or promises could move Charles Felix to recall him. When, in 1823, King Louis XVIII. of France sent his nephew and heir-presumptive, the Duc d'Angoulême, with an army into Spain to help Ferdinand VII. to put down the Constitutional Revolution, Charles Albert asked leave to join him. On the one hand, the prince wished to show his gratitude to Louis XVIII., who had pleaded for him with Charles Felix; on the other, his dislike, after the events of 1821, of constitutions and Constitutionalists, the cause of so much sorrow and trouble to him. After some months' delay, Charles Felix gave the desired permission, and the prince embarked at Leghorn for Marseilles with his equerries Robilant and Costa, and Isasco, officer of the staff. He arrived in time to take part in the campaign, and we all know how he distinguished himself at the Trocadero.[2] All

---

[1] Four miles south of Turin.—*Translator's Note.*

[2] The Trocadero, on the Isle of Leon, near Cadiz, was stormed by the French on the night of the 31st August 1823. The Prince of Carignano, disregarding the entreaties of his attendants and the orders of the French general Obert, was one of the first to throw himself into the canal and wade across up to his neck in the water. Seizing the colours of a regiment of grenadiers, he led them against the enemy's batteries. The gunners were killed at the point of the bayonet, as the cartouches of the attacking party had been spoiled by water. Seeing some of the enemy escaping in boats, the prince himself laid and fired two of their guns, and sank one of the boats. Next day the Duc d'Angoulême decorated him with his own Cross of St Louis, and —a far higher honour—a deputation of the grenadiers begged his acceptance of the epaulettes of one of their regiment who had fallen in the attack, saying he was so brave that he was worthy of filling the place of their dead comrade.—*Translator's Note.*

through life he was as courageous and prompt on the battle-field as he was timid and irresolute in politics. The Duc d'Angoulême invited him to Paris, where for a winter he was the idol of society, and Louis XVIII. lost no opportunity of recommending him to Charles Felix.

After the death of Victor Emanuel I. in January 1824, Charles Albert received permission to return to Florence by way of Turin, and to pay his respects to the king. He was, however, ordered to enter the capital at nightfall, and the king only received him late the next evening, fearing lest his presence at the palace might attract a crowd. Charles Albert told me afterwards that his uncle let him understand that he knew the prince had urged Victor Emanuel I. to resume the crown, and that the preference he had always shown for the late king had annoyed him. But, on the whole, the interview was satisfactory, and shortly afterwards the Prince of Carignano was recalled to Turin with his family.

He was handsomer than ever, but had lost his *brio* and gaiety and love of fun; he spoke little, never raised his eyes, and appeared nervous and timid. In reality he was suspicious of everything and everybody. The events of 1821 and their consequences, and the diffidence the king always showed him, had taught him only too well how dangerous it is for a prince to be carried away by his first impressions, or to confide his thoughts to those around him. I was constantly with him afterwards, and do not think he ever opened his mind to, or felt any affection or tenderness for, anyone, save perhaps for the very few women who gained his heart and knew how to keep it.

Before leaving the subject of the Academy for ever, I must mention those among my companions whose names became celebrated in war and politics—Alphonse La Marmora, Camillo di Cavour, and Cavalli.

My cousin, La Marmora, was three years my senior; audacious, enterprising, and intelligent, he was addicted to laying down the law to his companions. He was far from studious, so his mother, dissatisfied with the small amount he had learned at the Academy, obliged him to study seriously after he left. He travelled and read much and gained by experience, but none could have foretold what a high position he was destined to occupy. Very different was Camillo di Cavour. When as a small boy he joined the college in 1820, he showed most uncommon acuteness and intelligence. Endowed with a wonderful memory, he was a prodigious reader, particularly of political and historical works, and he had a passion for mathematics. The events of 1821 had a strong effect on him, and he wanted to follow and know the conditions of Piedmont and of other countries. So he induced his elder brother Gustavus to come into the parlour at the Academy, which was always empty during play hours, and from behind the thick grating which separated the pupils from visitors he listened to the newspapers his brother read aloud. Habitually studious he was not, but during some weeks before the examinations he worked double tides, and always came out first. Cavalli, celebrated as the inventor of the rifled cannon called after him, even as a boy was always studying mechanics. His only amusement consisted in making models in wood, iron, or anything he could get hold of, to demonstrate his ideas for the improvement of implements of war. Shortly after leaving the Academy he invented the high-wheeled gun-carriage, which was, I think, first adopted in the Camp of Instruction instituted by Charles Albert in 1833.

In 1825 I left the Academy with the rank of lieutenant, and began my service as officer of the staff. My three elder brothers were already in the army, the three younger I left behind me in the Academy.

CHAPTER III

1825-1840

The Staff—General Paolucci—Death of King Charles Felix—Accession o
Charles Albert—His Character—Life at Racconigi—Young Italy—
My Journey to Sardinia—Bear Hunting with Duke of Savoy.

THE staff, which I entered towards the end of 1825, was very different from what it is now. At the Restoration, when Victor Emanuel I. reorganised the Piedmontese army, he left the staff very much as it had been before the Revolution. The officers were considered more as topographical engineers than as part of the army, and civil engineers often shared in their work, and after some years obtained permission to enter the corps. Charles Albert altered all this in 1831; civil engineers were no longer admitted, the number of officers was increased, and some of them were put either to active or to office work under commanders of the military divisions.

My brother Casimir was named aide-de-camp to General Paolucci, a Modenese who for many years had been in the service of the Czar. Owing to the menacing attitude of France, Charles Felix had invited him to come from Russia to reform, or rather reconstitute, the army. His reputation stood high after a brilliant campaign in the Caucasus, in consequence of which the Czar named him Governor of Livonia and Courland, but he did not possess the military talent Charles Felix attributed to him. I believe the principal, if not the only, reform he made in our army was the introduction of a huge bunch of white feathers on the hats of the generals, still called a *Paolucci*. Fortunately France left us in peace, so the idea of reconstituting the army was abandoned. Paolucci was made Governor of Genoa, with a large stipend, by Charles Albert when he became king, out of gratitude for his services in advocating the prince's cause with the Czar in 1821-22. He held this post till 1848, but how or when he died I do not remember; as happens to us old soldiers when we leave the army, he vanished in silence and oblivion.

In the beginning of 1831 Princess Marianne, niece of King Charles Felix and one of the twin daughters of Victor Emanuel I., married the Archduke Ferdinand, heir to the Austrian throne. The King, with all the Court, accompanied the bride to Milan, and on the homeward journey His Majesty fell ill, after drinking, it was said, a lemonade at Novara. On reaching Turin he got worse, and never left his bed again. The Queen, Maria Christine of Naples, was named regent, so as I had just been promoted to be a captain, my commission bears her signature.

On the 27th April 1831 Charles Felix died, and was quietly succeeded by Charles Albert of Carignano. Revolutionary ideas had calmed down, men's minds were quieter, and several of the Monarchists, trusting in the experience of a man of thirty-three, who lacked neither intelligence nor culture, hoped for a pacific and wise reign. Many, however, of every party felt the same suspicion of Charles Albert that the late king had always shown. The extreme Monarchists accused him of Liberalism, with them a synonym of Jacobinism; they never forgave him for granting the Constitution in 1821. The ultra-Liberals, in the minority in Piedmont, but numerous in other parts of Italy, regarded him as a *Carbonaro* who had betrayed his brethren. This general and unmerited distrust which Charles Albert was powerless to dispel or combat, all the necessary documents being buried in the State archives whence they were only disinterred fifty years later,[1] was the perpetual sorrow and torment of his life—a torment which caused him to appear false and hesitating, and made his conduct incomprehensible to those about him who did not possess the key to the enigma. I saw and heard many examples of such apparently astounding duplicity that, in spite of myself, my affection for Charles Albert was shaken. He still cherished the liberal ideas of his youth, and had inherited the ambition of the House of Savoy, but at the same time was so steeped in mysticism that he conceived himself to be destined by God to achieve the redemption of Italy on the condition of becoming a sacrifice. Tied by promises and pledges given before he came to the throne, he would not break them while the various persons concerned lived, or until he received some manifestation of the Divine will, which he fully expected and in which he devoutly believed. His ambiguous and tentative manners were a blind to deceive the world as to his real thoughts and intentions.

In the beginning of 1833 my aunt, the Marchioness Christina d'Azeglio, who had been in Florence during the exile of Charles Albert and often received him in her house, wrote to beg him to give her nephew, who had been one of his pages, a place at his Court. The king, who never forgot old friends, at once named me one of his second equerries.

I entered on my service in May at Racconigi, the favourite summer residence of the king. He was an early riser, and at half-past five we were on horseback. On our return we breakfasted in our rooms, and then attended mass with the royal family, after which the king retired

---

[1] N. Bianchi proved by documents from the State archives that there was no foundation for the accusations of treachery and duplicity in the prince's conduct in 1821. My relation is founded on those documents, and not on the common belief which prevailed in my youth and for many subsequent years.

to his study until luncheon time. In the evening the queen called two of us to play whist with her and one of her ladies; the others played billiards with His Majesty, or read. The pleasantest time was after the queen, with her ladies and gentlemen-in-waiting, had retired, and we equerries, with the aide-de-camp and any favoured guest, remained alone with the king. Sitting on the edge of the billiard table, and swinging his long legs, he would talk of the present and the past, recount his travels, and tell us about the war in Spain and the people he had met, mimicking their voice and manner to perfection.

1833 and 1834 were sad years for our small country. A new secret society, 'Young Italy,' an offshoot of the *Carbonari*, took up the idea of a united and independent Italy. Since the French Revolution, or rather the victorious progress of Bonaparte through the Peninsula, this had filled many an Italian heart, but the general wish was to effect the change gradually, and rather in a Monarchical than in a Republican sense. Joseph Mazzini, a Genoese, was the founder; Orsini, Ruffini, Gallenga, Cattaneo, and Vochieri, were the leaders of the new sect; and, with the inconsiderate and rampant imprudence characteristic of Republican youth, they thought to stir Italy into rebellion with three or four hundred followers, and without money or soldiers. Mazzini, however, understood the necessity of having an army and a Prince with him. Abandoning his Republican ideas, he wrote his famous letter to Charles Albert, inviting him to follow in his footsteps and become the liberator of Italy, declaring that he had twenty millions of men ready to follow the Italian flag.

The king, who had good reason to doubt the existence of those twenty millions of men and did not wish to offend Austria who was jealously watching him, turned a deaf ear. Sad experience had taught him prudence, and how little secret societies and revolutionists were to be relied on. He was determined to be independent of sects or parties, to do nothing hastily, but gradually to create an army capable of resisting the attack of an enemy. Driven out of France, the Mazzinians had taken refuge in Switzerland, whence they attempted to stir up disorders in Savoy. A paper, called *Young Italy* after the society, was widely distributed, particularly in the army. The contagion spread from Chambéry to Alessandria, and thence to Turin, and the king was made seriously uneasy by the reports of the military authorities. A special commission was named to search for the culprits, and a court of judges at Turin, with the Count di Cimier (or Cimella) of Nice as president. He exaggerated in everything, in accusations, in judging, in punishing, and was cruel and unjust. A copy of *Young Italy* found in a soldier's knapsack or in a house sufficed to send a man to prison, and more than one was shot or guillotined. Many arrests were made in Savoy, in Alessandria, and in Genoa among the aristocracy; most of the latter were absolved after some weeks of imprisonment, save V. Gioberti, who was exiled. Several soldiers were condemned to death, others to the galleys or to long terms of imprisonment, by the military tribunal. The rewards bestowed on the judges who had shown the greatest severity produced a painful impression; people looked grave and sad, and even at Court there were whispered lamentations as to the course of events. When the first arrests in April were known the members of 'Young Italy' fled from Piedmont, and order was apparently re-established, but men's minds were uneasy. I was on duty at Racconigi at that time, and after receiving despatches from Turin the king grew sombre and taciturn. No one spoke during our morning rides; we were all enveloped in the black cloud of melancholy which oppressed Charles Albert.

In 1834 the Mazzinians, trusting to the assurances of a few Savoyards that the troops would flock to the tri-colour flag, entered Savoy in two divisions, one led by Ramorino, the other by Antonini, who had served in the Polish army. Disappointed by their cold reception, and hearing that the Sardinian troops were advancing, the rabble dispersed and returned to France or Switzerland, Mazzini among the first. A few military executions, necessary for the maintenance of discipline, took place at Chambéry, but the stern court of justice of the pre-ceding year having been dissolved, the sentences of death passed on the leaders were only promulgated after they had left the country. Among these was Garibaldi, a master mariner of the third class. For some years there was comparative quiet, but during his whole reign Charles Albert was tormented by the threats of the Mazzinian Society on one hand and the Society of Jesus on the other—the first trying to lure him with the promise of a kingdom on earth, the second with one in heaven.

In the spring of 1835 my brother-in-law, Count of Bernezzo, general in command of the division of Cagliari, died, and my sister Louisa wrote to beg me to come to Sardinia to accompany her and her small children back to Piedmont. A journey to Sardinia in those days was a serious affair. There were no railways, no steamboats, no telegraphs. The post-boat went once a month, and took from three to fifteen days, according to the wind. The boat had left before I got my sister's letter, so not to lose time I embarked at Genoa on a small mercantile ship about twenty metres long. The weather was bad and the wind contrary, and for twelve days I lay tied to the mast on a rug by the side of the beautiful Countess Rignon, who was going with her brother, the Marquis of Boyl, to Sardinia. I never saw or spoke to her, for we were both frightfully ill. The sea was so rough that we had to put in at the island of Asinara, where we passed the night in a shepherd's hut, and next day crossed over to Sassari.   A wretched diligence was the only mode of transport from Sassari to Cagliari, so I thankfully accepted the offer of General Crotti to procure me a horse and give me one of the ' 31 ' as a guide.   The ' 31 ' was a society charged with the postal service, and took its name from the number of its members.   There was a postman for every day in the month, and as soon as the post-boat was signalled, the man whose number coincided with the day saddled his horse, threw the big saddlebags across his flanks, and went to receive the letters which he distributed at the different post-offices along the road.   I took two days and a half to traverse Sardinia, sleeping one night at Macomer in the house of a rich proprietor, and the second in a village, the name of which I forget.   As was the custom then I begged hospitality for the night at the house of the principal man of the place.   But finding the whole family lived in one room with various domestic animals I preferred to roll myself in my cloak and sleep outside.

Prisoners condemned to forced labour were in those days transported to Sardinia and employed in gangs on the estates of the great landowners, or permitted to take service in shops or private families.   My brother-in-law had taken a frank, honest, good-tempered young fellow as cook and servant, who had been a shop-boy at Stresa on the Lago Maggiore, and was condemned as a domestic thief for stealing twelve francs.   ' They did quite right to punish me,' he used to say.   ' I was a mere boy, and stole a trifle ; who knows what a scoundrel I might have become if I had not been found out ? '

My sister was so anxious to obtain his release and send him back to Stresa, that I wrote to the king, who pardoned him, and most graciously sent a corvette to take us back to Genoa. With us sailed my brother Emanuel, who had served three years in Sardinia and married there. His wife was of noble family, pretty and nice, but, like all Sardinians, full of prejudice and superstition. During the voyage I observed that she was always chewing pieces of paper with writing on them, which she took out of a small box. These were sentences out of the New Testament, and verses from the Psalms, which her aunt had written out for her as a sure preventive against sea sickness. The more sick she was the more paper she swallowed, so at last, after vainly trying to persuade her to stop, I took advantage of a bad bout of sickness and threw the box into the sea, which made her very angry.

In 1838 I accompanied the young Duke of Savoy to the Monte della Moriana, where a bear had been seen. We drove to S. Michele, and climbed to the top of Montembrun on foot, while the beaters drove the forest. But in vain ; the bear had already escaped into the valley on the other side, and the king having fixed the day and hour of our return to Turin we were forced to abandon our bear-hunt. Charles Albert was already beginning to show the tenacity and inflexibility of character which led to more than one disaster in 1848.

CHAPTER IV

1840-1841

RUMOURS of wars were rife in the spring of 1840. Russia
and Prussia, together with England and Austria, were
united to uphold the rights of Sultan Mahmoud in Syria
against his vassal, Mahomet Ali, Viceroy of Egypt. The
latter had received encouragement, if not actual aid, from
France, who, with one of those poetical ideas which ought
to be banished from politics, remembered her Egyptian
successes in 1798, and favoured Mahomet Ali in his
struggle against the Sultan. Offended at her exclusion
from the quadruple alliance, she revived the idea of fortifying Paris, and there were rumours of armaments on our
frontier which alarmed the king and ministers.

One September morning I was summoned by Charles
Albert, who, under a promise of secrecy—religiously kept
by me for many years—said he wished, independently of
his ministers, to know the truth, and desired me to obtain
information. As a simple tourist I was to go to Savoy,
and thence to Dauphiné and Lyons. I applied for leave,
and the king gave me a passport in which my military
status was not mentioned. Charles Albert bade me be

careful, as in case I was arrested by the French authorities, he would disown me.

Fully resolved not to be caught, I provided myself with a botanist's vasculum, and went to Chambéry, where I established my headquarters. I knew all the country round, and, with my collecting-box over my shoulder, crossed and recrossed the frontier several times without molestation. Gathering plants one hot morning under the walls of the fort of Barau, I saw a veteran watching me from the glacis, and hailed him. Approaching nearer, I asked him 'whether there was any spring near by, as I was thirsty.

' I know nothing about water,' he answered. ' My only drink is good wine, and if you'll come up I'll give you a glass.'

I did not wait to be asked twice. After drinking, I offered him a cigar, and strolled on to the parapets praising the view. Chatting and smoking we walked about and I saw all I wished. There had been no fresh movement of troops, so the veteran and his companions had no reason for suspicion.

At Grenoble I entered a tobacconist's shop, and thought I knew the handsome woman who stood behind the counter. She recognised me at once, and began talking in Piedmontese dialect. I stopped her with a glance, and, as soon as we were alone, told her not to talk Piedmontese, and above all, not to call me captain, as being absent without regular leave, I might get into trouble.

She had lived in Turin for some years with a cousin of mine, by whom she had a child, which was in the foundling hospital, and which she wished to claim. I promised to help her as soon as I returned to Turin, and, through my uncle who was director of the hospital, was able to do so.

A handsome and taking woman she was in great favour with the prefect, and procured me permission to visit the heights, which were fortified.   At Gap I gleaned much information from the officers of the garrison, who dined at my inn; but at Briançon, which was full of troops, incessant rain prevented me from herborising, and I soon found myself an object of suspicion.   The gendarmes came to my room, examined my passport and my portmanteau, which only contained linen and a notebook with washing bills, and lists of plants, arranged as a cypher to remind me of the news I had collected.   The police were nonplussed; but that afternoon I saw others arrive, and determined to leave.

On reaching Turin I reported myself to the king, and was surprised to find Charles Albert gay and bright as in former years, before 1833-1834 had set such an indelible stamp of melancholy on him.   The change was due to the visit his intelligent, lively, and beautiful sister, Maria Elizabeth, the Vice-Queen of Lombardy, had paid him with all her family.   The king was pleased with the way I had fulfilled his instructions, and promised to name me one of the first equerries to the Duke of Savoy, just engaged to the Archduchess Maria Adelaide, second daughter of the vice-queen.

During the winter of 1840-41 I was continually in attendance on the young duke, but in the spring I was ordered on ordnance service in the Alps, where I nearly lost my life.   Soon after my return I accompanied the Duke to Genoa, and for twenty-five years, with the exception of two journeys in 1843 and 1849, I saw Victor Emanuel nearly every day.   Whether he knew me better, or that my frank, open character pleased him more than the usual ways of courtiers, or that, though not sharing his vehement passion for all physical exercises, I liked open-air life and was an excellent walker, I know not, but even when not on duty I was always called.   I could ride all day long, or walk for ten or twelve consecutive hours, without feeling anything but a tremendous appetite, and, like the duke, I cared more for quantity than for quality in my food. One or other of the officers of the Court or their sons were invited to his shooting parties, and among these at first was Alphonse La Marmora, equerry to the Duke of Genoa. But his authoritative, rather overbearing manner soon annoyed Victor Emanuel, who had plenty of good sense, and accepted advice when given unpretentiously and at the proper time. La Marmora with the duke, as with us all, posed as a professor, and wanted to lay down the law. At the slightest opposition he was ready to exclaim, like an old uncle of mine, '*I l'eu viaggià e lett.*'[1] He had read and travelled much more than other officers, but he took care everyone should know it, and Victor Emanuel, who never imposed his high rank, although fully conscious of it, disliked these airs of superiority, often asserted with considerable brusqueness. I was also sometimes rather brusque with my young prince, and held to my own opinion, but only when he did something I knew his father would not like, so he took it good-humouredly, laughed, and said, '*Là, là ch'as calma, ch'as calma. Un autra volta i fareu coum a veul chiel.*'[2] With La Marmora, on the contrary, he got angry, answered curtly, and gradually ceased to invite him. His place was filled by the son of General Scati, a college friend of mine.

Scati was as bad a shot as myself, and one day Victor Emanuel, with a keeper, distanced us, and climbed the ridge of a mountain, shooting blackcock as he went. As the birds could not be found, he thought he had missed them, and was much put out. They had fallen close to us, so we picked them up, and when we joined him said nothing. The duke, who was a capital shot, could not understand how we, so far below him and such inferior

---

[1] 'I have travelled and read.'

[2] 'There, there, be calm, be calm. Another time I'll do as you wish.'

shots, had made good bags. When we told him all the birds were his, he was delighted, and ate them later with redoubled zest.

Charles Albert never allowed his son to be absent more than two or three days ; so to gain time he left Turin in the night, particularly when we went to Casanova, near Poirino, the Count of Robilant's large property, the shooting over which he reserved for the duke. One morning we were to start at one. Carriages had been ordered, and I was to fetch Victor Emanuel at the royal palace. With my gun over my shoulder, I passed the sentry at a quarter to one, and found the palace gate ajar without any porter. Entering the great saloon of the *Svizzeri*, I found several servants stretched on mattresses fast asleep, and two policemen snoring on a bench. At the top of the stairs leading to the duke's apartments I found two more servants asleep, all the doors open, and the corridors illuminated. Without any difficulty, and without being seen by anyone, I reached his bedside. In a few minutes he was ready, and I took the opportunity to tell him how, unseen and unchallenged, with my gun on my shoulder, I had been able to reach his room. ' What I have done, others may do with different motives,' I said. ' Allow me to give orders that the access to your room at night should be less easy.'

He shrugged his shoulders and laughed. ' Who could have any evil intentions against me ? Pray don't have me put under lock and key.'

The marriage of Victor Emanuel with his cousin Maria Adelaide took place on the 11th of April 1842, with great pomp. Charles Albert excelled in organising magnificent ceremonials, without throwing away money or making debts. When he came to the throne, the public treasury and the private patrimony of the House of Savoy were in bad order, but by constant and wise economy he cleared off all liabilities.

After the marriage at the royal castle of Stupinigi, the bride and bridegroom entered Turin with the same ceremonial as had been used in 1817, only the State carriage was different, and there were no pages on the steps.

Marshall Radetsky, commander-in-chief of the troops in Lombardy, accompanied the Italian royal family, and was received by Charles Albert an hour after his arrival. They little thought under what different circumstances they would meet seven years later in the Lombard Quadrilateral and on the disastrous field of Novara. The king treated the marshal with the greatest distinction, and on the latter expressing his disappointment at not being able to stay for the tournament that was to be held in Piazza S. Carlo, a rehearsal was ordered for him in the royal garden.

CHAPTER V

1842-1847

AFTER a month's sojourn at Turin, the Vice-King and Queen of Lombardy returned to Milan, and the Court relapsed into the usual routine and stern discipline. The sweet smile and angelic goodness of Maria Adelaide softened and illumined, but brought no life or gaiety to the palace, where all were awed by the presence of the solemn and silent king. The Duchess of Savoy resembled her mother in many things, but lacked the *brio* and vivacity which, like a trumpet blast, roused everyone who approached the vice-queen, scattering melancholy and misanthropy to the winds. Victor Emanuel loved his cousin from the first time he saw her, and his affection was lasting. But she failed to fill his life, devoid of all mental occupation, as Charles Albert never allowed his son to participate in affairs of State. The duke continued his bachelor habits, and having more liberty after his marriage, was often away on shooting excursions for days together. At Court, Victor Emanuel was the heir to the throne, a loving husband and a respectful son; but outside he gave full scope to his natural instincts and tastes, and became a *mousquetaire* of the seventeenth century. He dressed rather in that style, and physically resembled Dumas' heroes, but without their vulgar manners and tastes. Though on familiar terms with those about him, and neither proud nor haughty, he was jealous of his personal dignity and position, and for no man would he have lowered them. With women it was different. It was sufficient for them to be young, pretty, and not coy to gain his affections for the moment. But I am perfectly convinced that among the large number—a sort of magic lantern of pretty women of all grades of society—not one ever really touched his heart. That belonged entirely to Maria Adelaide. Absolute trust, respectful and passionate admiration, and all his tenderest feelings, were so entirely hers that none remained for others, not even for the woman who for many years shared his life far more than the duchess had ever done, who bore him children, and at last became his morganatic wife.[1] Without pretending to be what he was not, Victor Emanuel gave the best of himself to Maria Adelaide. He had no secrets from her, though he did not tell her everything, because the litany would have been long and monotonous and unfit for her chaste ears. What she knew she pardoned, and even justified—a miracle of supreme indulgence and goodness not easy to understand, save by those who, like myself, stood between the two lives of the duke. The only person who had any right

---

[1] In 1814 and 1815, when, as boys, we watched the soldiers exercising on the bastions, the colossal drum-major was an object of great admiration. When the band ceased playing he walked about, and sometimes smilingly bent down and lifted a child up on to his broad shoulders. It was like being on the top of a church tower, and we all admired and liked Vercellani. Thirty years later, returning from Racconigi with the duke, in the suite of Charles Albert, who had passed a regiment of the Grenadier Guards in review, I recognised Vercellani on the balcony of a small house. By his side stood a beautiful girl of about sixteen ; she was his daughter, the *bella Rosina*, the future Countess of Mirafiore.

to blame him abstained, wisely, I think, showing perfect
tact and an intimate knowledge of her husband's exception-
ally ardent temperament.   I always tried (without posing
as a mentor) to restrain him; the thirteen years' difference
of age between us, and the affectionate familiarity with
which he treated me, allowed me to speak with frankness
and a certain authority.   I must add that, although in
no way responsible for the actions of the duke, I soon
discovered that the royal family thought I had more
power over him than I possessed.   I perceived this from
the bitter-sweet words of the queen, 'Mais Monsieur de la
Rocca, pourquoi n'avez vous donc pas ramené Victor plus
tôt,' if by chance we were five minutes late for lunch
or dinner in consequence of a horse falling or a carriage
breaking down.   Charles Albert allowed no excuses, and
put his son under arrest, even when once he appeared
with his arm in a sling.   I saw it also in the soft and
entreating eyes of the Duchess of Savoy when she said,
'Monsieur de la Rocca, je vous en prie, ne laissez pas
passer Victor à cheval dans le torrent Sangone (when we
were at Stupinigi) dans la Polcevera (when we were at
Genoa) le courant pourrait l'emporter;' and still more in
the angry glance the king cast at me before looking at
his son.   So I did my utmost to prevent mishaps, and
gave stringent orders to the hunt and stablemen.   As
to preventing the duke from fording rivers or jumping
dangerous places, I did my best; but like all high-spirited
young men, particularly princes who think it their duty to
have a double dose of courage, he was often imprudent,
and liked to show off.   Gradually, however, I persuaded
him to be more careful, and he would say, '*Là, i veui nen
ch'a sia crià an causa mia.*'[1]   In the matter of morals it was
more difficult.   He was profoundly sceptical as to the virtue
of women, and so many gave him good reason to doubt it

1 'There, I don't wish you to be scolded on my account.'

that reasoning with him was useless, facts were always in his favour.

In the spring of 1843 I went with my friend, the Marquis of Monforte, to Paris. Cavour was there, and took us to dine at the fashionable restaurants, and introduced us to the clubs. I remember one day, in the Champs Elysées, he introduced us to Thiers, who was going to take his daily riding lesson. He wanted to become a good horseman in order to turn his military studies to practical use in case France should be involved in war. From Paris we went to Belgium, and thence to London, where we parted from Cavour and returned home, *vià* Holland, the Rhine and Switzerland.

In July 1845 the Austrian family of Lombardy came to Piedmont for the last time, and the entertainments given at Racconigi in their honour were even more splendid than those of 1840. Afterwards people declared this to be another proof of the double dealing and falseness of Charles Albert, and that, determined to declare war on Austria, he had tried to deceive her by the courtesy and magnificence of his reception of the Emperor's uncle and his family. This was not the impression made on anyone about the Court. Charles Albert was devotedly fond of his sister, and delighted in her society. The presence of Maria Elizabeth and the occupation of preparing amusements for her seemed, for the moment, to dull his bodily and mental sufferings. The excitement of the *fêtes*, and still more the presence of his beloved sister, brought the last flush of happiness and gaiety to his pale face. Soon after her departure his melancholy, favoured by physical suffering and religious aceticism, increased. He grew thinner and yellower, while doctor and confessor seemed leagued together to encourage, instead of restraining, his inclination to excessive austerity. The unhappiness and restlessness of the king were patent to all, even bodily pain could not triumph over his mental anguish. He read the books of Gioberti and Balbo, and gave private audiences to Massimo d'Azeglio, who, in his quality of painter and poet, had traversed all central Italy and came to inform Charles Albert of the rapid growth of the idea of an independent and united nation, and of the general conviction that the House of Savoy was the only possible factor in the redemption of Italy.

About this time the king caused a medal to be struck, a sphinx with lion's paws throttling an eagle, and the motto, *J'atans mon astre*, on one side (taken, they said, from an old seal belonging to the Counts of Savoy), and heads of Dante, Columbus, Galileo and Michelangelo on the other. Charles Albert evidently felt the time was approaching when the condition of Italy might be improved. He did not lack the enthusiasm which produces heroes and martyrs, but he had no trust in the character and moral force of the Italian people, and therefore did not consider the time for appealing to arms had come. Above all, the painful experience of former years had filled him with such a horror of secret societies and Revolutionists, that he declined to avail himself of aid that was daily proferred.

The Republicans, the most numerous sect, were waiting impatiently in Malta, Corfu, and Switzerland, for a propitious moment for stirring up revolution in Italy. They had attempted it in 1844 in Calabria, and in the Romagna in 1845, and failed. Aware of this, Charles Albert, while wishing to take decided action against Austria at some future time, was fearful of compromising himself in advance. Hence he appeared undecided, wavering, and even hypocritical, and by degrees the faith, esteem, and love of those about him diminished, even of those who for years had been his friends and faithful servants. They were astounded to see him one day applauding the

words and acts of La Margherita, Minister of Foreign
Affairs, a clerical and a partisan of absolutism, while on
the next he listened approvingly to the Minister of War,
Villamarina, a reputed Liberal. Such uncertain conduct
aroused the suspicion of foreign powers, especially of
Austria, whose ill-humour, fanned by the reports of her
emissaries, vented itself in commercial reprisals. These
so angered Charles Albert as to cause great uneasiness
in the diplomatic body and corresponding hopes among
the Liberals.

Meanwhile Pope Gregory XVI. died, and was succeeded
by Cardinal Mastei Ferretti, as Pius IX. He granted an
almost universal amnesty to the political prisoners of the
former reign, and was at once hailed as a Liberal Pope
and the arbitrator of a federated and constitutional Italy.
His real motive was simply an act of clemency towards
prisoners who had nearly served their time; but he was
driven farther than he intended by the acclamations and
ovations with which this concession was received. The
Italian people, possessed by the passionate desire of a
fusion between the Papacy and Liberal institutions, either
did not, or would not see this, and for two years were in
a state of feverish excitement, setting aside every thought
or deed that did not refer to the independence and liberty
of Italy.

The agitation in Piedmont increased daily. It was clear
that the mystic and religious king was strongly attracted
towards the head of the Church, and sooner or later would
follow his example. In 1846 Charles Albert took the
decisive step of dismissing La Margherita. Notwithstanding the marked coldness with which the king
had treated him, he clung to power as long as possible,
in order, as he said, to attenuate the consequences of the
Liberal tendencies of the sovereign, and to save monarchy
and country from the catastrophe which would inevitably

follow the proclamation of a constitution. A few among the old nobles shared his opinions, but nearly the whole army, and the men of middle age about the Court, were as keen for Liberal institutions as the younger generation.

In November 1846 the death of my dear father prevented my accompanying the Court to Genoa. As soon as the king left on his return to Turin, the Genoese celebrated the centenary of the expulsion of the Austrians with illuminations and singing patriotic songs. A few years previously this would not have been allowed, but the train was laid, and the spark from Rome soon set the Sardinian realm ablaze. Liberal ideas were in the air, and the scientific congresses and agrarian societies contributed largely to their diffusion.

Over two thousand scientific men attended the congress at Genoa in 1846. Laurence Pareto was the president, and the Marquis Brignole-Sale came from Paris, where he was Sardinian ambassador, to do the honours of his fine palace and magnificent galleries. In all the meetings, patriotism, independence and liberty were more talked of than science. The meeting of the Agrarian Society at Casale in 1847 was so enthusiastically patriotic that the president reported it to Turin as seditious. But the private secretary of the king gave a different version, and Charles Albert's reply was read to the assembled members amid frantic applause.[1]

When I remember what times those were, and that this letter was read to men from divers Italian States, its

---

[1] I give a few extracts from the king's letter which has been printed in his biographies :—

'MON TRÈS CHER DE CASTAGNETTO,— . . . Votre lettre contient des détails qui m'interessent infiniment. Si je vous écrivais au long, je ne pourrais que vous répèter ce que je vous ai dit a Racconis à l'égard des sentiments et des vues qu'il faut exprimer pour le présent et pour l'avenir. Ajoutez seulement que si jamais Dieu nous faisait la grâce de pouvoir entreprendre une guerre d'indépendance, ce serait moi seul qui commanderai l'armée, résolu à

very audacity convinces me that for years the king had cherished the idea of liberating Italy from a foreign yoke. I consider this was the first step taken towards *action*, the independence of Italy ceased to be a dream, and hundreds, nay thousands, were ready to aid in its realisation.

On the 30th October, Charles Albert granted reforms which were hailed with gratitude and joy. A few days later he left Turin for his usual visit to Genoa amid the acclamations of the people, and on passing through Asti the crowd round the carriage was so great that, only just recovered from a serious illness, the king fainted. At Alessandria, where he passed the night, and at Genoa the enthusiasm was indescribable, save on one Sunday, when a significative demonstration took place. On leaving the palace to go to mass, the king was, as usual, cheered vociferously, until the people saw that he was bound for the church of the Jesuits, when all cheering ceased. A cold and silent crowd awaited his exit, and cries of '*Down with the Jesuits!*' '*Long live the National Guard!*' were heard.

Triumphal arches and addresses were prepared at Turin for his return; but Charles Albert, who was very ill, drove straight to the palace without even showing his face at the carriage windows. After resting, he was able to appear on the balcony and receive a fresh ovation from the crowd.

It has been said the king traversed the city without stopping to hear addresses, because he had been informed that paid agents intended to raise the cries of '*Down with*

faire pour la cause guelphe ce que Schamil fait contre l'immense empire russe. . . .

'. . . Les autrichiens ont donné un mémoire aux puissances pour chercher à faire croire qu'ils ont le droit pour eux, et ils ont déclaré qu'ils resteraient en possession de Ferrare, et que d'autre part ils interviendraient dans le pays où ils le croiraient nécessaire pour le intérêt. . . .

'. . . Ah! le beau jour que celui ou nous pourrons jeter le cri de l'indépendance nationale!

'TURIN, *le 2 Septembre* 1847.

Reform !' and *'Long live the Republic !'* But no one about the Court ever heard of this or of the scene between him and the queen before their departure for Genoa, when she is reported to have thrown herself at his feet, begging him not to go for fear of being assassinated. This is absolutely incredible to anyone who knew the queen. In the latter years she only approached the king with fear and trembling, without daring to speak.

In October 1847, Maria Pia, Princess of Savoy, was born, who afterwards married the King of Portugal. Her godfather was Pope Pius IX., who soon afterwards sent the traditional golden rose to her mother the Duchess.

CHAPTER VI

1848

1848! These four figures call up a host of fervent desires, hopes, anxieties, and joys, followed by cruel disillusions and bitter sorrow. It is impossible for me, a spectator— often an actor—in the great drama which even now, after forty-five years, agitates my very heart, to speak with the serenity of one who only knows the facts from books or by hearsay. I fear being carried away; of being, perhaps, even unjust in recounting what I have seen and heard. Our misfortunes and sufferings have not been in vain; one man was the victim and martyr, and we, the survivors, have reaped the benefit. Still, time has not lessened the indignation I felt against those who denied the valour of the small Piedmontese army, and dared to call its leaders traitors. If treachery there was, it existed among those who promised so much, and, when the first enthusiasm was over, did little or nothing.

In the beginning of January a Genoese deputation came to Turin to consult with the heads of the Liberal party and the leading newspaper editors. Among the latter was Cavour. They intended respectfully to demand the king to order the expulsion of the Jesuits, and the institution of the National Guard. The members were lodged at the Hotel d'Europe, exactly opposite the royal palace, so their advent and the visits they received from the recognised leaders of the Liberal party could not be ignored. The king was, of course, informed of all that passed, generally by men hostile to new ideas and to all public and private demonstrations. Irritated and annoyed, he refused to receive the deputation, alleging its illegality, and sent orders, through the police, that it was to return immediately to Genoa. On the 7th July the Genoese left, but, under pretence of assisting at the Carnival festivities, many provincial notabilities came to Turin. Everything said in the small parliament of journalists, of which Cavour was the leading spirit—and much that was not said—was immediately repeated all over the town. The editor[1] of the *Risorgimento* at once took a leading position and displayed extraordinary activity. Besides articles in his own paper, he wrote reviews in French and Genoese magazines, preparing the way for the redemption of Italy to be accomplished by the Piedmontese and, above all, by himself. Then came tidings of the rebellion of Sicily against her Neapolitan rulers, of violent demonstrations in Naples itself, and of the change of ministry, followed, like a thunder-clap, by the incredible news that the King of Naples, the most autocratic of sovereigns, had granted the Constitution. A few days later it was rumoured that his example had been followed by Leopold II. of Tuscany. The agitation in Piedmont increased. People no longer demanded reforms—the expulsion of the Jesuits—the institution of the National Guard—but the Constitution, enjoyed by France for many years—the Constitution, just granted by Francis and Leopold to their subjects.

The Duke of Savoy, wanting to hear and see for himself, went out at night, dressed like a well-to-do farmer, in a

[1] Cavour.—*Translator's Note.*

big cloak, with a slouch hat drawn over his eyes, and mixed with the crowd. He wished to go alone, but I always kept near him, afraid, not of his being hurt, as he was popular, but that some expression of public sympathy might get him into trouble. One night, also in disguise, I was in the crowd behind Victor Emanuel, listening to a group of men who were talking vehemently, when I was violently pushed. I was about to retaliate, when the man approached and whispered, ' I am Alexander La Marmora. Look out, you are known.' Warning the duke, we quietly withdrew. The police were aware of our nocturnal excursions, as I found out from the old marshal, Baron La Tour, governor of Turin, to whom the duke often sent me with messages. Fearing lest my frequent visits to the governor's palace should attract the attention of the idlers always stationed in Piazza San Carlo, the baron told me to enter by the small door in a back street, which led to the apartments of his son. I remember, as though it had occurred yesterday, the conversation between us one February morning after the baron returned from his daily visit to the palace. Seated in an armchair, and caressing his beloved snuff-box, he said the king was constantly being entreated to grant larger concessions and political reforms. ' They want the Constitution,' said His Majesty to me, ' and I will never grant it.' Stopping to take a pinch of snuff, the old marshal continued, ' You understand ? the king said he will not grant the Constitution. Well then he will, and very soon.' The baron was right. On the morning of the 8th February, Turin awoke to the news that the king had granted the Constitution. Charles Albert must have had a bitter struggle. He was intimately convinced that his people were, as yet, unfit for liberty, and he meditated a war with Austria, for the conduct of which he considered the absolute independence of the sovereign was necessary. He was tormented by the recollection of his promise made at Paris through the Sardinian ambassador to the Emperor of Austria, that if his succession to the throne was unopposed, no essential changes should be made in the institutions which had endured for eight hundred years. On this latter point the Archbishop of Vercelli succeeded in calming his conscience. Charles Albert gave the Constitution unwillingly, and against his own convictions, to please his subjects, but, unlike the Bourbons of Naples, with the resolve to keep his word.

The Constitution, announced on the 8th February, was promulgated on the 4th March. Those twenty-five days were passed in demonstrations of rejoicing—*Te Deums* in the churches, and processions. It was Carnival time, so Piazza Castello was crowded with masqueraders and sight-seers from other parts of Italy. Many were dressed *à l'Italien*, which at first looked like fancy dress. The ladies wore a long riding habit of black velvet looped up over a tricolour silk skirt, or a short velvet dress, with a tricolour scarf, and all had high calabrese hats, with white, red, and green feathers and ribbons. The men had shooting jackets and breeches of black velvet and tricolour waist scarfs, and their calabrese hats were decorated with tricolour braid and tassels. While we were singing, making speeches and walking in processions, grave events were happening in France and preparing in Austria. A fresh revolution had burst out in Paris ; the Orleans had fled, and the Republic was proclaimed. The poet Lamartine, President of the Republic, could not understand that the sons of the *terre des morts* had resuscitated, and the idea that Piedmont might expand into a powerful Italian state did not please French political men.

It was clear that, in the event of a war with Austria, we had nothing to hope from France. But in the first flush of enthusiasm that seemed of no account. 'What care we for allies? Italy will act by herself!' ('*l'Italia farà da se*'), was the cry. A few days later Charles Albert repeated in public, '*l'Italia farà da se.*'

There was some justification for this. Deputations came daily from central and southern Italy of leading men and of amnestied political prisoners, who had suffered for the Italian cause, to implore aid from the Piedmontese army, promising the support of all their fellow-citizens. Not only the king, but all we young officers, shared the illusions of the populace, and the streets resounded with patriotic songs. The excitement increased when the revolution burst out in Vienna, followed by the famous 'five days' of Milan and the rising in Venice. A Lombard deputation arrived to entreat the king's help to turn the Austrians, not out of Milan—that was done—but out of the Quadrilateral. Charles Albert promised his aid, and immediately ordered the troops nearest the frontier (the brigade Piedmont, and the Pinerolo and Piedmont cavalry regiments, with the 1st field battery, about four thousand men in all) to cross the Ticino and march to Milan. At the same time, the whole army was to be placed on a war footing.

After the promulgation of the Constitution the ministry resigned. Sclopis, failing to form a new one, the king called Cesare Balbo, requesting him to give a portfolio to the Genoese, Laurence Pareto. The new ministry assumed office on the 16th March, and the duty fell to Franzini general of the staff, as Minister of War, to organise the army for active service.

The task was an arduous one. Since 1815 there had been peace, and during the ten years' reign of Charles Felix military discipline had been neglected. Charles Albert had to reform everything. The Camps of Instruction, instituted by him, and which were held nearly every year from 1833 to 1847, had imparted some practical knowledge, especially as to the combined action of the various arms.

In a few days Franzini succeeded in placing twenty-five thousand disciplined troops on a war footing, to be joined by twenty thousand provincials,[1] thus bringing the army up to forty-five thousand men. With the announced support of the whole Lombard population, and the Roman, Tuscan and Neapolitan troops promised by their respective sovereigns before our departure, we calculated on having over a hundred thousand men, and, like Bonaparte in 1797, imagined ourselves already near the gates of Vienna. Such were the brilliant illusions, too soon, alas! to be dispelled.

Franzini, who had known me for some time and honoured me with his esteem, named me colonel, and chose me as chief of the staff of the reserve division, to be commanded by the Duke of Savoy. I was ordered to leave at once for Casale to organise it.

The division of the Duke of Savoy was composed of—

1st. The brigade of Grenadier Guards, the first and finest in the army; and the Sardinian Sharpshooters, under the command of General Count Biscaretti.

2d. The brigade Cuneo, commanded by General d'Aviernoz.

3d. The regiment of Aosta cavalry, in which my brother Frederick was captain, commanded by Colonel Castelborgo, which was substituted by that of Genoa when we arrived at Piadena.

4th. Four battalions of Bersaglieri, a detachment of engineers, and three batteries of artillery under Major Alphonse La Marmora, besides ambulances, commissariat, etc., etc.

---

[1] Reserves formed of soldiers discharged before finishing their time with the colours (eight years), and allowed to marry.

As I am not writing a history of the campaign, I shall only jot down from memory, aided by my notes, the part played by the reserve. On the 24th March the king, with the Duke of Savoy, left Turin for Alessandria to take command of the troops assembled there. As soon as our division was ready at Casale the duke joined us, and we left to meet the king on the road to Pavia. Before entering the town, tricolour cocardes and flags were distributed to the men. From a sentiment of delicacy Charles Albert ordered them to be substituted for the blue of the House of Savoy, as once the Ticino was crossed war and army became Italian.

The entry of the king into Pavia on the 29th March, at the head of some twenty thousand men, roused extraordinary enthusiasm, and the city was decked with the Italian colours. The townspeople were unanimous in desiring to drive the Austrians out of Italy. Not so the villagers and peasants, generally Conservatives, and afraid lest the passage of troops and a change of government would only bring requisitions and fresh taxes. We had proof of this at Borghetto, our first halting-place. Resenting our camping in their fields, the peasants prepared to open the sluices of the canals to flood the country. I sent for the syndic, and finding my appeal to the sentiment of Italian brotherhood, proclaimed by Lombardy, useless, threatened to burn the village if my men were not allowed to sleep in peace on dry land.

From Borghetto we went to Cremona, where the king had established his headquarters. Most of the generals had arrived, and the more distant garrisons of Nice, Savoy and Genoa, with many of the provincial regiments, were continually coming in. A council was held, and the formation of the army into two corps, divided into five divisions, was decreed. The 1st corps, under General Eusebius Bava, consisted of two divisions; the 2d also of two divisions, was commanded by General Hector de Sonnaz ; and the 5th formed the reserve under the Duke of Savoy. The Duke of Genova commanded the artillery, and supreme head of the army was the king. General Salasco, the chief of the staff and his deputy, Colonel Cassato, were disciplinarians, cultured, and honest, but wanting in initiative and military tuition. The Minister of War, Franzini, who accompanied the army, was, from a military point of view, the better man of the three, but he had no command, and only a consulting vote.

The choice of Salasco as chief of the staff was a grave mistake. He ought never to have accepted a post of such responsibility, for which he was unfit. He lacked the authority which it was his duty to exert ; under him everyone wanted to give orders, and that unity of command, so indispensable to an army, did not exist with us in 1848.

It was natural that Charles Albert, who risked everything in the cause of independence, should wish to accompany the army. But either his chief of the staff should have been enterprising, intelligent, and highly educated, with an ascendancy over the sovereign such as Berthier possessed in the first wars of Napoleon, or the command should have been entrusted to an experienced general who had the practice and knowledge of military matters. Bava, De Sonnaz, Franzini, and perhaps Bes, might have been capable of so great an enterprise.

The Duke of Savoy was impatient to enter the field, but rather as a common soldier than a commander. Courageous, like all his race, he would have enjoyed rushing into the thick of the fight, and charging the enemy with his lance at rest, like a knight of old. Without much instruction or knowledge of military matters, he had excellent common sense, listened to advice, and followed it when he saw it was good.

The Duke of Genova was said to be better informed

than his brother; he was certainly more thoughtful and less expansive, but equally courageous.

We continued our march towards the Mincio, between which and the river Chiese the Austrians were strongly entrenched. They however fell back, and our advanced guard soon came within touch of them. At Cremona it had been decided to attempt the passage of the Mincio and advance on Mantua, so the king went towards Piadena and Macaria. An Austrian reconnaissance from the fortress caught a small detachment of our cavalry asleep in a dairy farm, and took them prisoners to Mantua. The officers were in despair at this first check, but had their revenge at the Bridge of Goito on the 8th and 11th April. Only the 1st and 2d corps were engaged; the reserve was not called up. The Marquis Ceva had been despatched from headquarters to inform the Duke of Savoy of the affair, and when we were between Castelgoffredo and Castiglione delle Stiviere, Ceva arrived at full gallop, pulling up short on seeing the duke. Too excited and out of breath to speak, he opened and shut his mouth like a fish out of water, without producing a sound. At last he gasped, ' A i soun, Altessa, a i soun!'[1] The Bersaglieri especially distinguished themselves by pursuing the enemy across the ruins of the bridge, and their commander, Alexander La Marmora, had his jaw fractured.

The Austrians, driven out of Goito and Valeggio, retired towards the Adige, and our troops occupied Monzambano and Borghetto. The king established his headquarters at Volta, whence he attempted to attack Peschiera on the 13th April. He had been informed that there was only a small body of troops, with many Italians among them anxious to join their brethren. The fortress, on the contrary, was strongly garrisoned chiefly by Croats. After bombarding the place for a whole day the king saw

---

[1] ' They are there, your Highness, they are there.'

that, without the siege train which had been left in Alessandria, nothing could be done.   Alphonse La Marmora, one of the chief partisans of this attack on Peschiera, and who had persuaded the Duke of Genoa to suggest it to the king, offered to treat for the capitulation of the fortress. Astounded at such audacity, the commander refused to receive him; so the king sent Major Cavalli to Alessandria to fetch the siege train, and retired, leaving Federici's division to prepare the earth works.

From Castiglioni delle Stiviere we had meanwhile marched to Cavriana, where we remained for nearly a fortnight, and whence the duke went to visit his father at Peschiera.   Soon afterwards the king transferred his quarters to Monzambano, the duke went with the Grenadiers to Valeggio, while the Cuneo brigade remained at Volta.   On the 29th we heard cannon in the direction of Santa Giustina, whither the king had gone in the morning.   In the distance I saw moving masses, but could distinguish nothing; so, setting spurs to my horse, galloped up a winding path, cut so deeply in the hillside that I could not see to the right or left.   Finding that I was approaching within gunshot of the enemy, and from one moment to another might be seen, I urged my horse up the steep bank, whence, plunging into the wood, I returned to Valeggio to give the alarm.   The Austrians, however, did not attack us, and we were not summoned to support the other division.   In the evening we learned that the enemy had been driven back to Pastrengo, whence Charles Albert determined to dislodge them on the following day.

The king's object in taking the offensive was to drive the enemy away from Peschiera, which he was about to besiege, and to open the road to Verona.   Emissaries of a patriotic committee, who afterwards paid dearly for putting themselves into communication with him, were daily appealing for help.   The population, they declared, was ready to rise and drive the Austrians out, as the Milanese had done, if the army would support them. These repeated assurances, at first only listened to by the king, in the end convinced Franzini and Bava, and on them were based the military operations of the end of April and the beginning of May.

In April large reinforcements reached us. Immediately after driving out their princes, Parma and Modena declared in favour of a great northern kingdom of Italy, and despatched troops to join us. Those promised by Tuscany, Rome and Naples also came in, so that, with the contingent of provincials, about fifty thousand men were added to the fifty thousand we already had on the Mincio. The companies, consisting of one hundred or one hundred and fifty men, were raised to two hundred and fifty, a thing never seen before or since. Several provincial regiments were in the affair at the Bridge of Goito, and, although all married men with families, had fought well, and were obedient to discipline. For the moment the Italian army was superior in number to the Austrian; but the half beyond the Po included many volunteers—men who knew nothing of warfare, and hindered us more than they helped. Before we could discipline them, they disbanded and vanished, while the Romans were recalled by the Pope, and the Neapolitans by King Francis. The Pope, the initiator of the revolution, who two months before had blessed the troops, changed his mind, and, in an allocution of the 29th April, sounded the note of alarm which caused the recall of the Romans, and soon afterwards of the Neapolitans.

All this we, of course, did not know in the latter days of April; and men from Piedmont, Lombardy, Parma and Modena fought bravely side by side on the 28th and 29th at Colà, Sandrà and Santa Giustina, and on the 30th at Pastrengo.

The engagement at Pastrengo only began towards eleven, either because Charles Albert, in the fervour of his religious mysticism, insisted on first praying and hearing mass, or that De Sonnaz, who had only just been put in command, had not had time to prepare things before. Five hours later the heights were ours.

The command of the Duke of Savoy was divided, the brigade of Guards being on the right, the Cuneo brigade in the centre ; De Sonnaz's divisions were on the left and also in the centre. Officers and men scrambled impetuously up the steep hill, the top of which was fortified and occupied by the Austrians. I have seen many skirmishes and battles since then, but the ardour, the enthusiasm, displayed in the first days of the campaign of '48, I never saw again. The Piedmontese and the other Italians, who daily joined the regular army, presented the moving spectacle of a whole people rising to drive the stranger out of their country.

While the combat was raging on the steeps of Pastrengo, I perceived that, by advancing on our right from Verona, the enemy might strike us on the flank. The danger had not been foreseen, and points of defence had been left unmanned. Communicating my fears to the duke, I asked permission to go and reconnoitre. With full powers to make all necessary dispositions, I took Lieutenant Avet of the staff with me, and galloped towards Santa Giustina. From the strong battery posted there, I saw through my field-glasses several columns of the enemy's infantry leaving Verona for the Osteria del Bosco, on the Peschiera road, at the foot of the Sona Hills—a position that had been almost denuded of troops that very morning to reinforce the attack on Pastrengo. I immediately ordered the artillery to fire on the advancing columns, which was done with excellent results. Meanwhile I despatched Avet to Sona to ask General Sommariva, commanding the Aosta brigade, to send down part of his men on to

the Verona-Peschiera road, to oppose the enemy's advance.
Before arriving at the Osteria del Bosco, the broad and
straight causeway is cut through a hill, and has steep
banks on either side. Just there, whence nothing could
be seen, I found the brigade of cavalry commanded by
Major-General Sala awaiting orders, which never came.
I warned him of the enemy's approach, and of the necessity
of preventing it, to which he objected his lack of infantry,
there only being sixty grenadiers near by, sent to bring in
supplies, under Lieutenant Villafalletto. The latter, fully
alive to the danger, had disposed his men in skirmishing
order, ready to support the cavalry or the nearest battery.
I advised Sala to dismount a certain number of his cavalry
in order to strengthen the defence. The general acceded
to this, and soon afterwards, seeing part of the Aosta
brigade coming down the hill, I returned to Pastrengo to
tranquillise the duke, and take part in the last exciting
moments of the engagement.

Although the Austrians were in great force, and had
the advantage of a dominating position, they were rapidly
driven down towards the Adige, which they crossed on
pontoons, with the fear, naturally, of being pursued by us.
But the elementary rule that a victory should always be followed up was neglected. The order to cease the pursuit was
given too soon, and this grave mistake was repeated many
times during the campaign, to the despair of the officers.

Finding the road under the Sona barred, and probably
informed of the defeat of Pastrengo, the Austrians retreated
again into Verona.

During the battle Charles Albert rode from place to
place with a small suite, chiefly composed of non-com-
batants, such as the Lombard envoys and the representatives of various cities. Suddenly meeting a company of
Tyrolese, Sanfront, the colonel commanding the escort of
carabineers, gave the order to charge, when Charles

Albert drew his sword, and dashing forward with the men drove the enemy up the hill.

After the battle our army encamped between Sandrà and Santa Giustina, the king and the Duke of Savoy establishing their headquarters at the latter place.   In the evening there was a slight altercation between the duke and Alphonse La Marmora, who was so convinced of his own superior knowledge that, instead of obeying orders, he generally went his own way. The Duke of Genova's admiration and high opinion of La Marmora was not shared by Victor Emanuel, who, using a Piedmontese phrase, called him a *venditore di vasetti* (seller of pots), meaning a man who knows how to cry up his own wares. He esteemed La Marmora's high sense of honour, and made use of him when necessary, as he was popular, determined, and not afraid of responsibility. But Victor Emanuel never liked him, and resented his superior manners.[1]

In the first days of the campaign we were often on short rations, not entirely from the fault of the contractors, but from the peculiar conditions in which we were placed. It was impossible for us to behave as conquerors to our allies and brothers, who showed little generosity, and no inclination to assist the army which had come to their aid. This was one of the many disillusions to which I have already alluded.

The division of the Duke of Savoy, more fortunate than the others, suffered but little from want of food or

---

[1] Victor Emanuel's opinion of General Alphonse La Marmora is curiously confirmed by Theodor von Bernhardi.   In the seventh volume of his *Tagebuch-blätter* (1866-1867), just published, he talks of La Marmora as a narrow-minded Piedmontese, whose management of military affairs was childish. The king said to Bernhardi (p. 225), ' *Il n'a pas beaucoup de tête, ce pauvre La Marmora.*' On the other hand, La Marmora told him, ' *Prenez garde que le roi ne vous fasse quelque pâté . . . comme le roi n'est pas fort . . . il en a fait à moi.*'—*Translator's Note.*

forage. After the first days of confusion we arranged directly with the various syndics to furnish supplies on notes of hand, which were faithfully paid at Turin the following year when I was in the ministry.

From |Santa Giustina the king transferred his head-quarters to Sommacampagna, while the duke went to Guastalla.

The ministry at Turin, the provincial governments of Lombardy, and the Duchies were always urging Charles Albert to strike a decisive blow in order to maintain the popular enthusiasm (particularly in the Lombard provinces, where registers had been opened in favour of annexation); while the Veronese Committee assured him that the whole population would rise to expel the Austrian garrison.[1] So, for the second time, he determined to take the offensive, and attempt to lure the enemy out of Verona, in the hopes of gaining a decisive victory in the open to be announced at the meeting of Parliament, fixed for the 8th May. On the 4th he charged both Bava and Franzini to prepare plans of battle. He chose Franzini's—more complicated, but not very dissimilar from that of Bava. At a council of all the generals—saving, I never knew why, the duke— the king's opinion prevailed ; and Bava undertook to carry it out, demanding twenty-four hours in which to distribute orders to the troops destined to be engaged—the 1st corps, the reserve, and a division of the 2d corps. The king, however, and probably the other generals, insisted on the immediate execution of the plan, either in the hope of surprising the enemy, or because the Veronese Committee announced a rising within the city for the 6th.

Orders were therefore prepared and sent out during the

[1] The promises and affirmations of the members of this Committee, too lightly made in the name of the citizens, were most injurious to the Italian cause. They were the primary cause of the mistaken actions at Santa Lucia, at Tomba and Tombetta. The cruelty with which they were punished by the Austrians forbids us to judge them too severely.

night. But the time was too short. Many commanding officers were left in total ignorance of what had been settled and never moved, others received their instructions too late, or they were not clear, so they arrived when the battle was half over, some even when it was finished.

The orders were that at seven on the morning of the 6th May the army was to be under Verona. The 1st division at S. Massimo to form the centre; the 2d at Santa Lucia on the right; the 3d at Croce Bianca on the left; one brigade of the reserve, the Guards, were to go to Santa Lucia, the second was to support the centre.

But at seven o'clock no one had appeared at their appointed places save the king and Bava (who was in command) with their staffs, and the Aosta brigade with the 8th battery of artillery. Seeing this the king wished to postpone the engagement, but Radetzky, as usual, perfectly informed as to our movements, opened fire, and from an offensive ours became a defensive movement. We had received our orders at Guastalla, after ten in the evening, and I passed the night in distributing them to the various commanders. All were not ready at the appointed time, and the duke and I were kept waiting about an hour. However, the Guards reached Somma-campagna at half-past seven, and I sent them on to Santa Lucia to reinforce the Aosta brigade.

Passing through the small village of Tana, on our way to S. Massimo, I noticed a ladder against the church tower, and, interrogating some peasants, learned that Austrian troops had just passed through in the same direction as ourselves. Dismounting, I climbed to the top of the tower, and saw that S. Massimo was still unoccupied, and we reached there before the division of General d'Arvillars, under whose orders the duke was. After his arrival we saw that the enemy on the other side of the hill were continually receiving large reinforcements. The general gave the artillery orders to fire, but seeing the preponderating numbers of the enemy, and the strong position occupied by them, he waited for renewed orders before attacking.

A little after mid-day General d'Arvillars sent an aide-de-camp to the duke, ordering the Cuneo brigade to go to Santa Lucia. This seemed to me so contrary to all scientific rules, which forbid a column to expose its flank to the enemy's fire, that I feared the aide-de-camp, who was the general's son and very young, might have made some mistake, and sent to request the order to be repeated. On receiving the confirmation the duke immediately started, and I galloped off with the captain of the staff, Count S. Martino d'Agliè, to find Bava and ask what position the Cuneo brigade was to occupy. I found Bava at Santa Lucia, who told me the Guards had greatly distinguished themselves, but had suffered severely. Fearing that they would not be able to hold the position against a renewed attack, he had ordered the Cuneo brigade to take their place. Then he sent me to reconnoitre the ground in front of the first line.

Dismounting, I advanced, and at a bend of the road found General Sommariva (commander of the Aosta brigade) bending over the body of Count Balbis, his young aide-de-camp. Raising the handkerchief he had thrown over the poor fellow's face, he let me have a last look at him, then drawing a ring off the dead hand he said, with an unsteady voice, 'I shall give this myself to his parents.' He warned me that the road was swept by the fire of an Austrian battery, and for a moment I felt my heart beat, not for myself—a bachelor—but for d'Agliè, who had left his young wife, about to become a mother, to resume service in the army when war was declared. We walked on fast—not running, lest people might think us cowards—and when I had fulfilled my mission, returned to meet the Cuneo brigade. It came up with the artillery about four o'clock, having been knocked about during the flank march, but full of fight.

We had hardly taken up the positions held till then by the Guards when news came that the king had ordered a retreat. So astonished and disappointed were we that we refused to believe it. Shortly afterwards Bava arrived, in full dress uniform, with all his decorations (his habit was to dress so for battle), and bowing low to the duke, as a well-bred man would do to a prince in a ballroom, said, 'With your Royal Highness's permission, I take command of, and lead the retreat, requesting your Royal Highness to protect the rearguard.' Then, in a clear voice, impassible under the enemy's fire, he gave the words of command, 'Retreat by sections.'

Charles Albert had ridden several times during the engagement up to the walls of Verona, hoping to see the signal which had been agreed upon, or, at least, to receive some message. Once he was nearly made prisoner by a squadron of Uhlans; luckily they were put to flight by shells fired from two of our guns. No sign came from the town, and on hearing that the centre column had been unable to deploy in line for the capture of S. Massimo, which was well defended, while the Broglia division had failed in the attack on Croce Bianca, he deemed it better to desist and order the retreat. Santa Lucia alone was in our possession, and the error committed at Pastrengo was repeated there. Our troops were masters of the position, fresh ones were ready to reinforce them. The D'Arvillars and Broglia divisions might also have been called up to pursue the enemy into Verona itself, where the population, at the sight of the Italian troops, would probably have fulfilled the promises made by their representatives. It was a fatal mistake, and most painful for us to see victory always elude us when half won, more especially at Santa

Lucia, which had been taken at so great a sacrifice. We lost seven hundred or eight hundred killed and wounded, and the Austrian loss was greater.

Radetzky reoccupied the position immediately the duke left, but did not molest our retreat.

CHAPTER VII

1848—*Continued*

WE remained inactive at Guastalla for several weeks, riding now to Peschiera to watch the preparations for the siege, now to Sommacampagna, the king's headquarters, whence we always returned out of temper and disappointed at hearing and seeing no sign of intending hostilities. The 2d regiment of Grenadiers was at Guastalla, the 1st at Sommacampagna, while great part of the Cuneo brigade was employed in transporting the siege artillery which arrived from Alessandria towards the middle of May. Owing to the heavy rain the roads were almost impassable, and it required hundreds of men to move each piece. A few battalions of the Cuneo brigade were ranged in echelon behind the centre of the line, which extended from Rivoli to Villafranca, resting on Valeggio and Goito in order to assist the cavalry in guarding our flanks. Valeggio was defended by the artillery and the cavalry brigade.

These dispositions had been made to guard against a possible attack by Radetzky, who was expecting General Nugent with sixteen thousand or eighteen thousand men. The latter had crossed the Isonzo and was already in Friuli, but the Tagliamento, the Piave, and the Brenta still lay before him, swollen by the heavy rains. For this, or some other reason, his advance was so slow that General Durando had time to confront him with twelve or fifteen thousand Romans, Swiss, and Italians from various provinces, half regular troops, half volunteers. Knowing how little one could count upon men hastily collected and unacquainted with their officers, some of whom were unfit for their post, we trembled for the result.

For several days and nights I had been possessed with one idea—to prevent the junction between Nugent and Radetzky. Preparing a plan, hazardous I admit, but not impracticable, I submitted it to the duke. I suggested crossing the Adige, between Verona and Legnano, by a flying bridge at night, and marching to the assistance of Durando. If properly carried out, we ought to be at some distance before the enemy knew of our movements; and even had he followed and caught us up, I was confident of beating him with our brave fellows fresh from the victory at Pastrengo, the more so, that he would have been between two fires; Charles Albert, with two divisions, attacking Verona in front, and Victor Emanuel, with his division and the Savoy brigade on the side facing the Adige—in all sixty thousand men. If not molested, we should join Durando, and drive Nugent back beyond the Tagliamento.

The duke liked my plan, resolved to suggest it to his father, and rode off next morning in high spirits. But, alas! he returned dispirited and irritated. Never had his father treated him so harshly, or repulsed him so severely. The king said that if he considered himself a general because he wore a general's uniform, he would teach him that he knew nothing, that he could only repeat a lesson taught him by others, and that he appeared to have forgotten that it was not for him to give advice to his superiors, who had never asked for it.

Victor Emanuel, grieved and extremely mortified, was at first rather cross with me, the indirect cause of his annoyance. But, kind and just, that soon passed off, and he was soon convinced that we were not so much in the wrong. Durando, left to himself with his volunteers, was beaten; and first Nugent, then Thurn, joined Radetzky, who at once prepared to take the offensive. Finding our front and flanks well protected, he determined to attack us in the rear, and thus liberate Peschiera.

Besides instituting continual reconnaissances round Verona, I had arranged with some trusty Piedmontese, small traders in the district, to collect what news they could from their German clients. One of them brought me proof that some Italians, members of the Municipal Council of Villafranca, were in correspondence with General Radetzky's headquarters. Furious, I went to tell the duke, who commanded me to find out the culprits and reprimand them severely in his name. At Villafranca I discovered the whole story. Carried away by my indignation, instead of informing General Passalaqua, as I ought to have done, I went straight to the accused, and upbraided them in no measured terms. Of course they denied, and as soon as my back was turned went to Passalaqua to complain, and protest their innocence. The general reported me to the king, who condemned me to two months' imprisonment in the fortress of Pizzighettone. But my good friend Franzini interceded, and the sentence was revoked.

From my Piedmontese spies I learned that preparations were being made in Verona for a sortie in strength, which was soon confirmed by Lieutenant Marquis Trecchi, whom I had despatched with an escort to reconnoitre. He returned with the news that a large force of infantry, cavalry, and artillery with a siege battery, were leaving

Verona in the direction of Mantua. I sent at once to warn them at headquarters, and the same information arrived a little later from Passalaqua at Villafranca. We received orders to concentrate troops at Valeggio, and early on 30th May we left with the king in the direction of Goito, crossing the Mincio at Borghetto, on the way to Volta. On the march we met a Tuscan officer, who narrated the losses suffered the day before by the militia at Curtatone and Montanara. The troops we had seen leave Verona had made a sortie from Mantua, and in overwhelming force had fallen on the few thousand volunteers under General de Laugier, to whom Bava had not had time to send the promised reinforcements. The number of Tuscans and Neapolitans dead and wounded was enormous, the rest had retreated to Brescia.

From Volta we continued our march to Goito, which we reached before mid-day. The king took up his position on the rising ground of Somenzari, while the duke in the plain reviewed his division, already drawn up in line of battle according to the instructions sent by Bava. The engagement was to be fought by the 1st corps and the Duke of Savoy's division, in all a little over eighteen thousand men, a number about equal to the Austrian force. The two brigades (Guards and Cuneo) of the Duke's division were in position behind the artillery, one half of each in the first line, and with the Aosta brigade (division D'Arvillar) formed one right wing facing the road leading from Goito to Brescia, and parallel to that from Volta. The high road between Solarolo and Ceresara was thus guarded. On the left the division Ferrere was covered by Goito, and in a position to resist any attack, but the Guards on the extreme right, being quite in the open, might easily have been outflanked. Bava had, therefore, strengthened them with artillery and cavalry. His chief of the staff, sent to reconnoitre in the direction of Gazzoldo, returned without having seen any sign of the enemy; but Castelborgo, colonel of the Aosta cavalry, reconnoitring towards Sacca, reported that large bodies of troops were marching thence in the direction of Goito. Bava, who had expected to be taken in the rear from Gazzolo was reassured, and made up his mind the large bodies of Austrians were only small patrols, and that so late in the day (3 p.m.) there was no fear of any attack. Ordering the men to pile arms, and the rations to be distributed, he joined the king, and they rode slowly along the Volta road back towards Valeggio. The Duke of Savoy handed over his division to me and followed after them.

I had been too busy to eat anything before starting, and, passing a baker's shop on the march, bought a hot roll, which thoroughly disagreed with me. Feeling horribly sick, I had dismounted and stretched myself on the grass while the men were eating. Suddenly my brother rushed up. He also had seen a large Austrian force near Goito, and implored me to warn the king.

Charles Albert and his suite were riding at a walk, so I soon caught them up, and hardly were the words out of my mouth when a cannon shot confirmed them. Turning his horse, the king galloped back to Goito to give fresh orders, immediately executed, because Castelborgo, on his return from reconnoitring, had, in passing, told the officers of the artillery and of the brigades that he was convinced an attack was imminent.

At 3.30 p.m. the Austrians, as Bava had supposed, attempted to turn our right where the Grenadiers and artillery were posted; the latter immediately opened fire upon them. I was behind the Grenadiers, and as it seemed to me that General Biscaretti, absorbed in stationing his battalions, delayed the more necessary duty of launching them against the enemy, I gave the order to charge—'Battalion Marmorito, battalion La Rovere, forward ; charge with the bayonet !' Our splendid Grenadiers rushed forward with tremendous impetus; but many men and officers fell, among them Camillo Cavour's nephew. The Austrians withdrew, but only to bear down on our centre, which wavered for a moment at the point where the Cuneo and Aosta brigades touched. A battalion had given way, thus breaking the line. But the Duke of Savoy threw himself into their midst, shouting, '*Avanti, fieui; couragi, avanti !*'[1] infusing fresh ardour into them and reforming the line.

Major Mollard did the same with his battalion of the Aosta brigade. The artillery, hampered by the crowd of our own men advancing to meet the enemy close at hand, could no longer manœuvre. One battery, stopped by a ditch flanked by trees, ran imminent risk of being captured, when Mollard dismounted, seized a rifle, and at the head of his men charged with fixed bayonets. The Austrians retreated and then fled.

The bullets were whistling past our ears and falling like hail, killing men all round us. I leant towards the duke and whispered, ' I expect we shall find ourselves this evening *a ca d'Bergniff.*'[2]

'Not at all,' he answered; 'my plans are different. Someone is waiting for me this evening at Volta—but not *Bergniff.*' While thus joking, the duke suddenly put his hand to his right thigh, saying in the same tone of voice, ' I am wounded.'

Seeing him so calm, and that he had not changed colour, I felt sure the wound could not be dangerous, but insisted on his going to a surgeon, who was behind a mulberry hedge near by. We walked our horses quietly, as if we were only changing our places, and the surgeon pronounced the wound to have been made by a ricochetting

---

[1] ' Forward, my sons ; courage, forward !'
[2] ' House of the devil' (hell).

ball, and not serious, though it bled a good deal.   As soon as the duke heard this he refused to have the wound dressed, and remounted to show himself to the troops, among whom the news that he was wounded was already circulating.   I then asked leave to go and tell the king, lest the news might reach him in an exaggerated form.

Charles Albert had not heard of his son's wound, and was listening to my report, when Captain Franzini, the general's youngest brother, came from Peschiera with a letter from the Duke of Genoa.   The king opened it without dropping his reins.   Before he had time to read a word a projectile fell a few feet in front of his horse, which reared.   The king drove his spurs into the beast and forced him to stand over the shell.   We all remained motionless, but reflected, 'If that grenade bursts, the king will be blown up and all of us with him.'   The shell did not burst; the king read his letter, and with perfect calmness looked slowly round at us and said,—

'*Messieurs, Peschiera est a nous.*'[1]

We saluted these words with a tremendous hurrah, which was taken up all along our line, followed by a general and voluntary attack with the bayonet, which sent the enemy flying.

This engagement, and that of Pastrengo, were the most glorious days for the small, but courageous and well-disciplined Piedmontese army; defended by excellent artillery, and composed of men who knew and trusted their officers.   Had its leaders possessed resolution and audacity, the fate of Italy would have been decided in a few months.   The hesitation and want of initiative and unity among the commanders, the weakness of the head of the general staff, and the badness of the commissariat damped its enthusiasm and destroyed many of its good

---

[1] During the whole campaign Charles Albert preserved his habit of talking French to us.

qualities; but not, as has been said and written, to such an extent as to cause insubordination or cowardice. Till the end of the campaign of 1848, in spite of attempts at corruption, the men were valorous and faithful to the king and the House of Savoy.

As soon as I heard the good news that Peschiera was ours I started back to tell the duke, although I felt so ill that I could hardly sit my horse. He left for Volta after giving me his orders for the night's bivouacking, and I sent out to bring in the dead and wounded. The excitement which had sustained me all day then ceased, and I fell flat on the ground.

Count Piatti, a Veronese, one of the officers in the duke's suite, came to my assistance. We saw a cart drawn by a donkey coming along with a wounded man in it, who turned out to be my cousin, Major Marmorito. I was lifted in, and we reached Volta late at night. Next morning I was all right again.

The weather had changed to rain during the night, and our men suffered much, particularly from want of food. The commissariat broke down completely; the contractors lost their heads, and could not follow our rapid movements. In less than twenty-four hours we had concentrated eighteen thousand men at Goito. Not knowing the available force of the enemy, whose second line was not far off, we were obliged to await the arrival of De Sonnaz's corps, summoned to Volta by Bava. Meanwhile we prepared for a more important battle to be fought on the same ground.

There were a few trifling skirmishes between the Austrians and our outposts on the 1st and 2d June; on the 3d the 2d corps arrived; and on the 4th the staffs left Valeggio for Goito, where the army was in battle order. But it was too late; the enemy, who were at Sacca, Ceresara, and Solarolo the night before, had disappeared

A few thousand retired to Verona, but the greater number marched towards Mantua. The retreat was a blind to cover Radetzky's real destination—Vicenza—whence he proposed to drive Durando.[1] Our troops advanced as far as the dyke of Curtatone and Montanara, but only found traces of the recent passage of the enemy, and returned in the evening to their old camping ground. The king and the duke went back to Valeggio, where we passed the month of June. The former was, however, often absent; first going to take formal possession of Peschiera, and then passing some days at Garda, where he received Count Casati with the Lombard deputation, who presented the registers with 561,000 signatures in favour of immediate annexion to Piedmont. Modena, Parma, Piacenza, and other cities on the right bank of the Po, had already sent in their votes.

Several generals were summoned to Garda to discuss the various projects the king had under consideration. As soon as Franzini knew that Radetzky had marched on Vicenza he strongly advised following him ; while the king thought we had better take advantage of his absence to attack Verona. Bava was not averse, but insisted that the central positions round Goito should not be abandoned, or our retreat, in case of disaster, would be cut off. General de Sonnaz and others affirmed the necessity of driving the enemy from Rivoli before attempting to take Verona, and also suggested a rapid advance from Villafranca in order to cut off Radetzky's return. Charles Albert decided on attacking Verona during the absence of the Austrian commander-in-chief, and orders were given to concentrate at

---

[1] Unfortunately, he effected his purpose on the 9th and 10th June. Durando had beaten off the Austrians on the 23d and 24th May, but now succumbed to superior numbers. Colonel Massimo d'Azeglio (volunteer) and Colonel Cialdini, lately come from Spain to offer his services to the Italian cause, were wounded on that murderous day at Vicenza.

Villafranca on the 12th, and march thence on Verona, Tomba and Tombetta.

Leaving Villafranca on the morning of the 13th we reached our destination the same evening. The duke's division was the first to reach Tomba, and on the way the superior officers heard the bad news that Vicenza had fallen and Durando had been forced to capitulate. This implied the probable return of Radetzky. We bivouacked that night (over 40,000 men) under the walls of Verona, hourly waiting for a signal that Caliari, a member of the famous Veronese Committee, was to give on the outbreak of the revolution inside the town.

We looked in vain, no signal came; and at dawn on the 14th we received orders from headquarters, where Radetzky's return was known, to retire.

At Valeggio ambassadors, diplomats, intermediaries, bringing advice or proposals for peace or mediation, were perpetually coming and going. A deputation arrived from Sicily to offer the crown to the Duke of Genova; ministers came from Turin to take orders, and to entreat that the war should be rapidly pushed on; Parma, Piacenza and Modena sent members of their provisional governments begging for aid to counteract the intrigues of the deposed dukes and the retrograde party; while the Lombard representatives insisted on immediate action and the employment of the contingents sent by Lombardy, whose number they exaggerated.

General Hector Perrone was organising these, a difficult task, and one not to be accomplished in a few days; and meanwhile their impatience reached fever heat. Enthusiasm turned to criticism; odious suppositions and calumnies were rife, attacking even the king.

Our numbers were immensely exaggerated. People talked of 120,000 or 130,000 men as against 70,000 or 75,000 Austrians. In reality, we had fewer men than the enemy

—6500 were in hospital, and their number increased daily; 18,000 were in Venice, and about the same number were immobilised by the capitulations of Vicenza, Treviso and Palmanova.[1]   So that in July we had only 65,000 men under arms, and in worse condition than Radetzky's 75,000. Nevertheless, something had to be done.   Charles Albert, daily importuned to move, waited in vain for the enemy to attack us.   At last he charged Bava to prepare a plan of campaign, and the general suggested the blockade of Mantua.

I saw Bava several times while he was working at his plan and made objections to it, partly on strategical grounds, but chiefly on account of the time of year, which in that marshy country would be fatal to the health of our troops.   However, he persisted in his idea, and gave me a copy of his plan for the Duke of Savoy, who, remembering how his proposal to prevent Nugent's juncture with Radetzky had been received, refused to look at it, determined never to speak about the conduct of the war with his father.

Charles Albert resolved to execute Bava's design, but declined to recall the troops from Rivoli to form a second line and strengthen our weak centre.   Never was a position so ill chosen or so contrary to military tactics as ours in July 1848.   From the extreme right to the extreme left our line covered thirty-one miles; our right, near Mantua, was strong, our centre weak, and our left too far off to render any help.

Bava had command of the right wing, consisting of from 30,000 to 36,000 men, soon reinforced by the arrival of General Perrone with his Lombard division of 9000; the left, under De Sonnaz, extended from Sommacampagna to Rivoli, and numbered little more than 15,000;

[1] One of the chief conditions imposed by the Austrians was not to bear arms against them during the war.

in the centre, between Peschiera and Goito, was Broglia's division of about 10,000 to 12,000 men.

On the 13th July the blockade of Mantua began, the divisions of the Dukes of Savoy and Genoa being stationed between Roverbella and Castel Belforte.

The king's headquarters were at Marmirolo, ours at Roverbella, with rice fields to our left. The soldiers slept on the damp ground, the duke with his officers on straw in a miserable hut. In the early morning, when the *réveille* sounded, the fog was so dense over the fields that when we passed the men in review at a little distance we only saw their heads and shoulders. They looked like an army of busts.

On the 23d July we heard cannonading in the direction of Sona and Sommacampagna. Sent by the duke to Marmirolo to ask for orders from General Salasco, he told me the army was to concentrate at Villafranca, charging me to send word also to the Duke of Genoa. I ventured to suggest that Villafranca was not a fortunate choice, but Salasco brusquely repeated his orders.

At mid-day the division d'Arvillars, that of Victor Emanuel, and half the division of the Duke of Genoa, were marching towards Villafranca. Before leaving, the duke, with La Marmora, went to the king, and the latter made the same observation about Villafranca to Charles Albert as I had to Salasco, with the same result. On the way he again said that not Villafranca but Valeggio, a good defensive position, being surrounded by hills, would form an excellent support to the army. The king curtly replied, 'We go where the enemy's cannon calls us.' An excellent answer for whoso wishes to see a battlefield, but not for one who has to lead an army and place it in a position adapted for defence.

A few hours later, having driven our left wing beyond Peschiera, and our centre across the Mincio, Radetzky took

Valeggio. Fortifying himself there, he established his right wing, extending it past Custoza to Sommacampagna. He strongly occupied Monte Torre and Staffalo, opposite Villafranca, where the king had insisted on placing himself.

Officers and men passed the night ready for the battle, which might begin at any moment. Charles Albert, irresolute and hesitating, was anxiously awaiting the arrival of Bava, who was at Governolo, where he fought a brilliant action on the 17th and 18th, and could not reach Villafranca before 9.30 on the morning of the 24th. He showed great abnegation, unacquainted as he was with the position of the troops, in accepting the supreme command, immediately handed over to him.

All the hills opposite Villafranca, from Monte Torre to Staffalo and Berrettara, were occupied by the Austrians, so near to us that we saw them without glasses. Bava determined on an immediate attack, sent the Duke of Genoa to Sommacampagna, and ordered the Duke of Savoy to storm Monte Torre. With splendid dash our brave fellows rushed the position, and before night the tricolour flag waved from the heights whence the enemy had been driven.

The haste with which we had raised the blockade of Mantua and the usual improvidence and irregularity of headquarters in imparting orders, reacted on the commissariat. Hardly any rations reached us during the night, and the men had not sufficient food to carry them through the second day's struggle on the heights of Custoza.

On the 25th our line of battle extended from Sommacampagna to Valeggio, the centre being occupied by our division. We were to attack the Austrian centre at Custoza ; the Duke of Genoa to recapture Sommacampagna ; and the king, with Bava, intended to drive the enemy from Valeggio.

At daybreak the Duke of Savoy left Monte Torre for Custoza, expecting to find the enemy. They were, however, drawn up at the foot of the heights which they had abandoned during the night. Victor Emanuel took up his position on the highest point, above a castle flanked by a group of cypress trees forming part of the large park, and I extended the line of the two brigades so as to keep in touch with the Duke of Genoa on one side and the troops on the Valeggio road on the other. About 11 a.m. the Austrians advanced in strong force and attacked the heights towards Berrettara, aiming especially at our front, defended by artillery to the right and left of the cypress wood. Heavy cannonading was followed by repeated charges of infantry, gallantly repulsed by our men.

The heat was intense. Not a drop of water could be found on the top of the hill, and the morning's rations had been infinitesimal. Our men dropped from fatigue, sunstroke, hunger, and thirst, so that after a few hours' fighting the companies were reduced from two hundred men to fifty or sixty. From the furious and repeated attacks of the enemy the duke and I concluded that he intended, at any cost, to carry our position, and thus cut our army in two, facilitating his operations under Valeggio and at Sommacampagna, or, at least, enabling him to cut off the retreat of the Duke of Genoa's division.

At 1·30 Victor Emanuel sent me to headquarters to say that without immediate reinforcements our position could not be held. The heat was suffocating, and I could not resist drinking at the first rivulet, dirty though it was. In twenty minutes I found Bava, who, with the king, was in a field within range of the enemy's guns. At the same moment a messenger came with a note from De Sonnaz. His troops had fought on the 22d at Rivoli, on the 23d at Sona and Santa Giustina, and after leaving Peschiera, had marched for over twelve hours with the intention of reaching Borghetto or Volta about 5 p.m., and falling on the enemy's rear. On reading this Bava exhorted me to use every effort to hold out, as not only could he not send us help, but he was anxiously expecting it himself from De Sonnaz. With this answer I galloped back to Custoza a little before 3 p.m. The enemy's cannon was sweeping our position; we saw them below preparing for a fresh assault, and our companies were reduced by one-half! I had all the doors and shutters of the castle taken down to serve as litters to transport the wounded, as fast as they fell, to Villafranca. The duke determined to go in person and tell Bava and the king that unless reinforcements were sent we should have to evacuate Custoza before we succumbed to the ever increasing Austrian forces. He handed the command of the division over to me, and only a few minutes after his departure we were vehemently attacked. Once more, shouting ' *Savoia*,' we drove the enemy down the hill at the point of the bayonet.

The Austrians, unaware how small our force was, probably thought that, like their own, it had been renewed; so at 4·30 we were still masters of the position. Impatiently I awaited the return of the duke, but while continuing preparations to resist I got ready for a retreat on Gherla, which seemed to me inevitable. Fresh Austrian columns were seen advancing, when Count Zamojsky, a Pole in the suite of Charles Albert, galloped up with the order to retire. Being prepared, we were able to withdraw before the arrival of the enemy, who only found an abandoned position. Worn out, they did not follow us, and the division, ranged in order of battle on the plain of Gherla, was joined by the duke, with orders to protect the retreat of all the troops coming from Valeggio. Our retreat was undisturbed, save by a few detachments of cavalry. Even the Austrians did not know how to follow up a victory!

The battle was lost for want of men. Had the division,

uselessly left behind at Mantua, been brought up, reinforcements might have been sent to the divisions of the Dukes of Savoy and Genoa, and to the force before Valeggio.

Late in the evening we reached Villafranca, and abundant rations were distributed to prepare the men for the march and expected battle next day. The duke and I, tired out, lay down in a freshly-ploughed field; it rained all night, but we slept too well to feel it, and were wet through and stiff next morning. There was, however, no time to think of myself, as our division had to protect the rear during the retreat on Goito. I was extremely anxious, as I expected the enemy would attack our flank from Valeggio, or our rear guard. But Radetzky let slip the opportunity to crush us, and our flank was only attacked once by cavalry, easily repulsed.

To our surprise, on crossing the Mincio, where we took up a position fronting the river, we found De Sonnaz, with his men utterly exhausted. It was reported that, on reaching Volta much later than he expected, he found orders leaving it to his judgment to hold the place or abandon it. He chose the latter course; why, I never knew. The king was very angry, as the Austrians occupied Volta the instant De Sonnaz left, and curtly bade him go back and re-take the position.

He left about 6 p.m. with the brigade Savoia, on the promise that the brigade Regina should follow soon. The attack was made at night, and half way up the hill the confusion was terrible—so great, that our men killed each other in the dark. Nevertheless, they got to the summit and reached the piazza in front of the church. Here the Austrians, pouring out of every street, overpowered and drove them back, the promised brigade never having arrived.

The return of these beaten troops had a most disheartening effect on the rest, who, that very morning, had seen contractors, civil servants, representatives of provisional governments, and country folk, flying panic-stricken at the announcement of the Austrian successes.

Supplies failed entirely on the 27th. The staff had nothing but green cobs of maize gathered in the fields, which they dipped in brandy and water. In the evening the army was so demoralised that the king called a council of generals for 8 o'clock next morning to propose a suspension of hostilities. Seeing La Marmora, as chief of the staff to the Duke of Genoa, preparing to attend the council, I was going to accompany the Duke of Savoy, when Bava called me. Expecting to be engaged for some time, he put me in command of all the troops round Goito, with orders to place part in line of battle in case of an attack, and at the same time to make preparations for a probable imminent retreat.

While I was carrying out his orders, the Generals Bes and Rossi, with La Marmora, who knew some of the Austrian commanders, were sent to the enemy's headquarters. Radetzky's conditions were peremptory. The king must retire beyond the Adda, give back Peschiera, recall his troops from the Duchies, and immediately treat for peace. Without hesitation the king refused.

When Bava joined me, I told him everything was ready for retreating across the Po, which seemed our wisest course. By putting the river between us and the enemy, and preparing to be ready at any moment to attack his flank, we prevented his advance on Milan. For this reason I had already sent several columns towards Borgoforte.

'You are perfectly right,' he exclaimed. 'But everything must be changed. The king is absolutely determined to retire on Milan.' 'Then,' I replied, 'we shall draw the enemy on, and be powerless to impede or even repel him.' 'I know,' said Bava; 'but the king thinks it his duty to become the paladin of the Milanese and lead his army under their walls. A chivalrous idea, if you like; but it will probably be our ruin, and he will not understand this.'

From the Mincio we retreated to the Oglio the king, with the 1st corps, marching towards Bozzolo; and on the morning of the 30th the army was under Cremona, which Charles Albert had thought of defending. When he examined the environs of the city, he saw it was impossible.

At Grotta d'Adda the army crossed the river (Adda) on a bridge of boats thrown over during the night. The division of the Duke of Savoy formed the rearguard, and the bridge was broken up before the Austrians arrived.

Charles Albert's intention was to defend the line of the Adda as far as Lodi. Two excellent brigades, three batteries, and three squadrons of cavalry had been sent there by Bava, under a general who was to be reinforced by the Lombard division. On the 1st August we heard that the Austrians, protected by the fire of an admirably placed battery, were throwing a bridge over the Adda opposite our position, and that the general, convinced he would not be able to resist, had retreated on Piacenza. This desertion of his post displaced our right wing and exposed our army to be taken in the rear. The general probably thought, as did many others, that the army would retreat on Piacenza; but his orders were precise, and by not carrying them out he placed us under the necessity of retiring beyond the Adda towards Milan.

Our division left Grotta d'Adda for Codogno, where we hoped to pass the night; but orders came to continue the march towards S. Angelo and Borghetto. All that night, all next morning, and all through the hottest hours of that sultry 2d of August, our poor soldiers tramped on towards Milan. On the 3d we were in the suburbs. Bava disposed the troops in a semi-circle, extending from Chiesarossa and Naviglio di Pavia on the right to Porta Orientale on the left. The division of the Duke of Savoy was encamped on the bastions of Porta Renza (now Porta Venezia), reaching beyond Porta Romana. The king established his headquarters in a small inn at S. Giorgio outside Porta Romana. To defend the Milanese, Charles Albert had placed the army in jeopardy, and staked his kingdom and throne. Believing in the fine promises of the Lombard representatives, he had come to Milan expecting to find the city fortified and well provisioned. On his arrival, Generals Chiodo and Rossi, who had preceded us, met him with the news that no preparations had been made for the troops. The city was silent and deserted ; the few inhabitants who remained were cold, disappointed, and reproachful.

At daybreak on the 4th the large Austrian army came in sight, and the first shots were fired about 10 a.m. The king at once, as though he courted death, threw himself in the thickest of the fight. The Porta Romana had been barricaded, and from the bastions the Grenadiers kept the enemy at bay till the evening, when they gained ground, and at nightfall had advanced close under the ramparts. S. Giorgio, the headquarters of the king, was in the line occupied by them, so he was forced to enter the city, and took up his abode in the Greppi Palace.

The duke and I, after visiting Charles Albert, returned to our men and passed the night on a heap of stones by the roadside. Meanwhile the king, by the advice of some of the generals summoned to a hasty council, had sent two of them to Radetzky late in the evening, offering to surrender the city on the condition that the lives and property of the inhabitants should be respected, and that the Sardinian army was allowed to retire unmolested to the right bank of the Ticino. Radetzky immediately accepted the offer made by Charles Albert under the stress of dire necessity. The main park of artillery had been sent to Piacenza ; the provisions of the smaller parks had been exhausted during the battle ; there was no ammunition in the city, and very little powder. The supply of provisions was barely sufficient for three days, and no preparations had been made by the provisional government of Milan for defending the town or victualling the army. Resistance was therefore impossible.

As soon as the terrible news of the capitulation was known the whole city rose. Incited by the Mazzinian Republicans and the Anarchists, a howling mob assembled round the Greppi Palace, hurling abuse at the king and his officers.

Towards mid-day I begged the duke to allow me to take a battalion and liberate the king. Knowing the usual cowardice of a mob, I was sure the sight of our Grenadiers would be sufficient to disperse them. But the duke refused, fearing lest maddened by the sight of the troops, they might invade the Greppi Palace, abandoned by the Civic Guard, and endanger the life of the king.

With great difficulty Bava escaped out of the palace in the afternoon, and came to concert with the Duke of Savoy what measures to take in case the enemy, hearing of our internal discords, should attempt an attack. He said the Duke of Genoa, who went to see his father, was imprisoned with him, and that the mob had fired at the windows of the palace and at the balcony when the king showed himself; while those inside left him no peace, and at last induced him to say, 'Well, as you desire it, we will continue the struggle.'

Continue the struggle! Without artillery, money, or food, and after an armistice had been asked for and granted! Yet even Bava, to whom Charles Albert turned for advice, had answered that war with the Austrians was preferable to tearing each other to pieces under their eyes.

At nightfall, when the city seemed calmer, Victor Emanuel allowed me to go with a battalion of Grenadiers to the king's aid. I took Lieutenant Piati, a Veronese, with me, as he knew Milan well and could guide us by side streets. At Porta Renza we heard that Colonel La Marmora, with a company of Bersaglieri, had just left on the same errand as ourselves, and determined to take an opposite direction in order, if necessary, to take the mob between two fires.

We arrived at the Greppi Palace as the king crossed the threshold. He was on foot, deadly pale, and aged in face and figure. He held his sword tight under his arm, and, when he saw me, said, 'Ah, mon cher La Rocca, quelle journée, quelle journée.'

I shall never forget the tone of his voice.

He ordered me to tell his son to come and meet him, and when I returned with the duke we found Bava, who had also brought troops. These, with the Grenadiers and Bersaglieri, formed an escort ; and Bava begged the king to take a few hours' rest at his quarters in the Calchi-Taeggi College. The duke and I then returned to ours—the heap of stones by the roadside.

At daybreak the king mounted his horse and, followed by the army, left the city by Porta Vercellina. Taking three different roads, we began the march towards Piedmont.

The Austrians entered Milan on the 6th, the city being made over to them by Major Robert Morozzo, my brother, commanding one of the two battalions of the Grenadier Guards, which had been left in charge outside Porta Romana.

CHAPTER VIII

END OF 1848. BEGINNING OF 1849

Vigevano—Armistice signed at Milan—General Bava's Account of the Campaign—Is dismissed and succeeded by General Czarnowsky—His Plans—I am named Major-General—Our Retreat on Novara—Hard Fighting at Bicocca—We are driven back on Novara—Charles Albert abdicates—Victor Emanuel becomes King—I rally Fugitives—Am called to Turin by Victor Emanuel, and become Minister of War.

OUR division left Milan for Vigevano, followed by all those who had participated in the 'five days'[1] of March, and the revolutionary movements of the following months, or who had fought in our ranks as volunteers. So little did they trust the promises of the Austrians, that they preferred condemning their families to exile. Women and small children were seated on the artillery waggons and even on the cannon, and the burning August sun added to the misery of our march. But, once across the river, things changed for the better. We were at home. At Vigevano one of the best houses had been assigned to the duke and his staff, and as soon as I could leave him I went in search of a haberdasher's shop. In the confusion of the last few days our baggage had disappeared,

[1] On the 18th March the Revolution burst out in Milan. During the night of the 19th seventeen hundred barricades were erected in the streets; on the 21st the palaces of the viceroy and of the police, and the cathedral fell into the hands of the people. There was fighting in every street, and the Croats committed horrible outrages on women and children. On the night of the 22d the citadel was set on fire by the Austrians, and Radetzky quitted the city with his troops.—*Translator's Note.*

and since my arrival on the ramparts of Milan I had not changed my clothes. The sensation of a clean shirt was delightful.

As soon as the king arrived he was besieged by deputations and politicians; everyone wanted to condole, advise and suggest. Casati, President of the Council, and Count Borromeo visited the king to express, in the name of many Milanese, their sorrow at the scenes which had occurred under his windows; and the king assured them that he believed the mob was composed of strangers directed by the Republican party. Be that as it may, I am impartial enough to understand the anger of the Milanese at seeing their city once more in the possession of the Austrians, whom they had driven out five months before. Still, they had no right to lay the whole blame on Charles Albert and the Piedmontese army, in which, I must confess, there existed deep and undisguised indignation against the Lombards.

The armistice was signed at Milan on the 9th August. Charles Albert relinquished Peschiera, Lombardy, Parma, Piacenza, Modena and Venice, from which places all Italian troops were to be immediately withdrawn. The armistice was to last six weeks, with power to prolong it indefinitely by mutual assent, or to renew hostilities after a week's warning.

The king transferred his headquarters from Vigevano to Alessandria, and soon after went to Turin, leaving Bava in supreme command. The Duke of Savoy had established his headquarters at Valenza for the winter, and sent me almost daily to confer with the commander-in-chief, who knew and liked me, treating me as a friend rather than a subordinate. Bava was profoundly hurt by the criticisms and accusations of the common herd, which made no allowances for his exceptional position with Charles Albert, who often obliged him, as at

Custoza, to assume the command of an army already placed by others in a badly chosen position.

The ministry—Alfieri, Revel, Pinelli, with General Dabormida as minister of war—and those immediately round the king, suggested that the commander of the next campaign should be one who had held no command in the last war, or, better still, a foreigner. Marshal Bugeaud, who had distinguished himself in Africa, was mentioned; failing him, Changarnier or Lamoricière, and so on, down to the youngest of the French generals. Alphonse La Marmora, a great friend of Dabormida, accepted the arduous task of going to beg a commander for a beaten and disheartened army, whose confidence in its old commanders was thus utterly destroyed. His mission was a failure; and before he returned to Turin a new ministry, with Gioberti at its head, was in power— the third since the armistice.

General Czarnowsky, a Pole, was sent to Alessandria as chief of the staff to Bava, who said to me next day, 'They have sent me a Pole, a perfect monkey, small, ugly, with the voice of an eunuch, as chief of the staff, in case hostilities should be resumed. You, who know what the duties of a head of the staff are, can perhaps tell me what I am to do with a foreigner who does not know the country, the language, the officers, or the men.'

Soon after the storm burst, which Bava drew upon himself by publishing his account of the campaign of 1848, written in reply to a circular from the minister of war, Dabormida, to all the generals in command. I also received one, and related the general movements of our division, and the actions at Pastrengo and Custoza led by myself. The duke signed the former, I the latter.

Bava's relation created considerable sensation, and was blamed for the extreme severity of some of his criticisms on soldiers and officers. The scandal determined the ministry to take a step which had already been mooted. The minister of war ordered him to hand over the command to General Czarnowsky, and at the same time Gioberti, President of the Council, wrote a private letter, expressing sorrow at being obliged to dispense with his services on account of the stir made by his book.

Gioberti's ministry fell a few days later, to be replaced by one in favour of war at any cost. General Chiodo, one of the first pupils of the polytechnic school instituted by the French, was President of the Council with the portfolios of War and Marine. He knew little about military matters, and, like the rest of his party, chiefly lawyers, thought everything must go well with a foreigner as commander-in-chief. Czarnowsky was proposed to the king by his countryman Zamojsky, whom I have already mentioned during the campaign of 1848. Had he possessed all the military qualities which he lacked, he would have failed in reorganising such an army as ours then was, composed of discordant elements, and unprepared for entering on a campaign. The ministry which pushed king and nation into war assumed a tremendous responsibility. They risked the future, not only of Italy, but of Piedmont, which, once our troops were annihilated, might have ceased to be a European state, and become a Lombard province of the Austrian empire.

Recruits had been trained during the armistice, volunteers had joined from Lombardy and other parts of Italy, and the regiments had been augmented from eighteen to twenty-three; but everything was in disorder, all ranks were disheartened and utterly averse to renewed hostilities. Ten or more generals had left the service, and there was a dearth of officers to instruct the raw troops.

A few days after General Czarnowsky assumed the

command he came to Valenza to pay his respects to the heir of the throne. The duke sent me to receive the general while he finished some work he had on hand, and my reception was not a warm one. I liked and esteemed Bava, and the presence of this Pole as commander-in-chief of Piedmontese troops seemed to me a gratuitous insult to the army I belonged to. He did not notice my coldness, and at once began to talk about his plans for the approaching campaign. I soon saw that he would repeat the errors which had already been committed on the Mincio—too extended a position and a lack of reserves. He talked of occupying the right bank of the Ticino, from the Po under Pavia to the Lago Maggiore, and of sending small detachments on to the right bank of the Po to confront the Austrians in case they tried to enter Piedmont; but all was based on the idea that they would start from Milan. As he spoke I had a presentiment of coming misfortune, and he said, 'Vous n'avez pas l'air d'approuver mes projets.' I had barely answered, 'Il ne m'appartient pas de les critiquer,' when he was summoned by the duke, to whom he repeated the same story. It was like a lesson learned by heart, which he recited to all those he thought had any authority. If they talked about it to others it was more than likely that Radetzky knew the whole plan before the campaign began.

On the 12th March 1849 Major R. Cadorna was sent to denounce the armistice for the 20th. On the 16th I was summoned by the king to Alessandria, where he had just arrived with the new commander-in-chief. His Majesty told me I had been named major-general in command of the brigade Acqui, composed of the 17th and 23d regiments. I bowed my thanks, but begged to be allowed to refuse promotion, and to remain with the duke. The king frowned and insisted. So miserable was I at the thought of leaving Victor Emanuel just as war was declared, that I ventured to express my fears for the issue of the campaign. Charles Albert listened and replied, 'Vous vous trompez, tout ira bien. C'est moi qui vous le dit'. And as I again begged not to be promoted, 'Plus un mot. Allez tout de suite prendre le commandement de votre brigade; je vous l'ordonne.'

On paper our army consisted of over one hundred and twenty thousand men, but our real number was under eighty thousand, while Radetzky had ninety thousand.

At mid-day on the 20th March, Czarnowsky, absolutely ignorant of the enemy's movements, but having made up his mind that they would march towards Magenta, crossed the Mincio in that direction with Charles Albert. Instead of the Austrian outposts he expected, only terrified and discontented inhabitants were seen, who reported that large masses of Austrian troops had gone towards Pavia some days before. In fact, at that very hour, 60,000 Austrians were passing the Ticino on three bridges to occupy Piedmontese territory in the direction of Mortara. Only a few troops of the Lombard division confronted this invasion, among them the battalion of students from Milan and Triest, who, under Lucien Manara, defended the position of Cava with the greatest bravery. On the 17th General Ramorino had already received orders to place the whole Lombard division on the left bank of the Po; but he disobeyed, and kept his men on the right.

I reached Montara early on the 21st, and found the troops in marching order. My brigade was in column, so, instead of putting them in line to receive me as is the custom, Bes rode with me through the ranks to introduce me to my men. Their appearance was satisfactory; one regiment was composed of old soldiers, the other of recruits instructed by Colonel Cialdini. After a short march, Austrian outposts were reported; so, skirting Vigevano, we entered a large farm surrounded by walls, which we proceeded to loophole, while Bes drew up the division in order of battle, to arrest, partially at all events, the enemy's advance on Mortara. My brigade was thus in the first line of the attack, to which the 17th opposed a steady and gallant resistance. The 23d charged the enemy's infantry with the bayonet, but as they tried to surround us, I ordered my men to form squares. In one of these the major fell mortally wounded, and the flagstaff was broken. In an instant the square broke. Cialdini and I threw ourselves among the men, and by dint of blows with the flat of our swords stopped their flight. It was a momentary thing, and the men fought well afterwards. Late in the afternoon the brigade Casale, which had lost its way, came to our aid, and the brigade Savoia, excellent troops, and so full of dash that notwithstanding the large reinforcements perpetually received by the enemy, we had hopes of converting an undecisive but brilliant action into a great victory. But Czarnowsky, with Charles Albert, came from Vigevano and decided the decisive action had better be fought next day. At the same time, bad news came from Mortara, where the divisions of Durando and the Duke of Savoy had been beaten. Fearing to be taken in the rear, Czarnowsky resolved on retreating towards Novara, where he sent fifty thousand men to cut Radetzky's road. We passed the night on the farm, and Charles Albert insisted on sleeping in the midst of the Savoy brigade on the bare ground. I suppose he was very tired, for he slept so profoundly that the constant passage of officers and men, who came to look at his tall, fateful figure and worn, pale face, did not wake him.

A little after dawn on the 22d March we began our march on Novara, and only arrived under the walls of the town at nightfall. On the way I had to pass, at the head of my brigade, before the king and Czarnowsky. In spite of the change of uniform, Charles Albert recognised me at once and, with the old gesture used at Racconigi years ago, beckoned me to his side. Complimenting me on the behaviour of my men the previous day, he continued, 'Ne vous avais-je pas dit à Alexandrie, La Rocca, que tout irait bien?' These were the last words I heard Charles Albert speak, and it was the last time I saw him. For many years he was a strange enigma to me and to many about him. Only in 1847 did we begin to have an inkling of the true reason for his contradictory conduct—a fixed resolution to free Italy from the Austrian rule; a resolution carefully hid from others, because he did not think the time for acting had yet come.

We camped under the walls of Novara, and at dawn the army was in order of battle. The Duke of Savoy passed close to me on the way to his position, riding a wretched horse belonging to his household. On seeing me he exclaimed, 'You don't know how I wished for you yesterday. We were utterly beaten at Mortara; all my equipage and my horses were taken, so I had to send for this brute, in order not to lead the troops on foot. Let us hope to-day will not be a repetition of yesterday.' I did not see him again for five days, when, after our defeat and the abdication of Charles Albert, he sent for me at Turin to entrust me with the Ministry for War.

On the 23d March about fifty thousand men were drawn up in order of battle a kilometre to the south of Novara. Three divisions in two lines covered three kilometres—Durano on the right, Perrone on the left, and Bes, to which my brigade belonged, in the centre. Some battalions of sharp-shooters covered my front. The divisions of the Duke of Genoa and the Duke of Savoy were in reserve, the first on the high land behind Bicocca, a small village on the very summit of the hill; the second, behind Durazzo, was stationed between the *place d'armes* and the road to Vercelli. Our position could only be turned at a considerable distance towards Trecate or Vercelli. The disposition of our troops was excellent; but, as in 1848, and later in 1866, the quarter-master-general's staff was absolutely in the dark as to the movements of the enemy.

Both Radetzky and Czarnowsky had the same design of concentrating their troops between Novara and Vercelli, but we had outmarched the Austrians on the 22d; so their first troops, under General d'Aspre, who had no idea how large our force was, only appeared in sight about 10 a.m. in the direction of Olengo. He deployed the division of the Archduke Albert in front of our left at Bicocca, and in front of Perrone's division; then, seeing how numerous his adversary was, sent in haste to warn Radetzky and ask for reinforcements. Czarnowsky, on the contrary, never noticed the smallness of the Austrian force, and, instead of immediately assuming the offensive, stood on the defensive, and only pushed forward by degrees the troops of the divisions of the Duke of Genoa and Perrone towards Bicocca.

The Piedmontese army opposed a stolid resistance to the enemy's attack; and Bicocca was lost and retaken five times. General Passalaqua, commanding the Piedmont brigade, wrested several positions from the Austrian, and fell mortally wounded, while the Duke of Genoa had three horses killed under him. The enemy was driven out of Olengo, and at 2 p.m. d'Aspre, not having yet been reinforced, retired from all his positions. About an hour later, his reinforcements began to arrive in small quantities, when Czarnowsky ought to have attacked vigorously and driven the enemy back across the Ticino. But he stood the whole day on the defensive, moving forward small bodies of troops at intervals. Not only did he let slip the favourable moment, but he recalled the Duke of Genoa, who had driven d'Aspre beyond Castellazzo. This mistaken movement gave fresh courage to the Austrian general, who immediately reoccupied Castellazzo. At that moment General Perrone, encouraging part of his division, which had given way, to advance, received the wound of which he died two days later.

The Austrians were gradually gaining ground when Czarnowsky ordered up two regiments of the reserve, and one (the 17th) of our division, and again the enemy was forced to retire. But General Thurn now came up with large reinforcements. Crossing by the Bridge of Agogna, where only one detachment of cavalry was posted, Colonel Montevecchio was unable to stop the advance of so large a force. Radetzky, who was on a small hill on the Mortara road, watching the battle, sent orders to attack Bicocca vigorously in front, and only then did Czarnowsky resolve to move forward on the front and right. While Bes and Durando pushed back the weak body of Austrians that fronted them, Czarnowsky hastened towards Bicocca. But the enemy had already taken Castellazzo and the surrounding positions, and entered Bicocca. In vain Czarnowsky attempted to reconquer it ; in vain the Duke of Genoa, who having had his horses killed under him was fighting on foot, made a desperate effort with only three battalions ; Bicocca had to be abandoned to the enemy. Our army, attacked in front and on both flanks, was driven back on Novara. The crush and confusion at the city gate was terrible, of which, fortunately, the enemy did not take advantage, but, halting at some distance from the walls, bivouacked for the night under pouring rain. By the defeat of our left, the centre and the right were placed in a most perilous position, so Colonel Alexander La Marmora (chief of the staff) took it on himself to order a retreat before receiving orders from Czarnowsky. The engagement of our division had hardly begun when the aide-de-camp of Czarnowsky came to tell Bes to retire. 'In what direction?' asked the general. 'I don't know,' was the answer. Bes consulted with us and replied, 'Tell whoever sent you that I shall retreat in the direction of the Agogna, and thence to the province of Biella.' Then, turning to me, he added, 'Will you, who only left the staff a few days ago, resume your old functions for the moment and be our guide?' I accepted and, taking a battalion of infantry, a squadron of cavalry, a battery of artillery and a company of Bersaglieri, reconnoitered in the direction of Romagnano. 'I will collect one division,' said Bes, 'and before long will join you.' At about 8 p.m. the body of the army retreated in dire confusion. The soldiers, who had eaten nothing all day, dispersed in the city, sacking the bakers' shops and eating-houses. Our defeat was utter. Charles Albert, who, towards the end of the day, had in vain courted death, by exposing himself to the enemy's fire on the old city bastions, was taken almost by force by General G. Durando, his aide-de-camp, to the headquarters. There he called a few generals, the minister Cadorna, and the representatives of the provisional governments who were in camp, and laid Marshal Radetzky's hard conditions before them. The king could not bring himself to accept them, so resolved to abdicate in favour of his son Victor Emanuel, hoping that he might succeed in obtaining better terms. That same night Charles Albert left with a passport in the name of Count of Barge, accompanied by a cabinet courier and a valet.

I was meanwhile proceeding in the direction of Biella with about eight hundred infantry and two hundred cavalry. After an hour's march on the road leading to Romagnano I halted to give the division time to come up. Fugitives of every arm were perpetually passing, flying more for want of a leader than from fear. With the aid of Captain Cugia, I stopped and rallied them, and in a few hours found myself at the head of several thousand. At last Bes arrived, but without the troops and without his head of the staff, who had remained behind to guide the division. We waited for them in vain. By Czarnowsky's orders they had entered Novara, surrounded on three sides by the enemy, and thence retreated to Momo. At daybreak we reached Romagnano, fed our men as well as we could, and at mid-day we arrived at Biella, where Bes called a council of war of all the officers to deliberate on what we should do. Opinions differed ; some proposed returning to Novara, others to march to Turin, while Bes wished to gain the Val d'Aosta in Savoy, and raise the population to fight the Austrians. He made sure that the army had laid down their arms, and that the whole country behind us was in the hands of the enemy. From the first I had advocated the necessity of reconnoitering to find out what had happened in our rear, and at last offered to go myself. Our horses were worn out, so, with the help of the syndic, I got a small gig with a bad horse, and, with Major d'Auvare, returned by the road we had come by. It was snowing hard, and after some hours we met, near Cossato, the regiment of Novara cavalry under Colonel Maffei. He reported Austrian troops a little to his rear, and that we should be taken prisoners if we went further. Returning to Biella, we found that Bes had already left taking our horses with him. So, leaving our vehicle, we set out on foot for Ivrea, and made our report to the general, who, convinced that the army was utterly beaten, decided we ought to march directly on Turin to defend the capital.

We had collected over seven thousand men during our retreat, and at Castellamonte, where we halted for the night, the syndic gave us notice that Charles Albert had abdicated, and Victor Emanuel been named his successor to the throne. Bes immediately handed over the command to me, with directions to go to the Veneria and await his orders, saying, rather mysteriously, that political events called him to Turin. At Biella and Ivrea, I had noticed that the general was surrounded by men belonging to the Democratic party, and supposed they wanted him to enter into some ministerial combination. On the 26th I reached the Veneria with my defeated troops, and soon after our arrival a royal courier brought a letter from the new king, Victor Emanuel, calling me to Turin. At the royal palace I found several officers by whom the portfolio of war and marine had been refused. The king greeted me with great cordiality, described the scene of his father's abdication and the conditions of the armistice, and told me of his meeting at Vignale with Radetzky, and his return to, and glacial reception at, Turin. He found that the Chambers, ignorant of the disastrous events of Novara, had sat all night, and taken upon themselves to decide the fate of the country and oblige the nation to continue the war. Victor Emanuel did not appear the least affected by the unfavourable aspect of affairs. He had been trying to form a ministry, but could get no one to accept the portfolio of war. Knowing my devotion to himself, he begged me to undertake the ungrateful task. I was not afraid of the responsibility, or of the official work of a ministry, but the idea of having to present myself before the Chambers was most alarming. Victor Emanuel said he was going to dissolve Parliament and appeal to the country, so the Chambers could not meet again for two or three months. Again begging me to accept, at all events for the moment, he added that if I found the work distasteful we could then look for a successor. Under these conditions I accepted.

CHAPTER IX

1849—*Continued*

The First Ministry of King Victor Emanuel—Stormy Scene in the Chambers
—Revolt in Genoa — Disbanding the Lombard Legion — General
Ramorino condemned and shot—Victor Emanuel and Radetzky meet—
Negotiations for Peace—D'Azeglio becomes Prime Minister—Peace is
ratified—Death of Charles Albert—I leave the Ministry and marry.

GENERAL COUNT DE LAUNAY, the head of the first
ministry of Victor Emanuel, had been recommended for the
post by Charles Albert when he abdicated. A Liberal in
politics, he was a man of good common sense and great
determination, a perfect gentleman, and devoted to the
House of Savoy. The other members of the Cabinet were
Pinelli, a lawyer, who had been a minister before; Nigra,
the banker, well known as the most honest of men; C.
Mameli, De Margherita, F. Galvagno and myself. On
the 28th March the new Cabinet presented itself to the
Chambers. Hostile murmurs greeted De Launay, and
continued as we took our seats on the Ministerial bench;
directed chiefly, as it appeared, against the president's and
my military uniforms.[1] De Launay drew himself up and,
looking straight at Bunico, Vice-President[2] of the Chamber,
began to introduce his colleagues. Bunico immediately

[1] We had just come from Palazzo Madama, where we accompanied the
king to swear to uphold the Constitution, and had not had time to change our
clothes.

[2] Pareto, the president, had gone to Genoa to foment the disorders which
had broken out there against the conclusion of peace.

interrupted him, saying that as he had not asked permission he could not speak. 'Then I demand leave to speak,' answered De Launay, with wonderful calmness. 'Who are you?' replied Bunico. 'I am General de Launay. named President of the Council and Minister of Foreign Affairs by King Victor Emanuel.' 'Speak,' was the curt answer. De Launay presented us by name; and then began a series of interpellations on the causes of our defeat, and the conditions of the armistice were demanded. Pinelli rose and read them aloud, 'Dispersion of the Lombard legion; the fleet to be withdrawn from the Adriatic; our territory between the Po, the Sesia, and the Ticino to be occupied by the Austrians; the withdrawal of our troops from all territory belonging before the war to the Lombard-Venetian States; and a mixed garrison in the citadel of Alessandria. Every article was hailed with indignant shouts, and insults were hurled at those who had accepted such conditions. Speeches were made by lawyers, who, knowing nothing about military matters, or about the real state of the country, accused this person or that of stupidity, incapacity, and even of treachery. One of them spoke, as it seemed to me, so offensively against the army, that, forgetting where I was, I sprang up, and was rushing at him with doubled fists, when Pinelli gripped one skirt of my tunic and tore it, so I was obliged to sit down again. Then rising, with a calmness I envied, he denied the truth of the deputy's assertions. The noise, however, still continued, and Moffa di Lisio, a Democratic member of Parliament, rose, and in a fine speech declared that any idea of treachery was out of the question. Listened to by all, he succeeded in gradually calming the agitation of the House. But this one sitting sufficed to confirm my resolution not to form part of a Cabinet exposed to the insults and varied opinions of members of Parliament. Not that I am averse to a Constitutional government; on the contrary, I always upheld Liberal institutions; but my character and my habits were not those of a politician, who, adapting himself to circumstances, can rebut false assertions with dignity and calmness. The habit of always talking the Piedmontese dialect rendered it difficult for me to speak Italian fluently, and I was naturally impatient and quick tempered. Brought up as a soldier, the sword was the only argument I understood. I was made to serve my country in the army, not in Parliament, and I hope I have done so conscientiously and well.

The Chambers were prorogued on the 29th and dissolved on the 30th; so, relieved from the nightmare of another sitting, I began to put the war office in order. and to reorganise the army. In my department all work had been suspended; letters and despatches had been left unopened for weeks and even months. The military incapacity and the negligence of the late ministers and their subordinates were but too patent; there was no regularity in the administration, no steps had been taken for feeding or paying the soldiers, and the sum I found in the chest was barely sufficient for the expenses of one day.

This was soon remedied by the finance minister, Nigra, who was able, thanks to his high personal credit on the principal foreign exchanges, to negotiate a loan on comparatively easy terms. Twenty-four hours after I joined the ministry news of the disturbances in Genoa reached Turin. The troops, badly led by an old Genoese officer, had allowed the rebels to seize some of the forts, and it was imperative to act with energy and stifle a revolution which might compromise the whole kingdom. I offered to go at once, and the king accepted, when despatches arrived announcing that my brother, Casimir, had been killed at the head of his regiment by a shot from a window. Of course I withdrew my offer, as every punishment inflicted by me would have had the air of avenging my brother's death, and I proposed Alphonse La Marmora, who reduced the city to order in a few days. At the same time I was occupied in carrying out one of the stipulations of the armistice—the disbanding of the Lombard legion, which had been so miserably betrayed by Ramorino. Summoned to headquarters on the 20th March, to explain his disobedience to orders, he attempted to fly, but was arrested and taken to Turin to be tried by court-martial. General Fanti, his successor, was left entirely in the dark by Czarnowsky and tried in vain to send messengers to Mortara on the 21st and 22d March. At last, fearing the enemy might march on Alessandria, which had a very small garrison, he led his men thither. After the disaster of Novara, he received orders to leave for Tortona, and on the march the news that one of the conditions of the armistice was the disbanding of the Lombard legion became known. The men were very indignant, as they feared being left to the tender mercy of the Austrians, and their discontent was fomented by agents sent by the Republicans of Genoa. A few tried to desert, but were stopped by General Fanti's influence, who, on arrival at Tortona on the 30th March, called his officers together, and explained the sad necessity the Sardinian government was under to disband the Lombard division. He suggested that for the Italian cause it would be more advantageous to remain united, and offer their services to the provisional governments of Rome or Tuscany. The idea was admirable, and served to tranquillise the troops and keep the division together. Old Marshal La Tour accepted the task of presiding at the court-martial which tried Ramorino. The crime of high treason, suspected by many, could not be proved; but his disobedience was flagrant, the punishment for which, by the military code, is death. As I have already said, he had received a written order from Czarnowsky, on the 17th March, to take up a strong position with the Lombard division at and round Cava, on the left bank of the Po. With the bulk of his troops he remained on the right bank, and thus facilitated the Austrian invasion of Piedmontese territory.   The court-martial condemned him to death. He appealed against the sentence, and his old mother came to Turin to implore the king's pardon, who refused to receive her.   Several ladies, more tender-hearted than patriotic, also attempted to approach the queen to beg her to intercede, but without success.   The whole ministry were against granting any mitigation of the sentence, and on the 22d May Ramorino was shot on the Champs de Mars at Turin.   He refused to be blindfolded, and met his death with courage.

Besides the painful duty of disbanding the Lombard division, and sending out of Piedmont so many men who had fought with us for the liberation of Italy, I had to recall our fleet from Ancona to Genoa.   Left to her own resources, it is a matter of history how gallantly Venice, under Daniel Manin, defended herself against the Austrian fleet and army.   She only succumbed when sickness and a close investment by the enemy made resistance impossible.

Meanwhile, negotiations for the peace, of which the armistice had been the prologue, were proceeding. Immediately after the abdication of his father, Victor Emanuel sent the minister Cadorna and Colonel Cossato to General Hess to treat for an armistice.   General Hess, chief of the staff to Radetzky, showed himself as unbending towards the young king's envoys as Radetzky had been to Charles Albert, and maintained certain conditions absolutely offensive to the Constitution, which Victor Emanuel was about to swear to uphold.   They were returning to Momo, when they heard that Radetzky had asked and obtained an interview with Victor Emanuel. The meeting took place at Vignale, half way between the two headquarters. As already stated, the old marshal had accompanied the young archduchess, Maria Adelaide, to Turin in 1842, on the occasion of her marriage to Victor Emanuel. He had been received with all honour by the Court, and had made the young prince's acquaintance. Setting aside, for the moment, the conditions under which they met, the marshal greeted Victor Emanuel with great cordiality, and begged to be allowed to embrace him. He expressed a sincere desire to conclude not only a treaty of peace, but a durable friendship between his own sovereign and the young king. For this reason he strongly advised Victor Emanuel to renounce the new form of Constitutional government, which might become a source of continual disagreement between the Courts of Vienna and Turin. The young king's manner was most friendly and deferential towards the old marshal, but he resolutely declared his intention of preserving the Constitution, given to his people by Charles Albert, intact, as he considered a revocation would be an insult to his father. After this, Radetzky could not insist, and the conditions of the armistice remained as before. While it was in force we had to submit to the occupation of our territory, lying between the Po, the Sesia and the Ticino, by eighteen thousand infantry and two thousand cavalry. Half the garrison of the citadel of Alessandria was to consist of Austrian troops (Radetzky allowed it, however, to be understood that this clause would not be insisted upon unless difficulties arose about the ultimate treaty of peace). The Sardinian troops were to abandon the territory on the right bank of the Po, which before the war had not belonged to us. The king bound himself to disband the Lombard, Hungarian, and Polish legions, and to recall the troops stationed outside the confines of Piedmont for the defence of territory which was again to fall under Austrian rule. These hard conditions were signed by Victor Emanuel, who only stipulated a complete amnesty for those Austrian subjects who had fought under the Italian flag. This was promised by the marshal.

On this basis, negotiations for peace were begun at Milan, between the minister De Bruck for Austria, and Dabormida and Boncompagni for Piedmont. Our plenipotentiaries were instructed to obtain some relief from the hard terms of the armistice; but not only did they fail in their intent—new pretentions were raised, especially with regard to the indemnity for which De Bruck claimed 220 millions.

After futile endeavours to come to terms, our plenipotentiaries were recalled to Turin, and negotiations were broken off.

The Austrian troops, in observation round Alessandria, immediately entered the citadel and occupied one half, as had been established in the protocol of the armistice, notwithstanding the protest of our government that they refused to recognise those conditions during the preliminaries for peace, even at the risk of a new war. To tell the truth we were neither desirous nor prepared for fresh hostilities; and the same was reported of the Austrians.

Meanwhile dissension broke out between De Launay and Pinelli, Minister of the Interior. Public opinion wrongfully accused De Launay of Conservatism, whilst he was a sincere Liberal. But he would not hear of allowing the Radicals, who wanted war at any price, to get the upper hand and ruin the country. The king and De Launay agreed to choose another president of the Council, and, I believe, Massimo D'Azeglio was suggested by De Launay himself. D'Azeglio had no desire to enter the government, and still less to become president of the

Council; he made every sort of excuse, but at last saw, as I had done on the 27th March, that it was a patriotic duty. He entered the ministry on the 7th May, and his great popularity immediately made itself felt. In the beginning of June the negotiations of peace were reopened, after demanding the withdrawal of the Austrian troops from Alessandria, which was done in twenty-four hours. Count di Pralormo, who had been our plenipotentiary in Vienna for several years, was added to Boncompagni and Dabormida, and under his guidance things went better. De Bruck came down from 220 millions to 75, the amnesty of the Lombard-Venetians was published before peace was ratified, and in eight days the Austrian troops evacuated the kingdom of his Majesty the King of Sardinia.

The majority of the nation was devoted to the royal family, but occupied themselves little with politics, and lacked the energy to insist on peace and tranquillity, compromised by the Radical party. On the 30th July the new Chambers opened with the same elements of opposition as the last. The electors returned their former members, and Marquis Pareto, one of the instigators of the revolution at Genoa, was again elected president. No sooner did D'Azeglio announce that peace was about to be signed, and ask a vote for 75 millions, than violent uproar arose in the Opposition benches. The death of Charles Albert caused a momentary lull. On hearing how ill his father was, Victor Emanuel had sent Riberi, his own doctor, to Oporto, who remained there till the 28th July, when the king died. His death was only known in Turin on the 8th August, the day peace was ratified at Milan. The sittings of Parliament were suspended for a week, and when it met again the Opposition was more violent than before, and the vote for the payment of 75 millions only passed by a very small majority. These perpetual Parliamentary struggles kept the country in a ferment, and were most damaging to all business and commerce. The odious insinuations of treachery in the army were again circulated, and the government was accused by the Radicals of seeking to destroy the new order of things by secret treaties. D'Azeglio was furious, but restrained himself, and kept a firm hand on the helm of the State. As to myself, I confess I was delighted when the day fixed between the king and myself came, and I handed over my portfolio to Bava.

I quitted the ministry on the 7th September, and on the 12th I married the young Countess Irene Verasis di Castiglione, to whom I had been engaged for some months.

The king had given his permission to our marriage, and asked me if the future Countess Della Rocca would like to be named one of the ladies about the queen, whose Court was just being formed. Irene accepted, and it was settled that when we returned from our honeymoon I was to present her to their Majesties.

CHAPTER X

END OF 1849 - 1855.

VICTOR EMANUEL took up his residence at the castle of Moncalieri, whence he rode or drove every day to Turin. The Court was in mourning, not only for Charles Albert, but for the disasters which had befallen our country. All the rigid etiquette of the former reign was abolished by the young king ; Maria Adelaide, brought up in simple German fashion, disliking it as much as he did himself. The grave and unbending widowed Queen Maria Theresa remained the only representative of the solemn Court of Charles Albert, as Maria Adelaide, always kind and amiable, had insisted on her mother-in-law living with her. My wife had been named one of the ladies about the young queen, and her waiting began in December 1849 ; so the king allowed me to choose the same month for my duties as one of his four aides-de-camp.

On our return from our honeymoon, in November, the political horizon was gloomy. Several of my colleagues were no longer in the ministry—Galvagno had taken the place of Pinelli, and was succeeded as Minister of Public Works by Paleocapa, a Venetian ; while Alphonse La Marmora was Minister of War and Marine, instead of

Bava. The Chambers, restless and noisy, refused to listen to logic or reason. They clamoured for war at all hazards, without reflecting that quiet and order were necessary to recoup our strength and reorganise the army. Fortunately, our ministers and diplomatists were patient and clever, and succeeded in obtaining large reductions from the first demands of Austria. Now it seems almost impossible to realise how little Piedmont, vanquished, without allies, and unaided by any of the great powers, should have accomplished what she did. It was sheer folly not to see that everything that was possible had been done. The deputies demanded that new conditions, chiefly in favour of the emigrants, should be added to the treaty, and, by seventy votes against sixty-six, refused to sanction it. This was about the middle of November, and the king immediately dissolved Parliament, and appealed to the country for the second time. On the 20th, by the advice of the prime minister, d'Azeglio, he published the famous 'Proclamation of Moncalieri.'

The Parliament, which met in December, was better constituted, and Pinelli was elected president. In a few days the treaty of peace with Austria was ratified without a dissentient voice. The session was opened with a speech by the king, expressing his satisfaction, and he was heartily cheered in Piazza Castello on leaving the Chambers. The first debates were on ecclesiastical jurisdiction,[1] a thorny subject, which provoked stormy discussions, and lasted for several years, during which Piedmont was at open war with the Holy See. Deplorable acts were committed on both sides ; when, for instance, the Roman Curia refused the sacrament to the dying minister Santa Rosa, because he voted for the abolition of ecclesiastical privileges, and when the government arrested the Archbishop of Turin,

---

[1] For abolishing the privileges and immunities enjoyed by ecclesiastics in legal questions.

condemned to a month's imprisonment and finally exiled, for having publicly prohibited his clergy to obey any citation before a lay tribunal.

In the spring of 1850 a marriage was arranged between the Duke of Genoa and the daughter of Prince John, brother and heir to King Frederick Augustus of Saxony. I was sent to Dresden by Victor Emanuel to ask the hand of the Princess Maria Elizabeth for his brother, and was accompanied by my cousin, Major di Cigala, one of the handsomest men in the army. Travelling post by way of Strasburg and Berlin, we reached Dresden in five days. I was most graciously received, first by the King of Saxony, then by Prince John, and finally by the Princess Maria Elizabeth, and the marriage was arranged to take place soon.

Meanwhile I went to Prague to deliver a letter entrusted to me by the Queen Maria Adelaide for the archduke, her brother, who commanded the garrison. Whilst there, I asked leave to pay my respects to the ex-Empress Marianne of Austria, one of the twin daughters of Victor Emanuel I., who married the Crown Prince Ferdinand in 1831. He became emperor four years later, and abdicated owing to epilepsy and madness in 1848. The empress was most gracious, and addressed me in the Piedmontese dialect, asking after all the royal family. While talking to her near a window in the large saloon, a man, wrapped in a long mantle like a monk's cloak, crossed from one door to another. Divining that it must be the emperor, I was about to rise, when the empress laid her hand on my shoulder and said, 'Ca fassa finta d'nën,'[1] and went on with her conversation. Soon afterwards she dismissed me, and I returned to Dresden to receive the Duke of Genoa and attend his marriage.

----

[1] 'Pretend not to see.'

In December 1850 my daughter Nathalie was born, and the following spring I was made chief of the staff. It had rather lost ground in the last three years as many of the older officers had been placed on the retired list, and their places had not been filled by younger men. I presented a list to the minister of war, but La Marmora was too authoritative to admit that the chief of the staff should enjoy the position and privileges enjoyed hitherto, and I had some trouble in obtaining the nomination of six of the officers named in my list. They all turned out well, and did honour to the corps, so that, altogether, the years 1851-1855 were among the happiest of my life. Victor Emanuel was always kind and gracious to me. Though residing at Moncalieri he often passed whole weeks at Turin, so that our daily intercourse was almost uninterrupted.

All the rigid etiquette introduced by Charles Albert had been abolished at the Court of Victor Emanuel. The sweet smile of the Queen Maria Adelaide, her kindly manner to all, her perfect temper, and the unaffected cheeriness of the king, rendered life at Moncalieri easy and pleasant, and allowed no scope for the usual intrigues and petty jealousies of a Court.

The queen was very delicate and her health was visibly declining, but she preserved her beauty and angelic expression. She was very religious, but without any ostentation. Much of her time was passed in writing to her relations at Milan and Vienna, and she embroidered most beautifully in various coloured silks. Her conversation was simple and ingenuous as a girl's; highly educated, her modesty was so great that she seemed afraid of showing how much she knew.

As there were four aides-de-camp, I was only on duty three months in the year, but I was often summoned to take the place of one or the other of my companions, who were not strong enough to follow Victor Emanuel in his shooting expeditions and excursions. I took no direct part in politics during these years, but seeing so much of the king I heard all that was going on. My cousin, Massimo D'Azeglio, showed great tact and energy, although the Radicals, furious at his thwarting their policy, accused him of being idle, too fond of his painting, and unfit for the cares of office. The position was a difficult one; the European powers were against us, and gave us advice, which in fact was an expression of their disapprobation of our Constitutional institutions which, to them, were odious. England alone was friendly, and her representative, Sir James Hudson, who came to Turin about this time and remained until the kingdom of Italy was an accomplished fact, gave constant proofs of this. Republican France was hostile, although her president, Prince Louis Napoleon, was favourable. He had not forgotten that, with his brother, he had fought in 1831 for the independence of Italy; but for the moment he was forced to dissemble. Victor Emanuel and D'Azeglio were astute enough to divine this, and to cultivate his friendly feelings by their cordiality at a time when he was regarded with suspicion by all the sovereigns of Europe. During a visit the president made to the Savoy frontier, the king sent an envoy to greet him with a very complimentary letter. I am almost certain that Napoleon's resolve to come to the aid of Piedmont dates from that interchange of letters and friendly messages.

The *coup d'état* which made Napoleon emperor took place on the 2d December 1851, and the friendship between the two sovereigns became firmly established.

Our home affairs were not more satisfactory than our relations with foreign powers. The debates on ecclesiastical immunities, civil marriage and the suppression of convents were stormy. They aroused the enmity of Rome and tormented the conscience of the king, who changed his ministers several times, though Massimo D'Azeglio held the presidency from 1849 till 1852. Victor Emanuel liked, esteemed and confided in D'Azeglio; at that time he rather dreaded the audacity of Cavour, who was in bad odour at the Roman Curia. Though alien to the religious bigotry of the Bourbons, the king was a professed Catholic, and his mother and wife kept alive his sentiments of respect for the Church of the Holy See. He feared that if Cavour became prime minister, the Pope would turn completely against Piedmont and himself, and also that his minister might embroil him with Austria and Russia.

After one of the many ministerial shufflings there was a warm discussion between the king and D'Azeglio, who declared his resolve to abandon political life. Victor Emanuel tried to form a Conservative Cabinet before summoning Cavour, but the attempt failed; and as soon as the latter became prime minister he proposed Rattazzi, leader of the left centre, to the king as minister of the interior. A union between the right and the left centre had already been initiated by Cavour in the Chambers; but the king, who then hardly knew Urbano Rattazzi, and was afraid lest his party might undermine the monarchy and join with the extreme Radicals, refused.

Cavour now became arbiter of the destinies, not only of little Piedmont, but of all Italy. With marvellous ability he took advantage of the political emigration to Turin. From southern and central Italy, and from the Lombard-Venetian provinces, men came to Piedmont to enjoy the liberty, momentarily conceded by their own sovereigns only to be cruelly snatched away. The exiles were received with open arms; nearly every house had one as a lodger. Cavour made their acquaintance—nearly all men of mark in science, literature and art—and helped them. Gradually a large number of Republicans, struck by the loyalty and good sense of the king and the extraordinary intelligence of his minister, were persuaded by him to join the party of Constitutional monarchy. He was already laying the foundation of an independent and strong Italian kingdom.

The conduct of foreign affairs by Cavour had been so successful that, profiting by the condition of Europe, little Piedmont made a treaty with France and England for the defence of Turkey against the arrogance of Russia, on condition of furnishing a contingent of fifteen thousand men.

The Duke of Genoa was destined to command the army, with Alphonse La Marmora as chief of the staff. But in the autumn of 1854 the duke fell seriously ill. It became evident that he could not embark for the Crimea, and that La Marmora, who had been minister of war for five years, would have to take the command. The preparations took several months, and the Duke of Genoa died before our little army started in the spring of 1855.

CHAPTER XI

1855-1857

AT the end of 1854 the queen, accompanied by her mother-
in-law, came to Turin for her confinement. Maria Theresa,
as I have already said, was extremely religious, and rarely
left the palace, save to visit various churches. During one
of these visits she caught cold and died of inflammation of
the lungs on the 12th January. Her death was kept a
secret from Maria Adelaide, who had just given birth to
her seventh son. The child died almost immediately, and
his mother on the 20th January, eight days after Maria
Theresa. A few weeks later the Duke of Genoa, to whom
the king was tenderly attached, breathed his last. As
always happens in such cases, there were rumours of
poison, while many talked of a divine punishment for the
laws relating to the confiscation of church property and
the suppression of convents, which were under discussion
in Parliament. The death of the two queens was attributed, in great measure, to grief at the expected vote in
favour of these measures, and it was affirmed that their
last prayer to the king had been not to sanction them.
My wife, who was in almost constant attendance on the

Queen Maria Adelaide, and was present when she died, heard nothing of this. The queen was too weak to speak, and only now and then murmured a loving word to her husband while he held her hand. The king told me that during that time men of various parties left him no peace, attempting to influence him one way or the other. He did his utmost, while remaining staunch to the laws sanctioned by both Houses, to come to some understanding with Rome. But when he saw that, to the proposals made in his name by the bishops of Chambéry and Mondovì, Rome replied by threats of excommunication, he at once acceded to the wishes of the majority, and gave his sanction to all that had been done. As a distraction from his family sorrows, he occupied himself with the preparations for the Crimean war, and in the spring gradually resumed his active life.

I must confess that public opinion was decidedly unfavourable to the Franco-Anglo alliance, and still more to the expedition to the Crimea. Count Cavour was hotly attacked, and the king was also blamed, as very few people understood the advantages which were ultimately to accrue to us from such a policy. Our part of the war resolved itself into the brilliant battle of the Tchernaja, which was to have considerable influence on the destinies of Italy. It demonstrated to Europe that France and England had sought the alliance of little Piedmont, that our army was well disciplined and brave, that our sovereign was courageous and ready to enter into any undertaking likely to serve, not only his own reputation, but the general interests of the Italian peninsula, and that his prime minister was a man of extraordinary ability, and surrounded by a bevy of clever men from all parts of Italy. This was the first link of the chain, forged by the skilful hands of Cavour, which was to rivet Piedmont to the rest of the peninsula; the second was his taking his place among the representatives of the great European powers at the Congress of Paris.

Despite the intrigues of Austria, Cavour succeeded in obtaining a position in the Congress equal to that enjoyed by the other representatives, and he was thus enabled to put the Italian question officially before Europe. He took advantage of the admiration expressed by England of our troops to suggest that Queen Victoria should invite our king to pay her a visit, and arranged that at the same time he should also be the guest of Napoleon III. in Paris. Cavour foresaw the success that Victor Emanuel, so original in manner and character, would have abroad. The king was frank and expressive, nay, even familiar, but, at the same time, he was proud and fully aware of what was due to him as the representative of a princely family, dating from more than eight centuries.

On 23d November the king arrived in Paris, accompanied by Cavour and Massimo d'Azeglio, the leaders of the Liberal and the Conservative parties, and myself as first aide-de-camp. We were lodged in the Tuilleries, and the emperor, who had not long been married to the Countess of Montijo, gave a series of *fêtes* in honour of Victor Emanuel.

At the end of November we left for London. The railway was the property of the Baron James de Rothschild, and he accompanied us to Calais. As soon as the train started Cavour and Rothschild retired into another compartment. Half an hour later the former returned rubbing his hands, an habitual trick of his when pleased, and with a jovial, sly smile on his face. 'Well?' said the king, by whom Cavour had seated himself. 'Everything is settled, your Majesty; I am quite satisfied.' 'And you, Baron?' continued Victor Emanuel to Rothschild, who had followed Cavour. 'I am also satisfied,' he replied; 'everything is in order.' 'Then I must congratulate both of you,' said the king, shaking hands with them. During those few minutes Cavour had arranged the first loan, to be followed by many others, with the house of Rothschild. He never lost a moment ; walking, travelling, or eating, he accomplished some financial or political business.

The reception accorded to the king in London was extraordinary. We traversed the town at foot's-pace, in the midst of a compact, loudly cheering crowd. This went on for two hours, so great was the distance between the station where we disembarked and the one where we entered the train for Windsor.

The Prince Consort met the king at the foot of the stairs and accompanied him to the top, where he was met by the queen. Soon afterwards Prince Albert conducted Victor Emanuel to his apartments, where cigars of all sorts had been put into every room. The English, who were never seen with a cigar in their mouths, had heard the king smoked all day long, and the cigars had been provided as a kind of intimation that he was to make himself at home.

From Windsor we went to London for two days, where we heard a speech from the Lord Mayor, complimenting the King of Sardinia, the ally, friend, and guest of England. Emanuel D'Azeglio, nephew of Massimo, had already translated it into Italian for the king's benefit, and Massimo had written a reply in French.

Again the enthusiasm was tremendous, and the carriages could only go at foot's-pace through the crowd, which waved handkerchiefs and shouted. Smiling gaily, the king said to me, 'You'll see how well I shall bear myself to-day and bow my acknowledgments properly at the pathetic passages.' In public Victor Emanuel never lost his self-control, and he played his part admirably in the great hall of the Mansion House. Listening to the speech of the Lord Mayor, as though he understood every allusion, he bowed his thanks with the greatest dignity; then, handing me his cocked hat, replied in French, accentuating well, in a sonorous voice, and with a kingly air which elicited loud applause.

Before leaving London the king was invested with the Order of the Garter. Warned that he must wear the special dress of the knights of the Order, a tailor was summoned and told to have it ready in twenty-four hours. The uniform was made, but fitted very ill, as I saw before and after the ceremony, for only the knights are allowed to be present at the investiture.

We left England on the 5th December, and the emperor insisted on the king spending two days at the Tuilleries. He told me that Napoleon made particular inquiries about his family, and strongly counselled him to marry again. Similar advice had been given by the Queen of England, and the beautiful Princess of Cambridge had been vaguely mentioned. But Victor Emanuel, though he admired her exceedingly, could not make up his mind to the marriage, and Queen Victoria let the subject drop. Napoleon, on the contrary, insisted, and proposed a princess of one of the oldest, but not the richest, families of Europe. Although the king had not the slightest intention of marrying a second time, he did not wish to offend his powerful ally, or give him reason to suspect that he had already married, or was about to marry, Rosina Vercellani morganatically. He knew it would have as bad an effect on Queen Victoria as on Napoleon, so he affected to entertain the idea, if he could be assured that the princess was handsome, intelligent, and amiable, as the Queen Maria Adelaide had been. The emperor then suggested that I should be sent to see her; a mission not at all to my taste, but which I had to accept. So when the king left for Piedmont I went to Germany, without any letters of introduction, as the object of my journey was to be a secret. After two days of travelling I arrived in Dusseldorf, where I visited the churches, the public gardens and the theatres, without ever seeing Prince Hohenzollern Sigmaringen or his family. I began to despair, when the happy thought struck me of asking leave to visit the prince's stables. Whilst talking to the director the prince rode up in uniform and asked my name. One of his sisters had married Marquis Pepoli of Bologna, with whose family I was acquainted, so he invited me to dinner, and I was thus able to see the Princess Stephanie. She was only eighteen, and, though charming, was very shy and not likely to induce a sovereign who was averse to matrimony to change his mind. My mission, therefore, as I had foreseen, was fruitless, and I returned to Turin in time to pass Christmas with my family.

In March 1856 I was again in Paris with my wife and two little daughters, to consult the famous physician Blache about one of them. We saw the baptism of the Prince Imperial, and were invited to all the Court *fêtes* at St Cloud and in Paris. Here we saw the beautiful Countess di Castiglione, whom we had known as a child in Piedmont. It was the beginning of her great favour with the emperor, which lasted six or seven years, and aroused the jealousy of the empress. The richness and daring originality of her *toilettes* were celebrated. At a fancy dress ball at the Tuilleries the lovely countess appeared as Queen of Hearts, in a very transparent dress open on one side up to her hip, and displaying her magnificent figure clothed in scarlet silk 'tights.' Round her neck was a gold chain, from which hearts, encrusted with precious stones, were suspended, and a large heart hung from her girdle in front. Court gossips said that the empress exclaimed, '*Quels beaux bijoux, mais le coeur est placé bien bas !*'

The Congress for the peace with Russia was then

sitting in Paris, and the successes of Cavour, his wonderful cleverness, and his eminent qualities as a statesman, were themes of general conversation. I felt proud to see the admiration my compatriot excited, and was disagreeably surprised when, on my return to Turin, the king told me it was rumoured that I had been sent by him on a kind of secret mission to report on the acts of Cavour and the impression they made on the Tuilleries and elsewhere. These reports reached Cavour, who showed his displeasure to the king. He imagined that I had great influence with Victor Emanuel, an opinion shared by many others, and which was the cause of considerable mischief to me in after years. The truth is that the king was always extremely kind to me, and treated me, if I may use the term, as a sort of elder brother-at-arms, who could advise him in matters of private life, and to whom he could talk about political concerns, without however permitting any discussion on his duties as a Constitutional sovereign. He had a keen perception of those about him ; some he both liked and esteemed, but not all. Several of the men whose character and intelligence he admired were personally distasteful to him, yet he called them several times to power, sacrificing his likes and dislikes to the good of his country and the Italian cause, which was his one object in life, and in which he always believed when others had lost heart.

The same party in Piedmont which disapproved of the Crimean expedition could not seize the importance of the success obtained by Cavour at the Congress of Paris in 1856, or the impulse he had given to Italian affairs. Many Turinese grumbled that nothing had been stipulated for Piedmont, who gained no material advantages from the alliance and the war. But the Milanese, the Venetians and the Liberals of the divers Italian provinces were more clear-sighted, and the aspirations of 1848 again made themselves heard. The king *Galantuomo* and his incomparable minister were overwhelmed with thanks, encouragement and prayers. I think I am correct in saying that the designs and expectations of Cavour increased so largely towards the end of 1856 and during 1857 that he foresaw possibilities he had not dared to calculate on. By the help of several Lombards, of various Sicilians led by Farina, and of the more remarkable members of the Centre, he began to weave the net which was to enfold all the children of Italy, and realise his ideal of seeing all the independent provinces united into one country.

On 4th July 1857 I became lieutenant-general by seniority, which confirmed me in the position of first aide-de-camp and one of the chief officers of the Court, so that I was more than ever about the king.

There were violent debates in the Chambers about transferring the naval station from Genoa to Spezia. The latter port was preferable in case of a war, which seemed probable, as Austria was playing the same game she had done ten years before. The Genoese were less annoyed than had been feared by the passing of the law. Since the question of Italian independence had been raised they understood that Piedmont was the only possible champion. Mazzini, however, thought otherwise. Desirous of effacing the memory of the failure of his enterprise in southern Italy, he was planning fresh revolts on the Neapolitan coast and in central Italy. For some months he had been moving between Leghorn, Spezia and Genoa with some of his followers charged to collect men and arms. Counting on the ill-humour of his Genoese compatriots he determined to try and seize the naval arsenal and the artillery depot, and capture a frigate that lay at anchor in the port of Genoa. A warning had reached Rattazzi, the minister of the interior, but he did not believe the conspiracy was serious, and his information as to Mazzini's movements was defective. The French police, however, discovered the plot, and revealed it to our government, who immediately reinforced the garrisons of the places menaced by the Mazzinians; the result was their precipitate retreat, with the exception of a small detachment in the fort *Diamante*, who were not warned in time. During the night they fell upon the small garrison, killed the sergeant and took the men prisoners. There was some agitation next morning in the city, but rather in favour of the government than of Mazzini. Seeing the unfavourable turn of events, he took his departure; but, before leaving, arranged one of those foolhardy enterprises which only served to increase the number of victims to the Italian cause, or, as some said, to keep the idea of union alive in the peninsula.

Misled by reports from some of his emissaries, who assured him that on the Neapolitan coast, at Padula and at Sapri, thousands of men only awaited his orders to rise, he persuaded Pisacane and Nicotera, with a merchant captain and some volunteers, to embark as passengers on board the *Cagliari*, a Sardinian vessel trading between Genoa and Tunis. On the high seas they made the Sardinian captain prisoner, put their man in his place, forced the sailors and the two engineers, who were Englishmen, to obey him, and sailed for the coast. Not a man met them at the appointed places, but at Ponza they succeeded in liberating and enrolling three hundred prisoners. At Padula they were met by a battalion of Neapolitan troops and utterly beaten; Pisacane was killed, Nicotera wounded and arrested. The captain of the *Cagliari* left the conspirators on shore and started for Tunis; but the ship was captured in the name of Ferdinand II. and taken to Naples. Our government protested in vain, until at last England insisted on the release of her subjects the two engineers, the restitution of the vessel to Sardinia, and the payment of an indemnity.

CHAPTER XII

1858. BEGINNING OF 1859

IN January 1858 all Europe, and Piedmont in particular, was startled by the attempted assassination of Napoleon III. by Felice Orsini. The emperor wrote to the sovereigns of Europe, requesting them to take severe precautionary measures against the Republican and Radical Italian emigrants and exiles who had taken refuge in their several states. Many of them sent special ambassadors to Paris to compliment Napoleon on having escaped unhurt, and Victor Emanuel, in concert with Cavour, confided this difficult mission to me. Our government especially had fallen under the displeasure of the emperor on account of the number of exiles from the various Italian states who had taken refuge with us. I arrived in Paris with my aide-de-camp and secretary, Count Charles di Robilant, captain of artillery and an intimate friend of ours, at the end of January. At an official audience I delivered to the emperor an autograph letter from the king, informing his *bon frère* that his ambassador extraordinary was charged to give the fullest explanations on all matters connected with the circular and subsequent notes sent by the Imperial to the Sardinian Government.

Several days passed without our receiving any invitation to the Tuilleries, and I became anxious. Unaccustomed to the tortuous ways of diplomacy, I knew not whether to ask for another audience or to await the pleasure of the emperor. Both the king and Cavour were anxiously waiting to hear the result of the private audience which they expected would follow immediately on the delivery of the letter. From the Marquis of Villamarina, our minister plenipotentiary at Paris, I heard that, after the attempt on his life, the emperor had expressed great anger against the Sardinian Government, exclaiming, 'Piedmont is a nest of revolutionists and assassins. Orsini has stayed there several times, and Mazzini is continually in the country, without the police taking any notice.' These words, and the delay in granting me an audience, seemed to augur badly, especially as the Prince of Liechtenstein, Austrian ambassador extraordinary, who arrived in Paris after us, was said to have been very well received at Court. At last in the beginning of February came an invitation to dine at the Tuilleries, with a letter from the minister of the household, intimating that his H.I.M. the Emperor would see me in private the same evening. After dinner Napoleon took me into his study, and said the tone of the king's letter was very friendly, and that he intended to reply at some length. Then he paused, and I thought I might venture to draw his attention to several matters I had been instructed to submit to him. But seeing that he wished to formulate his accusations before I could attempt any defence, I stopped short. Requesting me to listen attentively, as he wished his precise words to be reported to the king, he began with vehement, I may say unjust, charges against our government. He complained especially of a newspaper, *La Ragione*, and of the judges who, after trying the editor for abusing monarchical governments and publishing something very like an apology for political assassination, had absolved him. Such acts, continued the Emperor, were calculated to cool the friendly relations hitherto subsisting between his government and Piedmont, and showed that our ministry, particularly Count Cavour, was in league with the extreme left. Our laws, he added, were quite inadequate to cope with the disorder born of political assassination, or with the disgraceful press which glorified such deeds. Recalling our alliance with him and with England in 1855, he impressed upon me how little we had to hope from the latter power, while all our interests lay in a close alliance with him. For this it was absolutely necessary that those emigrants, who constituted a perpetual source of danger to ourselves and to him, should be banished from Piedmont. He said that, owing to his complaints, Geneva, till now a refuge for assassins, had expelled a large number of exiles who had gone to Savoy, where the police not only failed to denounce them, but allowed demonstrations of welcome in their honour. From the provinces, from public bodies, and from the army, Napoleon stated that he had received addresses expressing the utmost horror of the attempted assassination by Orsini, and that the army *was ready to march against any place known to be a refuge for assassins.*

The threat contained in the last few words was menacing. To conceal the impression made upon me, I again tried to persuade the emperor that the accusations against our government were unfounded, and assured him of our unceasing endeavours to restrain revolutionary tendencies and repress disorder. He listened courteously, but retracted nothing, and again requested that his exact words should be reported in writing to the king. Reluctantly I had to obey, and the same night our courier took my letter to Turin.

The emperor had been as courteous towards myself

as he had been harsh towards my government; when I took leave he told me to come to the Tuilleries any morning between nine and ten, when he was generally at liberty. So, before the courier returned, I saw him several times, and, according to my instructions, attempted to lay the condition of Piedmont since 1849 before him. From observations and questions addressed to me at the Tuilleries and in Paris *salons*, I saw that Piedmontese affairs were utterly unknown in France. We were regarded as more or less revolutionary, and accused of giving refuge to exiles and political criminals. I told the emperor that the first years of Victor Emanuel's reign had not been easy; but now, thanks to his loyalty, the prudence and firmness of D'Azeglio, and the clear-sighted policy and powerful genius of Cavour, he had gained the confidence and love of his people. Social revolution would not break out in Piedmont, but was imminent in other Italian provinces, especially in those ruled by Austria. The only way to prevent this, and pacify those who were appealing to us for help, would be the intervention of a great power in favour of Italian independence. With regard to Mazzini, I assured him that we knew his influence was on the decline, owing to his foolhardy enterprises, which only served to augment the number of martyrs to the Italian cause; and I gave the true version of the affair of the *Cagliari*, which had been misrepresented in France.

By the time the courier returned with answers to my letters, I saw the emperor was better disposed towards us; so I ventured to obey the orders contained in one of the letters of Victor Emanuel—*to commit the imprudence* of reading the other aloud to the emperor by *motu proprio*, as it were. Napoleon listened attentively, smiled at some passages, and expressed his admiration of the proud dignity of the concluding words, '*D'après ce que je viens de vous dire, mon cher La Rocca, l'empereur doit être bien persuadé de mes bonnes intentions, et voir que les faits ont été executés même avant qu'il les eut demandés. S'il voulait que j'use de violence ici, qu'il sache que je perdrais toute ma force, et lui toutes les sympathies d'une genereuse et noble nation. . . . Si les paroles, que vous me transmettez, sont les paroles textuelles de l'empereur, dites lui dans les termes que vous croirez les mielleurs, qu'on ne traite pas ainsi un fidèle allié, que je n'ai jamais souffert de violences de personne, que je suis la voie de l'honneur toujours sans tache et que de cet honneur je n'en reponds qu'à Dieu et à mon peuple ; qu'il y a huit cent cinquante ans que nous portons la tête haute, et que personne ne me la fera baisser, et avec tout célà que je ne désire autre chose que d'être son ami.'*

'*Voilà ce qui s'appelle avoir du courage,*' exclaimed the emperor. '*Votre roi est un brave, j'aime sa réponse.*' He continued talking about the king, and repeated several times, '*Je suis sûr que nous nous entendrons,*' and then told me to write immediately to reassure Victor Emanuel, and say he was sorry to have caused him any uneasiness, and that his opinions with regard to Piedmont were modified. In another audience I touched upon a reported scheme of alliance between France and Austria, and the emperor replied, ' I love Italy, and shall never ally myself with Austria against her. Had I occupied the place I now fill in 1849 I should certainly have gone to the aid of Charles Albert.'

At a great review the emperor beckoned me to his side, pointing out one regiment after another as they marched past. The same evening a paper was sent me through the post, with a notice of the review, saying that the emperor had conversed with the Austrian and English ambassadors, but only said a few words to the King of Sardinia's envoy, '*Car ici les Piemontais ne sont pas aimés.*' At the Tuilleries ball that night the empress stopped to inquire about the king and his children, and asked after my wife. Immediately after her came Princess Mathilde, sister of Prince Jerome Bonaparte, one of the few persons then in France who liked the Italians, and who was supposed to enjoy the full confidence of the emperor. '*Dites moi, Monsieur Della Rocca*,' she exclaimed, in her clear, high voice, '*avez vous vu le journal de ce soir? Ces gens là ont bien raison de dire que nous ne vous aimons pas, car*' . . . pausing a moment, '*nous vous adorons*,' she continued, laughing, and glancing archly at me. The Prince of Liechtenstein was‑standing close by, and his yellow face turned green at these words.

A few days later I received letters from Turin. Cavour wrote :—'*Je te félicite sincèrement de tes debuts dans la carrière diplomatique. Placé dans une position extrèmement difficile, tu as su t'en tirer avec une rare habileté et un tact parfait. Le roi a été très satisfait de ce que tu as dit et de ce que tu as fait. Je pense qu'il te l'écrira lui même*' . . . and the king added, '*Je vous embrasse et je vous remercie de tout mon cœur ; vous m'avez rendu un grand service, et vous vous êtes tiré d'affaire d'une manière merveilleuse, mieux qu'un diplomate*.' . . .

At my last audience, on the 20th February, the emperor declared himself perfectly satisfied with all I had told him in the name of Victor Emanuel and of Cavour, and with my explanations about the condition of Piedmont. He authorised me to tell the king confidentially that in case of a war between Piedmont and Austria he would come with a large force to fight side by side with his faithful ally Victor Emanuel. '*Dites aussi*,' he added, '*a M. de Cavour, qu'il se mette en correspondance directe avec moi, et que nous nous entendrons certainement*.'

It was a fortunate coincidence that, just as the emperor was beginning to mollify towards us, Pietri, the prefect of police, gave him a letter from Orsini, written in prison, containing almost the same words I had spoken—that the

Italians were resolved to bear a foreign yoke no longer. 'I conjure your Imperial Majesty,' continued Orsini, 'to bestow on Italy the independence her sons wanted in 1848 and 1849. Be assured that until they have it there will be no tranquillity for Europe, or for your Imperial Majesty. Deign to listen to the last request of a patriot on the steps of the scaffold—free my country, and the benedictions of twenty-five million people will follow you to posterity.

On arriving at Turin I hastened to inform the king and Cavour of the formal promise, to come to the aid of Piedmont in case of war with Austria, given by the emperor at my last audience. I saw that Napoleon had some other idea with respect to an alliance with us, and hinted as much to the king. To Cavour I spoke more plainly, and he rubbed his hands, and smiled rather sardonically with an air of superior knowledge.[1]

It is a matter of history that, immediately after the meeting of the emperor and Cavour at Plombières in 1858, war was talked of as imminent. The propaganda of the Italian cause in the provinces redoubled in zeal, aided by the *National Society* of Central Italy, under La Farina, who worked with Cavour. After the reception at the Tuilleries for the New Year, when the emperor said to Hübner, Austrian ambassador at Paris, 'I regret that our relations with your government are not as cordial as they were,' and Victor Emanuel's speech on the 10th January 1859, at the opening of Parliament, the agitation increased. Austria sent reinforcements to her Italian army, and war, unpopular in France, but hailed with joy by the Italians, was considered inevitable. Our finance minister, Lanza, asked for a loan of fifty millions, troops were summoned from the more distant garrisons, and in March all our reserves were called under arms.

[1] The marriage of Princess Clotilde, daughter of Victor Emanuel, and the cession of Nice and Savoy, were probably in the thoughts of both.

France armed slowly. Public opinion was generally hostile, and politicians, aware of Napoleon's predilection for the country which had given birth to his forebears, declared the war was a sentimental one and injurious to France, who could reap no advantage. They were ignorant of the treaty at Plombières, which gave her two rich provinces. We, on the contrary, pushed forward our armaments with all speed. By the middle of April an army of five divisions, each consisting of from twelve thousand to fifteen thousand men, was ready. Victor Emanuel was commander-in-chief, and he named me head of the staff; La Marmora accompanied the king as minister in attendance. Volunteers from Lombardy, Venetia, Parma, the Roman States and Tuscany, flocked to join us on the first rumour of war, and were placed under the command of General Garibaldi. Two thousand Tuscan regular soldiers also assembled under General Ulloa, but they only arrived when all was over—after San Martino and Solferino.

La Marmora (minister of war), thinking the enemy would march straight for Turin, ordered the right bank of the Dora Baltea to be fortified, and retained the command of the troops destined to defend the capital for himself. These preparations alarmed everyone, and there was a general exodus. The entrenchments were hardly finished when Marshal Canrobert, who was to command one of the French army corps, and General Froissart, head of the engineers, arrived in Turin to concert matters with the king and the minister of war. They were invited by the king to visit the line of fortifications, and the minister of war, the chief of the staff, and the heads of the engineers and artillery (La Marmora, Della Rocca, Menebrea and Pastore) were asked to meet them. Canrobert immediately declared himself against the defence of Turin from that side, but courteously praised the way the work had been carried out under La Marmora's supervision. Froissart, on the contrary, roughly—almost aggressively—criticised everything. We were rather hurt, but managed to conceal our feelings, all except Cialdini, aide-de-camp in attendance on the king, who was very hot-tempered. He contradicted Froissart so wittily, and with such knowledge of military matters, that we began to fear war might be declared between France and Piedmont instead of between Piedmont and Austria. With some difficulty Menebrea and I contrived to change the conversation.

On the 23d April Baron von Kellersberg brought a letter from the Austrian minister, Buol, inviting Count Cavour to reply within three days whether the government of the King of Sardinia would place his army on a peace footing and dismiss the volunteers or not. On the 26th Cavour gave the Austrian envoy a negative reply; the king having issued a proclamation on the 24th, calling his troops to arms and announcing the imminent arrival of a large French army, commanded by the emperor.

On the 28th April Francis Joseph announced to his people that the Austrian army had been ordered to cross the Piedmontese frontier, and next day the regiment of hussars, King of Prussia, met our light cavalry near Zinasco, and the advanced guard crossed the Ticino at Beregnardo by a military bridge. On the 30th April the strategical development of the Austrian army was accomplished behind the Terdoppio, and on the same day the first French troops entered Turin.

L'armée d'Italie, as it was called, consisted of about one hundred and twenty thousand men in five army corps, four of twenty thousand men, one of twelve thousand, and fifteen thousand men of the Imperial Guard under General Regnault de Saint-Jean d'Angély. The first corps was commanded by Marshal Baraguay d'Hilliers, the second by General MacMahon, the third by Marshal Canrobert, the fourth by General Niel, and the fifth by Prince Jerome Napoleon.

The Austrians were said to be over two hundred thousand men; but in the first battles they could only muster one hundred and twenty thousand, divided into five army corps; the rest formed the garrisons of the fortresses in Lombardy, Venetia, Mantua, Verona, Peschiera, etc. The commanders were Prince Liechtenstein, Count Schwartzenberg, Count Stadion, Baron Nobel, and Von Benedek. The division of reserve cavalry was under Baron Mensdorf, and a division of independent infantry under Urban. Field-marshal Count Giulay was commander-in-chief, with Count Valmoden *à latere;* the emperor's chief of the staff was Baron Hess, Count Giulay's Baron Külme.

By the 10th May all the French troops had arrived in Piedmont; the 1st and 2d army corps and the Imperial Guard disembarked at Genova, and marched by Novi on Alessandria; the 3d and 4th came over the Mont Cenis and Monginevra; the 5th disembarked at Leghorn for Florence, and, crossing the Apennines, did not join the army till after Solferino. The first four corps took up their positions with us between S. Salvatore and Casale.

The king left Turin on the 30th April and established his headquarters at S. Salvatore, near Casale, when my hard work and responsibility as chief of the staff began. La Marmora had sent twenty thousand men to occupy the triangle between Alessandria, Casale and Bassignana on the right bank of the Po, as soon as Kellersberg left Turin. His orders had been given without consulting the commander-in-chief, and still less the chief of the staff. When the king and I visited the troops we saw how hazardous their position was, opposed to an enemy more than four times as strong on the Sesia and the left bank of the Po, occupying the positions of Vercelli, Novara,

Vigevano, etc. Giulay, leaving a corps in observation before Casale and Valenza, might easily have crossed the Po, attacked us on the right bank, and, placing himself between Alessandria and Genoa, have arrested the French as they descended from Novi towards Alessandria. Had Giulay known his numerical superiority, and been capable of using it, he might have prevented the junction of the two armies.

It was fortunate for us that the enemy, far superior in number, was led by an irresolute and hesitating commander. We stood opposite him for nearly twenty days, during which time he made no serious move, and only attempted small attacks on our outposts, which were invariably repulsed. When, in after years, it was proposed to raise a monument to Victor Emanuel in memory of the campaign of 1859, he used to say, 'The monument should not be dedicated to me, but to Giulay, for having been so good as to spare us until the arrival of the French.'

One of my first acts was to recall Cialdini and his division from his position on the Dora Baltea, and establish his headquarters at Casale near us. On the 3d and 4th May he frustrated the enemy's attempts to cross the Po at Frassineto, and forced them to abandon the positions of Balzole, Villanova and Terranova. On the 9th and 10th the Austrians advanced towards Trino and Crescentino, thus approaching nearer Turin. I sent Castelborgo to attack their left flank during the march, but before he could deploy his troops, the enemy, to our surprise, retreated and retired across the Sesia.

We spent ten days at S. Salvatore, where Garibaldi, in his new uniform of general of brigade, came to see the king. Victor Emanuel sent him to Ivrea to take command of the volunteers, ordering him to cross the Ticino at Sesto Calende and advance on Varese, where there was a strong Austrian force. The terror and disorder into which he threw the right flank of the enemy is a matter of history. On the 11th May we left S. Salvatore for Occimiana, where Victor Emanuel received Don Neri Corsini, sent by the provisional government of Tuscany to entreat him to accept the sovereignty of the Grand Duchy. The king's reception was extremely cordial, but he would give no promise. This was the first of the many offers which reached the *Re Galantuomo* (Honest King) from the various provinces of central Italy.

CHAPTER XIII

1859 (SECOND PART)

ON the 12th May Napoleon III. disembarked at Genoa, and on the 14th established his headquarters at Alessandria, assuming the supreme command of the allied armies. My work was then doubled. I was perpetually summoned from Occimiano, where the king had his headquarters, by the emperor or by General Vaillant, his head of the staff, to give information about the roads and the means of communication; so to my other duties was added that of courier and *éclaireur* to the French headquarters. I had to think, not only of my own sixty thousand men, but of the whole allied army.

The emperor immediately grasped the incapacity of the Austrian commander-in-chief, who, for nearly three weeks, had kept one hundred and twenty thousand men in line without attacking the opposing force of between twenty-five and thirty thousand. Giulay had made up his mind that the first battle was to be fought in the great plain of the valley of the Po, and kept his army stationary between Casale and Mortara, and Mortara and Novara, in order to defend Milan from that side. Napoleon resolved to draw the enemy in another direction, and made a feint to enter Lombardy by way of Piacenza, where he sent a considerable body of troops and part of his camp equipage. The battle of Montebello was the consequence of this move, and Giulay was for some days in doubt as to the real intention of the emperor, which was a counter-march towards the Ticino. The idea was a bold one. It necessitated crossing the enemy's front, and marching round his flank. Falling back from Alessandria towards Casale, and advancing on Vercelli and Novara, the French troops, describing a semi-circle, were to cross the Ticino at the most undefended point and march on Milan. This was to be done as quickly as possible, while the Austrians, misled by the movement towards Piacenza, were on the right bank of the Po. The Piedmontese were to cross the Sesia, and station themselves in the centre of the semi-circle on the road between Mortara and Palestro, to protect the French advance from Casale on Vercelli. This plan resulted in the two splendid days of Palestro, and in the battle of Magenta on the opposite side of the Ticino.

On the 20th May, the day on which our cavalry fought so well at Montebello, the king transferred his headquarters to Casale. The Austrians, after some days of inactivity, at length prepared to cross the Sesia nearly opposite Terranova, a position occupied by General Fanti's division. Victor Emanuel had ordered a bridge to be thrown across an arm of the river to a small island, whence the passage of the enemy could be observed. They did not attempt to molest our engineers, but two sharp skirmishes took place near by.

On the evening of the 23d there was a continuous interchange of telegrams between Alessandria and Casale. Napoleon, badly informed, announced a gathering of the Austrian's in force near Voghera, and he feared an attack on the small body of French troops sent on the feint towards Piacenza. He begged the king not to divide his forces, to recall Cialdini, who was already on the other side of Vercelli, and to send reinforcements towards Voghera. After I returned from Terranova to Casale, having executed the emperor's wishes, a telegram with counter orders came in. Napoleon having received more correct information, notwithstanding the official bulletin, announced his departure for Voghera. The news was false, but served its purpose; as the enemy, after vainly trying to take the islet, which had been well fortified, and was defended by General Mollard's brigade, disappeared from the banks of the Sesia, and hurried to prevent the advance of the French towards Voghera.

On hearing this, the emperor resumed his plan of a counter-march, which he had hesitated to carry out owing to various false alarms. Late on the 26th he wrote to Victor Emanuel, and next morning we rode over so early to Alessandria that Napoleon was still in bed. The concentration—crossing from the right to the left bank of the Po—of both armies began that evening, with the happiest results for us.

The positions held by the allies on the 27th May were as follows — Marshal Baraguay d'Hilliers and General MacMahon were at Voghera, Casci, Castelnuova di Scrivia and Sale, on the right bank of the Po; Marshal Canrobert was at Ponte Curone; General Niel at Bassignana and Valenza; the Imperial Guard at Alessandria. Our divisions Fanti, Durando, and Cialdini occupied Motta de' Conti, Caresana, Pezzana, Prarolo, and Vercelli, on the right bank of the Sesia; Castelborgo's division was half at Casale, half at Terranova; and Cuchiari held the right bank of the Po, from Monti to Frassineto, with his division.

The first corps to leave Alessandria was Canrobert's, in whose staff was General Trochu, whom I had often seen at Paris, at the house of our mutual friend Alexander

Bixio. Canrobert was exactly what the French call *un bon enfant*, and had none of the pride and conceit of other French marshals, particularly apparent in those who showed least ability in the campaign of 1859. His divisions always arrived in time and in good order. From Alessandria he went to Casale, and thence to Prarolo, where he halted to construct bridges of boats across the Po, opposite Palestro, for the passage of the Imperial Guard and the troops of Niel and Baraguay d'Hilliers, who were to push forward to Ortengo.

Our divisions Fanti, Durando and Castelborgo marched towards Vercelli on the night of the 28th, to take up their respective positions; Fanti at Confienza, Durando at Vinzaglio, Castelborgo at Casalino. Cialdini recrossed to the left bank of the river, and on the 29th occupied Porrione, not far from Palestro. The division Cucchiari, as I have already said, was left at Frassineto to guard the Po. On the same day Victor Emanuel, who was delayed a whole day by the block on the railway, left Casale for Vercelli. He traversed the French camp on horseback, and was cheered to the echo by the officers and troops. The soldiers crowded round to see him, and Cler, the brave and beloved general who lost his life a few days later at Magenta, addressed the king in words expressive of admiration and praise. At Vercelli, which we entered about mid-day, the population received Victor Emanuel with acclamation. He dismounted at the palace of Count La Motta, and soon afterwards came despatches announcing the victories of Garibaldi, who had driven the cruel and hated General Urban out of the province of Comasco. On reaching Vercelli I went to inspect a bridge which our engineers had been ordered to make; to my surprise, I found it was hardly begun, because the French had insisted on doing the work, and being unacquainted with the country, they did not know where to get materials. I had rather an altercation with Froissart, who would not understand that to gain time it was better to leave the execution of such things to us. Of all the French generals he was the most difficult to get on with.

At daybreak on the 30th I rode over to inspect the positions of Confienza, where my brother Robert was stationed with his brigade Pinerolo. On my return I found the king on the railway bridge watching our troops march past and Canrobert throwing bridges over the river, nearly opposite Palestro, on which our right wing was advancing. About eleven a cannonade announced that the battle had commenced, and we galloped off in the direction of Palestro.

Palestro is impregnable in front. There is only one road through the rice fields, and the place is protected on that side by an earthwork, whence four pieces of artillery could stop several thousand men. Cialdini had cleverly turned the position on the right. We followed in his footsteps, and entered the village, as our troops, to the cry of 'Long live the king!' 'Long live Savoy!' were driving back the enemy at the point of the bayonet; while another Austrian brigade was hurrying up to their aid. The struggle was tremendous. The Austrians defended every house, firing from the windows, the roofs and the walls, whilst our men pushed forward with indomitable pluck. The loss of life was great, but we expelled the enemy. On our left, Durando captured the position of Vinzaglio, after some brilliant bayonet charges. Captain Vecchi, one of our staff officers, dismounted, and at the head of his men rushed, sword in hand, at the barricade erected at the entrance of the village. Springing on the top, he pulled up those below, stormed the second barricade, and with his handful of men drove the enemy before him without receiving a scratch. General Fanti drove out the small body of Austrians who held Casalino, and then hurried to Confienza, where he again repulsed the enemy. Our victory was complete, and all the more glorious because gained without extraneous help.

In the evening, the emperor rode over from Vercelli to congratulate the king, and on his return sent a regiment of Zouaves, about two thousand four hundred men, under Colonel Chabron, with orders to place themselves at the disposition of Victor Emanuel. Napoleon foresaw that the enemy would receive reinforcements during the night, and at daylight try to recapture Palestro.

The king passed the night in a house adjoining the big farm of Torrione; and in the early morning of the 31st, while Cialdini and I were taking our orders for the day, a cannon shot warned us that the enemy was approaching. Cialdini's divisions and the Zouaves were the only troops near Torrione, and forty thousand men were marching to attack us. We immediately mounted and sent off a considerable body of troops towards our left; but suspecting that the enemy's advance on that side might only be a feint, the king and I climbed up the *campanile* of the little church and found our surmise to be correct. The greater portion of the Austrian army was to our right, with the intention of turning our position and cutting us off from the bridge over the Sesia, prepared for the passage of Canrobert's troops. Our right was weak, but fortunately the Zouaves came up at double-quick time, followed by four pieces of artillery. As they debouched on to the piazza in Palestro, the king descended from the *campanile* and took his place in their ranks. I remained for a short time on the tower, but, anxious not to lose sight of Victor Emanuel, soon joined him. We were in the midst of the Zouaves, who rushed like lions upon the Austrians, drove them back, and threw many into the canal. Colonel Chabron approached the king and said, ' *Sire, retirez vous, ce n'est pas ici votre place.*' ' *Dans le danger,*' replied His Majesty; '*ma place est au milieu des miens, et aujourd'hui vous êtes des miens.*' The slaughter was great. Our brigades Regina and Savona and the Zouaves covered themselves with glory, took many prisoners and several cannon.

In the midst of all these horrors comic scenes occurred. One of the enemy's ammunition waggons was driven up at full gallop by two of our infantry soldiers as postillions, while another on the box shouted, 'Faster; go on, postillions; let us enjoy our carriage and horses now we've got them!' Then came several of our men, with some Zouaves harnessed to cannon taken from the enemy, hallooing, 'Make way for the new artillerymen!' followed by prisoners of every arm. The poor fellows made signs that they were suffering from hunger and thirst; and the Zouaves, so terrible whilst fighting, were kindly and compassionate. They produced bits of bread from their pockets, and ran to the fountain to get water, which they offered, with caressing gestures, such as one might use to children.— ' *Tu as faim, mon petit? Mange, mange, moi ça. Et avale ce verre d'eau fraiche.*' We remained masters of the positions, victorious all along the line. The emperor came from Vercelli to compliment the king and thank him, for this victory enabled Canrobert to execute his march from Vercelli to Novara, and secured the success of the enterprise.

On his way back to Vercelli, Napoleon met a detachment of the Nizza cavalry escorting prisoners. The young officer in command halted to render military honours to the emperor, who returned his salute and said some courteous words about the successful issue of the day. The sublieutenant replied in such pure French that Napoleon was struck, and asked who he was. ' I am the Duke of Chartres,' was the answer.[1]

·During the night of the 31st May a deputation of Zouaves came to our modest quarters at Torrione and insisted on seeing the king. Tired out, he was fast asleep; but his servant woke him, and, half dressed, he came out to see his comrades of the day's fight. They were soldiers and corporals, with an officer as spokesman, who presented Victor Emanuel with the stripes of a corporal of Zouaves. He thanked him heartily, and they cheered him as they had done when he fought in their ranks like a simple corporal—' *Vive notre chef. Vive le preux Victor Emanuel de Savoie.*'

Next day the king visited the battlefield, received with acclamation by the Zouaves and other troops. We found wounded men lying in the wheat, who had passed a night of agony without succour and without a drop of water. For several days water was hard to get; so many corpses had been thrown into the canals that even the mills were clogged by them. In the evening the emperor transferred his headquarters to Novara, which the French had taken after very slight resistance.

On the 2d June the chief part of the French army concentrated at Novara, while an advanced guard pushed on towards the Ticino, which the Austrians had crossed the day before by a forced march. They tried to blow up the bridge of S. Martino di Trecate behind them, but their powder was so bad that the damage done was slight. Nevertheless, Napoleon caused another bridge to be thrown across for the passage of his troops. That same night three of our divisions—Castelborgo, Fanti and Durando—ad-

---

[1] Robert Ferdinand d'Orleans, Duke of Chartres, had been sent to our Royal Military Academy to study, and had just left it with the grade of sub-lieutenant in the cavalry. He was a handsome, intelligent youth, and glad to undergo his first baptism of fire in the company of his compatriots.

vanced from Palestro towards Galliate, followed by Canrobert. Cialdini remained at Vercelli to guard the Sesia, and Cucchiari was at Casale to guard the Po.

Giulay, who only understood after the battle of Palestro that the whole allied army was on his flank, retreated, abandoning Vercelli and Novara. With unusual rapidity of conception and movement, he summoned his troops from Vigevano and Abbiategrasso and massed his forces at Magenta. It was an excellent tactical position; more extensive, more open, in every way better than Palestro, and well protected by the double line of the Ticino and the canal called the Naviglio, which supplied Milan with water. On the 3d the Austrian commander-in-chief had made all his arrangements for concentrating his forces at Magenta to oppose the advance of the allied army on Milan, when Field-Marshal Baron Hess, chief of the staff, arrived from Verona with full powers from the Emperor Francis Joseph. News of the defeat at Palestro had reached him, but he was not aware that the army was in full retreat, and his orders were to hold the district of Lomellina[1] at any sacrifice. Giulay had to confess that it was already abandoned, and that the allies were menacing Milan. Baron Hess changed some of the dispositions made by Giulay, and sent orders to part of the Austrian troops to remain at Vigevano and Abbiategrasso, thus diminishing their available number at Magenta, where they only had fifty thousand men on the 4th May. Napoleon had given orders that the corps of MacMahon, Niel and Baraguay d'Hilliers, and our divisions Castelborgo, Durando and Fanti, were to cross the Ticino from the right to the left bank on that same day. He was ignorant of Giulay's movements, so the engagement of Robecchetto, which took place early in the morning between the troops of MacMahon and those of Clam Gallas, and the battle of Magenta in the afternoon,

---

[1] Lomellina is in the province of Pavia.—*Translator's Note.*

were surprises. The affair of Robecchetto retarded the crossing of the river by MacMahon's corps, so the divisions of Fanti and Durando, who were to follow in his wake, had to wait from six in the morning until eleven. While the king stood near the bridge to see the troops march past, we heard that General Urban was in the neighbourhood. Garibaldi had driven him out of the district of Comasco, and he was reported to be somewhere near Monza. I immediately sent out small detachments to reconnoitre, and before one o'clock, while Fanti and Durando were crossing the river with their divisions, the news was confirmed.

As soon as our troops reached the left bank their progress was arrested. We could not make out the nature of the obstacle, so the king sent me to Fanti to ask what had happened. MacMahon's military train stopped the way, and there was no hope of our troops advancing for hours. I went in search of MacMahon, who was pushing forward to get up with the enemy, whom he found near the bridge of Buffalora. The marshal was anxiously awaiting his second column under General Espinasse, who had mistaken the road, and was much put out at the enforced delay of our divisions, on whose aid he was counting, particularly as Espinasse was not to be seen. But he could suggest no remedy save patience; his baggage was so hopelessly entangled in the midst of the troops that the road could not be cleared. I returned to tell Fanti to try and advance by lanes and across fields to join MacMahon, and ordered Durando to change front and intercept Urban on the left. MacMahon had opened fire at Buffalora for more than an hour, but ordered it to cease while, with a small cavalry escort, he went in search of Espinasse. This placed the emperor, with part of the Guard and a brigade of Zouaves, in considerable peril, he having hurried from the bridge of S. Martino to the Naviglio as soon as the cannonade began at Buffalora. Before he arrived the

Austrians had blown up all the bridges, and he was forced to throw over new ones while exposed to a murderous fire from the enemy's guns on the left bank of the canal, which was considerably above him. Several small but bloody engagements took place on either bank, and the hours passed slowly to the emperor, who began to be nervous about the issue of events.

Suddenly, towards evening, came the good news that MacMahon had found Espinasse, outflanked the Austrians on the right, and was pressing them hard on every side. Soon afterwards we knew that he had driven them out of their position ; and, helped by Fanti, who arrived late, but in time to be of use, had destroyed the barricades at the station and driven the enemy from their last entrenchments The allies were victorious, and the troops passed the night on the battlefield.

On the 5th, when the emperor knew the particulars of the battle, he made up his mind that the victory was due to MacMahon, whom he created a Marshal of France and Duke of Magenta. Considerable envy was aroused by the bestowal of such high honours, and MacMahon's want of forethought and clearness in giving orders were much criticised ; by his delay he upset the plan of attack and nearly caused it to fail.

The Austrians retreated in the direction of the Adda during the night after the battle of Magenta. Faithful to his first idea of fighting a great battle on the plains of Lombardy, in the vicinity of the Quadrilateral, Giulay left the road to Milan open to the allied army, and was only attacked by the French at Melegnano, when Baraguay d'Hilliers drove the last of their troops towards the Adda on the day of the entry into Milan.

The crossing of the Ticino by a large body of the allied troops was retarded by the unexpected battle of Magenta, which was a surprise. The baggage and military train of all the French corps were far too numerous, and their leaders miscalculated the time they would take to pass over, so that we were kept waiting the whole of the 5th May before our divisions could cross the river. The king was obliged to remain at Galliate during the night of the 4th and next morning at daybreak he went to see the emperor at S. Martino di Trecate, and visited the battlefield of Magenta with him. Victor Emanuel hoped to see our troops defiling across the bridges in the afternoon. I went to ask at what hour I was to order our divisions to be ready, and found the emperor seated on a rickety chair near a bridge with Baraguay d'Hilliers, whose men were marching past. Turning to the marshal, Napoleon said, '*Voyons, à quelle heure nos troupes auront-elles fini de passer?*' Pulling out his watch, Baraguay answered, '*Il n'est pas encore deux heures. Canrobert qui va venir après moi, aura fini à quatre heures, Niel à six.*' '*Vous entendez général,*' said the emperor to me, '*Baraguay croit qu'après six heures les ponts seront libres.*' I saw that Baraguay was quite out in his reckoning, and that the French army could not cross the Ticino, there being only two bridges, before late in the night. Pretending to have understood six in the morning, I answered, '*C'est bien, sire, demain matin bien avant six heures nos troupes seront prêtes pour passer le fleuve.*' '*Mais non, mais non,*' exclaimed Napoleon, '*Baraguay entend dire ce soir a six heures.*' I bowed, but my face must have shown that I was not convinced. As a fact, the bridges were not free until two o'clock that night.

The next morning the king again visited the emperor at S. Martino, and in his presence received the Milanese deputation, which came to announce the evacuation of Milan by the Austrians, and the proclamation by the municipal council of Victor Emanuel as king. They begged him to come as soon as possible and take possession of the city. Victor Emanuel accepted the sovereignty, and promised that the troops should start immediately on their way to Milan.

Leaving Magenta, the king crossed the Ticino by a bridge of boats and went to our headquarters at Lainate. The emperor sent to warn us that an Austrian corps, under General Urban, menaced our flank, and as the letter contained no instructions the king was in doubt whether to remain on the defensive or go in search of the enemy. To put an end to this uncertainty I asked his leave to take a small division of six squadrons of light cavalry, artillery and Bersaglieri, and scour the country. I soon found out that the enemy's rearguard was only a few hours' march distant, and that they were exhausted by fatigue and privations. My men, on the contrary, were fresh, well fed and eager to fight, so there was every probability of my catching up the Austrians and forcing them to fight or surrender. We gained rapidly upon Urban, who had halted at Vespolate to flog some men who had fallen out of the ranks ; and in forty minutes we expected to come up to him, when some French officers galloped up with a white flag of truce. General Desvaux had sent them, in the name of the emperor, to call upon the Austrian commander to surrender. We were, of course, obliged to stop and await their return. In vain we waited till night closed in, when I sent back to Lainate to inform the king, who despatched Count Charles di Robilant to the French headquarters at Magenta to ask for an explanation. The emperor was already in bed, but received Robilant at once, and said there must have been some misunderstanding. He had given Desvaux permission to pursue Urban with his regiment, but could not conceive why a flag of truce had been sent. The mystery was afterwards solved Desvaux took the wrong road, and only discovered his mistake too late. Then, counting on the exhausted condition of Urban's troops, he thought they would surrender. But he was wrong ; and the delay of the French officers in notifying his refusal deprived me of the honour and satisfaction of inflicting a lesson on the imperious and cruel Austrian general.

CHAPTER XIV

1859 (THIRD PART)

ON the 7th June we arrived outside the walls of Milan, and next morning entered the city by the Porta Sempione, where a division of infantry and one of cavalry was drawn up. The procession was opened by a squadron of the Cents Gardes, followed by all the aides-de-camp of the king, then by those of the emperor ; the two sovereigns rode together, and after them came the officers of the staff of both armies, and another squadron of Guards closed the *cortège.* At about nine o'clock we passed under the magnificent triumphal arch raised to the memory of Napoleon I., and transformed by the House of Austria to a monument to their own glory. The streets were crowded with people and decked with the Italian and French colours. A continuous rain of flowers and enthusiastic cheers for the emperor and for the king, for the Piedmontese and the French, accompanied us all the way. Involuntarily I thought of poor Charles Albert when, in August 1848, he turned to me on the steps of the Greppi Palace and said, ' *Ah, La Rocca, quelle journée ?* '

Lodgings had been prepared for the emperor in the villa of the public gardens built for Prince Eugène Beauharnais, Viceroy of Italy, by Napoleon I., and afterwards inhabited by the Austrian archdukes. The king took up his residence in the splendid palace Serbelloni-Busca.

The sovereigns went in state to the cathedral on the 9th June to hear the *Te Deum* for the liberation of Milan, when a disagreeable incident happened for us Italians. When the mass was over, the Abbé Laine, chaplain to the emperor, intoned the *Domine, salvum fac Imperatorem nostrum, Napoleonem*, answered by the band of the Guides, The same *oremus* ought to have been sung for Victor Emanuel, but his chaplain never thought of arranging with the emperor's chaplain or with our military band; so nothing was done, and we left the church with a painful impression.

Napoleon and Victor Emanuel remained a day or two at Milan, where General Castelborgo was left as governor. I was obliged to leave after the service to obtain precise information about the engagement of Melegnano, and give orders in case the enemy should attack us on the other side of Milan.

From the day we left the Lombard capital until the Austrians retreated beyond the Mincio—from the 11th to the 21st June—with the exception of a few days spent at Brescia, we were always engaged in forced marches ordered by the emperor. Evidently we were sent as an advanced guard, while his own troops marched leisurely; so that we arrived under the walls of Brescia many days before them. He was puzzled as to the ultimate designs of the Austrian commander-in-chief, who seemed inclined to cross the Chiese and concentrate his forces at Montechiari in readiness for the great battle which had been talked of for more than a month. There were constant false alarms; and as soon as our troops advanced the enemy retreated, wearing our men out in fatiguing and useless marches.

. Victor Emanuel left Milan for Vimercate on the 11th, and after crossing the Adda and the Oglio, arrived near Brescia on the 15th without meeting the Austrians. He did not wish to enter the city so long before Napoleon arrived, so established his headquarters at Castegnato near by—an excellent position for observing the enemy's movements—under the impression that Giulay intended giving battle at Montechiari. Our troops were stationed in the strong positions of Castenedolo when he retired and crossed to the left bank of the Chiesi. We thus lost a good opportunity of fighting him.

Meanwhile, Garibaldi had attacked and beaten the Austrians at Tre Ponti, aided by Cialdini, who had been sent, by desire of the emperor, to assist the movements of the volunteers in the valleys of the Oglio and the Mella, whence the Austrians might have attacked us on the flank. As soon as Cialdini reached Salò, on the lake of Garda, he constructed a battery to sink the enemy's boats, who precipitately retired.

, On the 17th June, the day before the arrival of the French, we entered Brescia. The reception was, if possible, more enthusiastic than at Milan. Not a window but was decorated with the national colours, and flowers rained thick on us and our horses. We spent three days there, well lodged and well fed—a pleasant change after so many privations. On the 20th I celebrated my fifty-second birthday, thankful for my robust constitution, which enabled me to resist fatigue better than many a younger man.

The French troops were forced to halt for a few days for want of provisions. Their commissariat was inferior to ours, and there was considerable disorder and peculation. Many years afterwards I was at the Chartreuse of Grenoble, and the abbot told me one of his monks had been in the campaign of 1859, but was so horrified by the carnage at Magenta that he left the service and entered the convent. As the monks passed to go into church, the abbot pointed the man out, and I recognised a French officer who had disappeared, with some others, when an inquiry into the disorders of the commissariat department was made. Leaving Brescia, we crossed the Chiese at Calcinato, where the king established his headquarters. On the 21st June all the divisions were on the left bank; the 1st and the 5th at Lonato, the 2d at Calcinato, the 3d at Desenzano, and the cavalry between Bedizzole and Lonato. Deputations from the cities of Trent and Bologna came to Calcinato to express their desire to be annexed to Piedmont. The king thanked the latter, but said for the moment he could only accord them military protection, with a view to their assisting in the great cause of Italian independence. The deputies from Trent he received with courtesy, without pronouncing a word that could raise any hope that he would accede to their wishes. Italian Tyrol formed part of the German Confederation, with which it was not our interest to interfere.

On the 23d the emperor came to visit Victor Emanuel at Lonato, and inspect the positions to be occupied, with a view to crossing the Mincio and besieging Peschiera or Verona. It was near lunch time when Napoleon, dismissing the suite, asked the king to ride up a hill near by, whence a view of all the positions might be obtained. No one had been invited to follow the sovereigns, but after they had gone a few steps, Victor Emanuel, always accustomed to have me by his side as a guide, looked back and beckoned to me to join them. I soon saw that the emperor did not care about examining the positions, but that his object was to be alone with the king in some quiet place. We were more than half way up the hill, and I thought they would ride to the summit while I remained on the slope.   But the emperor pulled up his horse close to where I was, and taking a letter from his pocket, read it aloud to Victor Emanuel.   I feigned to examine the country through my field-glasses, but could not avoid hearing every word.   The letter was from the empress, who had been named regent during her husband's absence, and was evidently one of a series.   Alluding to certain designs of the German Confederation, and to the approach of Prussian troops towards Coblenz and Cologne, she complained of the insufficient forces left in France in case of a possible Prussian invasion, and requested the emperor to come to an immediate decision, and send back part of the *Armée d'Italie*.   She bade him consider the terrible consequences of a defeat on the Rhine, and advised him to take advantage of the victories already won to conclude peace, and return to France to stem the growing discontent at the menacing advance of Prussia.

Victor Emanuel listened in silence; he understood, as I did, that all was finished, and that the emperor would not risk his own throne to serve Italy.   Slowly and silently the two sovereigns descended the hill, without giving another thought to the siege of Peschiera or Verona.   Reading the letter of the empress, without any comment, was a tacit retraction by the emperor of his promise to free Italy from the Alps to the Adriatic. It was the first intimation that he meant to stop short at the Mincio.

At the lunch given by the king to the emperor at Lonato I sat opposite the latter, next to an officer of his suite.   We were talking of the more or less probability of a pitched battle, and my neighbour asked my opinion. ' Hitherto,' I answered, ' my forecasts have been pretty good ones.   I suspect we shall see no more battles on the right bank of the Mincio.'   The emperor, whose sense of hearing was extraordinarily acute, laughed and said, ' What a prophet! How can there be any battle when there is no enemy on this side?'

No one could imagine that a few hours later the Austrians would cross the river and attack us in our positions on the right bank. The order of the day, published in the evening of the 23d for the 24th June, was as follows:—
' 1st, 3d and 5th divisions are to leave Lonato for the siege of Peschiera, keeping on the right bank of the Mincio. The 2d division, with the cavalry, will remain at Lonato in reserve; headquarters to be moved to Rivoltella.' But that night the enemy threw a large number of bridges over the Mincio, and before daylight their army had crossed. Colonel Cadorna fell in with some Austrian outposts, and the fusillade gave the alarm. By the king's order, I at once sent an officer to Castiglione, where the emperor had just arrived from Montechiari, to warn him, and soon afterwards came a note from him, saying, ' Eighty thousand (there were over one hundred thousand) Austrians have suddenly appeared on my front. Send a strong reinforcement in the direction of Solferino.' The king replied, ' I send part of divisions Fanti and Durando. At this moment I am informed that the enemy is advancing in force on our right, at Madonna della Scoperta, and on our left at S. Martino. I must retain the rest of my troops in those positions for our own defence.'

Napoleon had advanced cautiously, and kept his army well together until he reached the Chiese, when, seeing the enemy withdraw to such a distance, he thought he might allow a larger space to intervene between the different corps. Thus, when the engagement on the 24th began, he found himself with only the Imperial Guard and MacMahon's corps at hand. Baraguay d'Hilliers, however, soon hurried up, and reinforcements were despatched to Solferino, where the battle began to rage furiously about mid-day. The Emperor Francis Joseph led the Austrian army in person, and the struggle was a tremendous one. Napoleon, with the two army corps, gained a complete victory at Solferino, and was master of the field of battle about one o'clock; while at Robecco, Casanova, Montefontana and Cavriano the corps of Canrobert and Niel beat off repeated attacks, and at length forced the centre of the Austrian army to retire.

We were not so fortunate in the early part of the day. Durando's advanced guard repulsed a first attack by four brigades of Stadion's corps at Madonna della Scoperta, but, overcome by superior numbers, were driven back into the Val di Quadro. Benedek, concentrated at Pozzolengo, repeatedly charged Mollard and Cucchiari at S. Martino, whose forces were insufficient to defend so extended a line, and at last gave way. Towards mid-day I was warned there was no unity of command, and consequently no concentration of forces, which were, on the contrary, broken up into various detachments. Knowing that General Alphonse La Marmora was on the spot as a simple spectator, I sent one of the king's aides-de-camp to order him to assume the command of the two corps Durando and Fanti. This he did with considerable success, but the enemy was so superior to us in number that a victory could not be hoped for.

The king and I were on rising ground in front of Castelvenzago, whence we could follow the phases of the battle through our field-glasses. The enemy had retired from Madonna della Scoperta, but occupied the position of S. Martino in great strength. Our 2d division had been ordered up to support the other two, and Victor Emanuel was fuming with impatience at seeing our men worsted and not being among them. In spite of my remonstrances, he insisted on descending into the plain to join the troops and encourage them. Followed by several aides-de-camp, he started for S. Martino, which was much further off than he thought, while I remained to fulfil my duties as head of the staff at Castelvenzago.

My anxiety that our troops should be victorious increased when news came of the great victory at Solferino, and the probable successes of Canrobert and Niel; so when seeing how useless his presence was in the plain, the king returned, I submitted to him a project of attacking three different points with our four divisions at five o'clock, and driving the Austrians out of the position of S. Martino at any sacrifice. He approved, and orders were sent to execute my plan. Our troops had started, when suddenly the sky became black as ink, and the fury of the wind was such that men were blown off their horses, while the rain fell in torrents. The hurricane lasted twenty minutes, during which movements were impossible. Only Fanti, with part of his division, reached his destination. Durando never arrived, and La Marmora, with a small following, marched towards Monzambano, to attack the left flank of Benedek.

The storm ceased at half-past five, and our troops attacked with splendid dash. Step by step they gained ground, and took battery after battery. Before night the enemy was driven out of his position, and retreated in complete disorder. Towards nine we heard the last cannon shots, and darkness forced us to stop the pursuit. This victory cost us five thousand five hundred and twenty-two men—one thousand three hundred and fifty soldiers and fifty officers killed, the rest wounded, and five hundred prisoners, but not a single officer among them.

The king bivouacked for the night at Castelvenzago, and the emperor established his headquarters at Cavriana, in the same house Francis Joseph had occupied that morning. The French drove the Austrians out after the great storm. I went off to Lonato, our headquarters, to give orders for the ambulances and the food supplies for the next day, and telegraphed immediately to Cavour:—
' A great battle; victorious all along the line; enemy in

full retreat; recrossing the Mincio.' I hoped the glorious news would be known at Turin next morning, but for some unknown motive my telegram was not published till the 26th, and on the evening of the 25th the papers had a copy of the despatch sent by the emperor to the empress in Paris. At two in the morning I returned to Castelvenzago to make my report to Victor Emanuel. Embracing me, he said he had decided to give me the Order of the Annunziata, and invited me to lie down by his side on the bare earth, where we slept till daylight. We expected to be attacked again, and all was ready to repulse the enemy; but we soon heard that the Emperor Francis Joseph was at Villafranca, and that his whole army had crossed to the left bank of the Mincio.

The king took up his headquarters at Rivoltella, and early in the morning we rode over the battlefield of S. Martino. Many unfortunate wounded men still lay where they had fallen; the houses and the churches near by were all full. The 3d division alone had two thousand two hundred wounded; among them was my nephew Constantine. A ball had broken his jaw, and he could not speak, but was perfectly conscious. He was so disfigured that I did not recognise him; so, writing on his notebook, 'I am your nephew Constantine,' he handed it to me, as with the king I passed close to him. The brigade of my brother Robert also suffered severely.

The 26th was a Sunday, and after hearing mass in the parish church, we rode to Desenzano to visit the hospitals, which were crowded with wounded, as well as all the houses of the village. On the 27th the king returned to S. Martino, where a large body of troops were still encamped. Count Fabio Tracagni, owner of the land where the last tremendous struggle had taken place, was presented to the king. Farmhouses and villa were a mass of ruins; gardens, meadows, and fields were devastated.

The king expressed his sorrow for the damage done, but Count Tracagni did not allow him to finish his sentence. He declared that he regretted nothing, but, on the contrary, felt proud to possess a property hallowed for ever by the valour of the Italian army. Touched by these words, the king held out his hand, which the count tried to kiss, but Victor Emanuel prevented this, and shook hands cordially.

In the afternoon the Emperor sent General Froissart of the engineers, and General Leboeuf of the artillery, to concert measures with Menabrea and myself about the siege of Peschiera. After the excursion of the two sovereigns on the 23d, and still more after the battle next day, I was convinced that the siege would not take place, and that negotiations for peace were being carried on. I did not even mention the matter to the king. He perhaps still cherished some hope; I had none. But, of course, I carried out the orders sent to me, and prepared everything for the investment of Peschiera.

On the 27th and 28th June the troops destined for the siege crossed the Mincio without being disturbed by the enemy. On the 29th I went with the commanding officers of the engineers and artillery to trace the lines of cir-cumvallation agreed upon with Froissart, and that same evening our guns opened fire. The enemy answered immediately, and as we were beyond the outposts there were a few skirmishes, in one of which two officers of Grenadiers were killed and several soldiers wounded.

On the 1st July we transferred our headquarters to a house in Pozzolengo, which had been inhabited by Charles Albert in 1848, and by Benedek on the eve of Solferino. The 3d and 5th divisions crossed the Mincio at Salionze, together with the 1st French corps, to invest Peschiera from the left bank. The headquarters of the emperor were at Valeggio, where the 3d corps was stationed with one division at Goito. Next day we moved to Monzambano, and remained there till the 12th July. The French army was holding the positions we occupied in 1848; but Napoleon, whose one idea was to concentrate his troops, thought the line too extended, and on the nights of the 3d and 4th withdrew and formed a line with one wing on the lake of Garda, then from Castelnovo along the Tirone, through Oliosi and La Gherla, on the road from Villafranca, to Valeggio, and from Pozzuolo and Goito extending to the Mincio.

Meanwhile, General Hess, who was at Verona with the Emperor of Austria, sent the son of General Urban with a flag of truce and a letter to Marshal Vaillant. Napoleon wished to speak to the young officer himself, and forgetting the oldest and most elementary rule of military discipline, the French allowed him to traverse their whole camp without being blindfolded. When too late they perceived their error, and committed the absurdity of blindfolding him on his return, when he had seen everything. The Austrians behaved very differently two days later. When the king visited the wounded Austrian officers, who had fallen into our hands, they begged so earnestly to be allowed to return to their compatriots that he resolved to give them up unconditionally, and ordered me to write to General Hess and send Count di Robilant with a flag of truce. He started for Verona with a small escort, which was stopped at the outposts, and he was blindfolded and sent on alone in a closed carriage.

General Hess knew Robilant, and introduced him to the Emperor Francis Joseph, who, with true military courtesy, praised our troops, particularly the Bersaglieri and artillery, and asked after the king, to whom he sent his compliments. On leaving, the count was again blindfolded and driven back to where his escort was waiting.

On the 6th, Victor Emanuel mounted his horse early

and went to meet his son-in-law, Prince Jerome Napoleon, who preceded the 5th French corps and the Tuscan troops under General Ulloa. I was busy all day carrying out the emperor's orders to prepare for a defensive battle, in which I did not believe. While visiting the positions next day, General Cadogan, the English officer attached to our army, asked me where he could get a good view of the intended battle. I advised the top of a hill overhanging the river, and next morning he went there at daylight and remained some hours without seeing anything. On returning to headquarters he was very angry at hearing that I had gone with Vaillant and Martimprey to Villafranco to meet General Hess and sign a truce agreed upon between the sovereigns. Napoleon had sent his aide-de-camp, General Fleury, on the evening of the 7th, to the Emperor of Austria with a letter proposing a suspension of hostilities, to be followed by an armistice. Francis Joseph demanded the night for reflection, and next morning delivered his acceptance to Fleury, who brought it to Valeggio. Napoleon then sent him a second letter, stating the conditions on which he would treat for peace, adding, that if the Emperor Francis Joseph was inclined to accept them, he wished for a personal interview; if not, he would prefer not to meet him, as it would render the continuance of war more painful. The conditions were accepted, and the meeting fixed for the 11th July at Villafranca. Our troops meanwhile took up the positions indicated in the armistice.

On the 10th Count Cavour arrived at our headquarters, accompanied by his secretary, Constantine Negri, afterwards Italian ambassador at Paris, and by Alexander Bixio, who in 1848 was the envoy extraordinary of the French Republic at the Sardinian Court, and a strong partisan of the unity of Italy. He came straight to me to announce Cavour's arrival, and warned me of the state of irritation and excitement the news of the armistice had thrown him into. He had forbidden the publication of the news by the Turinese papers, but it had been divulged by the French journals, who only mentioned the Emperor Napoleon, without even alluding to the king. Cavour at once went to Victor Emanuel. The meeting was a stormy one. The prime minister denounced everyone in bitter words of reprobation, and, irritated by the calmness with which the king listened and answered, at last lost all self-control and forgot the respect due to royalty. Victor Emanuel and Cavour were alone, and their conversation could not have been heard by anyone, so that all the accounts published of their interview are imaginary. Later in the day the king told me Cavour had been absolutely insolent and disrespectful, and that, feeling he could no longer contain himself, he had turned his back on the prime minister and left him.

Cavour then came to my tiny room, which contained a camp bedstead and two chairs. Bixio was sitting on one, and immediately rose and went into the passage outside. Just as Cavour was declaiming against the king and everyone else, the door opened and Prince Jerome Napoleon entered. He took part in the discussion, which was embittered by his abrupt roughness. Cavour declined to entertain the idea of a prolonged armistice, or of treating for peace, save under the condition of the liberation of Northern Italy — from the Alps to the Adriatic — as announced by Napoleon III. The prince replied that we ought to be only too glad to get Lombardy and the Duchies. I remember he wound up by exclaiming, 'Do you expect us to sacrifice France and our dynasty for you?' Cavour doggedly replied that promises were promises, and ought to be kept. He threatened to promote and head a revolution rather than leave the work half done, and complained bitterly of the emperor, of the king, of La Marmora, of me. I could not blame him. For years he had worked to form an independent kingdom of Italy, and now he saw his labour stultified, his enterprise diminished and again reduced to anxious expectation. He could not be expected to resign himself and bow to dire necessity as we had done, who, day by day, had watched all the phases of the emperor's enforced withdrawal. Cavour, as a last resource, wished to carry on the war alone; but 1848 was too fresh in our memories, and, as military men, we declined the responsibility. It would have been folly, or worse, to pit fifty thousand or sixty thousand men against over two hundred thousand, who, although beaten, had shown such discipline and courage at Palestro and S. Martino. Victor Emanuel absolutely refused to stake the certain against the uncertain. The annexation of Lombardy and the Duchies doubled his army and increased the chances of ultimately liberating Venice and uniting Tuscany and the Legations, which had repeatedly invoked his aid, to the kingdom of northern Italy. For my part, I trusted in the great political sagacity of Napoleon III. The ability with which he had prepared the Franco-Sardinian alliance, and gained his end, convinced me that necessity, not caprice, induced him to abandon us.

But Cavour would not listen to argument, and finding the king, the emperor, and Prince Jerome Napoleon inexorable, resigned, and left for Turin as soon as he knew the first conditions of peace had been established.

After the meeting of the two emperors at Villafranca, some modifications were made in the preliminaries, and on the 12th they and Victor Emanuel signed the treaty which united Lombardy, the Duchy of Parma, and Piacenza to Sardinia and Piedmont. On the original document the king added, by the side of his signature, '*J'accepte pour ce qui me concerne,*' thus accepting the increase of territory without entering into the other questions or prejudicing his future action.

The emperor, Victor Emanuel and Prince Jerome dined together at Monzambano on the 12th, and afterwards Napoleon left for Desenzano, where he established his headquarters until he went to Milan. Next day the king announced his departure to the troops in an order of the day, and visited the emperor at Desenzano, where they drew up the proclamation to the Lombard people. The rough draught was dictated by the emperor, and after Victor Emanuel had altered and rewritten a sentence, he handed it to me to telegraph to the syndic of Milan. That afternoon the king left by special train, received with enthusiasm all along the line, and at seven reached Milan. Amid the acclamations of the populace he drove to the royal palace, where he occupied the apartment once inhabited by the viceroy of Lombardy, father of Queen Maria Adelaide. Next day we went to the station to meet the emperor, and the two sovereigns drove together in the same carriage. There was much cheering for Victor Emanuel and some for Napoleon. On the whole, the resentment against the emperor, who had put a stop to a war begun under such fortunate auspices, was not too openly displayed.

Early on the 15th the king visited the sick and wounded in the hospitals, and as we were leaving the palace one of the French officers asked whether I had not forgotten to order the escort. He was extremely astonished when I told him that Victor Emanuel always went about alone with his aide-de-camp. Later, when the emperor drove to the French hospital, the carriage was surrounded by his Guards. At two the sovereigns again traversed the city together on their way to the station, and were warmly cheered. At Turin, on the contrary, their reception was icy. Hardly a cheer was raised for the king—not one for the emperor. After the State dinner Napoleon withdrew to his apartments, and had a long interview with Cavour. Early next morning he left for France, accompanied by the king as far as Susa. He intended to spend two days at Turin, but the coldness of his reception the evening before probably hastened his departure. When we returned to Turin the king granted me a few weeks' leave, and I went to join my family at Luserna.

CHAPTER XV

END OF 1859. BEGINNING OF 1860

Marshal Vaillant—Napoleon objects to the Annexation of Tuscany—Cavour
returns to Power—Persuades Napoleon to agree to the Annexation of
Tuscany—I am named Commander of the 5th Army Corps—Annexation
of Tuscany, Emilia, and the Romagna—Garibaldi upbraids Cavour.

AFTER spending some weeks with my family at Luserna
I returned to Turin on the 1st August, and on the 7th
accompanied the king to Milan, where he was received
with demonstrations of frantic enthusiasm. Marshal
Vaillant, in command of the French troops, which were
gradually being withdrawn from Italy, was still living in
the Villa Reale, and I went one morning to see him. He
was just going out, and, dressed in a light suit, looked quite
a young man, spite of his seventy years. We strolled
about the park, and I found he believed in the possi-
bility and the advantages of a confederation of the Italian
States under the presidency of the Pope, as announced by
Napoleon III. in his last order of the day to the troops. I
had the strongest doubts as to the working of such a plan,
and I believe the emperor, whose suggestion it was, and
who earnestly advocated it with Victor Emanuel and
Cavour, had already realised its impossibility. At Villafranca it had been agreed that the deposed princes
might return to their States, but were not to call in the
aid of foreign troops. Now it was most unlikely that,
after declaring in favour of annexation to an Italian

kingdom under Victor Emanuel, and sending deputations to beg his assistance, the people would tamely consent to again receive the rulers they had expelled.

Vaillant, like many Frenchmen, did not believe in the spontaneity or the unanimity of the revolutionary movement in Italy. Not wishing to contradict him, I turned the conversation to military matters, and soon after left him to continue his walk to a mill near by, where he went every morning to catch crayfish. 'There,' he said, 'I sit on the bank of the little stream and fish while preparing my orders for the morrow. They are not complicated, as everything is well prepared and goes by itself. Then I ponder over the events of my long life. The hours pass, and I go home to lunch with many memories . . . and very few crayfish.'

Born in 1790, Vaillant became an officer in 1811, and was in the Russian campaign and at Waterloo. Set aside by the government of the Restoration, he was again employed after 1830 and sent to Algiers. When the empire was re-established after the *coup d'état* he became a Marshal of France, and was several times minister of war; in 1859 he held the post of general chief of the staff to the French army. Although not of high birth, he was a perfect gentleman, and shone among the other marshals and generals by his courteous and charming manners. In 1870 I heard that being too old for active service, he was on the ramparts of Paris in plain clothes and was mistaken for a spy by the Communists, who arrested and imprisoned him. He was exiled, and returned in 1871 to Paris to die the following year.

The king, after visiting other cities in Lombardy—Brescia, Bergamo, etc.—greeted everywhere with great enthusiasm, returned to Turin on the 17th August. During the autumn he received deputations and delegates from cities in the Emilia, in the Romagna, and in

Tuscany, all wanting to be annexed to the Constitutional monarchy of the *Re Galantuomo* (Honest King).

D'Azeglio, Boncompagni, Farini, Ricasoli, and many others had been ably working to this end with untiring patriotism ; and the people now came to solicit annexation to the kingdom of Victor Emanuel and the aid of his army against those who opposed the desires and will of the nation. During the war the king had refused to accept any proposals of allegiance, but now, with certain official restrictions imposed by foreign politics (explained away afterwards in private audiences), he promised that the popular desire should be gratified ere long, and the delegates left Turin trusting in the prompt realisation of his royal word. This was somewhat delayed by the hesitation of the Rattazzi-La Marmora-Dabormida ministry, who came to power after the resignation of Cavour at Villafranca. What with the serious discontent of Austria, who threatened to break off the negotiations at Zurich for peace if the Convention of Villafranca was not rigorously observed by the King of Sardinia ; and the hostility of France to the creation of a stronger Italy, our poor ministers sometimes lost their heads, and by their vacillation threatened to compromise and destroy the brilliant hopes of the future.

Whilst declaring that the Convention of Villafranca must be respected, Napoleon allowed it to be understood that if Savoy, the cession of which, together with Nice, had been arranged at Plombières (but not carried out at the close of the war because he had not fulfilled the conditions of the contract), was handed over to him, no objection would be raised to the annexation of Emilia and the Romagna. He absolutely objected to the annexation of Tuscany, of which he proposed to make a kingdom of Etruria under some prince who had nothing to do with Austria. The popular report was that the emperor wished to reserve the throne for his cousin Jerome, husband of our Princess Clotilde; but the real reason was his conviction that the annexation of Tuscany would hasten the formation of a united Italy, distasteful to all the great powers, with the exception of England. He also knew that they considered him in a great measure responsible for the Italian movement, and he was unable and unwilling to compromise himself further for us.

In the Liberal party, especially among the lately annexed Lombard subjects, the unpopularity of the ministers increased daily; while the king, by nature prompt and resolute, was in perpetual disaccord with one or the other. He said nothing, but in his heart of hearts regretted Cavour. Taking advantage of one of the frequent disagreements with La Marmora, which generally ended by his tendering his resignation—hitherto refused—the king took him at his word, dissolved the ministry and sent for Cavour. This was towards the middle of January 1860, when Victor Emanuel was ill in bed. I left the king's room when Camillo entered, and waited in the study, as His Majesty had orders to give me. Half an hour afterwards Cavour came out of the room with a smiling face and rubbing his hands, a sure sign that he was pleased. 'Well,' he said, looking straight at me over his spectacles, 'the reconciliation is complete.' 'Really?' I answered. 'Don't pretend to be a simpleton,' replied he; 'you knew it. And now,' he added in rather a sarcastic tone, 'many things will be accomplished.' Of that I had no doubt; but I never imagined, and I do not think Cavour himself thought, that before the end of the year we should be masters of the whole boot, with the exception of Venice and Rome. The alliance with Garibaldi, which brought about the union of the south with the north, only occurred some months later. At that moment he was in bad odour with the government. It is true they had put him in command of the Tuscan contingent, but Fanti, commander-in-chief of the army of the central provinces, was ordered to keep watch on him, and had found means to remove him. The first act of Cavour, on his return to power, was to name Farini Minister of the Interior, and Fanti Minister of War. The latter had shown great ability in organising the army of the central provinces, raised by him in a few months to forty-five thousand well-disciplined men. They had now to be incorporated and amalgamated with the Sardinian army and the Lombard troops, and he did the work well. Meanwhile, Cavour dissolved the Chambers, fixed the elections for the end of March, and the opening of the new Parliament for the beginning of April. His chief object was to repristinate the good relations existing before Villafranca between Victor Emanuel and Napoleon. Cavour understood what services the emperor might yet render Italy, and wished to secure him, not only as an ally, but, if I may use the word, an accomplice, having a direct and positive interest in the realisation of Italian aspirations. Aware of Napoleon's desire to possess Savoy and Nice, he therefore immediately reopened the question of their cession. Fond of Italy, and admiring and trusting Cavour, whom he regarded as the good genius of his mother-country, Napoleon III. promised his assistance. Meanwhile, Cavour and Fanti worked together to change the whole organisation of the army and facilitate its mobilisation. They divided it into five great *corps d'armée*, each forming a small army, with its head of the staff, artillery, heavy and light cavalry, Bersaglieri, commissariat, ambulances, etc., etc., complete in number, easy to call together and put on a war footing in a few days. For more than two months no one was aware of what was going on; I only knew it when the king offered me the command of the 1st or the 3d corps, which I refused, as I wished to retain my post at his side. De Sonnaz was named to the 1st, La Marmora to the 2d (the Lombard), extending from the Ticino to the Mincio, and from the Po to the lake of Garda. The 3d, under Durando, was destined to defend the line of the Po from Ferrara to Casalmaggiore.

All this occurred in March, and Cavour had meanwhile induced the emperor (by the promise of Nice and Savoy) to agree to the annexations, including that of Tuscany. The king wished to pay a visit to the Empress of Russia, widow of Nicholas I., who was about to leave Nice, where she had passed the winter. But his presence there at such a moment was considered inopportune, and he decided to send me to compliment the Czarina in his name, and explain why he had not come in person. Victor Emanuel had said nothing more to me about the commands of the five army corps, but a few days after I reached Nice, my brother Frederick, then aide-de-camp to the king, wrote, by his orders, to advise me not to persist in my refusal. The commanders of three divisions had already been appointed; the ministers had asked for one for Cialdini, and the king had reserved the last (the Tuscan) for me. An immediate answer was necessary, as the Parliament opened early in April, and there was every prospect of another campaign. I should have liked to have spoken to His Majesty, and to have consulted my family, but it was impossible for me to leave Nice, as the Czarina had asked me to dinner on purpose to meet one of her sons, who was to arrive next day. Russia was one of the great powers who disapproved of the formation of a northern Italian kingdom, and I could not let slip an opportunity of conversing familiarly with the Grand Duke, and attempting to persuade him that Victor Emanuel was not influenced by personal ambition, and that his ministers (Cavour and Rattazzi) were not revolutionary Jacobins, making use of the democracy for their own ends. So I sent my servant back to Turin with letters for His Majesty, for my wife, and my brother, frankly stating my own wishes, but telling the two latter to decide as they thought best for my interests, and, above all, to conform to the wishes of the king. When I returned home everything had been settled ; I was gazetted commander of the 5th *corps d'armée* (the Tuscan), resident for the present at Turin. Victor Emanuel meanwhile told me that I was to retain the position and the functions of his first aide-de-camp.

The king, in his speech at the opening of Parliament on the 2nd April, announced the treaty for the cession of Nice and Savoy. In the stormy debates which followed, Cavour made two or three admirable speeches, and bore down all opposition. The cession of the two provinces was voted, and the annexation of Tuscany, Emilia and the Romagna to the kingdom of Victor Emanuel, who lost two or three millions of subjects and gained seven or eight. Garibaldi, deputy for Nice, made his first appearance in the House, and furiously upbraided Cavour, who certainly did not merit such treatment. It was reported that Garibaldi never forgot or forgave the cession of his birthplace, and that his bitter words always rankled in the mind of Cavour.

CHAPTER XVI

1860

AFTER the vote in the Chambers the king, who had already received all the deputations bringing the results of the various *plébiscites*, went to visit the new provinces. His entry into Florence on horseback, surrounded by a brilliant staff, was a triumphal progress, and in all the cities of Tuscany, in Parma, in Piacenza, in the Romagna, in Bologna, etc., the enthusiasm was extraordinary. Either at Prato or Pistoia, I forget which, lunch had been prepared, to which I felt disposed to do full justice, when the king called me aside and ordered me to take post-horses and go to Viareggio to compliment his cousin, Maria Theresa, ex-Duchess of Lucca.

Maria Theresa of Savoy, one of the four daughters of Victor Emanuel I. and Maria Theresa of Este, married Charles of Bourbon, a wretched madman, who made her life miserable. He abdicated in favour of his son, who was as bad, or worse, than his father, and died by the hand of an assassin. His son Robert succeeded him under the tutelage of his mother, the Duchess of Berry. The ex-duke went to Paris, where he led ·a dissolute life, and Maria Theresa had retired to a villa near Viareggio, entirely buried in the pine woods. With some difficulty I persuaded the porter to let my carriage drive up to the door, and the duchess was summoned from the chapel, where she passed the day praying for the repose of the soul of her son. She had no ladies or gentlemen-in-waiting; her sole companion was her chaplain and confessor; her only visitor a Florentine nobleman, who administered her property. When I mentioned Victor Emanuel she had difficulty in understanding who I meant; and when I said I had come from Florence, she asked after the grand duke. I told her he had been at Vienna for more than a year, and as she made no sign for me to leave, I explained as well as I could that, by a *plébiscite*, Tuscany had united herself to Piedmont, where her own family, the House of Savoy, still continued to reign. I saw that the word *plébiscite* was utterly unknown to her, and that she did not understand what I was talking about. She looked at me with astonishment, and then half closed her eyes, and clasped her hands as though in prayer. At last she rose and told me to thank her cousin, but she did not give me her hand to kiss.

The demonstrations of joy which greeted Victor Emanuel in his new dominions found an echo in the south of Italy, and aroused the patriotic aspirations which had been crushed in Naples and Sicily by the implacable despotism of Ferdinand II. On his death, in the spring of 1859, the Liberal party took fresh heart, as the mother of his eldest son and heir Francis was Maria Christina of Savoy, another of the four daughters of Victor Emanuel I. On the strength of this, Count Cavour attempted to make a treaty of alliance between Piedmont and the young sovereign. He sent Count Ruggero di Salmour as ambassador extraordinary to explain to Francis II. that he might free Italy from serious complications, and probably save his own throne, by allying himself with us.   But Franceschiello, as he was called in Naples, refused to listen, and swore he would adhere to his father's form of government and policy.   A few months later, when the revolution broke out, he sent one ambassador after another —first to Cavour and then to Victor Emanuel—to express his willingness to enter into a treaty of alliance, and even to grant a Constitution.   But it was too late.   King and minister were morally bound to Garibaldi.

At Palermo a large body of Bourbon troops had quashed the revolution, the leaders of which were, oddly enough, saved and harboured by the monks of a large convent.   But the impulse was given, and the whole south of Italy only wanted a vigorous leader to rise and declare for union under Victor Emanuel.   Garibaldi had promised two of his friends—Nino Bixio, a Genoese, and Francesco Crispi,[1] a Sicilian, ardent partisans of the unity of Italy— that when a favourable occasion came he would put him- self at the head of an expedition to liberate the southern provinces.   But after the vote in April for the cession of Nice and Savoy, Garibaldi drew back.   The two patriots, however, at last persuaded him to reconsider his decision ; although the official aid of the government was refused, he had reason to hope for their indirect assistance, and determined to act.   The immediate result was the em- barkation at Quarto[2] of the 'Thousand,' on two boats seized by Bixio.   The incidents of that adventurous expedition are well known.   They necessitated our march

---

[1] Crispi, a Mazzinian Republican, had, it was said, accepted the idea of unity under Victor Emanuel, by the advice of Mazzini himself.   Whilst keep- ing to his own opinions, Mazzini's passionate love and desire for unity induced him to permit his followers to abandon the form of government he preferred, rather than risk the formation of a united Italy.

[2] The splendid villa of Quarto, whence the Garibaldians started, once belonged to the Spinola family.   Now it is the property of Signor Carrara, a Garibaldian.

across Umbria and the Marches, as triumphant, in its way, as that of Garibaldi.

In the beginning of August the minister of war sent all the troops stationed in Piedmont to the Camps of Instruction on the Vauda of S. Maurice (Canavese), placing them under my command during the manœuvres, which were to take place from the 1st September to the 15th October. I took a villa near by, intending to receive all the superior officers, and the king announced his intention of assisting at the first sham fights. All was ready, when I received orders from the War Office to concentrate my corps (the 5th) and start immediately for the Umbrian frontier, and with the 4th corps defend, so said the order, our frontiers menaced by the foreign legions of the Pope. At the same time (31st August) Fanti wrote me a private letter, containing these words: ' Spread the report that we are concentrating our troops to quell the revolution, and, if necessary, to march on Naples.'

I cannot say this order surprised me. The rapid spread of the revolution in the kingdom of Naples, where the people greeted Garibaldi with enthusiasm, and the garrisons laid down their arms and joined his army, had been known for some days. Poor King Francis, betrayed by his relations, by his ministers, and by those he esteemed his most faithful servants, was about to leave Naples and take refuge in Gaeta with the remnant of his army, about fifty thousand men.

Seeing the kingdom of Naples a prey to a double revolution, fanned by Mazzini on one hand and Garibaldi on the other, Cavour decided on throwing off the mask and openly assisting the latter. The time was propitious, but it was a perilous and decisive step to take.

The king and Cavour took advantage of the presence of Napoleon III. in his new province of Savoy to send

Farini and Cialdini, under pretext of complimenting him, to represent the terrible condition of Umbria and the Marches, exposed to the incessant depredations of the mercenary Papal troops. They were to obtain a promise from the emperor that the French garrison in Rome should not be permitted to assist Lamoricière, and also to make sure that His Imperial Majesty would raise no obstacle to the entry of our troops into Umbria, or to the *plébiscite* of the people, who had asked to be annexed to the kingdom of Victor Emanuel.

Napoleon, always favourable to the Italian cause, and at that moment under the impression of the brilliant reception accorded him in the provinces just ceded to France, promised to recognise the action of our government, provided the work was done quickly; it was necessary that Europe should only know it as an accomplished fact. The injunctions verbally made to our envoys were repeated in an autograph letter from the emperor to Victor Emanuel, which I saw :—'*Allez, allze, et surtout faites vite.*' We went and we made quick work of it.

I had orders from Fanti, Minister of War, and commander-in-chief of the expedition, to have my troops on the frontier by the 10th September. He gave me full powers, and placed the railway at my command. Thanks to this, but still more to the excellent organisation introduced by Fanti himself, I was there before the date named. The mobilisation of my corps only took three days, and within a week thirty thousand men were on the frontier.

I must confess that I was hurt and angry when Fanti, my junior, whose grades had been gained in foreign service, was named commander-in-chief of the expedition. I thought he might have joined the army, as minister of war, and left me the honour of directing the expedition.

But I soon recognised his superiority and his great military intuition; and during the whole campaign I took counsel with him on all essential matters.

The 2d and 3d corps, under La Marmora and Durando, were entrusted with the defence of the kingdom, in case the Austrians attempted to take advantage of our southward march and attack us on the rear.

On the 3d September I left Turin with my staff, and embarked at Genoa for Leghorn, where we arrived during the night of the 4th. Next evening we were at Florence, and on the 6th I left for Arezzo to reconnoitre the country while waiting for my troops, who, on account of the defective railway service, could only arrive on the 8th. Next day my corps—about eleven thousand men, the rest having been left to garrison Turin and Florence—was concentrated on the frontier, near Arezzo, where Fanti established his headquarters.

Cialdini, in command of the 4th army corps, had received orders to concentrate his troops at Cattolica, between Pesaro and Rimini. He had two strong divisions, numbering about fourteen thousand men, and could also summon Cadorna to his aid, whose division was destined to reinforce whichever corps needed strengthening. Altogether we had about thirty-two thousand to thirty-three thousand men in five divisions. My numerical inferiority to Cialdini was blamed by some, as the 5th corps was likely to be the first to meet the enemy, and ought, people said, to be the strongest. But it was just in these dispositions that Fanti showed his intuition and military genius. He so completely deceived Lamoricière as to our real intentions, that he abandoned his sole line of retreat in Umbria and concentrated his troops around Ancona, threatened by the 4th corps, leaving the road open for our rapid advance. Fanti also estimated that eleven thousand picked troops, such as I had, were more than sufficient to engage any number of mercenaries, even without the aid of Cadorna's division.

The strategic plan for the 5th corps was to avoid the narrow pass of Lake Thrasimene, march by Citta di Castello and Fratto on Perugia, and seize the fortress which commands the city. Once masters of Perugia, we were to proceed to Foligno, the centre of communication of the Papal States, and effect a junction with the 4th corps. From Foligno we could operate on Spoleto or Ancona, according to the movements of the enemy.

On the 9th, Fanti sent a letter to Lamoricière by Lieutenant Farini,[1] informing him that he had orders to cross the frontier, if the manifestations in the cities of Umbria and the Marches in favour of annexation to the monarchy of Victor Emanuel were interfered with.

Three days before, Cavour had written to Cardinal Antonelli, to announce that the people of the Marches and of Umbria had appealed to the King of Sardinia to defend them against the aggressions of the mercenary troops, who, in the name of the Pontifical government, threatened their lives and their honour.

The reply given by Cardinal Antonelli may be imagined. The Pontifical troops were not withdrawn, but were ordered to resist the invaders to the utmost. Lamoricière looked on Fanti's letter as a declaration of war, and replied that he was ready to defend himself.

We crossed the frontier on the 10th. On the 11th I encamped near Monterchi, sending on the brigade of the Sardinian Grenadiers to Citta di Castello, which they entered at one o'clock, after a slight resistance at the city gates and the governor's palace by seventy-six gendarmes, who were taken prisoners. The rest of the troops entered the town next day amid the rejoicing of the inhabitants, who distributed refreshments among them

[1] Now President of the Senate.

from a *café* on the piazza, whose name had been changed during the night to *Café General Della Rocca*. In a few hours we organised a grand ball in the municipal palace for the officers and gentry, and another on the piazza, in which the soldiers had permission to join.

While part of the troops were dancing and amusing themselves, the Sardinian Grenadiers, the Bersaglieri, the artillery, and a squadron of cavalry advanced towards La Fratta, while the engineers and pioneers threw a bridge across the Tiber, near S. Maddalena. On the 13th the headquarters were at Pierantonio, whence I sent on General Maurice de Sonnaz with a column of the Sardinian Grenadiers, a squadron of the Nice cavalry, Bersaglieri and artillery to Bosco, in preparation for the morrow's attack on the fortress of Perugia. It was only defended by a few hundred Papal troops, General Schmidt being out reconnoitring with fifteen hundred men. Schmidt was the man who had been charged to quell the rising in Perugia during our campaign in June 1859, when the city first declared for annexation to the Constitutional kingdom of Victor Emanuel. He permitted his troops to commit every kind of atrocity, and was execrated by the inhabitants. His men were too tired to reach Perugia before us, but during the assault he managed to enter the fortress unseen.

De Sonnaz had my orders to attack the city from above, and struck his camp early in the morning of the 14th. He advanced to reconnoitre and pick up what information he could from the inhabitants, as we possessed no topographical maps of any sort. On reaching the walls he decided to divide his troops into two divisions ; one was to enter the city by the gate of S. Antonio, the other by the gate of S. Margherita, and, protected from the fire of the fortress by the cathedral, attack the front and the exterior door of the citadel. Both city gates were closed and barred, but the former had been left unguarded, so the

Perugians were able to open it and let in the first column. Major Pallavacini, with his battalion of Bersaglieri, rushed into the town, followed by three battalions of Grenadiers, a squadron of cavalry and a battery of artillery. They were received by a sharp musketry fire from the fortress. Major-General Camerana lost a good many men while crossing the piazza to take up a position on the opposite side. Detachments of the enemy in the streets leading to the fortress were put to flight by our soldiers, who were fired upon from the windows of houses occupied by Schmidt's men. Aided by the inhabitants, we hunted them out, and making barricades of furniture and mattresses, which were offered without stint, at last became masters of all the surroundings of the citadel.

In one street a shot from a window mortally wounded the handsome drum-major of the Grenadiers. Eyewitnesses swore that the shot came from the room of the parish priest, and was fired by him. A court-martial was immediately held, and sentence of death pronounced. The execution was, however, deferred to the next day, it being contrary to the rules of war to carry out a sentence during a siege.

While the first column entered the gate of S. Antonio without difficulty, the second had to wait, under a heavy fire from the walls, at the gate of S. Margherita until the engineers and sappers came up to burst it open. They then rushed in, made some sixty prisoners in the barracks close by, and crossed the city in the direction of the gate of S. Pietro. Part of the troops were stationed in the public gardens opposite the citadel; the others guarded the road to Foligno to prevent any attempt at flight. I left Pierantonio in the morning for Bosco with the rest of my troops, and, marching round the hill of Perugia, debouched on the Foligno road at the bridge of S. Giovanni. Towards mid-day De Sonnaz sent to inform me that Schmidt, with fifteen hundred men, reported to be well provided with artillery, had got into the fortress, and to ask for reinforcements. Fanti joined us at that moment, and approved of my resolve to start at once with the Lombard Grenadiers, under General Brignone, to the aid of De Sonnaz, and to send Colonel Ceresole with two squadrons down into the plain to cut off a possible retreat of the enemy towards Rome. Finding the gate of S. Pietro undefended, we entered, ranged the troops in front of the church and convent of S. Pietro, and placed a battery of eight guns in readiness to bombard the citadel. All was quiet in the city, which made me think a parley was going on. I sent the head of my staff to see, and he returned with news that Schmidt, having found out that he had to do with regular troops, and not, as he supposed, with volunteers, had asked for a suspension of arms with a view to capitulate. De Sonnaz had agreed, and for two hours had been discussing with two colonels sent by Schmidt, who refused to accept the conditions drawn up previously by Fanti.

In order to accelerate matters I galloped up the steep paved incline from S. Pietro to the cathedral piazza, and joined De Sonnaz and the Colonels De Curten and Lazzarini, sent by Schmidt, who did not venture to show himself in the town. Finding them intractable, I drew out my watch and said, ' It is now five ; if at five forty-five the citadel has not surrendered, I open fire from S. Pietro.' Then ordering De Sonnaz to retreat, I went back to my position. There I found Fanti, who had come with an aide-de-camp to know what had happened. He approved of my ultimatum, being anxious to come to a conclusion, as he had heard that Lamoricière was hastening towards Ancona, and wanted to launch the 5th corps in pursuit. Cialdini, with the 4th corps, was to intercept him, and Fanti hoped to crush the mercenary troops between our two armies ; Cadorna, with his division, having meanwhile advanced towards Gubbio to reinforce the 4th corps. Time passed without any sign of surrender, and after looking at his watch several times the commander-in-chief gave the order to fire, and our eight guns did considerable damage to the fortress. Immediately afterwards De Sonnaz sent in hot haste to beg us to cease firing, as the citadel had capitulated.

Fanti, De Sonnaz, I and some of our staffs entered the convent of S. Pietro, where the Colonels De Curten and Lazzarini soon joined us, with full powers from Schmidt. We asked the custodian to give us a room, which he declined to do, adding, that in any case we could not have ink or pens. 'Really!' answered Fanti. 'Go to your superiors, and say that if a room is not opened at once, and pens, ink and paper provided, I shall call in a battalion of soldiers, who will know how to open doors and find what is necessary.' In a few minutes a room on the ground floor was opened for us, and paper, pens and ink were brought. The conditions of surrender were signed by De Sonnaz and the two Pontifical colonels in Schmidt's name. Thus, on the 14th September 1860, Perugia was avenged for the maltreatment she received on the 20th June 1859 at the hands of Schmidt. He was made prisoner, and we sent him out of the town under a strong escort at night, as the people threatened to tear him to pieces.

That same evening Fanti sent off part of the troops to Foligno, leaving a garrison at Perugia, and despatched General Brignone to take the fortress of Spoleto, defended by eight hundred Irish mercenaries. As the fortress commands the road to Rome, it was important for us to hold it to prevent reinforcements reaching the enemy.

Just before leaving Perugia for Foligno with Fanti I met the detachment of soldiers with the condemned priest. A fine, tall man of about forty, he walked slowly but firmly, and never raised his eyes from his breviary. Although a gun, lately discharged, with the barrel still warm, was found in his room, he persisted in declaring that he had not fired the fatal shot, but declined to name the culprit. I should have liked to pardon him, but Fanti, although not more bloodthirsty than myself, thought an example was necessary in order to prevent a recurrence of such treachery. Some hours before, the Archbishop of Perugia (Cardinal Pecci), now Pope Leo XIII., sent to say he wished to see me, but as I had a shrewd suspicion what he wanted I excused myself on the plea of important business. The death of the priest was greeted with shouts of applause from the crowd, who remembered the atrocities of 1859 and the oppression suffered since.

Our march in pursuit of Lamoricière was not accomplished with the rapidity planned by Fanti. The excessive steepness of the road between Foligno and Colfiorito retarded the commissariat waggons and the artillery. The troops had to bivouac for a night and wait for them, which gave Lamoricière the advantage of two marches over us.

Having taken the fortress of Pesaro on the 12th, Cialdini made an admirably planned forced march on Iesi and Osimo, positions which effectually barred the advance of the enemy towards Ancona. On the 16th he reached Castelfidardo and Le Crocette, where he met the Papal troops on the 18th and completely beat them. Nothing therefore remained for us (the 5th corps) but to besiege Ancona. I remember we met the courier from Rome to Tolentino, Macerata, etc., on the summit of the Apennines, and, according to the right, or at any rate the usage, of war, Fanti stopped the coach and seized the mails. We returned most of the letters to the bag, only keeping those which contained information which might be of use to us. Among them was one to Lamoricière from a rich landowner at Macerata, offering to lodge and feed a portion of his troops on his farms, and placing his house and all it contained at his service. On arriving at Macerata, Fanti sent for this gentleman and informed him that a certain number of men would be quartered on his farms, and that he and his staff intended to lodge in his house. Lamoricière's friend declared his farms were few and ill-provided, and his house small and quite unworthy to receive so great a general and his suite. Fanti suavely replied that he and his soldiers would be quite satisfied with what he could provide, and then handed him the letter intended for the Papal general. The poor man's face was a study!

We had met fugitives from the Papal army at Tolentino, where we halted on the way to Macerata, among them several officers riding at full gallop. With some difficulty we succeeded in stopping one, and heard of the battle at Castelfidardo, which was probably still going on.

On the 20th I entered Macerata, where I heard more details about the victory of Castelfidardo, and next day met Fanti at Loreto. Soon afterwards Cialdini joined us, and we started for Ancona to besiege the fortress. Cialdini was to invest it on the left side, I on the right, and the fleet had orders to assist our operations.

My right wing rested on the high rocks overlooking the sea, my left extended down towards the Pia gate, where Cialdini had his headquarters. Fanti established his at the Favorita, near Castro, and I took up mine at the Villa Bosdari, on the heights of Monte Acuto. Opposite me were the two strong redoubts of Monte Pelago and Monte Pulito. We threw up batteries, and on the fourth day opened fire. On the 25th the enemy made a sortie to interrupt our work, but the Bologna brigade, which was at the outposts, drove them back under the lunette of fort Pelago. Here our men had to wait for reinforcements in order to surround the position. Soon afterwards the Bersaglieri came up, and the enemy were driven back at the point of the bayonet. The flag of the Bologna brigade was planted on the conquered positions of Monte Pelago and Monte Pulito, which the enemy in vain attempted to wrest from us.

A large number of Papal troops were in the Gardetto fort, which my corps attacked on the 28th, supported by the fire of the fleet, whose shells passed over our heads. At the same time Cialdini made a feint attack in another direction to draw off part of the enemy's forces. The day —a brilliant one for our navy and our army—ended with a tremendous explosion ; a dense cloud of smoke, torn by long tongues of flame, rose into the sky. A shell had exploded in the powder magazine. Soon afterwards a white flag ran up on the citadel where Lamoricière was, and firing ceased on both sides, only to recommence at eight in the evening, as he demurred to our conditions. I ordered Colonel Ferrero, with the 4th Lombard regiment, to occupy the suburbs during the night with three battalions and two guns, and destroy the Calamo gate, which would admit me into the fortifications. He reached the gate, but unfortunately one of his guns. burst, which somewhat retarded operations. Next morning the capitulation was signed, and the inhabitants tore down the battered remains of the gate to let my men in. I telegraphed to Fanti for permission to enter Ancona, and at five in the afternoon marched in with my staff at the head of the 4th Grenadier regiment, destined to garrison the citadel. The same evening the 12th regiment of Bersaglieri and the marines joined me, and on the 30th the 4th corps entered the town with Generals Fanti and Cialdini at their head.

The king arrived off Ancona in the *Maria Adelaide* on the 3d October, and after reviewing the troops by the seashore, rode to the government palace, where he spent twenty-four hours in listening to our reports and to those of the government commissioners. Then he despatched Fanti and Cialdini to Turin to consult with Cavour, and during their absence confided the command of the army to me. I was also charged to prepare an itinerary for the march of the two corps to Isernia on the crest of the Apennines.

His Majesty took up his residence on the hill outside the Pia gate, and as I was perpetually backwards and forwards between my headquarters and his villa, I met the Countess Mirafiore, whom I had not seen for years. Though she had been living fourteen years with the king, and must have been thirty, she looked wonderfully young and had not lost her beauty. But she dressed very badly in a theatrical style. I remember one morning the king made me stay for lunch, as he had not finished signing the orders for the day, and Rosina appeared in a voluminous and immensely long sort of dressing-gown, with a diadem of brilliants on her head, strings of pearls, reaching to her waist, round her neck, and her arms and fingers covered with jewels. I was no favourite of hers, and she showed it; for though I knew her as a girl I had never been near her since she became the king's mistress. But Rosina was not a bad or intriguing woman, never tried to injure me, and I do not believe she ever did an ill-natured thing to anyone.

On the return of Fanti and Cialdini the king expressed his sorrow at not being able to keep me as his chief of the staff. Having taken over the supreme command of the army, he felt bound to give Fanti the position I had filled in 1848 and 1859. Policy, or rather Cavour, who, since Villafranca, had borne me a grudge, thus ordered it. But with his usual kindness Victor Emanuel arranged that my corps should march with him. Only long afterwards I learnt that, seeing I disliked Cavour's idea of leaving me in command of the troops in Umbria and the Marches, instead of taking an active part in the Neapolitan campaign, the king had insisted on my retaining the command of the 5th corps, which was under his direct orders.

CHAPTER XVII

FROM Terni I rode with a small escort across the Neapolitan frontier to Citta Ducale, and thence to Antrodoco. On the 20th October I was at Aquila, where everything was quiet. Popoli, which I reached late in the evening, was crowded with the military train of my corps and with commissariat waggons. Groups of volunteers on their way to join Garibaldi were shouting, singing and drinking success to Italy in every street. At daylight I started for Sulmona, and wishing to see the voting for the *plébiscite*, entered the town on foot. The crowd was extraordinary, and nearly every man had a bit of paper with a big *Si* (Yes) stuck in his hatband; very few bore a *No*. I was watching the scene, when screams and angry shouts of 'Death to the Bourbons!' 'Long live Victor Emanuel!' 'Hurrah for Italy!' arose, and I saw an officer of our carabineers attempting to protect a Neapolitan general from the fury of the people. Seeing the officer would not be able to save his prisoner, I made a rush with my two aides-de-camp through the crowd. 'Save me! save me!' cried the poor wretch; 'these madmen want to kill me.' Cigala and Gianotti placed themselves on either side of the general, while I harangued the crowd, telling them that no barbarous action should be committed in the name of Victor Emanuel and of Italy, that the laws of civilised nations commanded prisoners to be respected, and that no one would be allowed to hurt a man who was in our hands. I had hardly finished speaking, when a ruffianly-looking fellow came up to me and said, 'Who are you, to mix yourself up in our concerns?' 'I am General Della Rocca, commanding one of the *corps d'armée*, who have come to liberate you,' I answered. The names of Fanti, Cialdini, and Della Rocca, were probably known through the newspapers, for as soon as I pronounced my name the crowd began to cheer, 'Long live Della Rocca!' 'Long live Fanti!' 'Long live Cialdini!' My aide-de-camp Cigala conducted the Bourbon general, a certain Scotti Douglas of Parma, whom Cialdini had taken prisoner on the Apennines, half fainting to the barracks of the carabineers, whence he was sent to Piedmont, and, I believe, soon set at liberty.

From Sulmona I went to join the king at Castel di Sangro, and heard His Majesty had been received everywhere with enthusiasm. At Isernia, where we arrived on the 22d, a council of war was held. It was decided to advance on Naples, which had been abandoned by King Francis and immediately occupied by Garibaldi in conjunction with our troops. Naples was to be our new base, and our line of operations the Garigliano. I was to take Capua, which intercepted our advance on Naples, while the king, with the 4th corps and the chief part of mine, marched towards the Garigliano in search of the Bourbon army. Owing to inexact information given by prisoners as to the strength of the garrison at Capua, and counting on the aid of the Garibaldians, who had been for nearly a month investing the place, I only took a few battalions. At Teano I separated from our main body, turning off on the road to Alife. Soon afterwards the king met the Bourbon troops, and defeated them after three hours' fighting.[1]

Between Venafro and Alife I met General Garibaldi and his aide-de-camp in search of the king. I put him in the right direction, and heard afterwards that he found Victor Emanuel at Quadriglia, and for the first time saluted him enthusiastically as *King of Italy.*

At Alife the bishop, an excellent, high-minded man, came to see me. He belonged to the Liberal section of the Neapolitan clergy, who hoped that a new government might sweep away the corruption and abuses which had infested the country for centuries. We talked for more than an hour, and I remember my astonishment when, among other things, he said, 'You will easily beat the Neapolitan army, the soldiers are cowards, they have no backbone; but you will find it difficult to overcome the immorality of the Neapolitans, particularly of a great part of the clergy. I have lived in the south for more than twenty years, and sad experience has taught me how little one can do for their amelioration, even by incessant work. You will not really conquer the Neapolitans until you succeed in teaching them the holy truth of moral order, and, I warn you, that will take time and labour.' I heard afterwards that the good bishop had talked in the same sense to the king and to Farini, insisting on the necessity of reforming the universal immorality of all classes of the population.

[1] He wrote to me :—

'TEANO, *27th Oct.* 1860.

'MON CHER GENERAL,—Hier soir j'ai trouvé l'ennemi en force à moitié route, entre Teano et Sessa, sur les hauteurs. Le combat dura trois heures, l'ennemi fut repoussé à Sessa, je crois en retraite vers le Garigliano. Il avait seize bataillons de chasseurs et, je crois, grande partie on toute l'armée. Les prisonniers m'assurent n'y avoir en Capoue qu'un regiment et un bataillon. Portez vous aussitôt sur cette ville . . . et tâchez de la faire rendre au plus tôt, ceci est très important pour notre politique très tendue.

'Tenez moi au courant de tout. Je vous embrasse.—Votre très affectionné,

'VICTOR EMANUEL.'

N

On the 28th October I arrived at Santa Maria (di Capua). Immediately after the victory of Volturno, in the beginning of the month, Garibaldi, with about thirty thousand men, called the Southern Army (*Esercito Meridionale*), had surrounded Capua, but, lacking artillery, was able to do nothing. They were stationed at Santa Maria, at Caserta, at Avellino, and on the road called Formicola, on the right bank of the Volturno. After going over the lines fronting the fortifications of the town, I went to Monte Sant' Angelo, where Garibaldi had established himself. He told me the king had informed him of the orders given to me, and added, ' My opinion is that in war unity of command is indispensable.' I had expected some such objection, and it never entered my head to claim the supreme command of his troops; still, it was impossible for me, in spite of my respect and admiration, to serve under him. I therefore answered that while surveying the lines of attack I had seen the positions of his troops on the heights to the right of the fortress and on part of the narrow plain on the slopes, and had come to the conclusion that, if I occupied the plain to the left, we could work together with good results and without interfering with each other. He listened in silence, and after some minutes said, ' If not inconvenient to you, we can meet again to-day between four and five, and I will give you my answer.' A little before five I was at his quarters, and found the Dictator surrounded by all his generals— Cosenz, Medici, Sirtori, etc. Garibaldi introduced us, saying I had been charged by the king to besiege Capua and take the fortress without loss of time ; and that, being averse to any division of command, he placed the whole of his army under my control for this undertaking. But, fearing lest his volunteers might raise difficulties if this were known, he wished them to believe that he was still in their midst. ' I therefore beg,' he continued, ' General

Della Rocca and all of you to keep this secret. General Sirtori, in whom I have absolute confidence, will transmit the orders of General Della Rocca to my men, as though they came from me. I am called to Naples on urgent business relating to the Dictatorship, but shall be ready to return at once should my presence be necessary.' He then shook my hand and wished me good luck. Everything being thus satisfactorily arranged, I sent my head of the staff to General De Cornè, commanding in Capua, with a letter informing him that I had orders to take the fortress, and enough troops to do it with. Resistance being useless, I invited him to surrender in order to save the town and its inhabitants the horrors of a siege. Meanwhile, with Meneabrea and Colonel Bottacco of the artillery, I chose the places for establishing the batteries. These were begun the same night, General De Cornè having refused to surrender.

Having only batteries of sixteen, I sent to Naples for heavier guns. Twenty-four hours later Valfré, commander-in-chief of the artillery, arrived himself with twenty heavy pieces, and in less than three days they were in position. Just as we were firing the first shots to get the range, the king, impatient for an answer to a letter he had written from Sessa,[1] rode up, accompanied by only one aide-de-

---

[1] 'SESSA, *le* 31 *Octobre,* 1860.

'MON CHER MACIGNO,*—Donnez-moi des nouvelles exactes de Capua, et dites moi quand vous croyez que cela sera fait ; plus ce cera vite, mieux ça sera. En attendant, avant hier on m'a fait une bêtise. Je donnais l'ordre à . . . de reconnaitre le Garigliano, lui, croyant bien faire, s'avança vers le pont avec trois régiments de cavalerie, quatre bataillons de Bersaglieri et deux batteries sans me le dire. Aussitôt le feu s'engagea avec deux bataillons de chasseurs qui étaient de ce côté-ci du pont, et la cavalerie, portée très en avant, fut fortement mitraillée. En entendant le feu, je me portais sur place avec Sonnaz, mais c'etait trop tard, c'etait le bon de l'action. Les Napolitains de l'autre côté du fleuve faisaient un feu d'enfer, je donnais l'ordre de retirer les troupes, chose désagréable, mais nécessaire : on avait déja tué et blessé

* *Granite*—a play upon General Della Rocca's (*rock*) name.

camp, running some risk of being taken a prisoner. With my habitual frankness I told His Majesty that his presence at that moment was very inconvenient, and after asking me how long I thought the siege would last, and receiving my assurance that, although the garrison consisted of several thousand men instead of a few hundred, as we had been informed, in three days Capua would be ours, he shook hands and rode off. Heavy firing began at 4 p.m. on the 1st November, to which the fortress replied. Towards evening I was forced to slacken fire for want of ammunition, and only sent two or three bombs an hour during the night. Some of these burst in the town, and, among other buildings, set fire to the palace of the bishop, who immediately went to the commandant and advised him to surrender. Before six in the morning of the 2d November two superior officers came to my headquarters;

35 hommes du septième bataillon, 5 officiers, et pris du même bataillon 30 prisonniers qui bêtement s'étaient poussés de l'autre côté du pont, croyant de devoir le prendre et qui furent entourés. Une 20.ne de chevaux de Piêmont Royal y resterent. Dans la retraite les chasseurs Napolitains repasserent le pont et nous suivirent un peu et puis s'arrêterent. Maintenant leurs avant postes sont plus près de nous, nous n'avons pas encore pu faire de pont. Celui de Gaiazzo n'est pas arrivé, nous avions combiné avec la marine d'en faire un à l'embouchure du Garigliano, mais l'Amiral français vient se mettre en bataille en face de nos navires, et déclare les couler à fond si on tire un coup de canon, et si on met le pont. Je suis sûr que c'est de son crû, car l'empereur n'a pas de ces ideés ; aussi je viens d'ecrire une lettre plus qu' enèrgique que Persano lui enverra. Entr' autres choses l'Amiral dit que le Garigliano fait partie de la place de Gaëte, et que lui se trouverait avec la flotte entre deux feux, de la place et les nôtres, lorsqu'il y a 14 kilomètres entre la place et nous. On dit que c'est un ami de Lamoricière. C. . . . est celui qui a eu le plus de tort dans l'affaire de l'autre jour, car il a fait mitrailler la cavalerie, et a ordonné aux Bersaglieri de passer le pont où il n'y avait qu'une planche oui et une non. J'ai donné perruque à tout le monde.

'L'ennemi est en force de 45,000 hommes de l'autre côté et quantité d'artillerie.

'Demain nous verrons si on peut faire mieux et passer en faisant mettre un pont 6 milles plus haut.

'Je vous embrasse.—Votre très affectionné,   VICTOR EMANUEL.'

one, a General Liguori, asked me for a free pass for Gaeta in order to consult with King Francis. I explained the impossibility of granting such an extraordinary request, showed him the very easy conditions of surrender I had already drawn up, and advised him to return to his commanding officer and induce him to accept them. Firing had been stopped on their arrival, and I gave the general till nine o'clock to bring me an affirmative answer. As the clock struck nine I sent my aide-de-camp to order the batteries to open fire, and directly afterwards Liguori arrived in hot haste and accepted my conditions. The garrison, eleven thousand five hundred strong, were fine men and well dressed. They could not conceal their satisfaction at the cessation of hostilities and danger, and were sent to Naples with their families, about five thousand old men, women and children. The Bourbons favoured matrimony in their army, and gave rations to the soldiers' families.

Garibaldi said, when he left on the evening of the 28th October, 'I am going to Caserta, but to-morrow shall be at Naples, where I have much to do.' On the 30th I heard he was still at Caserta, and ill; so, while the engineers were working at the batteries, I rode over to see him. With his usual simplicity in private life, he had declined to inhabit the palace at Caserta, and I found him in a little room above the guardhouse at the entrance. On dismounting, I observed several barrels of powder, and when I entered the room of the Dictator noticed his bed was exactly over the spot where the powder had been placed. I begged him to move immediately; and, smiling, he promised to do so. Propped up with pillows, he was wrapped in a military cloak, a little cap on his head, and a silk handkerchief knotted round his neck. As I entered, he held out his hand, and seemed quite touched when I told him I had only come to ask how he was. He was still more pleased when I told him how well I got on with his generals, Cosenz and Sirtori, notable personages and most excellent men, and how I regretted the enforced absence of Bixio, who had been sent to hospital in Naples owing to a fall from his horse. Mine were no idle compliments; I meant what I said, and I saw Garibaldi was pleased that I appreciated his friends.

As soon as the capitulation was signed I sent off my aide-de-camp, Cigala, to Garigliano with a note to the king. When he had read it, he exclaimed, 'Capua is ours! Hurrah for La Rocca!' 'Hurrah! Hurrah! Long live La Rocca!' was repeated by all his staff. The king asked for a pencil, and sent me a note ordering all the guns taken at Capua to be sent to him, and bidding me go to Naples and take over the command there.

I confess that I was delighted, but not astonished, at the description Cigala gave me of the reception of my news, for I knew that in the small military Court circle of Victor Emanuel I was liked and esteemed. But lately, in the Memoirs (*Ricordi*) of General Genova Revel, I see it is broadly hinted that I opposed Fanti about the disbanding of the Garibaldians, and suggested to the king to be over-indulgent towards the Southern Army to the detriment of the regular army. Fanti, as minister of war, foresaw the disorders and annoyances which the volunteers might cause when the war was over, and very properly advised the king to disband them at once. Victor Emanuel, knowing that it would grieve Garibaldi, whose great services and perfect loyalty and generosity he fully recognised, was averse to such prompt action. I well remember his saying to me, 'They are in too great a hurry; they make me cut a sorry figure. I cannot show less generosity than Garibaldi.' These were entirely personal impressions of the king's, and suggested by no one. But having a strong admiration for

Garibaldi, who had behaved so well and nobly to me at Capua, I certainly could not combat them.

Before leaving Capua I went over the citadel, and in the prison found and set at liberty Arrivabene, the correspondent of the *Morning Post*. He had been taken by the Bourbons during the battle of Volturno and imprisoned as a spy. On the 4th November I left for Naples, with rather a perturbed mind. It was all very well for the king to tell me to go there and take the command. At Naples there was a Dictator, Garibaldi; a pro-Dictator, George Pallavicino; General Türr, and several other commanders of large bodies of troops, all men of note. For me to arrive, perhaps without having been officially announced, and say, ' Here I am, now you can all go,' was no easy task. I could only do as I had done before—trust in the star of Victor Emanuel. Garibaldi was at dinner with twenty-five guests, and I sent in to beg him not to leave them, as I would wait to give him a message from the king. In a few minutes the Dictator appeared, and, taking me by the hand, presented me to those who had followed him into the drawing-room—' Gentlemen, I present General Della Rocca, who only took three days to besiege and conquer Capua.' After a few complimentary words, I drew Garibaldi aside, and said, ' To-night my troops arrive from Capua with eleven thousand five hundred men of the Bourbon garrison; barracks and forts must be ready for them.' ' I understand, of course,' he answered, ' room must be found; tell me where you live.' ' Close to you, in the royal palace; but my headquarters will be in the palace of the Prince of Capua; and now I am going to dine at the Calata del Gigante.' ' Very well, in half an hour General Türr, who was in command of the city during my absence, will be with you. He will tell you where the troops can be lodged, and will place himself at your disposal, in case you wish him to superintend their billeting.' General Türr joined me soon afterwards, and I asked him to dine with me. We arranged everything; and I accepted the command of the city handed over to me by the orders of the Dictator.

Thus all was settled without the slightest difficulty, and with the simple cordiality of brothers-at-arms. I did not even produce Fanti's order, countersigned by Victor Emanuel, which I had with me.

On the 7th November the king entered Naples. He arrived an hour before the appointed time; but part of the troops were drawn up in the streets he was to drive through, and, luckily, I got to the station in time to accompany him. It was raining hard, and the royal carriages were not to be seen, so the king entered a large tent, where he received the government officials and the officers of the municipality. When at last the royal carriage drove up, Victor Emanuel invited Garibaldi to sit by his side. The Dictator, dressed in his usual red shirt, grey cloak and small cap, was wet through. Opposite them sat Pallavicino, pro-Dictator of Naples, and Mordini, pro-Dictator of Sicily. I rode on the right hand of the king, with my drawn sword.

All the clergy, with the exception of the archbishop, who was at Gaeta, received Victor Emanuel with great pomp at the door of the cathedral. After a solemn *Te Deum* had been sung, the king and his suite went into the chapel of San Gennaro, where, after the miracle had taken place, the holy relic was given him to kiss. A few days before the question was discussed, Victor Emanuel asked me what I should do in his place. 'I should inaugurate the new era of things by showing respect to religion and the church,' but I should abolish superstition.' He was very much of my opinion; but Farini and several other members of the government said that, the miracle having taken place when Garibaldi visited the chapel, there would be great risk of setting the clergy and the common people against the king if he declined to go through the ceremony. So he determined to bow to their opinion, and to kneel before the miraculous phial. The suite of the king not having reached the cathedral as soon as ourselves, I dismounted to accompany His Majesty, but his aides-de-camp appearing just as he was entering the chapel of San Gennaro, I was enabled to retire and remount my horse outside. In spite of the heavy rain, there was tremendous enthusiasm when the king drove to the royal palace.

After the state dinner that evening, Victor Emanuel took Garibaldi into his study, and they remained talking for a long time. His Majesty told me that the Dictator, speaking about the great difficulties of governing the Two Sicilies, had suggested and offered to remain as viceroy, if not as dictator, for some time longer, in order to use his popularity for the good of Italy. He sincerely thought that his influence, especially in Sicily, was so great that he would have more chance of success than the government of the king. Victor Emanuel listened without giving any opinion, and said he would give an answer after consulting Farini and the members of the government who were at Naples. Fanti and Farini naturally opposed any such arrangement, and they were right. Garibaldi was sincere and honest, but he suffered himself to be surrounded and led by persons whose only desire was to detach the south from the north and create a Republic. among them was Mazzini, who, in the neighbourhood of Caserta, was trying, through his partizans and emissaries, to foment disorder and insubordination, particularly among the young officers of both armies.

After the *plébiscite*, Mazzini did not go into voluntary exile, as modern writers affirm. He remained at Naples, and with the Garibaldians who had been, or were to be, disbanded ; the brigands, and the two Alexandre Dumas' (father and son) gave me a world of trouble and annoyance. The elder Dumas had taken possession of a villa which, he pretended, the Dictator had given to him. He lived there with an actress of I forget what theatre, and his son and Mazzini often stayed with him. A clever police agent, charged to watch the agitator, and who knew how dangerous he was, proposed to get rid of him in a way which would appear perfectly natural, and have saved the government many an anxious moment. It would have been a criminal act, and I refused to sanction it. I contented myself with having him closely watched and traversing his designs, and, after a time, he momentarily disappeared from the scene.

The king only refused the offers of Garibaldi after the official presentation of the *plébiscite* on the 8th November. On the same day the rank of a general in the army, the Collar of the Annunziata, and a considerable pension was offered to Garibaldi; but he refused everything. Considering himself still as Dictator, he made a large number of promotions and appointments, and demanded the Collar of the Annunziata for Pallavicino and for Mordini. The king had already determined to give it to the former, not so much for his services under Garibaldi as for his splendid patriotism and the sufferings undergone at Spielberg for the Italian cause, for which he had spent the greater part of his large fortune.

Late in the afternoon the king informed Garibaldi his councillors disapproved of his offers, and that, to his regret, he must refuse them. Neither anger nor disappointment was shown by Garibaldi, who, the same evening, published a proclamation to the Italian people, calling them to rise in the following spring and complete the unity of Italy by liberating Rome and Venice. He then embarked for Caprera with a few of his immediate adherents.

Next day, 9th November, Farini was appointed Viceroy of the Two Sicilies by the king.

CHAPTER XVIII

1861

I MUST confess that my impressions of the inhabitants of Naples during the first weeks I passed there were most unfavourable. Later, when I made friends with many excellent men, born and educated in the southern provinces, among my colleagues in the Senate and in the army, they were modified. Among these was Poerio, the type of everything that was great and noble.

The king and the government were impatient for Gaeta to fall; they wished the capitulation to take place before His Majesty left for Turin. Ancona and Capua had accustomed Victor Emanuel to quick and successful operations, and he did not take the far greater obstacles, chiefly owing to the presence of King Francis and the royal family at Gaeta, into account. Matters were also complicated by the uncertain and hesitating conduct of Napoleon III., who maintained a French fleet in the waters of Gaeta, which prevented any action being taken by our ships. One morning the king said he should send me to hasten the siege ; but I declared it would be impossible to supplant Cialdini, and declined any such mission. A few days later he again broached the subject, proposing to charge Cialdini with the amalgamation of the three armies, Sardinian, Neapolitan and Garibaldian—and give him the supreme command in southern Italy. 'I know and I like Cialdini!' I exclaimed, 'and I am sure he would be hurt and would accept nothing until he has taken Gaeta.' The matter then dropped for the moment.

Meanwhile, it became imperative to reorganise the army. Among the many decrees brought from Turin by Fanti for the king to sign was one naming me president of the commission to reform and weed the Garibaldian army: a perfect hornets' nest to be put into! However, the commission only met once in Naples, when I read the royal decree of 11th November 1860, granting six months' pay to the officers and soldiers of the Southern Army. A discussion arose as to whether those who had no regular nominations from General Garibaldi ought to profit by this decree; by far the greater number of officers were in this category, and it was decided to give them only three months' pay. Such protests and difficulties were, however, raised by the Garibaldians, who were in Naples, that the new ministry, the last one formed by Cavour, decreed the transfer of the commission to Turin.

One day Fanti met me and said, 'Let me be the first to congratulate you.' 'What for?' I answered. 'The king has named you to the military command of the kingdom of the Two Sicilies; it is a splendid position, one of the first, if not the first, in the new kingdom.' 'I am much obliged to His Majesty,' I replied, 'but, to tell you the truth, I have no wish for such a post; and when the war is over, my only desire is to return to where and what I was.' I was fully resolved only to give my services in the southern provinces temporarily, and to resign sooner than take up my residence there. As the king said nothing to me, I held my tongue, but determined to speak frankly to him next morning. Very early, before I was dressed, he sent for me, and at once asked why I had been so out of temper the day before. 'For many reasons,' I answered; 'and as your Majesty is good enough to ask me, I will tell you them.' Repeating Fanti's words, I reminded him that early in the year I had repeatedly refused the command offered until I knew war to be imminent. 'I think I have done my duty,' I added, 'and been of some service to the Italian cause; but in time of peace my only wish is to remain with your Majesty. As first aide-de-camp, I can follow and serve your Majesty in the field, and be near you in time of peace.'

After a moment's silence the king came up to me, and taking my hands, said he was as jealous of my military reputation as I could be, and would never permit me to leave the service, but that for his sake I must undertake to arrange military affairs in the southern provinces, and accept for the moment the military command of the ex-kingdom of the Two Sicilies. I promised him to do my best, on condition that the government sent me men and money when I required them. This condition was not kept, as will be seen hereafter.

The king passed Christmas at Naples, and left for Turin on the 26th December. Soon afterwards Prince Eugene of Carignano came as viceroy, and occupied the state rooms of the royal palace. Thanks to his gracious manners and his generosity, he was very popular at Naples. To me he was always kindness itself, and overwhelmed my family, who lived on the second floor of the palace, with attentions. I was so busy that, with the exception of state dinners, when my wife, as lady-in-waiting to the late queen, was asked to receive the wives and daughters of the guests, I declined all invitations. The Southern Army, *i.e.*, the volunteers, gave me plenty of work, and the re-actionary party was busy in various districts of the ex-kingdom. The country was infested with armed bands, augmented by malcontents and men out of work, led by a few officers of the Bourbon army, or by discredited Garibaldians, such as La Monaco, who stirred up disorders in Sicily. Outbreaks occurred in various places, and I had to divide and sub-divide my troops in order to protect the inhabitants. After the departure of the king things grew worse. The greater part of the troops were engaged at the siege at Gaeta, or in Sicily under Brignone, and I applied in vain to the ministry for reinforcements. The brigands were so numerous, and so many were shot, that orders came from Turin to execute only the chiefs. My officers, realising the necessity of capital punishment in certain districts where it was only possible to govern by fear, telegraphed, 'four, five, six armed brigand chiefs arrested in such a place'; to which I replied, 'Shoot them.' After a time Fanti, struck by the extraordinary number of chiefs, sent orders that they were not to be shot, but taken prisoners. Prisons and barracks were soon insufficient to contain the prisoners; and, after the capture of Gaeta, the disbanded Bourbon soldiers and the volunteers, who had spent what money they had, joined the rapscallions.

Disorder was also rife in Naples. Mazzini made his appearance, wearing the Garibaldian uniform, and sent his agents into the provinces to stir up discontent in the army. This I knew from a letter to the police which was communicated to me. He was carefully watched, and soon afterwards disappeared for the second time. Then the government, in spite of my reiterated demands, did not send money from Turin for the monthly pay of the troops and the Garibaldian volunteers, who made a row outside the gates of the Treasury. I wrote to Fanti and to Cavour for money and reinforcements, without any result; the only consolation I had was that the disgust of the Prince of Carignano equalled my own. He threatened to return to Turin and let them give the vice-royalty to anyone who would accept it. At last I had the following letter from Cavour in January:—

'DEAR LA ROCCA,—. . . After some trouble, I have at last induced Fanti to send you a brigade. I hope they will embark on the frigate which is expected from Naples; make the most of them. I must beg, however, that you will not leave Sicily without help in case of any serious disturbances in the island.

' After much negotiation I have come to an understanding with the emperor. The whole fleet will leave on the 19th, and on the 20th we shall be free to attack the place (Gaeta) from land and sea.

' I am not afraid of the reactionary movement, or of the help afforded to it by France. I am used to a double current from Paris. Rondon, the minister of war, is most useful to us. His orders must come from a Bourbon source. But, once the fleet is withdrawn, I hope the behaviour of the French soldiers will undergo a change. In any case, it is useless to worry about it.

' Fanti has also decided to summon the Garibaldian and Neapolitan officers here. I shall do all I can to assist you in this arduous matter. I know I can rely on your firmness and shrewdness. The prince is well disposed ; Nigra[1] is clever. Working well together, you will succeed in restoring order in the kingdom ' (of Naples). ' It will be an immense service rendered to Italy. . . . Adieu.

'C. CAVOUR.'[2]

---

[1] Secretary of State to the Prince of Carignano, who was beginning his brilliant diplomatic career under the auspices of Cavour.—*Translator's Note.*

[2] 'CARO LA ROCCA,—. . . Ho deciso non senza fatica Fanti a spedirti una brigata. Spero imbarcarla sulle fregate che aspetto da Napoli ; fanne buon pro'. Ti raccommando però, in caso di disordini gravi in Sicilia, di non lasciare l'isola senza aiuti.

'Dopo infinite pratiche sono giunto ad intendermela con l'Imperatore.

The brigade sent by Fanti was that of Pisa, small and badly commanded. Fortunately troops were not needed in Sicily; but I considered the reinforcement insufficient, and asked in vain for others. My discontent was augmented by the conduct of the minister of war, who suspended General Pinelli and sent General Mezzacapo in his stead, without consulting me, and made him independent of my command. I sent in my resignation, but the king refused to accept it. The temporary suspension of Pinelli, who was doing excellent service against the brigand and Papal troops in the Abruzzi, was rendered necessary by a violent proclamation he published after falling into a trap laid by the Communal Council of a reactionary village. He actually called the Head of the Church, 'that clerical vampire, who for centuries has sucked the blood of our mother with his foul lips.'

On the 14th February our troops entered Gaeta. Early in the same month there was a revolt among the convicts employed in the harbour. This was to be expected, because, after the departure of the Bourbons, secret agents were at work among the lowest classes of the population. The police were not as good as they ought to have been, and we were unwillingly obliged to inculcate respect for law and morality by force.

Tutta la flotta partirà il 19, ed il 20 saremo liberi di attaccare la piazza per terra e per mare.

'Non mi spavento della reazione e degli aiuti che la Francia le dà. Sono avvezzo a veder partire da Parigi una doppia corrente. Il Ministro della guerra Rondon ci è utilissimo. Le sue istruzioni debbono essere borboniane. Spero però che, ritirata la flotta, il contegno dei soldati francesi muterà ; ad ogni modo non bisogna darsene soverchio pensiero.

'Fanti si è pure deciso a chiamare qui i Garibaldini ufficiali e gli ufficiali Napoletani. Faccio quanto sta in me per agevolarvi l'ardua impresa. So di poter fare assegnamento sulla tua fermezza e il tuo accorgimento. Il Principe è ben disposto ; Nigra ha ingegno. Tutti insieme camminando d'accordo riuscirete a ristabilire l'ordine nel regno. Sarà un servizio immenso reso all'Italia. . . . Addio.   C. CAVOUR.'

In the middle and upper classes the sense of morality was exceedingly low. During the dictatorship of Garibaldi abuses had crept in which had to be reformed. Under the pretext of lodging soldiers, every disposable house was occupied. Some of the Garibaldians had taken possession of rooms, not only for themselves and their families, but for letting. I appointed a commission of inquiry of some of our generals with those of the Garibaldian army, and of the members of the Communal Council who had been charged with distributing the billets. It was difficult to make them understand that this abuse must be put a stop to; but at last it was decided that in thirty days the houses were to be cleared of all who had no right to be there.

Some days later I received a visit from one of the members of the Council. With perfect self-possession he said, 'Listen, dear friend. My brother occupies several rooms in such a street. Poor fellow! he has such a lot of children that he is forced to turn his hand to anything in order to gain a living; he only keeps two rooms for himself, and he lets the others. Can you not allow him to keep them? Though he is my brother, I cannot do much for him. What do you say?' I looked at him with astonishment. He bore a great name, and he was rich, or, at all events, well off, yet he coolly proposed not only to disobey the very decision he had voted, but to do a dishonest action in favour of his brother. Other people were waiting to see me, so I rose, saying, 'Your brother and his tenants must be out before the end of the month; and remember that you have said nothing and that I have heard nothing.' He was rather taken aback, but left the room.

Another day a rich contractor came to beg me to recommend him for an important government contract. I told him to leave his proposal for examination, because I was busy. As he was going I saw him put something on the mantelpiece — evidently a rouleau of gold.

‘I beg your pardon,’ said I ; ‘what is that ? ’ ‘Only a small offering,’ he quietly replied, ‘for the person who assists me in this matter.’ ‘I’d throw you and your money out of the window,’ I exclaimed ; ‘but I see you don’t know what morality means. Take what belongs to you; go, and don’t come back.’

A gentleman, well known in science and politics, called on me and said, ‘My son is an officer, and has been at the siege of Gaeta. Now, they say, he is to be sent to that of Messina. Not to mention the fatigue, there will also be danger, and he would rather go to some garrison town.’ ‘My dear sir,’ I replied, ‘our officers ask to be sent on active service. I will not do your son the injustice to think he would act otherwise, or imagine that you care more for his life than his honour. We will forget that anything has been said, and your young officer will go wherever he is ordered.’

I got very tired of this sort of thing, and of writing over and over again for troops and for remittances. Instead of accepting my resignation, Fanti proposed that I should exchange the command of the 5th *corps d’armée* for that of the 6th, which was to be sent to the southern provinces, and retain the position of commander-in-chief at Naples, in obedience to the wishes of the Prince of Carignano. This I refused; and after waiting in vain during the month of April for my successor to be appointed, I seized the pretext of an important discussion in the Senate early in May, took leave of the prince (who I knew intended to follow my example), and returned to Turin.

The kingdom of Italy had only been constituted a few months before by Parliamentary law, a natural consequence of the *plébiscite*, and Victor Emanuel had at once been acknowledged as King of Italy by England. Save Austria, the Pope and the ex-princes, no other power had protested, and evidently were inclined to follow the example of England. Internal affairs, however, were not so promising. Stormy scenes occurred in the Chambers. While La Marmora, in bitter language, opposed the new organisation of the army, Garibaldi flung insults at Cavour, and Cialdini violently, but justly, criticised Garibaldi. I then saw that these internal difficulties had prevented the government from giving more attention to the affairs of the new provinces. That terrible struggle between Cavour and Garibaldi, the two greatest factors after Victor Emanuel of Italian unity, was at its height. The death of Cavour, which took place forty days later, was attributed by many to the mental sufferings he underwent at that time. I saw Cavour a few days after I arrived at Turin, and related my impressions of the Neapolitan provinces. Struck by the gravity of the report, he summoned me to a council of ministers to repeat publicly what I had told him in private.

On the 6th June all Italy went into mourning for the death of her great son. He was, and he will remain, one of the greatest figures of the nineteenth century—if not the greatest. Without Cavour it would have taken centuries to form a united Italy ; thanks to him, it was done in little more than twenty years. The prologue was in 1848, the epilogue in 1870, after the death of the great minister.

CHAPTER XIX

1861-1864

THE Prince of Carignano left Naples for Turin soon after
I did. Count Ponzo di S. Martino was named in his
stead as viceroy, and General Durando assumed the
military command. He had no more luck than myself,
and, after begging in vain for more troops and more money,
sent in his resignation after a few months' service.

The 5th *corps d'armée* had meanwhile been sent to
Tuscany, and I gladly resumed the command. In the
autumn, just as my wife was preparing for the move to
Florence, the king sent for me, and offered me the first
military command (Turin). General Hector de Sonnaz
wished to go to Florence, and I was only too glad to
return to Turin, and thus be enabled to continue my
service of first aide-de-camp to the king. Victor Emanuel
had kept his promise and fulfilled my dearest wishes.

Some weeks later I was sent as ambassador extraordinary to Berlin, to attend the coronation of William I.,
who succeeded his brother King Frederick William IV.
of Prussia. All the great European powers were to be

represented, and although the new kingdom of Italy had not been recognised by Prussia, the friendly relations which had always existed between that State and Sardinia made it advisable to send an ambassador to the coronation.

The mission was not so difficult or so important as that of 1858 to the Emperor Napoleon III.; still, La Marmora having failed several months before to obtain the recognition by Prussia of the new kingdom of Italy, it was not quite plain sailing. My business was to do nothing and say nothing about any recognition, but quietly to assume the position, not of ambassador of the King of Sardinia, but of the King of Italy.

In the second week of October I left with a numerous suite of officers, all clever, handsome, well-bred young fellows, who did their country credit. The day after my arrival at Berlin I presented my credentials to Baron von Bernsdorf, Minister of Foreign Affairs. They were made out for the ambassador extraordinary from King Victor Emanuel to His Majesty King William I. Glancing at them, the minister said, 'Why His Majesty King William, and not His Majesty the King of Prussia?' Feigning ignorance, I answered, 'If this form does not please your excellency, I will at once send to Turin and have it changed into ambassador from the King of Italy to His Majesty the King of Prussia.' 'No, no; it does not matter,' he said. Bernsdorf did not seem altogether satisfied, but made the best of it, and was very courteous. Two days afterwards I was received by King William I. with the same ceremonial as the French and English ambassadors. He greeted me personally with great cordiality, having known me in 1850. The coronation took place a few days later, and I summoned the little diplomacy I possessed to my aid to avoid making some false step, as the ex-King of Naples had not recalled his ambassador, who was invited with the other members of the diplomatic corps in Berlin, and, poor fellow! cut a sorry figure.

A special train, with a reserved carriage marked by a card for each ambassador, was to take us down to Kœnigsberg. Walking down the platform with my suite, I saw a card with 'His Excellency the Ambassador of the King of Sardinia,' attached to a carriage. We passed without noticing it, and meeting a court official, I said, 'Excuse me, but I cannot find the carriage for the ambassador of His Majesty King Victor Emanuel.' The official disappeared, and soon returned and conducted me to where I had seen the first card, now changed for one bearing the words, 'His Excellency the Ambassador of His Majesty King Victor Emanuel.'

The coronation took place in the chapel of the castle of Kœnigsberg, where Frederick I., the great Elector of Brandenburg crowned himself King of Prussia in 1701. Long, wide galleries, leading to the chapel, flanked the huge halls, and in one of them were ranged the foreign princes, ambassadors, ministers and distinguished visitors. The king, who walked under a canopy, was dressed in red velvet embroidered in gold, and a long ermine mantle; in one hand he held the sceptre, in the other a globe surmounted by a gold cross, exactly like the pictures of Charlemagne and the old German emperors. After him walked numerous German princes and knights in rich robes, and officers in every kind of uniform. The picturesque procession passed slowly before us, and people generally thought it very impressive; I confess it appeared to me rather theatrical.

I was treated by everybody on the same footing as the ambassadors of France, England, and other great powers, to the annoyance of the Austrian ambassador, that same prince of Liechtenstein who took such a dislike to me in Paris in 1858. It was common talk among the members

of the diplomatic body that the other powers would soon
follow the example of France and England, and officially
recognise the new kingdom of Italy.   Some of them offered
me their services with the Prussian Court, with a view to
accelerate the recognition ; especially Lord Clarendon,
Ambassador of Her Britannic Majesty, Queen Victoria.
But I had no authority from Ricasoli[1] to accept any such
offers ; on the contrary, absolute neutrality had been

---

[1] I"give some of the telegrams bearing on this question.

'BERLIN, 13 *Octobre* 61.

'*A. S. E. Ricasoli.*

'Lord Clarendon m'a offert ses services demandant s'il pouvait être
agréable au Roi et gouvernement de parler à Bernsdorf et Roi lui même, si
occasion se présentait, pour reconnaissance nôtre royaume, ou du moins con-
naître raison du retard.   Jen 'ai pas laissé gnorer que ne puis faire politique,
ni prononcer mot reconnaissance avec Gouvernement prussien, mais pas cru
devoir refuser bons offices ; je pense que Clarendon veut pas ceder à Mac-
Mahon honneur obtenir notre reconnaissance.   En tout cas ma politique est
profiter des circonstances et bon vouloir Clarendon.   J'ai prévenu Comte de
Launay de tout ceci.   DELLA ROCCA.'

'14 *Octobre* 61.

' Réponse Ricasoli :

' Nous avons promis au Gouvernement prussien de ne faire aucune démarche
pour reconnaissance à l'occasion du couronnement, par conséquent si Clarendon fait ouverture, doit être bien entendu sera sans aucune participation de V.
E. Veuillez causer avec De Launay.   RICASOLI.'

' KŒNIGSBERG, 17 *Octobre*.

'Je fais trop mauvaise figure ne pouvant répondre à certaines questions,
Veuillez me tenir au courant politique, desire savoir si Général La Marmora est
nommé à Naples.   Reçu dépèche, ne me suis 'amais ecarté vos instructions ;
toutes questions etiquette marchent d'une manière satisfaisante jusqu' à
present.   DELLA ROCCA.'

' Réponse Ricasoli :

'Je réponds sans delai à votre télégramme d'hier.   La Marmora vient
d'accepter commandement des troupes à Naples et temporairement les
fonctions de Préfet de la province Naples.   L'abolition de la Lieutenance de
Naples et du gouvernement de la Toscane est decidée, et le decret relatif sera
publié prochainement avec la loi de décentralisation administrative.   Les
choses à Naples marchent assez bien, et j'espère marcheront mieux.'

imposed upon me. A few months afterwards, Prussia, Russia, Belgium and Portugal recognised the new kingdom.

I only alluded to it once. A new Catholic church was consecrated with great pomp while I was at Berlin, and everyone had been invited except the Ambassador of King Victor Emanuel. I was dining at court that night, and King William, raising his voice, asked me, across the table, if the ceremony had been a striking one, and whether there were many spectators. Answering, so that everyone might hear, I said, 'I don't know, your Majesty. I was at the hospital, where there are several Italians I was charged to assist by the King of Italy.'

The leading personalities then in Berlin were the English and French ambassadors. The latter had been allowed a million for his expenses, the empress had lent some of her jewels to the Maréchale MacMahon, and workmen had been sent from Paris to decorate the French Legation, and turn the courtyard into a huge ballroom. Clarendon ridiculed such extravagance as pertaining to a *parvenu*, and neither he nor the rich Duke of Ossuna imitated it.

On the termination of my mission I returned to Turin, and was able to pass a few weeks at Luserna with my wife and little girls. The first three years of the new kingdom of Italy were among the happiest and most fortunate of my life; I wish I could say the same for my country.

When in 1860 Cavour returned to power, he induced Napoleon to relinquish his idea of a congress for settling the so-called Italian question, and persuaded him to consent to our annexation of the Duchies and the Legations after a *plébiscite*. This was paid for by the cession of the two frontier provinces, Nice and Savoy. But after the death of Cavour the emperor drew back, and the negotiations relating to the recall of the French troops from Rome were dropped. Matters went pretty smoothly in northern and central Italy, but in the southern provinces our representatives were incessantly being changed without contenting either the population or the government.

In spite of his hesitating policy, the emperor was faithful to Victor Emanuel, and sent a fleet to salute him at Naples, when he passed through from the inauguration of the railway between Pescara and Foggia. Victor Emanuel went on board the admiral's vessel, and was received with enthusiasm by the French sailors. Rejoicings at Naples were cut short by his sudden departure. He was recalled to the capital by the events which preceded the sad affair of Aspromonte. Home politics were upset. Rattazzi, who had succeeded Ricasoli, fell, and poor Farini, a shadow of his former self, was called to form a new ministry. After a few weeks he was forced to resign the presidency to Minghetti. Ministers changed, but the difficulties, chiefly caused by the presence of a French garrison in Rome, remained. Without demanding any guarantee, the emperor, trusting in Cavour's political sagacity, had promised him that in 1861 it should be withdrawn. But Napoleon had no faith in his successors; he feared arousing the enmity of the Catholic powers, who wished to keep the Pope at Rome, and he insisted on some pledge or guarantee that Rome should not be wrested from the Sovereign Pontiff. Hitherto none had been found which seemed calculated to assure him against the machinations of the revolutionary parties. At last, in the summer of 1864, a way out of the difficulty was suggested by an Italian relation of the emperor, and Turin was called upon to make the sacrifice. Turin would have gladly made it had it been asked for the good of Italy, but it was torn from her by treachery and force. As I was intimately mixed up, not in the conspiracy (against Turin), but in its consequences, I must explain what occurred after the so-called Convention of September.   The negotiations, which had been begun in June by the Minghetti ministry, were continued by Visconti-Venosta, through the agency of Menabrea, who went several times to see the emperor; finally the Convention was signed in Paris on the 15th September 1864.   The important article was the removal of the capital from Turin.   Outside government circles nothing was known in Turin till the 20th, the day after a council of generals was held, under the presidency of the Prince of Carignano.   This council was simply a farce, held in order to be able to tell the Chambers that the generals had been consulted as to the strategical advantage of transferring the capital.   The prince declared that he was only authorised to ask us to name which city, with the exception of Rome and Naples, was most fitted to be the capital of Italy.   The question was put first to our *doyen*, General Hector de Sonnaz, who tried to couple his answer with certain objections.   Prince Eugène at once stopped him, saying, 'I can listen to no comments and no appreciations.   I can only receive the name of the city which strategically in your opinion is most suited for a capital.'   We agreed that, strategically speaking, the best capital, that is the easiest to defend, was Florence.   This sufficed for telling the Chambers that the generals had unanimously indicated Florence as the future capital of Italy.   The Convention had been signed some days, and the king had already suggested Florence, because it lay on the road to Rome, which he did not intend to renounce. Victor Emanuel was not easy to persuade; he often combated the ideas of his ministers, and occasionally insisted on carrying out his own.   But once convinced (Cavour generally succeeded in convincing him), he frankly accepted what he considered his duty, and never wasted time in vain words of regret.

CHAPTER XX

1864

THE negotiations for the Convention had been conducted
with such absolute secrecy that, on the 19th September,
when the generals met, the public suspected nothing.
Vague reports circulated next day, but the news was
only definitely known when published in the ministerial
papers, the *Opinione*, the *Stampa* and the *Gazzetta di Torino*,
on the 21st. The *Stampa* and the *Opinione* made no comment, but the *Gazzetta* accompanied the announcement
with hurried words, containing veiled irony and covert
threats against the people of Turin. Demonstrations
were immediately made in front of the ministries to
the cry of ' Down with the ministers ! ' ' Rome or death !'
Rioting also took place near the office of the *Gazzetta
di Torino.*

Nearly the whole garrison had been sent, by ministerial
orders, to Cigliano, beyond S. Maurizio, to take part in
some sham battles.   On the 20th I reviewed the troops,
and sent them off, and next day, at dawn, left Turin with
my staff to assist at the manœuvres. Returning at dusk,
I saw Major Corvetto, of the staff, at the station of
Chivasso, evidently waiting for me. I made him get into

my carriage, and he then told me what had happened in Turin, and also gave me an official letter, which had reached my headquarters after three in the afternoon. The ministers were evidently alarmed, as they had called a Cabinet council at the first news of the rioting, which, after all, was not very serious. No one knew better than themselves that the commander of the territorial troops was absent, yet the letter said 'Your Excellency is requested to commission Colonel Formenti, commanding the 1st Legion of Gendarmes, to take command of the troops necessary for the repression of present disorders, or of those which may occur to-night or to-morrow.' The handwriting was unknown to me, but the minister of war, General Della Rovere, had added these lines: 'When the territorial commander arrives, he will take whatever steps he considers best.—THE MINISTER OF WAR.' I reached Turin between nine and ten at night and was at once informed that an excited crowd was going down Via Nuova, towards Piazza Castello, which was occupied by young, untrained gendarmes. Police, known by their accent not to be Piedmontese, were stationed at the corner of every street; they were Milanese or Neapolitans, and instead of calming the populace, seemed to excite them.

I sent one of my aides-de-camp back to Cigliano to order the troops to return, and then walked to the ministry of war. With the exception of Piazza Castello, Via Nuova and part of Via del Po, the city was perfectly tranquil. After waiting more than an hour, I was leaving the war office, when Della Rovere arrived and told me what had just happened. Piazza Castello had been invaded by a mob from Piazza San Carlo, furious with the gendarmes and the police, who had hit the people with the flat of their swords to make them disperse. A shot from some unknown hand, followed by a second, was taken as a signal by the gendarmes to fire a volley. Over fifty people fell dead, wounded, or senseless from fright, and in an instant the square was deserted. Della Rovere expected more serious rioting next day, and ordered me to accelerate the return of the troops from the Camp of Instruction. He told me nothing about the cabinet Council held that day. Afterwards the ministers Minghetti and Peruzzi said that it had been decided to unite the civil and military powers under my command. This is very improbable, as no alarming riots had taken place ; indeed, I should say there never was any occasion for alarm. The number of idle lookers-on largely exceeded the rioters, and would have been easily dispersed by the usual bugle call without using firearms.

Leaving Della Rovere, I went to headquarters to send off the orders and prepare for the morrow, and then to the minister of the interior to inform him of my arrangements. I found the corridor of the Home Office guarded by gendarmes, and the ministers, with one or two exceptions, in a state of excitement and anxiety, which astonished me. I told Peruzzi (minister of the interior) that six thousand men would arrive from Cigliano early in the morning, to be followed before noon by others, and made some suggestions for tranquillising the population. It was agreed between the ministers of the interior, of war, and myself that as soon as the troops arrived they should patrol the streets.

Early in the morning the troops were there ; but I waited in vain for the police delegates, without whom the patrols could not legally act. At last they arrived, and soon afterwards the police magistrate, Chiapusso, sent to ask for troops to protect the vicinity of Piazza San Carlo. I went to the Home Office, and, among other things, asked Peruzzi if the National Guard was to be employed together with the troops. He said, ' Certainly not ; the whole service would be confided to the regular troops.' At mid-day I heard, to my astonishment, that the National Guard had just been called out. The truth is, the ministers had lost their heads. Meanwhile, a mob had collected in Piazza San Carlo, throwing stones at the office windows of the *Gazzetta di Torino*, and shouting, 'Down with the *Gazzetta!* Down with the traitorous ministers! Rome or death!' Chiapusso, misled by the exaggerated reports of an agent, sent a small force of gendarmes and police, who were received with hisses and abuse. The bugle note of warning, calling the people to disperse, was sounded, but the row prevented those at any distance from hearing; so the doors of the police office were flung open, forty young gendarme recruits rushed out, broke through the line of infantry, and threw themselves on the crowd. A shot was heard, then another, and the troops, thinking they were attacked, fired. Owing to the unfortunate manner in which they had been stationed (by Chiapusso's orders), at the corners of the square, they shot, not only people in the crowd, but their own comrades. The colonel and the ensign of the 17th regiment were severely wounded, and several soldiers killed and wounded.

I found the ministers in a state of great agitation—so alarmed that Minghetti actually proposed to declare martial law. I could not refrain from combating this with considerable warmth, and then assured them, if they would withdraw magistrate, police and gendarmes, and entrust the maintenance of order to the troops, tranquillity would soon be restored. When Della Rovere, who had been ill and was lying on the sofa, heard me oppose the proposal of Minghetti, he jumped up, exclaiming, 'La Rocca is right! I, minister of war, am absolutely against any such measure.' 'But you have sent in your resignation,' observed Minghetti, ironically. 'Quite true, on account of ill-health; but, seeing the dangerous condition of things, I have withdrawn my resignation. I remain at my post, and such material and moral injury shall not be done to Turin with my consent. She has been sorely tried, and will have more to bear!'

On the night of the 22d, or rather at two in the morning of the 23d, I returned home, and thought it my duty to draw up a report of what had happened for His Majesty. Contrary to my usual habit, I ventured to add that, in my opinion, he ought to dismiss the present Cabinet. My messenger crossed Count Castiglione, who brought me a letter from the king, stating his intention of dismissing the ministry, but directing me to consult first with the Prince of Carignano. If, as was most probable, the prince approved, I was ordered to go to the prime minister, and invite him and his colleagues to send in their resignation.

The Prince of Carignano agreed that the sooner the ministers resigned the better. So I went to Minghetti, with whom was Peruzzi, and delivered my message. Minghetti angrily refused to accept verbal orders, and telegraphed to Sommariva for an order signed by the king. An hour later the answer came, but he did not show it to me. Sneering ironically, as when he spoke to Della Rovere, he said, 'We resign, and hand over all civil and military powers to you. Now, see whether you can tranquillise the people and prevent fresh disturbances.'

I could not refrain from saying, 'Rest assured there will be none, save, perhaps, a slight demonstration in an hour or so—but of a different kind.'

'I understand, of course,' replied Minghetti, 'demonstrations of joy for our fall.'

From the ministry I went to Hotel Fœder to see La Marmora, who had just arrived from Switzerland, to give him an order from the king to form a Cabinet. He had been absent during the negotiations for the Convention, of which he disapproved, and brusquely said, ' Yes, yes ; follies are committed, and then I am charged to remedy them.' In spite of his reluctance, however, he undertook the task, and secured the co-operation of Giovanni Lanza, respected and esteemed by every Piedmontese.

During the day (23d) numerous detachments of infantry traversed the city, which was perfectly tranquil in every direction. I had confined the gendarmes to their barracks, sent the extra police out of Turin, and Chiapusso to pursue his avocation in another city. I ordered the theatres to be reopened on the 25th, which diminished the crowd in the cafés, and the city soon resumed its usual aspect. There was a slight effervescence on the day (24th October) of the opening of the Chambers, but chiefly in the clubs and cafés. The truth is, the Piedmontese were profoundly irritated. The so-called pledge, which had not been demanded by Napoleon of Cavour, when in 1861 the latter stipulated the withdrawal of the French troops from Rome, was now to be dearly paid by the people of Turin. They had been ready—nay, anxious—to make any sacrifice for the union of Italy, with Rome as capital, ever since the day when Camillo Cavour summoned the Parliament in the small Piedmontese capital to proclaim that Rome must be the great capital of the new kingdom of Italy. But now that our going to Rome seemed almost hopeless, the Piedmontese were furious, and insisted that the national programme, according to the policy of Cavour, should be carried out. In vain we endeavoured to convince them that from Florence we should proceed to Rome ; in vain Victor Emanuel exclaimed, ' Florence is but a stage on the way ; to Rome we shall go.'

The discussions on the law for the transfer of the capital lasted all through November and part of December. In spite of violent, but useless, opposition, the king, having already, by virtue of the power given him by the Constitution, signed the Convention; the law passed by a great majority in the Chambers, and also in the Senate, although opposed by several leading men, particularly by Massimo D'Azeglio.

Excitement increased in Turin as the day approached for the opening of Parliament. The Turinese naturally resented the decapitalisation of their city without any apparent gain to Italy. Several deputies wanted to put the ministers, who had proposed and signed the Convention, on their trial for high treason, as having acted in contravention of the national vote, expressed and sanctioned in 1861 by the Parliament.

The situation was difficult and involved, and discord reigned between Italians. The patriot Bettino Ricasoli resolved to try and put an end to such a condition of things. He inscribed his name first on the list of intending speakers, and made an eloquent speech in favour of concord and brotherly love which ought to unite the representatives of the various Italian provinces. He appealed to the Piedmontese deputies to set the example, and add yet another sacrifice to the many made for the unity of Italy. His words touched all hearts, and carried the day; enmity and rancour were, if not forgotten, at least momentarily stifled in a wave of patriotism.

I soon saw that the ex-ministers and their partisans could not forgive the accusations made against them by the Turinese; and also that they erroneously believed that I had induced the king to dismiss them on the 23d September, and intended that I should suffer for it. They discovered, what no one had suspected during the sixteen years the Constitution had been in force, that it was unconstitutional for one man to hold the offices of chief aide-de-camp to the king and commander of any considerable force, such as an army corps. Although this was something very like an insult to the most constitutional of kings, friends of the fallen ministry found influential people to listen to them, the more so that La Marmora, President of the Council, was on their side.

CHAPTER XXI

1865

The Mob insults the King's Guests—The King leaves for Florence—
Closer Alliance with Prussia.

ON the first of the year 1865 the king, according to old
usage, went in state to the theatre, and was very warmly
received, in spite of the discontent still existing among all
classes about the transfer of the capital. This discontent
was manifested by a small demonstration on the night of
the first Court ball, the 30th January. A crowd assembled
at the palace gates, and as the carriages passed hisses and
shouts of 'Down with Florence as capital! Long live
Rome!' were raised. Stones were thrown at the carriage
windows, while the National Guard looked stolidly on.

I was standing with His Majesty at a window of the
palace when the disturbance began, but there was no great
crowd, and neither of us thought there was any danger. I
begged the king to return to the ballroom, and went down
into the square. After seeing the last carriage enter the
palace gates, I followed and told the king everything was
quieter.

I was even more struck by the emptiness of the ballroom than by the row in the street. Many guests had not
come, and most of the ladies had been frightened and

returned home. The wives of the high Court officials were represented by my wife and the old Marchioness Spinola, a very small, thin woman, who always dressed in the fashions of 1830, a tight and short gown, which looked very odd among the crinolines and sweeping skirts.   It was said that she never discarded her old dresses, had not bought a new one since the death of her husband, and wore her old ones by turns at the Court dinners and balls. Anyhow, she made such a contrast to my wife that the king, in spite of his annoyance, was much amused.

Next day the papers were filled with exaggerated descriptions of the demonstration, and some of the ministers succeeded in representing the affair to the king in such a way as to give it considerable political importance.   The syndic of Turin, Marquis di Rorà, was also blamed for not going with the municipal authorities to present the excuses of the citizens of Turin, and beg the king to pardon the disgraceful scenes of the 30th January.   There was so much talk and fuss that the king lost all patience and decided to leave at once for Florence.   He was enthusiastically cheered during the journey, and received with every sign of love and gratitude.

I must now revert to my own experiences during the early days of 1865, certainly among the saddest in my life. On the last of January and the 1st of February the king was worried and preoccupied. On the 2d I was detained all day at my office and did not see him, so he sent Castiglione late in the evening to my house with a message. The ministers and some other persons had so effectually succeeded in rousing the anger of the king against the Turinese, and against their syndic, for not having offered any apology for the occurrences of the 30th, that he had resolved to leave Turin next day for Florence. 'The king imagines,' added Castiglione, after a pause, 'that you are as much disgusted as he is by all that has happened, and will have no objection to throw up your command here and follow him to Florence.'

I was so taken aback by these words, of which I at once saw the hidden meaning, that I remained silent for a moment. I then said, 'I am most grateful to His Majesty for wishing me to accompany him, but I cannot resign my command; if I am dismissed, the dishonour will be unbearable, as people would suppose that I had a hand in the slaughter of September, and in the recent disorders. I know there is the rumour that I am to lose one of my appointments, and, however painful it will be for me to leave the king, after passing twenty-five years in almost daily intercourse with him, I shall resign the post of first aide-de-camp to His Majesty.'

Castiglione assured me that the king knew perfectly well that no blame attached to me, but since the question had been raised, and the two appointments had been declared incompatible, the king thought I might retain the post of chief aide-de-camp and follow him to Florence. My cousin tried hard, probably by the king's orders, to gild the pill, but it was too bitter a one for me to swallow. La Marmora, in proposing these measures, had acted as I should not have done towards my worst enemy. In spite of what Castiglione said, I gathered that I was to be deprived of the command of the army corps of the department of Turin, and resolved to do my utmost to retain it. I therefore sent in my resignation as first aide-de-camp to His Majesty, fully determined to demand satisfaction of La Marmora if the command was taken from me. I wrote to the king to thank him for his constant kindness, and said that, though most painful to me to resign a post I had held for twenty-five years, my military honour demanded that at this moment I should prefer the command of an army corps to any other position. The king was already at Florence, so I sent my letter to my brother Frederick, who was on duty there, to give to His Majesty. Getting no answer, and no news from my brother or from Castiglione, I sent in my resignation to La Marmora, who, as president of the Council, had accompanied the king to Florence, adding that I should discard my uniform in order to be free to demand satisfaction for the unmerited affront received at his hands. The letter had just left when a telegram came from my brother, calling me to Florence. At the same time my wife received a letter from Castiglione, written by order of the king, to say that though, for political reasons, I could not be left in command of the Turin district, he had arranged with La Marmora that I was to be named to the military command in the new capital. This would enable me, even if I resigned my post of first aide-de-camp, to be about the king's person as before.

Victor Emanuel received me most cordially and kindly and described how furious my letter had made La Marmora; but he could not deny that all the trouble had been caused by my dear cousin Alphonse, for His Majesty knew better than myself how and why he disliked me. The king tried to prove that the military command of a district was a political post, but could not help laughing when I exclaimed, 'Since when? Only since I have held the post, and General Alphonse La Marmora has been president of the council!' He then added that he had induced La Marmora to promise not to answer my challenge by word of mouth or by letter, and that he hoped that I would show the same deference to his wishes, and meet La Marmora as though nothing had occurred between us. Touched by the kindness of His Majesty, I promised to avoid all scandal. A few days later I accompanied him to S. Rossore, near Pisa, where a deputation from Turin brought a petition, signed by many thousand Piedmontese, entreating Victor

Emanuel to return to his old capital. The syndic, Rorà, had already been to Florence with an address which the ministers rejected. The king, after some severe words of censure, resumed his habitual indulgent kindliness, and dismissed Rorà with a promise that he would spend part of the spring in Turin.

Poor General Fanti died early in April, and I must do La Marmora the justice to say that he at once fixed upon me as his successor to the military command of the capital. But the king, knowing how susceptible I was about my military honour, insisted on my being reinstated in my old command of Turin, thus giving me another proof of his benevolence. I believe it was also good policy, as he thus showed the people of Turin that he had found out they had been calumniated and was determined to give satisfaction to everyone.

We passed the winter of 1865 between Turin and Florence, where the king had given us a nice apartment in an annex of the Pitti Palace. The question of Schleswig-Holstein was being hotly discussed in all Europe, and threatened to be a cause for war between Austria and Prussia. Italian politicians took advantage of this state of things to draw the bonds of our alliance with Prussia closer, who, by using our troops against Austria, would give us the chance of obtaining the Venetian provinces.

La Marmora, as president of the council, was negotiating the alliance. At Florence the king spoke to me about it, convinced that it would lead to the fulfilment of his one desire in life—the independence and unity of Italy. He talked of the hoped-for war with Austria, referring frequently to the events of '48, '49 and '60, as though it was sure that I was again to be his companion in this new war. I listened, but said to myself, war there will be, but they will not let me be near the king as of old. In 1859 Victor Emanuel could impose his will on La Marmora, Minister of

War, and choose his own chief of the staff.   But in 1866 La Marmora was president of the Council, and for six months had been treating this alliance.   The king certainly could not give to anyone the post the minister had reserved for himself, and least of all to me.

CHAPTER XXII

1866 (FIRST PART)

False Statements of the Austrian Cabinet—Mobilisation of our Army—A
Newspaper Correspondent—Declaration of War by Prussia and Italy
—We cross the Mincio.

FOR a short time it seemed as though all fear of war had
passed, so my wife and daughters left for London, never
doubting that they would find me at Turin on their return.
About the 20th April the Austrian government, challenged
by several of the European Cabinets, declared that all armaments on the Italian confines had been countermanded, and
all bellicose ideas abandoned. This was trumpeted abroad
in the papers; but troops were meanwhile being rapidly
concentrated on our frontier. Called upon for an explanation, the Austrian Cabinet, as a justification of this sudden
change, gave two absolutely false reasons ; one, that Italy
was bringing numerous troops up from the south, and
massing them at Bologna and Piacenza, with a view to the
invasion of the Venetian provinces; the other, that Garibaldi, with his volunteers, had already entered Venetian
territory, near Rovigo. The so-called 'numerous troops'
were two cavalry regiments, which had been sent to the
Neapolitan provinces in 1864 to repress brigandage, and
were now returning to their garrisons. Garibaldi had not

moved from Caprera, and no Garibaldian had entered the Venetian provinces. But, on the strength of these inventions, Austria sent large contingents of troops from Hungary and Bohemia to our frontiers ; and La Marmora, finding his denials were not believed, determined to justify the assertions of Austria, and ordered the immediate mobilisation of our army.

I was rather afraid that, with La Marmora at the head of the government, I might have been left in command at Turin, and not sent to the front. But once more Victor Emanuel came to my aid and gave me the command of the 3d corps.

Early in May the army was ready to take the field— four army corps, twenty divisions, in all about two hundred thousand men. Durando commanded the 1st corps, formed of the four divisions Cerale, Pianell, Brignone and Sirtori ; General Cucchiari commanded the 2d, formed of the divisions Mignano, Cosenz, Angioletti and Longoni; the 3d (mine) consisted of the divisions Bixio, Cugia, Cadorna and Govone, but Cadorna's division was shortly changed, by the king's desire, for that of Prince Humbert. The 4th corps, under Cialdini, consisted of sometimes eight, sometimes ten divisions, and was called the army of the Po. The other three corps were commanded by the king, with La Marmora as chief of the staff, and was called the army of the Mincio.

As soon as I arrived at Piacenza I called on General Pettiti, the *alter ego* of La Marmora, and, of course, we began talking about the organisation of the army. I could not refrain from expressing my disapprobation of thus dividing our forces into two armies, independent of each other.

'You are right in theory,' replied Pettiti ; 'but our case is an exception. The Austrians, engaged in Bohemia, cannot throw a large army into Italy, so either of our two armies will be equal to the enemy wherever he may attack us—on the Mincio or on the Po.' 'Very well,' said I ; 'but remember the old proverb, "Union is strength." It seems to me the best tactics would be to keep together, await an attack, and repel it with our whole force.'

We parted mutually unconvinced, but I felt certain of the inevitable consequences of so fatal an error.

Either just before, or immediately after, my visit to Pettiti, the king came to Piacenza to review my troops and to ask me to take the 16th division, commanded by Prince Humbert, into my corps. Cialdini, to whose corps the 16th had been destined, absolutely refused to have a royal prince under his orders, alleging that his presence was prejudicial to the liberty of action of the commander. I was far too devoted to Victor Emanuel to refuse, and knowing that Prince Humbert was brave like his father, and eager to show himself obedient to military discipline, I welcomed him heartily, and trusted that the good star of the House of Savoy might preserve him from any mishap.

During his sojourn at Piacenza the king asked me if all essential preparations for the campaign were made, and whether all would be ready in a few days. 'Not at all,' I answered. 'We are no longer in the good old days of Fanti, when eight or ten divisions could be placed under arms in a week, thoroughly equipped.' 'Oh!' said the king, 'that is just what Cialdini said yesterday at Bologna. He said it was all the fault of Pettinengo.' 'The evil existed before he became a minister,' I replied, 'and he has not yet had time to mend matters.' But from that day I felt sure that Pettinengo would be made the scapegoat for the mistakes of others. I well remember the king saying to me during that visit, with all his old kindliness, that he already felt the want of my services as chief of the staff, and added that he would have a cipher sent, as he desired to correspond directly with me, and have my candid opinion on everything. His secretary, Castiglione, sent me not one, but two, ciphers; but I only made use of them once, for after 1864 politics, *i.e.*, the ministers, always stood between Victor Emanuel and myself.

After reviewing and superintending the instruction of the recruits at Piacenza during incessant and heavy rain I had an acute return of my old pain in the shoulder, and told the military doctor, Cerale, to bleed me. The doctor was horrified, and protested that he could not, and would not, obey me. 'Doctor,' I said, 'you are a major, I am a general. The advantage of being a superior is precisely that one can command; therefore, get to work at once.' 'But, general, I have not got my instruments.' 'Go and get them, and make haste.' Cerale went most unwillingly, and returned in an hour with all that was necessary. He visited me again in the evening, and found me much better; but being still in pain, I made him take off the bandages and let more blood. I slept well, and, though weak and pale, after two days' convalescence rode to Cremona to preside over the council for the national defence.

On my return Signor Petruccelli della Gattina, correspondent of the *Journal des Débats*, called upon me with a letter from my friend General Trochu. I received him coldly, and had it not been for this letter, probably should not have received him at all. In time of war I have little sympathy with these gentlemen, who, for the sake of sending a few columns of news to their papers, are capable of altering truth in a most dangerous manner.[1]

---

[1] The following are a few extracts of Sig. P. della Gattina's article, published in the *Journal des Débats* on the 6th June 1866 :—

'J'ai dit que le Général Della Rocca commandait le 3.me Corps d'Armée, J'éprouve un certain embarras à parler du Marquis Morozzo Della Rocca, qui m'avouait tantôt que s'il était Chef d'Etat Major général il empêcherait la presse de s'entretenir de la guerre. Je ne veux donc pas effaroucher le silence que ce Général désire faire autour de sa personne, et je me borne à rappeler ses états de service, du reste fort éloquents. . . .

Late in April and during May the Emperor Napoleon opened negotiations for convening a congress, with a view to prevent the war between Prussia and Austria, and also to obtain the cession of Venice to Italy against a large monetary compensation. But his attempt failed, the congress did not meet, and the campaign was retarded. I therefore wrote to my wife, who was determined to return to Piedmont, to come and join me at Piacenza, where I expected to be for another fortnight. She left London the end of May with our two daughters, and on the 2d June arrived in Piacenza, where I was able to lodge them comfortably, and show them various military evolutions, which pleased the girls. It was reported that Count Arese was going on a mission to Paris to secure the neutrality of France, and we officers feared that some diplomatic arrangement would give Venice to Italy without the chance of striking a blow, on condition that she

'Della Rocca fit la campagne de 1848 comme Chef d'Etat Major de la Division de réserve, commandée par le Duc de Savoie d'alors, aujourd'hui Roi d'Italie. Cette Division prit une part brillante à la campagne, surtout à Santa Lucia, ou elle couvrit la retraite et sauva l'Armée piemontaise, en soutenant pendant une demie journée le choc de l'armée de Radetzky, Elle contribua aussi à la défense de Custoza, où la défaite fut aussi glorieuse que la victoire.

'Della Rocca fit la campagne de 1849 comme Général de Brigade, ayant sous ses ordres les Colonels Mollard, aujourd'hui Général dans l'Armée française, et Cialdini, qui prise à un haut degré la capacité militaire, le coup d'oeil, la science, l'audace, au besoin, de son ancien Général. Dans la campagne de 1859 Della Rocca fut ce que La Marmora est aujourd'hui, Chef d'Etat Major de l'Armée. Dans la campagne de 1860-61, il commanda le 5.me Corps d'Armée avec lequel il assiegea Ancône du côté droit, et prit ensuit en trois jours la place de Capoue. Après de siège d'Ancône, Della Rocca fut nommé Général d'Armée ; après celui de Capoue, il obtint la medaille d'or de la valeur militaire. En 1859, le Roi lui avait donné l'ordre de l'Annonciade, qui est la Toison d'Or et la Jarretière de la dynastie de Savoie, et il obtint le lendemain matin le Grand Cordon de la Légion d'Honneur, Della Rocca a rempli plusieurs missions à l'étranger, et il est Sénateur.

'Sa figure peu expansive, ses manières aristocratiques, son maintien tout anglais, sa modestie qui le rend peu comunicatif, font du Général Della Rocca un homme peu populaire, mais sa capacité et son experience ne sont mises en doute par personne. . . .'

retired from the Prussian alliance. In fact, the Emperor Napoleon, who always wished us well, had started the idea of a congress with this very object, but owing to the absurd pretentions of Austria it. fell through. She demanded that the Italian representatives were not to mention Venice, and the Prussians were not to speak of the Northern Duchies. So France withdrew, and King William, who until then had turned a deaf ear to the warlike councils of Bismarck, suddenly resolved to vindicate his rights to Holstein, acquired by the Treaty of Gastein. On June 16th Prussia invaded the Duchies. I had already received orders on the 9th to move towards Chiesi, and on the 10th my troops started for Asola. Next day I spent at Cremona, where La Marmora presided at a council of war, to arrange the march towards the Mincio, and decide whether or no Cremona should be left armed. The heads of the bridges were already fortified, and it was determined to leave them so in case a retreat upon that town should be necessary.

What a miserable campaign it was. Not only for what the public knew and saw, but for all that was going on under the surface, and which only came to light on the eve of our departure. Prussia, as I have said, declared war on the 16th. Our government at Florence was at that time in the throes of a ministerial crisis, owing to the sudden departure of the president of the Council to join the army. At that moment a note reached Florence from the Prussian government, who, after trying in vain, through its agents, to combine a plan of campaign with the Italian government, suddenly proposed one which deprived our army of every liberty of action, and used it almost entirely to the benefit of Prussia. The note was sent first to La Marmora, who deemed it offensive and unacceptable, and having sent in his resignation, paid no further attention to the matter. Usedom, the Prussian minister at Florence, was charged to present another copy, which fell into the hands of the king. A reply at that moment was impossible, owing to there being no ministry extant; so the king named Jacini provisionally Minister of Foreign Affairs until the arrival of Visconti-Venosta, then our ambassador at Constantinople. A third copy was sent to Jacini, which, like all telegrams sent to Florence during those days of confusion, remained unanswered. Even La Marmora, in his headquarters, did not succeed in obtaining any reply from the capital. On the 19th June he telegraphed to Jacini, 'Si je ne reçois pas ordre contraire du Roi demain j'enverrai la déclaration de guerre à Mantoue.' The king himself telegraphed back immediately, 'Send declaration of war to Austria. —VICTOR EMANUEL.'

At six in the morning of the 20th June Colonel Bariola, assistant chief of the staff, sent a letter to the officer in command at Mantua, addressed to the Archduke Albert, commander-in-chief of the Austrian army in the Venetian provinces, to notify the declaration of war from Victor Emanuel to the Emperor of Austria. The same day I received orders to advance on Gazzoldo from Asola. The so-called army of the Mincio was well found and ready, and we supposed Cialdini to be in the same condition. We knew that the volunteers under Garibaldi were two or three times more numerous than had been expected, which, however embarrassing to the minister of war, who had to find provisions and arms, yet augured well, and the dash and enthusiasm of all those young fellows gave hopes of glorious deeds being accomplished. My own troops had shown satisfactory proofs of discipline and ardour. I forgot the bad impressions and presentiments, and hoped that our arms would be victorious.

On the morning of the 23d I left Gazzoldo for the

left bank of the Mincio.   The 1st and 3d army corps (General Durando's and mine) had orders to cross the river, while the 2d army corps (Cucchiari's) was to keep watch on Mantua, and form a reserve for the other two. His right was to extend from Goito to Curtalone, his left from Goito to Roverbella and Marmirolo.

On the 22d June the king and La Marmora came from Canneto to Gazzoldo to consult with me about the passage of the Mincio.   They were then convinced, owing to erroneous information, that the Austrians, about eighty thousand strong, were concentrated beyond the Adige round Verona, and that the Quadrilateral was free.   So we were sent to take up positions on the heights to the north, between Pastrengo and Villafranca.   At eight in the morning of the 23d the divisions of the 1st army corps crossed the Mincio—Cerale by the bridge of Mozambano, Sirtori by that of Borghetto, Brignone at Molino di Volta, while Pianell remained to the right in observation before Peschiera.   Three of my divisions—Bixio, Prince Humbert, and Govone—crossed by the bridge of Goito; the 4th, Cugia, by a military bridge at Ferri.   The division of the cavalry, commanded by General De Sonnaz, under the immediate orders of the chief headquarters, had crossed the bridge of Goito before us.

After taking leave of the king I remember stopping on the bridge to inform La Marmora of certain orders I had issued to my generals; for instance, to Bixio to place his column on the right flank, ready to oppose any attack which might be made from Mantua.   La Marmora shrugged his shoulders, and answered, 'Oh no, it is quite useless; you had better cancel that order.'   I had not time to do so, for Bixio had only gone a few steps when a small detachment of Austrians were seen on his right flank.   As these might have been followed by others I held to my own arrangement.

Owing to various circumstances we were later than we had planned. Crossing the Mincio took several hours, and night overtook us in the neighbourhood of Goito. The troops bivouacked in the open, and I and my staff slept in a cottage hard by.

CHAPTER XXIII

THE DAY OF CUSTOZA

Defective Reconnaissance—Prince Humbert under Fire—I search in vain for the Commander-in-Chief—I am ordered to hold Villafranca—Our Retreat towards Goito—La Marmora throws up His Command—Our Fatal Mistakes.

MUCH has been said and written about Custoza. My account is taken from my notes, and touches chiefly on the events in which I took part. Unfortunately, I did not set down the exact hours at which various engagements were fought; had I done so it might have served to correct many erroneous statements.

At dawn, on the 24th June, I was on foot to see my divisions start. The sleep of the men had been disturbed by high wind and showers of rain, which, however, cooled the stifling atmosphere for a few hours. Towards noon the heat was as bad as ever. The march had already begun, the division of Prince Humbert, taking the Roverbella road to the right, in the direction of Villafranca; in the centre, Bixio, with his division, was to occupy the Ganfardine, not far from Villafranca, on the road to Sommacompagna; while Govone's division, in the rear, formed the reserve on the Massimbona road, which led to Pozzo Moretta. The division of General Cugia, which had crossed the Mincio by the military bridge, marched towards Rosegaferro, to join at the foot of the hills with Bixio's division on one side, and the right wing of the 1st army corps (Brignone) on the other. The brigade Pralormo, consisting of the light cavalry of Saluzzo and the lancers of Foggia, followed Bixio. The Alessandria light cavalry were distributed among the various divisions, and part of them were attached to my headquarters.

The division of cavalry, commanded by General de Sonnaz, and under the orders of the commander-in-chief, had been the first to cross the bridge on the 23d. Charged with reconnoitring in the Quadrilateral, they did not go beyond Villafranca, and on the strength of this the general assured the commander-in-chief that there were no Austrians in the Quadrilateral. This report, which, unfortunately, agreed with news received by the intelligence department, persuaded La Marmora that he could, with impunity, send two army corps to take up positions on the hills between Salionze, Valeggio and Sommacampagna on the opposite side of the Mincio. The order of the day, communicated to me, said simply, 'Your Excellency will advance to-morrow morning before four, taking all due precautions, with your four divisions, and place them as you think best between Villafranca and Sommacampagna. On your right you will join with the 2d army corps at Roverbella and Marmirolo by means of the cavalry of the aforesaid 2d corps. The 1st army corps will extend by Sona and S. Giustina towards Pastrengo, with its headquarters at Castelnuovo. The commander of the 3d corps will inform the chief headquarters as soon as he can of the place he has selected for the headquarters of the 3d corps.' As I rode with my staff we heard the roar of cannon, and putting our horses to a sharp trot, we arrived just as the Austrian cavalry had made its first charge against the Parma brigade. This is what had occurred.

The divisions of Bixio and Prince Humbert were advancing by two nearly parallel roads—the 16th towards Villafranca, the 7th towards the Ganfardine—when they were informed that detachments of Austrian cavalry, followed by artillery, were scouring the country round Villafranca. Both commanders sent out staff officers to obtain news, and the prince was assured that, though a few scouts were to be seen in the direction of Calori, Villafranca was entirely free. He entered the town, followed by the Parma brigade, and marched through it as far as the farm of S. Giovanni. There he halted, covering the front and flanks of the brigade with battalions of Bersaglieri, while he sent back to order the mixed brigade to hurry up to his aid.

While getting the Parma brigade into line a large body of cavalry was seen in the distance—squadrons of the Emperor's Hussars and of the Trani Uhlans, with a battery of horse artillery. One squadron came up at a gallop to within five hundred paces, but some shells and canister from the cannon stationed in the road, and the hot fire of the Bersaglieri put them to flight. This must have been about a quarter to seven. At that moment the head of the column of Bixio's division came up, and he immediately sent his advanced guard to join the 16th division and cover Villafranca on the side of Sommacampagna, whence the squadrons of Colonel Pulz were advancing. After a short struggle the latter launched his men against the troops of Prince Humbert, upon which the commander of the Parma brigade, General Ferrero, immediately ordered the battalions to form squares to resist cavalry. Suddenly, from a dense covert, emerged Hussars and Uhlans, who charged at full gallop. The prince, followed by some of his officers, had ridden forward to make sure of the flight of the first squadron, and was still on the road, separated by a wide ditch from where the battalions of the Parma brigade were forming squares. He had barely time to jump the ditch and put himself, with his staff and Ferrero, in the centre of the first square in order to oppose the charge of the Austrian cavalry. The latter were soon thrown into confusion by the fire from the squares, and the furious attacks of the Alessandria light cavalry. The Uhlans turned and fled. Some fell into the deep ditch skirting the Verona road, others were killed by the fire of our infantry and artillery, and many were made prisoners. It was said that out of six hundred hardly two hundred answered the roll-call. The heir to the throne received his baptism of fire bravely, showing that he inherited the valour of his race. In that first encounter he manifested all the qualities of a good soldier—dash and ardour in the first instance, coolness and firmness during action.

I arrived at Villafranca as the first attack ended, and at once sent the squadron of light cavalry of Alessandria, which formed the escort at my headquarters, to the prince.

The day had begun favourably for the 3d corps, but badly for the 1st. How incorrect was the information given to the chief headquarters as to the movements of the enemy may be gathered by what happened to the 7th and the 16th divisions. During the day and night of the 23d the Austrians had occupied the heights, which were the very objects of our advance, and the divisions of Durando's corps had suddenly come face to face with the enemy. The advance guard of the 5th division (Sirtori) missed their way, and instead of taking the country road of S. Rocco and Palazzuolo, took the high road to Castelnuovo, thus outstripping the 1st division (Cerale), of which they became the advanced guard. The 1st division thus being uncovered, came upon the enemy, and were unable to execute their formation without confusion. On the other hand, the left wing of this division came unexpectedly upon the Austrians a mile from Oliosi, and was forced into an engagement, and routed before the other divisions were able to render assistance.

. General Cerale was warned of the presence of the enemy after he had started ; but, unaware of the mistakes already committed, he determined to carry out his orders, and advanced towards Castelnuovo. Seeing the heights facing Salionze occupied, he ordered the Pisa brigade to attack, when the commander, General Villarey, was killed. Cerale was himself severely wounded, and the division, overpowered by the ever-increasing numbers of the enemy, retreated in confusion upon Monzambano.

The Forli brigade, which had advanced as far as Oliosi, was attacked by a strong force of Uhlans and infantry, and driven back to Valeggio.

The 3d brigade (Brignone), which formed the extreme right of the 1st corps, had advanced to within a short distance of my troops, on the tableland of Gherla, a central point between the plain and the hills. There they met La Marmora. He always rode out in the early morning, and had unexpectedly found himself, with only one aide-de-camp, on the field of battle. Ignorant of the enemy's position, he ordered Brignone to attack the heights, which he found already occupied by the enemy. Both parties were surprised, and a fierce struggle ensued at Monte Torre. Brignone commanded the Lombard and the Sardinian Grenadiers ; the latter, led by Prince Amadeus, repulsed the Austrians several times ; but while they received continuous reinforcements our numbers diminished, owing to the many killed and wounded— among the latter the prince. These bad tidings were brought to me bit by bit by the various officers I had despatched to glean information ; so I gathered that I had better establish my headquarters provisionally at Villa-franca, whence I could prevent the enemy's advance upon

Valeggio, and send help where needed to the troops engaged near by. In obedience to orders, I sent one of my officers to Valleggio, where I supposed the army headquarters to be, to give information of the engagement of the 7th and 10th divisions, and of the place where I had established myself. He returned in about two hours, with his horse quite knocked up. Having found no one at Valeggio, he proceeded to Cerlungo, where nearly all the officers of the army headquarters still were; but La Marmora had not been seen since daybreak, when he rode off, without leaving any orders, while the king had mounted his horse at the first cannon shot, and no one knew where he or La Marmora had gone to. My aide-de-camp then went to Goito, with the same result. Unable to obtain any information of the movements of either the king or La Marmora, he galloped back to Villafranca. During the whole of the 24th June the headquarters of the commander-in-chief were non-existent.

I sent aides-de-camp in various directions to search for the king and La Marmora, and seeing that the divisions Bixio and Prince Humbert maintained their positions on the Sommacampagna and Povegliano roads, and that for the moment the Austrian cavalry and artillery had withdrawn, I went to congratulate the prince on his successful conduct, and then rode on to find General Bixio, and tell him that, after searching in vain for the commander-in-chief, I considered it advisable to wait for fresh orders before advancing towards Sommacampagna. I also informed him that a struggle was going on at Monte Torre, in which the left of the 1st corps was engaged, and we arranged a diversion to endeavour to take the enemy on the flank or the rear, and liberate Brignone. We settled, however, that he should wait for a positive order from General La Marmora or from me, and meanwhile retain his positions, which formed the extreme right.

of the long line of the 1st and 3d army corps, extending from Peschiera to Villafranca.

In the meantime, I sent two squadrons of the Saluzzo light cavalry and two of the Foggia Lancers to the 7th division, and ordered Cugia to join them, and extend his division towards Pozzo Moretta. He was slightly checked, and the division Govone was terribly retarded by the civil and military transport which encumbered the roads. As soon as I knew that Govone had arrived at Quaderni, I ordered him to advance with the Alpine brigade towards the foot of the hills, to unite with Cugia's division, and to send the Pistoza brigade to Villafranca in reserve.

I had just given these orders when General La Marmora arrived from Monte Torre between eight and nine o'clock. He had heard firing at Villafranca, and came to see what had happened, and at the same time to tell me to send help to the 3d division of the 1st corps. He was in a state of great anxiety, impressed by the imminent danger, and also by having just discovered that his sight had deteriorated so much that he was unable, even with field-glasses, to judge either of the number or the distance of the enemy's forces. He approved of the choice of Villafranca, and ordered me to hold the position at all hazards, and at the same time to send what help I could to Monte Torre. On leaving, La Marmora again bade me not abandon Villafranca until the plain on that side should be clear of the baggage waggons and military train. I did not see him all day, and had no orders from him after 11 a.m. until 6 p.m., when the retreat across the Mincio was commanded.

La Marmora had hardly left when the king arrived, also extremely anxious, having just seen Brignone's troops repulsed—almost put to flight—at Monte Torre. I do not remember his first words, but I know I could not restrain my indignation at the ignorance of the staff concerning the positions of the enemy. Trusting to false information that the Austrians were on the other side of the Adige, when they were in the Quadrilateral, they had thrown our army into the clutches of the enemy. I also alluded to the inexpedience of the long line extending from Peschiera to Villafranca, and to the lack of an army head-quarters. I related how my aide-de-camp had in vain gone from Valeggio to Cerlungo, and then across the Mincio to Goito, without being able to report the events of the morning, receive new orders, or make known where I had taken up my position. My words were bitter ; but the king knew I did not cast the responsibility of these errors on him, and he told me how he had been assured that the enemy were on the other side of the Adige, and how perplexed he had been at finding that the chief of the staff had left Cerlungo at dawn without having arranged any plan of attack with him, or confirmed the proposed transfer of the army headquarters from Cerlungo to Valeggio. I told His Majesty of the orders left by La Marmora, and he confirmed them, bidding me hold the positions until I received other orders from him or from his chief of the staff. He then left for Valeggio, where he expected to find La Marmora and the two divisions of the 2d corps (Cucchiari), which were to arrive there before noon. After the departure of the king an officer of General Bixio's staff came to ask me if the general could continue his march towards Sommacampagna or, at any-rate, towards the Ganfardine, whence the light cavalry of the brigades Pulz and Bujanowich were constantly attacking us. I was obliged to refuse his request, and told him of the commands left by General La Marmora and the king—that the 7th and 16th divisions were to keep on the defensive and hold their positions until further orders. After 11 a.m. General La Marmora sent me a few words by a light cavalry soldier from Monte Torre,

where he found that the Lombard Grenadiers had retreated, and part of the Grenadiers of Sardinia had given
way on hearing that their commander, Prince Amadeus,
was wounded.   Only one half stood firm, and heroic-
ally contested every inch of ground.   La Marmora informed
me that he had ordered General Cugia to go with his
whole division to Monte Torre and Monte Croce, and
General Govone to occupy Custoza and Belvedere with
his artillery and the Alpine brigade.   He again impressed
upon me the necessity of holding the positions at Villafranca, and asked me to send what aid I could to Govone
at Custoza, and by word of mouth he placed two regiments
of cavalry at my disposal.   Soon afterwards I heard that
Cucchiari's troops, which ought to have arrived at Valeggio
before noon, were not even in sight.   As I had sent every
man I could spare without dangerously diminishing my
own forces, I wrote to the commander of the 19th, General
Longoni, who I supposed had been at Roverbella for some
time, to tell him of the straits Govone and Cugia were in,
and ask him to advance on Custoza, preceded by his artillery.
I calculated the artillery ought to arrive at Custoza before
4 p.m. and that Govone would be able to hold out until
then.   The disastrous news that the 1st corps had crossed
to the right bank of the Mincio had just reached me,
and confirmed my determination to await formal orders
before moving from my positions.

About half-past three Govone sent word that all the
positions had been retaken from the enemy, whose guns
had not replied during the past hour.   But he feared
another attack, and his ammunition was exhausted.   So
I sent orders to Cugia to divide his ammunition with
him, which was done.   Shortly afterwards Cugia informed
me that an ever-increasing number of Austrians were
gathering in front of him on the heights of Beretara, and
more troops were pouring out of Verona.   His men

were so tired that he feared they could not stand against
these fresh troops, and he asked leave to retreat. I also
learned that Belvedere had been strongly attacked, and
that Govone's troops were beginning to give way.   To
both generals I sent orders to retreat on Villafranca.
When the order reached the 9th division it had already
fallen back on Valeggio. The 8th descended into Villafranca, leaving the 52d regiment behind, still defending
itself furiously. It ultimately reached Valeggio, where it
remained till the morning of the 25th.

Hardly had I sent the orders to retreat to the 8th and
9th divisions when Colonel Avogadro arrived from Goito
with a message from La Marmora. Repeating his injunctions to hold my positions, he asked for information
as to what was happening on the heights, and placed two
other regiments of cavalry at my disposal, in case a general
retreat became necessary. I charged Avogadro to tell
La Marmora that I considered a general retreat unavoid-
able, because the 8th and 9th were retiring, while Longoni's
division had never arrived, and the vicinity of Villafranca
was still encumbered with baggage waggons. The case
would have been very different if the 18th and 19th had
come up in time. Avogadro had passed my aide-de-camp,
with his horse dead lame, and brought me a message from
him that the artillery of the 19th must already be on its
way, as General Longoni had promised to despatch it
immediately. It only arrived when the troops were preparing for the general retreat, and was sent straight
back to Roverbella. Soon after Avogadro left I received
the order from La Marmora to retreat, with the whole
army corps, across the Mincio, sending on first all the
military and civil train.

For two hours the long line of waggons was defiling in
the direction of Goito, and it was dusk before the 16th
division took its place in the rear. To Bixio I entrusted

the protection of the retreat, during which the rearguard was several times hotly attacked by the Austrian cavalry. Half way I ordered my chief of the staff to establish our headquarters at Marengo, near Goito, and with an aide-de-camp I rode to Cerlungo to find the king and La Marmora, and obtain orders for the morrow. I started about half-past eight, hoping to arrive by ten, and to find them still up. But I became entangled in the confusion of the transport waggons, had to ride in the bottom of the ditches, and wait a long time before I could cross the bridge. It was one o'clock in the morning before I reached the army headquarters, and I found that the king and the chief of the staff had retired to their rooms, which were near each other. The king received me immediately, and said La Marmora insisted on resigning his post as chief of the staff, and wished me to assume it at once. But I pointed out that, in the present condition of affairs, I could not be of any service. The division of the army, and all the arrangements which could not be changed without turning everything upside down, would have paralysed my initiative. I could not eliminate La Marmora or deprive Cialdini of his command; it was therefore absolutely necessary that La Marmora should remain and carry out his plans. These and other arguments I used to the king, and begged him to let me try and persuade La Marmora to remain at his post. I found Alphonse walking up and down his room, half undressed, giving vent to his grief by broken words and gestures. Forgetting the past, I took his hand, drew him towards me, and embraced him. I tried to console him, but was so much moved I could hardly speak. I strove to persuade him that his plain duty at such a moment was to stand by the king, unite our forces, and take an immediate revenge, which would allow us to continue the campaign and attain what all desired. It was in vain; he refused to listen. Tossing his long, hairy arms about, he vehemently rejected every proposal as to keeping the command. At one moment he took up a revolver from the table and said, ' Rather than retain the command under such conditions, I will blow out my brains.' Then he sat down, with his head between his hands, and reiterated all he had told me that morning— the pain and humiliation when he found he could no longer see; that the battalions of the enemy and their movements had been pointed out to him in vain ; everything was indistinct. Sadly he repeated, ' All is over with me ; I am no longer fit to command.'

I went back to the king to announce my failure. ' I am not surprised,' said Victor Emanuel ; ' he said almost the same things to me, and he is determined to resign. He wants me to call Cialdini, but I feel that would be falling from the frying-pan into the fire.' ' If Your Majesty will take my advice,' I replied, ' you will make Bixio your chief of the staff.' ' Oh !' exclaimed the king, with a start, ' you are mad ! Bixio is very young, and the junior general. Who would obey him ?' ' I would. Bonaparte was a general at twenty-seven,' I answered ; ' and, believe me, Bixio is a great general.' ' That may be, but with Cialdini and the others . . . we should raise a hornets' nest. We must take some decision,' continued the king, thoughtfully. ' Then take Cialdini, Your Majesty. He is very popular at this moment, and all will go well if he accepts.' ' Well,' said the king, ' to-morrow we shall know what he has accomplished.' ' If he is ready,' I said, ' we might recommence without loss of time. In twenty-four hours my corps can be in fighting order. Cucchiari's has done nothing, and Durando can reconstitute his immediately.' ' Yes ; but first I must see Cialdini in private,' and the king inquired where he could find the general, as he would take my brother Frederick and meet him in some isolated cottage. His Majesty dismissed me, saying, 'I shall come and see you soon.' I went back to La Marmora, and again begged him not to abandon the king. He was calmer, and held out his hand, which I took warmly; I do not think I should have done so had I known of the disastrous telegrams which he had sent to the capital at half-past ten that night, and which struck the whole country dumb with grief next morning. (*See note*, p. 259.)

As may be gathered from the above description, the battle of Custoza took us by surprise. The want of foresight of the chief of the staff, then practically commander-in-chief of the army,[1] is, and probably always will be, inexplicable. The man who sent the declaration of war ought to have had a matured plan ready, and the commander of each corps should have been in possession of the minutest details. Instead of which, the crossing of the Mincio was treated as though it had been a simple change of quarters, and the instructions given to the commanders of the different corps contained no hint of any plan of battle. The army headquarters trusted blindly in insufficient and false information, and the orders given on the 23d to the general commanding the cavalry division were so indefinite and insufficient that he did not push his reconnaissance in the Quadrilateral beyond Villafranca, whereas he ought to have reconnoitred the positions of S. Massimo, Croce Bianco and Santa Lucia on the right bank of the river. Having stopped at Villafranca, he declared there was no enemy in the Quadrilateral, save a few scouts. This coincided with the information of the Intelligence Department, whereupon the chief of the staff took it for granted that the whole Austrian

---

[1] The ministry had submitted to the king for signature a decree naming La Marmora generalissimo of the army, as Czarnowsky had been in 1849. But Victor Emanuel refused to sign it, and substituted chief of the staff for generalissimo. La Marmora, however, very likely without intending it, thanks to his domineering nature, really exercised the functions of generalissimo.

army was concentrated behind the Adige, and that it was for us to drive them out on the 25th. General Durando, commanding the 1st corps, had received, or, at anyrate, had given, orders to his subordinates on the morning of the 24th to occupy the positions between Castelnuovo and Valeggio—the very positions which had been occupied during the previous evening by the Austrians, who atacked the divisions Sirtori and Cerale early on the 24th.

The primary, if not the most fatal, error of the chief of the staff lay in thus acting without exact information. Occupied in directing the politics of the government, which detained him in Florence far from the army until the last moment, he ought never to have assumed the responsibility of the command at the king's side. The political services rendered by him during the campaign 'were,' he writes,[1] 'of far greater importance than a victory on the plains of Custoza.' They would have been more efficacious had he remained at his post as president of the Council; he would then have been able to correct the erroneous opinions of the other ministers, who misunderstood or misinterpreted the conditions of the Treaty of Alliance with Prussia, and advanced pretensions which might have compromised not only the fate of Venice but of all Italy.

I have said that acting on insufficient information was the principal, if not the fatal, error which led to the disaster of Custoza. The first mistake was the division of the army into two independent parts. Cialdini, commanding the so-called army of the Po, received no orders— only suggestions, from the chief of the staff—suggestions to which, on two separate occasions, at least, he replied, 'I cannot come; I am not ready.' As a fact, on the 24th he was not ready to cross the Po, but he might have been on the 25th or 26th. The chief of the staff ought to have

---

[1] *See* Lettera al Massari, 19th August 1866, in *Ricordi Biografici*, p. 369.

been informed of this; the army of the king would then probably have either only threatened the Austrians from the opposite bank of the Mincio, or have crossed in force at Borghetto, and taken up a strong position at and around Valeggio to attract the notice of the enemy, and thus facilitate Cialdini's passage of the Po. Then Archduke Albert would not have been able to try and outflank us from Goito or from Mantua. We should have menaced his flank, and his communication with Verona might have been broken. He would have been forced to retire by the Tyrol or accept battle between two fires.

Had the army been kept together, our great superiority of numbers must have given us the victory. An encounter with the enemy was so little expected on the 24th at headquarters that, although the troops had crossed to the left bank of the Mincio, the headquarters remained on the right at Cerlungo, instead of moving to Valeggio, the central position of the line from Castelnuovo to Villafranca, so that the commander-in-chief had no headquarters during the whole course of the battle. Another grave mistake was allowing all the transport, ammunition and commissariat waggons to follow immediately behind the army, encumbering all the roads, causing endless confusion in the plain of Villafranca, and preventing reinforcements to arrive in time. It also greatly retarded the retreat of the 3d corps, and exposed the army to the danger of being attacked on the flank or the rear.

CHAPTER XXIV

1866 (THIRD PART)

AFTER leaving Victor Emanuel and La Marmora at Cerlungo, I rode to Goito in the hopes of finding my troops. But although the night was far advanced, few had been able to cross the bridges, and others were detained by the confusion of the waggons on the road. I succeeded, however, in getting through, and entered the first house in Goito I found open. In a big room on the ground floor were several officers asleep on straw, and on a mattress, with a rug thrown over him, General Cucchiari. Not to disturb him, I lay down quietly on the straw; no one had seen me enter, or knew I was there till I said good-morning at dawn, when my divisions, Bixio and Prince Humbert, arrived. After seeing them march past in splendid order, I returned to Cerlungo, where La Marmora had called a council of generals. We were to discuss and decide upon our future movements and plans—whether to retire or to summon Cialdini's army corps from the other side of the Po, and, with the united armies, reassume the offensive. But, as usually happens on such occasions, no one's opinion was positively asked. He who had summoned us stated his own opinions, which assumed the form of commands, and it was resolved to retreat upon the positions we had occupied on the 11th June—Piacenza, Cremona and its vicinity. And yet, on the 25th, General Pianell had been able to reorganise the 1st corps (Durando); the 2d (Cucchiari) had taken no part in the action of the preceding day; and the 3d (my corps) was also reorganised, and full of 'go.' We had, therefore, over eighty thousand men and one hundred and fifty guns in a strong position, with our right leaning on the Mincio, and the Pass of Goito in our hands. But La Marmora, either disheartened, or wishing to give the king and the ministers time to arrive at some determination about the nomination of a new chief of the staff, was about to issue orders for the retreat.

Although my opinion had not been asked, I could not refrain from going to La Marmora and to the king to say that I thought it would be most discouraging to send the troops back to their first positions, and thus acknowledge a defeat they had hardly realised. I implored that, at all events, mine should be stationed behind the Oglio, a strong position, whence we could soon return to the Mincio.

For once La Marmora listened, and approved of my idea. His first orders were maintained for the other divisions, but mine started on the 26th for Gazzoldo and Acquanegra towards the Oglio. Bixio was charged with the defence of the rearguard, and did it admirably. On the 29th my headquarters were at Piadena, where I received the first letters and papers I had seen since we crossed the Mincio on the 22d. For the first time I saw the telegrams despatched from Cerlungo to Florence on the evening of the 24th and the morning of the 25th.[1]

---

[1] The telegrams we now read in the files of the official papers of the 24th and 25th June 1866 are different from those I saw at Piadena. The former would hardly have caused the anger and indignation I felt. I quote a tele

I was still under the painful impression of the first telegrams, the effect of which there had been an attempt to mitigate,[1] when, soon after dawn on the morning of the 2d July, Victor Emanuel, his cigar in his mouth, entered my tiny room at Piadena. I was up, but not dressed, and my clothes occupied the single chair ; so the king sat on the bed and told me he had seen Cialdini, and La Marmora had gone to Parma to meet him. At first Cialdini absolutely refused to take the place of La Marmora, and advised the king to make me chief of the staff, assuring him that there would be no friction between us. Experience had, however, taught me that, with every good intention, my colleague could not curb his temper, impatient of any sort of control. Victor Emanuel knew this as well as I did, and assured Cialdini that I had refused, and it was no use to ask me again.

They then agreed that the whole army should be concentrated on the Po, and that Cialdini was to have the command of one hundred and fifty thousand men, forming an army for active operations, while the rest, nearly

gram of the 25th from the *Life of La Marmora*, by Massari (page 351). It is less offensive than the first (of the 24th), which is not given. I leave my readers to judge what a disastrous impression even this one must have made on the minds of Italians :—' Yesterday the Austrians attacked the army corps Durando and Della Rocca near Valeggio and Villafranca with their whole force, and routed them. The condition of the army is deplorable ; will be powerless for action for some time. Five divisions—Cerale, Brignone, Sirtori, Govone, Cugia—are disorganised. Austrians do not seem inclined to pursue for the moment. Goito, Volta, Cavriana, Solferino are being put into a state of defence. Our losses are very heavy, but cannot as yet be estimated. Generals Cerale, Dho, Gozzani, Prince Amadeus, wounded ; General Villarey, killed.'

[1] On the 27th June La Marmora despatched the following telegram from Redondesco :—' Now that the details are known, the battle of the 24th is more creditable to us than at first appeared. The Austrians remained masters of part only of the battlefield, we retained the rest. Our losses were heavy, but so were those of the enemy. Most of the troops performed prodigies of valour, and the Austrians are certainly convinced by now that the Italian is not inferior to the old Piedmontese army.'

fifty thousand, were to remain in observation in Venetia and round the fortresses, under the command of the king, with La Marmora as chief of the staff (provisionally, they said, but he kept the post until peace was concluded). After recounting this, the king at length told me what had brought him alone to me at such an hour.

The evening before news had come that the Archduke Albert had crossed the Mincio with part of his army on the night of the 30th June, and taken up a position to the right near Goito. On the 1st July the king and his chief of the staff settled to send a reconnaissance in force to drive the enemy into the Quadrilateral, and Victor Emanuel had come in person to bring me the good news that I was to have the command of the expedition. I already saw myself at Goito, ready to revenge the day of Custoza. On leaving, the king said, ' We have prepared everything ; make haste and start, I know all will go well.'

I made such haste that everything was ready that evening. We started at nightfall without trumpet or drum, the silence only broken by the tramp of the men and horses. The soldiers left their heavy knapsacks behind, and only carried provisions and ammunition for two days. We marched fast, and arrived at Redondesco, where we halted, much sooner than we expected. All were in high spirits ; they knew or guessed that we were going to take our revenge.

But just as we were preparing for a short rest an officer came up at full gallop with counter-orders from La Marmora. The affair was to be limited to a simple reconnaissance w.th a few troops, the rest were to return at once to Piadena. Curses were loud and deep, and I must confess I set the example. Charging my chief of the staff to see to the retreat on Piadena, I occupied myself in preparing the reconnaissance, which I ordered to advance as far as the Mincio. On the advent of our men, the Austrians, who were just dining, threw away pots and plates, and hastened to recross the bridges, which they barricaded.

It was the beginning of the great retreat, which they continued, across the Tyrol, beyond the Brenta, the Piave, the Tagliamento and the Isonzo, leaving only troops enough to garrison the fortresses. The main body had been summoned to replace the men who had fallen at Sadowa. Had the counter-order of the chief of the staff been less clear and peremptory, and deprived me of the full powers given by Victor Emanuel on the morning of 2d July, neither the enemy's flight nor the barricaded bridges would have prevented me from following him and forcing him to fight. In which case, even without the aid of Cialdini, there is no doubt Venetia would have been taken and occupied by force of arms.

I refrained from asking La Marmora why he sent that unfortunate counter-order, nor did I go near the king, whose headquarters at Piadena were close to mine—I was so angry that I feared I might say something I had better have left unsaid. A year later, at Turin, I asked La Marmora, and his reply was, 'You remember that I resigned after the battle of Custoza, but consented to remain as chief of the staff until Cialdini, designated by me as my successor, should have seen the king. At Parma I met Cialdini some days later, and we settled to concentrate the troops in a counter-march on Ferrara, when he was to have taken the command of three parts of the army, pursue the Austrians, and force them to deliver battle in the open before crossing the frontier. It was decided that from that day I was to communicate every movement of the army of the Mincio to him. His Majesty, having been informed that part of the Austrian army were moving on the opposite side of the Mincio towards Goito, insisted on making an attempt on Goito before undertaking the counter-march. He arranged everything with me, and went straight to order you to carry out his idea. This I knew late on the 2d, and, according to my promise, telegraphed your departure to Cialdini, and asked him to assist you if necessary. He answered that he was not ready to support the movement on Goito, begged me to suspend it immediately, and detain the troops at Piadena and Bozzolo, adding that he would advance his corps towards Borgoforte, which might be taken on the 5th. That is why I sent you orders to return to your encampments on the Oglio.'

Thus an operation ordered by the king, and approved by La Marmora, was countermanded by Cialdini—another proof of the evil of a divided command. Here I must put on record that of the three commanders, the one who on that occasion showed most military intuition was Victor Emanuel, and he keenly felt and lamented over the lost opportunity.

Before mentioning the political *imbroglio* which occurred in July, when we not only lost valuable time, but ran the risk of having to fight not only the Austrians, but the French and our allies the Prussians, I must touch on the retreat of the enemy.

The Austrian commanders evidently received news on the 3d July of the defeat in Bohemia, accompanied by orders to concentrate the troops and to retire upon Vienna, renouncing the plan begun on the 30th June by the passage of part of the troops to the right bank of the Mincio. Orders not to accept battle must already have been given on the 2d. Telegrams, announcing the defeat of Sadowa, arrived on the 3d and 4th July, accompanied by orders to send every available man to the frontier. The evacuation began on the 5th July ; twenty thousand men were left in Venice, but Verona, Mantua, Peschiera,

Legnago and Palmanova were denuded of all the troops, save those necessary to defend the material of war.

The archduke, with the greater part of his troops, retired during the 6th and 8th behind the Adige, leaving only one corps to cover his retreat, which had orders to make use of the railway, and from the Tyrol go straight to the Danube. We ought to have seized that moment to pursue the retreating army, take the fortresses, and carry out, in part, the plan sketched by Prussia in that famous note of 17th June, which so offended La Marmora, and which suggested our taking possession of Venetia and opening the road towards the Danube. We were prevented from doing this, not only by Cialdini's hesitation on the Po, but by the far more justifiable hesitation of the king and the government.

Then began the political *imbroglio*. Immediately after the defeat of Sadowa, Austria had made, through the Emperor Napoleon, the unexpected proposal to King Victor Emanuel to cede Venice and some of the fortresses to Italy, with the intention, naturally, of detaching us from the Prussian alliance, and being thus enabled to send all her troops into Bohemia. But this proposal of a cession and a retrocession was doubly offensive to the national sentiment; first, the refusal of the Emperor Francis to treat directly with our king; secondly, seeing all chance of our long-wished for revenge escape. There was a scream of indignation throughout the country and the army. The unpopularity of the measure, and the loyalty of the king, who insisted on at once acquainting his Prussian ally with the proposal, greatly embarrassed the government, and induced them, if not to refuse, at all events not to accept the advice of the French Emperor immediately. To increase the difficulties of our position Napoleon accused Italy of wilfully causing delay.

Several days passed in this uncertainty, during which

we consulted Prussia, who turned round and accused us of
double dealing and weakness, and then suddenly accepted
proposals made by Austria, and at Nikolsburg (July 21st)
signed, without the cognisance of the Italian government,
an armistice with preliminaries of peace, thus abandoning
her ally in front of the formidable army collected by
Austria against themselves.

All these circumstances called up a fourth direction of
the army, personified by the government, and representing
policy and diplomacy, which, I need not say, disagreed
with the three military chiefs already existing.

On 10th July I had received orders to execute a
counter-march from the Oglio to Ferrara, and by way of
Casalmaggiore, where the 1st corps met us, went to Parma,
whence Ferrara could be reached in a few hours. But we
were delayed twenty-four hours by a collision on the railway and the want of trucks.

While the Austrians were retiring from the Quadrilateral,
Cialdini was besieging Borgoforte. When, on the 8th July,
he crossed the Po between Carbonarola and Fellonica, the
commander-in-chief thought it a favourable moment to
transfer the army of the Mincio to the lower Po. Borgoforte was evacuated by the Austrians on the 13th July, the
last operations having been directed by General Nunziante,
Duke of Mignano, Cialdini having been called to Ferrara,
where, at a council presided over by the king, it was
decided to resume hostilities.

One army of about one hundred and fifty thousand
men, under General Cialdini, was to advance towards
Isongo and Trieste; another, of less strength, to remain
in Venetia, near the fortresses, under the king, with La
Marmora as chief of the staff. The first, composed of
fourteen divisions, forming five corps—Pianell, Pettiti,
Cadorna, Brignone, and Sonnaz—with two divisions of
cavalry, was called the active corps (*corpo di spedizione*).

The second of six divisions, forming two corps, Della Rocca and Cucchiari, was called the corps of observation (*corpo d'osservazione*).

On July 16th I left Parma for Ferrara to learn what arrangements had been made regarding my army corps. I went as seldom as possible to the palace, where the king and several of the ministers were staying, but on the 19th or 20th I was summoned, for some reason I no longer remember, and met Prince Jerome Napoleon, sent by his cousin, the emperor, to persuade Victor Emanuel and the ministers to accept the conditions proposed by France, *i.e.*, an armistice between Italy and Austria, on the basis of the cession of the Venetian provinces to Italy. The prince gave me no time to salute him, but said, '*Le roi m'a dit qu'il vous avait offert la place de La Marmora le soir même de la bataille de Custoza ; puisque vous l'avez si bien tenue en 1859 pourquoi ne l'avez-vous pas voulue cette fois ?*' '*Mais, monseigneur,*' I replied, '*j'avais pour célà de très bonnes raisons, que Sa Majesté a bien voulue comprendre et accepter.*' '*Ah ! bah ! il devait vous y contraindre, et si j'avais été à sa place, et que vous enssiez persisté dans le refus, je vous aurais flanqué un bon coup de pied . . . quelque part.*' '*Vous oubliez, monseigneur, qu'en ce cas j'aurais été obligé d'ajouter à mes autres méfaits celui de vous le rendre.*' The prince laughed, but afterwards inveighed against the state of affairs, and abused La Marmora, Ricasoli, Visconti-Venosta, Cialdini, and all who were in power. He declared that the king was compromising the existence of the country for questions of susceptibility, which he considered mere rhetoric.

In Italy we reason otherwise. The questions of so-called susceptibility Victor Emanuel regarded as the defence of his own honesty and the honour of the country ; he therefore resolved to reply—by continuing the war.

The intense desire of the king and of all of us officers to see the war recommenced and carried on energetically; Cialdini's activity in getting all his troops across the Adige, and sending one division to Maghera to watch the lagoon, another to the Val Sugana to help Garibaldi, and Cadorna's corps on a forced march towards Trieste; so well carried out that he would infallibly have reached his destination in five or six days, was all frustrated by the disaster of Lissa. That necessitated a suspension of arms on the 26th, and rendered orders and plans of battle useless. It was written that Venice was not to be ours by force of arms.

From Ferrara I was sent to Este, and later to Vicenza. With me was only one division (the 16th, Prince Humbert's), but the other two were to join me. I had been given no special orders, and, according to my wont, my first care was to be well informed as to the movements of the enemy. I learned that from Roverado he intended to try and surprise Medici, who was in the Val Sugana on his way to the Tyrol, by attacking him on his left flank and rear. I warned him, and sent several battalions of Bersaglieri with artillery, under Major-General Ferreri, whose expedition was, however, paralysed by the suspension of hostilities. I then received orders to go to Vicenza.

La Marmora was compelled to ask for an armistice by the force of circumstances. Prussia had signed preliminaries of peace with Austria, guaranteeing the integrity of the Austrian empire, with the exception of the Venetian provinces, without warning or consulting her ally. The moment the armistice was signed, Austria reconstituted her southern army, and the Archduke Albert turned his steps again towards Italy, with an army three times more numerous than his former one. His divisions advanced towards Isongo and the Tyrol. The Italian government—that is Ricasoli and Visconti-Venosta, as well as our representatives abroad, wanted to extend our frontiers so as to include the territory of Trent, or, at anyrate, whatever ground was occupied by our troops, *i.e.*, the *Uti Possidetis.* There was every prospect of a furious struggle, and La Marmora, fearing we might be worsted, asked for an eight days' armistice, in order to discuss matters and treat with the archduke. This the latter refused to grant until the Italian troops in occupation of the Trent territory and those marching on Trieste were recalled. At the expiration of eight days things stood at the same point as on the first. Meanwhile, the Austrian army was daily reinforced, and Prussia, who no longer wished to continue the war, assumed a threatening attitude, and tried to force us to conclude the armistice. The Emperor Napoleon, angry at his mediation not having been accepted, also threatened us, and accused us of risking a general war by refusing to simply accept Venetia. It was patent to all that an armistice followed by a peace was inevitable, and that we should be baulked of our revenge. A prolongation of the suspension of arms for another week was therefore asked.

On July 28th I entered Vicenza, to the relief of the inhabitants, who had been left without a garrison, and feared molestation from the Austrians at Verona. I should have enjoyed my stay in the beautiful city had I been less tormented by the fear of a more or less dishonourable peace. I did not ask what was going on, and no information was given to me, and although the king was near by at Padua, I avoided going there until called. Some days after the second suspension of arms Victor Emanuel sent for me ; he was ill and low spirited—a rare thing—and had been bled twice by the doctor's orders. Worried and perplexed as to what decision to take, he wished to have my opinion and advice. I answered briefly, not that I was offended by having been told so little about the political and military conditions of the country, but after witnessing almost daily for sixteen years the pitfalls and the difficulties which surround the life of a Constitutional sovereign, I knew what his good intentions were worth, and what practical use he could make of the advice of sincere friends, when that advice was contrary to the deliberations of the ministers. So I replied that I was not in a position to express an opinion, or to give any advice, as I knew nothing of what was going on. When I said this, Victor Emanuel looked me straight in the face with the half-affectionate, half-sceptical, but wholly good-natured expression I knew so well and loved so dearly, and half sighing, half laughing, with the same tone of voice in which twenty years before he had said to me, ' *Là, là c'am cria nen i fareu tut lo ch'a veul,*' he said, ' You are right; it shall not occur again. Henceforward I shall tell you everything, and you must advise me.' He then initiated me into the difficulties of his position, in the midst of a terrible struggle between the opinion of his ministers, the just wishes of his army and of the nation, which he shared, and the imperious will of three European powers far stronger than ourselves. He told me several facts which, to my mind, rendered the situation exceedingly grave.

Although La Marmora was no longer chief of the staff of the whole army, but only of the corps of observation (*corpo di osservazione*), he continued to exercise the functions of generalissimo, and was therefore far better informed than myself. He considered our position to be so perilous that to save the army and the country he resolved to sacrifice his popularity to the public wrath, and signed the armistice which, in despite of diplomacy, of the Italian ministry, and of public opinion, saved Italy from an Austrian invasion, and from still greater calamities.

The armistice had not been signed when I saw the king at Padua ; perhaps he hoped that my opinion would have been contrary to that of La Marmora. Twenty-four hours later, during the night of the 10th August, His Majesty telegraphed to me in cipher, peremptorily asking whether I thought the armistice arranged at Cormons, by order of La Marmora, between General Petitti and General Möring ought to be accepted or not. I replied, 'Considering our bad strategical position, I think the armistice should be signed.' My reply was immediate, and despatched at midnight, and I used one of the ciphers given to me by the king; yet next morning (I heard afterwards from Pettinengo) my telegram, translated, was in the hands of the ministers.

The armistice was signed that same day (11th August). I do not suppose my advice had any weight with the king, or that he desired to throw any part of the responsibility on me. La Marmora generously assumed it all. As president of the Council he treated with Prussia, Austria and France, and knew better than anyone what dangers threatened us. He was daring and resolute, as he had been on many other occasions. The evil having been done, it could not have been better remedied.

Cialdini and Garibaldi were ordered to retreat from the positions they occupied, and God alone knows with what a sore heart the hero of Nice answered the telegraphic order, with the simple and now famous word—*ubbidisco* (I obey).

CHAPTER XXV

1866-1867

Cialdini Chief of the Staff of the Army—Illness of Victor Emanuel—La
Marmora retires to Private Life—Annexation of Venetia—Enthusiastic
Reception of Victor Emanuel in Venice—Marriage of Prince Amadeus
of Savoy—Death of Count di Castiglione.

AFTER the armistice had been signed, peace was regarded
as a certainty, and all who were able left the camp and the
headquarters. I retained the 16th division at Vicenza, and
sent a large portion of the 10th to Padua to guard the
king's headquarters, which were not far from the Austrian
outposts, and entirely denuded of troops. Absorbed by
the difficulties of the situation, the chief of the staff had
given no more thought to the headquarters of the general
commander-in-chief. Victor Emanuel, with his usual active
habits, rode all over the country, sometimes at dawn, sometimes late in the evening, accompanied by only one aide-
de-camp. Fortunately, these excursions were not noticed
by the enemy. Imagine what consternation there would
have been in the army had the Austrians taken the king
prisoner!

At that moment no one thought of giving fresh orders.
La Marmora had resigned, and Cialdini had accepted the
position of chief of the staff of the army; but the former
still momentarily retained the signature, because Cialdini
had made certain conditions, and insisted on their fulfil-

ment before assuming office. One of the conditions was that La Marmora should have no active command, and not interfere at headquarters, or in any particular in which the responsibility of Cialdini was engaged. The latter was still very popular, and everything he asked was conceded, in the hope that he would succeed better than anyone else in making the nation understand the necessity of bowing to the political exigencies of the moment. On the 25th August everything was settled, and General Menabrea started for Vienna to treat for peace.

I wrote to Cialdini to congratulate him, and from that day our relations, which had been interrupted during the campaign, were renewed. His acceptance of such a position at the close of the war was incomprehensible to many; but people soon understood that he had taken it in order to become master of the army, and, in case of need, curb the storm which threatened from within.

On the 1st September I went to Padua to take leave of the king, who had been ordered by his doctor to return to Piedmont. But his departure had to be retarded for ten or twelve days, owing to a relapse—a threatening of paralysis—which fortunately passed off in twenty-four hours. The circumstances of the armistice, its antecedents and its consequences, had affected even the robust fibre of Victor Emanuel. He spoke but little of himself, and a great deal of me, and I was deeply touched when, on taking leave, he said, ' I wish I could compensate you in some way for the unjust accusations and unpleasantness you have had during this campaign. However, you will soon return to Turin. I have insisted on your being reinstated in your old command. Are you satisfied ?' ' Yes, your Majesty,' I replied ; ' but, if wanted at Verona or elsewhere, I should go with pleasure. I have no longer the same motives as some years ago to wish for the command at Turin at any cost.' ' I know,' said the king ; ' but you will be happier in Turin than anywhere else. Come and see me often at Florence.'

On leaving the king I stopped at Stra, a royal villa where Cialdini had established his headquarters. We talked over the war, and found that we agreed on many points. With more or less philosophy we discussed the painful impressions received since we last met. He told me about the political conditions of Italy from the 5th July to the 15th August, much of which I had already heard from the king.[1] The day before I left Vicenza for Ferrara, I returned to Stra to take leave of Cialdini. He was out, so I left a few lines. In his answer, though written with his usual humour, one can read between the lines the bitterness we all felt.[2] I also saw La Marmora

---

[1] *Extract of Letter from General Della Rocca to his wife.*

'VICENZA, 2d Sept. 1866.

'. . . I have paid my two visits. The king was still unwell, and not in good spirits. Cialdini, on the contrary, in high good-humour; he told me many things, some I knew already. . . . From what the king said, I hope to be in command at Turin again. . . . Judging by the telegrams of yesterday, one would say that in the high imperial and royal circles, French and German, they don't know what they are doing or saying :—

' 1st. "Austria cedes Venetia to the Emperor Napoleon."

' 2d. "By the Treaty of Prague she assures Venetia to Italy."

' 3d. "By the treaty signed at Paris on the 24th Austria cedes Venetia to France."

' 4th. "France cedes Venetia to the municipal bodies."

' 5th. "A national *plébiscite* will decide to whom Venetia is to belong."

' 6th. "Menabrea goes to Vienna to discuss what portion of the debt Italy is to assume for Venetia . . . which is not yet hers, and perhaps may never be !"

' What a mess ! . . .'

'STRA, 25th Sept. 1866.

[2] 'DEAR FRIEND,—Thanks for the courteous good-bye contained in your kindly lines of yesterday. . . . I have a presentiment that this is our last campaign, and as it seems that the country is not satisfied with its generals, we shall be beaten and demolished without ceremony. We stand in the way of growing ambitions, and we shall receive . . . the same kick we once gave to our predecessors. This is only natural, and I don't complain; but it distresses me to finish my career like a fool, by an odious campaign which has satisfied no one, and made everybody say that the Italian generals are so many matriculated asses.'

at Vicenza towards the end of August, a few days after he had definitely retired from public life. I think he was thankful to be quit of the responsibility, and although perfectly aware of the harsh judgments passed upon him (with the Treaty of Cormons he had voluntarily cast his popularity to the winds), he was perfectly tranquil, because persuaded that he had saved the army and the country from imminent peril. He attributed the many misfortunes of that unfortunate campaign to various things, which may have contributed, but were certainly not the principal causes of our disasters. In my opinion, these were—ignorance of the positions of the enemy, and the want of the general commander-in-chief's headquarters on the 24th July; want of unity in the command ; and the diplomatic negotiations (probably necessary and well conducted) which fatally interrupted and impeded the action of the army until the conclusion of peace between Austria and Prussia, which left us alone to face the enormous forces of the enemy.

On the 3d October the treaty ceding Venetia to France was signed, and immediately after the *plébiscite* the imperial commissary, General Lebœuf, made the territory over to the Italian government. His presence and manners were not calculated to calm the irritation existing between the Italians and the French. The *plébiscite*—647,384 favourable votes against 69 negatives—was a consolation to Victor Emanuel, who suffered more for the Italian cause in the year 1866 than ever before. Early in November I assisted at the reception of the Venetian deputation, which presented to the sovereign the Act of Annexation, the result of the *plébiscite*, and the homage of his new subjects.

The king had insisted on receiving the Venetian deputation in his ex-capital, where he had received the Lombard, Tuscan, Parma, Piacenza and Romagna deputations. It was a kind of last homage rendered to the city which had been the cradle and the centre of the movement for the renascence, the independence and the unity of Italy.

After the ceremony Victor Emanuel sent for me to his apartments, and invited me to accompany him to Venice. He then told me of some disagreeable things which had happened in his military and civil court. Good-natured General Rossi, who succeeded me as first aide-de-camp to the king, was indirectly responsible, as he had never made his authority felt over the military court. He had sent in his resignation on account of bad health, and the king asked if I would resume my old position. I thanked His Majesty for this fresh proof of benevolence, but observed that if I accepted I should have to resign my military command, and that on the morrow of so unfortunate a campaign I did not think I was justified to do so in order to take a pleasant and honourable position. I reminded the king that some years before, at Naples, he had insisted on my retaining the command when I wished to follow him to Turin, saying that he was as jealous of my military reputation as I was myself, and would not allow me to quit a position in which he was kind enough to say I rendered good service. Now circumstances were more serious, and I could not leave my position of military commander on active service for the attractive post of his first aide-de-camp. The king remained silent for a moment, then jumped up and shook my hand, saying, '*A l'a rason.*'[1] But his voice had a tone of regret which touched me.

The king entered Venice on the 7th November, amid such frantic enthusiasm that he was visibly moved. I doubt whether any sovereign was ever so heartily cheered as Victor Emanuel between 1859 and 1870.

According to the treaty of September 1864 the French troops evacuated Rome about two months after the peace

---

[1] 'You are right.'

of Vienna, and Ricasoli was treating with the Holy See on the lines laid down by Cavour—*a free Church in a free State.* Through my brother Frederick, who was on a secret mission to the pontifical government, Pius IX. sent affectionate messages to the king, who thought he might obtain better terms from the Pope than his government could hope for. But the Holy Father's benevolence was confined to words, and a few slight concessions regarding the vacant bishops' sees. Ricasoli was most anxious to come to some understanding, and made large financial concessions in the hope of tempting the Pope and the clergy. Although the negotiations were secret, some information had leaked out, and raised a storm of discontent in the Chambers and the country. The Venetians were particularly violent, and the ministry suspended public meetings in Venetia. But hostile manifestations still continued, and in February Ricasoli dissolved the Chambers. The new elections (10th March) greatly increased the power of the Opposition; Ricasoli fell, Cialdini attempted in vain to form a ministry, and Victor Emanuel then called in Rattazzi, who in a few days succeeded in presenting to the king a Cabinet, culled from every party in Parliament.

In the spring of 1868 the advocate Cassinis, an honest man, who had been a minister of the crown several times, and was a devoted adherent of the royal family, and a friend of the family Pozzo della Cisterna, suggested a marriage between Prince Amadeus, second son of the king, and the only daughter and heiress of Prince della Cisterna. The two young people were engaged for two months, and married at Turin on the 30th May. My wife was ill at Florence, so I was not at the marriage, and next day we heard the sad news of the sudden death of Count di Castiglione. Verasis di Castiglione was my wife's first cousin, and our intimate friend. He had just been named first equerry and director of the royal stables, and considered it his duty to accompany the royal princes from Turin to the castle of Stupinigi, where they were to pass the honeymoon. Just before reaching the castle Castiglione was seized with a fit of apoplexy, and fell dead from his horse, almost under the wheels of the carriage. He was the husband of the beautiful countess so well known under the Second Empire, and was still passionately in love with her, although they had been separated for several years.

CHAPTER XXVI

1867-1870

IN the spring of 1867 Garibaldi was in Tuscany, preaching rebellion against the government, which, he believed, had an understanding with the Pope, and urging the people to elect deputies capable of leading the Italians to Rome. His language was so violent that it became absolutely necessary to arrest him. He was taken to Alessandria and imprisoned in the fortress; but this raised such a storm of protests, and increased the unpopularity of Rattazzi to such an extent, that Garibaldi was released from prison and sent to Caprera, escorted by several ships of war, which remained to watch the island.

Notwithstanding the absence of Garibaldi, volunteers continued to assemble on the pontifical frontier. The French government sent a note to remind the Italian government of the conditions of the Convention of September 1864, which imposed upon France the duty of protecting the frontiers of the Papal dominions. Not receiving an immediate answer, the emperor despatched troops to Toulon to embark on the fleet destined for Civitavecchia. Rattazzi had delayed his answer, trying to strike a balance on the Roman question between the observance of the treaty and the wishes of the nation. Encouraged by the example of Cavour in 1860, when no convention existed between France and Italy, he secretly protected Garibaldi. It was also said that his wife, a cousin of the emperor's, wrote from Paris that he need pay no attention to the threats, which were only made to satisfy public opinion in France. Rattazzi, as I have said, treated the first French despatch as of no account, and contented himself with declaring in Parliament that the government had no intention of violating the Convention of September, but he took no measures against the invading bands.

Then came the news that Garibaldi had escaped from Caprera and was in Tuscany, and, immediately afterwards, that the emperor had ordered his fleet to start for Civitavecchia. Victor Emanuel understood the danger, dismissed the Rattazzi ministry and wrote to the emperor, to assure him that the Convention should be respected. Napoleon thereupon suspended the departure of the fleet, and awaited the end of the crisis.

Cialdini was charged with the formation of a new ministry, but, wishing to please all parties, was so slow that, after a week, the king lost patience, and took matters into his own hands. In twenty-four hours his chief aide-de-camp[1] had made a ministry, of which Gualterio and Cambray-Digny formed part. But precious time had been lost, and it was too late. The volunteers had crossed the frontier, Garibaldi had passed through Florence, and, joining his followers at Monte Rotondo, had beaten the Papal troops. Victor Emanuel issued a proclamation to protest against their action ; but meanwhile the French troops had disembarked at Civitavecchia, with orders to attack the invaders of the Pontifical territory. We were then forced

[1] General Menabrea.

to send our troops across the confines '*to assist in re-establishing order and law.*' Everyone knows how it ended. Caught between two fires, the Papal troops on one side and the French *chassepots* on the other, the Garibaldians were beaten at Mentana. Doggedly faithful to his programme, which was not that of September, Garibaldi crossed the frontier, was arrested, and taken first to the fortress of Varignano, and then to Caprera, under strict surveillance.

1868 and 1869 were uneventful years in the foreign politics of Italy. The French continued to hold Civita-vecchia, thus, in fact, abrogating the Convention of September. Relations between the two countries became strained ; the *chassepots qui avaient fait merveilles* against untrained and undisciplined youths certainly did not do *merveilles* in favour of French interests. The bitter and imperious words of certain ministers of the emperor— '*Que les Italiens n'auraient jamais Rome,*' and '*Que le drapeau français flotterait toujours sur le Vatican*'—had the natural result that, when France was at war with Prussia in 1870, she no longer found in Italy the ally she might reasonably have counted upon between 1859 to 1867.

In spite of ministerial changes Menabrea remained President of the Council until the last days of 1869. The financial question was always the difficulty. Italy was made, and had been on the eve of conquering her capital. But it had cost money. Every year showed a deficit of several millions, and during those years the unpopular laws of Ferrari, Cambray-Digny and Sella were proposed and passed—the tobacco monopoly, the grist tax, the tax on the public funds, etc., etc.

On 22d April 1868 the heir to the throne married his cousin, the young Princess of Savoy, daughter of the Duke of Genova and the Princess Elizabeth of Saxony. The marriage was extremely popular, especially in Turin, where Princess Margaret—handsome, good and intelligent—was adored. Her departure was a great loss to my daughters, who were companions of the young princess. The following year my eldest daughter married Count Francesetti di Hautecœur, lieutenant in the Piacenza Hussars.

Towards the end of 1869 the king was ill at San Rossore (near Pisa). The symptoms were so alarming that His Majesty asked for the last sacraments. Menabrea sent at once to the Archbishop of Pisa to request him to send a priest with the viaticum. The Archbishop sent a young priest, with orders to read a declaration to the king, and obtain his signature to it before granting absolution. This was nothing less than a formal retractation of all the acts committed during the reign of Victor Emanuel contrary to the rights of the Holy See. But the king, who was perfectly conscious, and preserved his strength of mind, refused to sign, on the plea that it was a public act, which he could only sign in the presence of his ministers. 'The prime minister is in the next room,' he said, 'go and show him the paper.' Agitated and trembling, the young priest obeyed. Menabrea, furiously angry, threatened to have him arrested and put in prison if he persisted in refusing absolution, as the law punishes severely any attempt to coerce the conscience of a dying person. The priest, thoroughly frightened, returned to the room of the king who received absolution and the last sacrament in the presence of the heir-apparent, of the Prince of Carignano, of the Countess Mirafiore (to whom he had been privately married a short time before), of Menabrea, and of a few of the high officials of the Court. A few days later Princess Margaret gave birth in Naples to a son, who was named Victor Emanuel, and received the title of Prince of Naples.

The new session opened with a series of hostile

demonstrations against the ministry, once more re-formed under Menabrea. The government put forward Adrian Mari as their nominee for the presidency of the Chamber, but he was beaten by a large majority by G. Lanza. In such cases, which are rare, Parliamentary custom demands that the new president of the Chambers should be called to form a ministry. The king had only just returned from San Rossore ; he was still unwell, and regretted the fall of Menabrea. Instead of receiving Lanza at once, he sent to propose various combinations for the new ministry, in which he desired to have, if not Menabrea, at all events Gualterio and Cambray-Digny. Lanza refused to accept any suggestions, and difficulties arose, which prolonged the abnormal situation.

Just at this time I was summoned to Florence by the illness of my brother Frederick, prefect of the palace. Lanza had just seen the king, and told him frankly that the majority in the Chambers was against Menabrea, and that he could not undertake to form a ministry in which any member of the Court entered. He quoted the example of England, the model constitutional kingdom, where not only men filling positions about the Court were debarred from becoming ministers, but even the high Court officials were changed with the change of parties. Lanza therefore declared that he felt constrained to decline the mandate, unless the king removed from his Court the three high officials who had been in the late ministry — Menabrea, Gualterio and Cambray - Digny. Victor Emanuel demanded two days for reflection, and then acceded to the request ; and Lanza at once formed his ministry.

In January my brother Frederick died, aged only 54, and I returned to Turin, where my wife and daughters (Countess Francesetti was there with her husband) did all they could to mitigate my sorrow. The following May she augmented our family by a baby girl, called Margaret after the Crown Princess, who was her godmother. The baby has in her turn grown up, is married to Colonel di Robilant, and has made me a great grandfather.

When the high military commands were abolished in 1867 I was asked to say what post, suitable to my seniority and rank, I wished for. I replied by placing myself unreservedly at the disposition of the government for any military service they considered me capable of. A few months later the minister of war offered me the command of the troops in the southern provinces. But the impressions received in 1861 had been too strong. I remembered the impossibility of obtaining men and money, without which it was impossible to attempt to cope with the brigandage which still infested the country, and I refused. My occupations were therefore reduced to the presidency of the military order of Savoy, and my work on the commission for the defence of the State. In 1867 I was occupied with the defence of the frontiers of the Venetian provinces, in 1868 with those of Naples, and in 1870 with the fortifications of Rome. I went to Rome a month after the entry of our troops, and was joined by my wife and second daughter. We were caught by a great inundation of the Tiber, and for two days could not get out of the Hotel de Rome in Piazza S. Carlo. The officers of the commission fished for and caught two or three tables as they whirled past our first floor windows, and cleverly used them as rafts. They went to the Piazza di Spagna and other dry spots, and brought us back the news.

The *plébiscite* in Rome and in the province, in favour of annexation to Italy, had taken place a few days before our arrival, and Michelangelo Caetani, Duke of Sermonata, went at the head of a deputation to Florence to announce it to the king. The Parliamentary elections took place in November, and on the 5th, for the first time, Roman deputies took their seats in the Italian Chambers. The day before, the 4th, the king received at Pitti Palace the deputation of the Cortes, which came to offer the crown of Spain to his second son, Prince Amadeus, Duke of Aosta. The transfer of the Parliament and government from Florence to Rome was to take place in June 1871, when the Quirinal would be ready to receive the royal family. There was a great difference of opinion between Lanza and Sella as to the best time for the king to visit the capital. Sella wanted him to go at once. Where His Majesty would have lodged, I know not. Lanza insisted that the king should not precede the government and the Parliament. He threatened to resign if his opinion was overruled, and Victor Emanuel was reluctantly about to give way when the inundation cut the gordian knot, inspiring him with the happy idea of going amongst his new subjects in their time of trouble. He arrived in Rome early in the morning, visited, amid the hearty cheers of the people, the parts of the city which had suffered the most and left late in the evening for Florence.

In January my wife and daughter went to pass some time in Florence, where they met Baron G. Sonnino, who, in April, became engaged to my daughter Helen. They were married at Turin in September, twenty-two years after my own marriage. My military career and my functions as father of a family ceased almost at the same time. I was consoled by the birth of five grandchildren, who have been the joy and delight of my old age.

TO THE READER

WHEN in October 1896 my husband dictated the last chapter of his memoirs, and declared the work was finished, the whole family protested. We endeavoured to persuade him that his grandchildren and his great-grandchildren would be but ill-satisfied at his biography being brought to a close without giving any account of the years between 1871 and 1896. The general thought to silence us by saying, 'A happy nation has no history. During these twenty-five years I have been a happy man, and therefore have nothing to narrate.'

'One of those years, 1878, was an unhappy one,' we objected; 'and you must say in what a grandfather's happiness consists. It will be a great joy to the children, and also redound to the honour of those who have made you happy.' He smiled and answered, 'Very well; I will talk about my family, and then?' 'Your agricultural pursuits, your wine-making, the Institute for Soldiers' Daughters, which has been your second family.' Thus, little by little, we arranged the plan of our work. But the autumn chills of Luserna drove us to the home of our second daughter in Tuscany; and then we went to Rome to stay with our eldest daughter. Everyone wanted to read the autobiography, and then declared it must be published. The general was, however, so averse to making public what had been written solely for the family that we were obliged to come to a compromise, and content ourselves with the permission to publish the first volume only.

The correction of the proofs kept us busy during the

winter of 1897, and the epilogue, already commenced, was laid aside. My husband was then in excellent health; the pages were read and re-read to him, and he suppressed or added paragraphs with perfect clearness of intellect. The first volume appeared on the 20th June, the general's ninetieth birthday, and had an immediate success, so much so, that a hostile paper called it the ' Idol of the Day.'

Twenty-two days afterwards, at Luserna, I read him a letter from the publisher, saying that the first edition was exhausted, and asking leave to publish a second—a popular edition. The general was not well; he was in the garden, where he had passed the day under the trees, and his chair had just been drawn into the open in order that he might enjoy the last rays of the setting sun. I see him now, his head resting on his hand, and his elbow on the arm of his chair, as with half-playful, half-sceptical smile, he said, 'Well, I suppose now I must believe it is a success. Money is not words. If the publisher is satisfied with the sale of the book, it means that people like it.'

A few days later the illness from which he had been suffering for some weeks made rapid progress, and a month later, on the 12th August, he passed from the arms of his dear ones to those of God. Eight months have elapsed. With a sad heart, I must finish alone the epilogue we began together.

COUNTESS IRENE DELLA ROCCA

EPILOGUE

1871-1893

THE last twenty-five years of the life of General Henry
Della Rocca, from 1872 to 1897, may be described in a few
lines by amplifying a saying of his on his return to Luserna
after the unfortunate campaign of 1866 :—The month of
October spent among my dear ones passed like a single
cloudless day.'

They were calm and peaceful years, clouded only by
the disappearance of one or another of those to whom he
had dedicated the devotion of a lifetime or a brotherly
friendship. The friends of his youth had been dead for
years, and this last period of his life was saddened by the
loss of many he loved, and who were much younger than
himself; above all, by the death of King Victor Emanuel,
whose character and disposition he probably knew better
than anyone, and to whom he was absolutely devoted.

Between 1870 and 1880 five grandchildren were born to
us—four girls and a boy. The children loved him dearly,
for he knew how to make himself a child with children.
One day, when past seventy, I found him in the garden
teaching the little girls how to skip. He was showing them
how to make the rope pass twice under one's feet in one
skip, and did it again and again with extraordinary agility
for his age.

As an outlet for his energy and vigour he took to farm-
ing, or, rather, vine-growing, in 1869 and 1870. On a small
scale, it is true, but with as much zeal as though the yield

286

of that small piece of land was 100,000 francs instead of 1000 or 2000.

Between 1870 and 1880, in obedience to my often-expressed wish, the general began to write down his memories. On loose sheets of paper he noted down an episode, an event, or a biography of some illustrious personage he had known, and threw them into a drawer without date or order. He consigned them all to me in 1884, when he ceased to write, and they were very useful when, in 1893, he began to dictate his memoirs. It is a comfort to me to think that this occupation was an amusement to him. We lived the old days over again together, and called up memories of beloved friends. He was proud of his excellent memory, narrated simply and ingenuously, and his descriptions were so graphic that one saw the people and heard them talk. Of himself he talked without ostentation or exaggerated modesty, describing what he had done and why he did it, and all he had seen and thought, never thinking that his words would be read outside his own family.

The general was one of the promoters of the National Institute for Soldiers' Daughters, and worked hard as vice-president from 1867, when it was founded, until 1874, when he was named president, an office he kept till his death.

1878 was the saddest, or, rather, the only sad, year of the last period of the life of General Della Rocca. It opened with the death of Alphonse La Marmora and alarming rumours about the health of the king. The general at once left for Rome, but arrived too late to see Victor Emanuel alive. On receiving my husband's telegram I at once joined him at Rome. Sad and miserable were the days we spent at the hotel, and saddest of all the 11th January, the day of the funeral. I assisted my husband to put on his uniform, covered with medals and decorations, and observed that he was deadly pale. I was unhappy and anxious, knowing what his feelings were, and would be, during the long ceremony and slow march beside the coffin, for he, as *doyen* of the Order of the Annunziata, was one of the pall-bearers.

We stayed a few days in Rome to tender our condolences and do homage to the new king and queen. Just as we were starting for Turin the general was informed that he had been designated as ambassador extraordinary to Paris and London to announce the death of Victor Emanuel and the advent to the throne of Humbert I., On our way to Turin he asked me to go with him, as none of the officers of the Embassy knew English.

At the Elysée the general met two companions-at-arms of 1859 — MacMahon, President of the Republic, and Marshal Canrobert. Canrobert told him it was the first time he had dined at the Elysée, though often invited, and that he had accepted only to meet him and hear about the last years of Victor Emanuel.

We waited several days in London, as the Queen had gone to the Isle of Wight ; and on her return we were invited to Windsor for two days. The Queen spoke several times to the general about Victor Emanuel, whose name had become the centre of a sort of heroic and popular legend, in which, as in all legends, some truth was mixed with fiction. Her Most Gracious Majesty, as they call the Queen in England, asked particularly about the events of the last twenty years, and courteously recalled having seen the general in 1855, when the king was in England. She ordered a picture of the military review given in his honour, and sent it to Turin as a present to my husband. With me she talked of Queen Adelaide, and made many inquiries about young Queen Margaret, for whom she gave me two richly-bound volumes—*The Life of the Prince Consort*, written by herself.

In 1881 a friend persuaded the general to send some of

his grapes and samples of his wine to a viticultural exhibition at Pinerolo. I seem to see his happy face on the arrival of a diploma of merit; I really think it gave him more pleasure than all the ribbons and decorations he had received from the principal European Courts. To these he attached little importance, he only valued his war medals and the decorations given for services rendered to his country.

In 1887, when he was eighty years old, though he still read without glasses, his sight began to fail. Incipient cataract, which never came to maturity, declared itself, and glasses were of no avail. Blindness came on gradually, but never became total; so to the last he had the comfort of seeing the light, especially the sun. How he waited for it! How he enjoyed it! He begged that his shutters might be left open in order to see the sun rise; he welcomed it every morning with fresh delight, because it told him that he was not totally blind. His great amusement at Rome was to hear the first news from Montecitorio, the Consulta, Palazzo Braschi and Palazzo Madama. He waited with evident impatience for the evening paper, and still more for the friends and some of the deputies who came to tell him the news of the day. During the last twenty-five years of his life he followed the vicissitudes of his country and the acts of our sovereigns with the deepest interest, and delighted in the popularity of the young princes. The last paper that was read to him, on the 9th August 1897, contained the news that the Count of Turin was going to vindicate the outraged honour of Italians, and he exclaimed, 'Bravo! Bravissimo!' His good wishes may have brought good luck to the young prince.

And now it may be permitted to her who passed forty-eight years by his side, and knew how frank and upright was his character, and how kind and good his heart, to say how he practised the philosophy of life. He liked neither the name nor the abstract science of philosophy, and often playfully rallied me on my taste for metaphysical reading. 'Philosophy, my dear, is to be practised, not read,' he would say; and he did practise it. He never exaggerated the misfortunes and ills of this life, but bore them, not with passive resignation, but with courage and serenity—*Loetus in fronte* and *loetus in pectore*—during the twenty years when he lived forgotten at Turin and Luserna, and during the three last years, when his residence at Rome, so to speak, exhumed him from oblivion, and when his presence in the Senate and at the Quirinal reminded people that the veteran of 1848 and 1849 was still alive. He carried it out when, in May 1897, he strolled down the Corso with his grand-daughter on his arm, to take his customary glass of vermouth, or go for flowers to bring home; and when he sat in the rocking-chair, singing old Piedmontese songs to himself, and smoking his cigar.

He was so absolutely truthful that his word could never be doubted. People who only saw him once or twice, or at long intervals, thought him cold, because he was reserved, and had an aversion to paying compliments or saying what he did not feel. But they were wrong; he was often silent to hide his emotion. This frankness, which in youth may have been a drawback, stood him in good stead with Victor Emanuel, who appreciated the truth spoken opportunely and for a good reason, as he appreciated that practical good sense, so much like his own.

To find a man so devoid of egoism as was the general is rare. He always thought of others first; and although in the last years of his life he disliked any change in his habits, he was ready to do anything he thought would be for the good or the pleasure of those about him.

On 12th August 1897 he received the last sacraments, and died in his villa at Luserna, sitting in his favourite armchair, calm and silent, with the sad look of one who deeply feels and sorrows over the separation from all his beloved ones, whose warm affection he felt till the last.

The body was taken to Turin, to the house he had lived in for more than forty years, and on 16th August—a sad, rainy morning—it was carried to the church on a gun-carriage, followed by the troops in garrison and carriages laden with wreaths. Thence it was taken to the cemetery of Turin, placed in a temporary sarcophagus, raised above ground like those of the ancients. The face was turned towards the hill of Superga, where rests the great initiator of the independence and unity of Italy, his wife Maria Theresa, and the gentle and saintly Queen Maria Adelaide, wife of the hero who sleeps in the Pantheon.

I must not lay down my pen without fulfilling a wish my husband expressed five years since, on an April morning in 1893. He was still in bed, dictating the autobiography with such rapidity that I could scarcely follow him. The arrival of the morning papers, describing the rejoicings on the occasion of the silver wedding of the king and queen, interrupted us. When in Rome, in March, we had presented our congratulations to their majesties for the coming anniversary, and had been asked to dine privately at the Quirinal. Afterwards the queen and the prince questioned the general about the customs of the old Piedmontese Court, which he had known so well. The general listened while I read the description of the beauty, the grace, the triumphs of Queen Margaret, who attracted all eyes amid the queens and princesses assembled to celebrate the silver wedding, and then said, 'Some day, perhaps, when I am gone, the queen may like to read my old stories. Were I a poet or a literary man, capable of composing a fine dedication, I would dedicate these pages to her; but I do not know how to say what I feel. Please, however, put on record that to-day, 23d April 1893, he who was sent to Saxony to ask the hand of her mother, the Princess Elizabeth, for the Duke of Genova, and who the following year was among the first to see the infant girl, sends her a greeting and a hurrah on the occasion of her silver wedding ; proclaims her the most popular, the most graceful and gracious of reigning queens, and himself the most affectionate admirer and devoted subject of the Queen of Italy, as he was of the youthful Princess Margaret of Savoy.'

INDEX

A

D